Shade Spells with Strangers

Shade Spells with Strangers

A Queer Historical Romance

Fae & Human Relations
Book 3

Sarah Wallace & S.O. Callahan

For those searching for magic against all odds, we hope you find it.

CONTENT WARNING

Shade Spells with Strangers is a cozy historical fantasy set in a queernormative world. As such, we hope our readers will find it a soft and light read.

But please note that this book will contain some on-page sex scenes and prejudice between human and fae communities.

CHAPTER 1

SILAS

Silas Rook-Worth stared up at the large country house; it looked majestic in the setting sunlight. He wasn't surprised by the grandeur. Anyone who commissioned a specialty magically-protected furniture piece to be used for a single event had to be grand. His father seemed impressed by the family name when the commission had arrived. Though Silas had little knowledge of prominent families, he knew enough to recognize the Wrenwhistle name. He had a particular interest in that fae family's propensity to marry non-fae members of society, so he looked forward to what the project might hold.

Silas and his family were directed to the servants' entrance and Silas caught a glimpse of a manicured garden filled with wedding decor. The housekeeper met them as they got out of the cart. Her hair was pulled back into a tight bun, revealing pointed fae ears. Silas stepped to the back of the group. It was an unspoken strategy that Silas' father, Mr. Rook, took charge when talking to fae customers and Silas took charge when talking to human customers. His own ears were pointed only faintly, making him appear human to many. The housekeeper beamed at Mr. Rook, as expected. Fae always seemed to prefer working with other fae, just as humans seemed more inclined to trust other humans.

Silas' father introduced each of his children: Briony, Quince, and then Silas. Mr. Rook prided himself on his children's unique talents and had raised each of them to assist in the family business in their own way.

Briony and Quince's mother had died when they were both very young. Mr. Rook later married Ruth, a human woman, and they'd had Silas. The entire family had the same dark brown skin and dark hair. Although Silas' mother had dark brown eyes and Silas had dark green eyes, compared to his father and siblings' fae green. Silas had always felt the small differences of his dark green eyes and softly pointed ears keenly, especially when the rest of the world seemed to agree that those differences mattered the most.

But Mr. Rook was always quick to point out where their similarities lay: powerful magical abilities, a willingness to work, and a strong family bond. He gave no indication that Silas was different from his siblings or that his magic was especially unique. Although, if Silas had to guess, he imagined the housekeeper had some thoughts and assumptions about the topic.

"Perhaps you'd like to see what you'll be working with," she said.

Mr. Rook indicated for her to lead the way and she walked briskly away from the house and into the garden.

"The wedding spell will be performed here," she explained, leading them to the front of the space. "As you can imagine, we are concerned about all of the foliage. Mr. Emrys Wrenwhistle has insisted on a fire spell, and we are doing our best to comply."

Mr. Rook smiled at her. "What better time for young people to be insistent than on their wedding days, eh?"

She seemed to relax at his attitude. "Yes. As you can imagine, this wedding is quite the event. So we have been working tirelessly to make everything perfect."

Mr. Rook nodded as he looked around the space. "Shouldn't be any problem." He tapped his foot on the walkway experimentally. "We can definitely work with this."

Briony stared up into the trees. "I think the foliage will work in our favor," she stated.

Silas followed her gaze. "What time will the wedding spell be performed?"

"Early evening," the housekeeper responded.

Mr. Rook gave his children a knowing smile. "A fire spell is sure to be impressive."

Quince paced around the little area sectioned off for the spell, no doubt measuring it mentally.

"Would you like to start working now or first thing in the morning?" the housekeeper asked.

"The morning will suffice," Mr. Rook said breezily.

Satisfied, the housekeeper turned to lead them inside, but stopped at the sight of two gentlemen approaching. "Mr. Wrenwhistle," she said, pasting on a bright smile. "The craftsmen are here for the new fireplace."

"For the wedding spell?" one of the gentlemen said. "How wonderful!" He eagerly stepped forward. "Everyone seems so anxious about us performing a fire spell, but I am completely confident I can keep everything safe."

The housekeeper's facial expression betrayed her doubt, but only briefly. Mr. Rook, however, gave Mr. Wrenwhistle a smile. "Of course, sir. I'm sure you can. However, we would like you to be able to spend all of your focus on your betrothed, yes?" He glanced at the other gentleman.

Mr. Wrenwhistle laughed. "Oh, this isn't Torquil. This is Keelan Cricket. We were just taking a walk. Torquil hasn't arrived yet, although I wish they'd get here soon."

Mr. Cricket rolled his eyes good naturedly in a way that suggested Mr. Wrenwhistle had said something similar already. "They'll be here, don't worry. It isn't as if we can start the wedding without them."

"I wouldn't put it past my mother to try," Mr. Wrenwhistle muttered.

Mr. Cricket chuckled and strode away, inadvertently retracing Quince's steps from mere moments ago. Silas found himself unable to look away. The gentleman was remarkably attractive. Hair the color of honey peeked out from beneath the curved brim of his hat, matching his full brows. The lines bracketing his amiable smile and crinkling the corners of his eyes only added to his handsome features. Silas noted that the fashionable clothes he wore did a fine job of showing off the man's trim figure as he disappeared around a corner of the neat hedgerow.

"Is there anything you'd like us to keep in mind, Mr. Wrenwhistle?" Mr. Rook asked.

"Oh, I don't think so," he replied breezily.

"Then I'll lead the Rooks to their rooms, shall I?" the housekeeper said.

Mr. Wrenwhistle waved his approval and followed his friend further into the garden. Silas and his family trailed behind the housekeeper back to the house.

Silas was unsurprised to be led to the servants' quarters. Nor was he surprised to be sharing a room with his brother.

Quince peeled his shoes off and sank onto one of the beds, spreading his legs out. "Sorry you have to share," he said.

"I don't mind it," Silas said, opening his small trunk and pulling out his clothes.

Quince gave a small snort. "Oh really? I rather thought you had hopes of sharing with someone very different tonight."

Silas raised an eyebrow.

"You weren't exactly subtle."

Silas shrugged. "Does it matter? He isn't the one getting married."

"What would poor Ruth say if she knew how badly we'd influenced her sweet little son?"

"My mother is well aware of my...activities." He piled his clothes neatly on top of the trunk to better allow for an efficient morning. "And you can't tell me you aren't hoping for something similar."

"True," Quince said, leaning back on the bed with his arms crossed behind his head. "It will be nice to have a wide array of choices."

Silas grunted in response and looked around the room. It was small, but not uncomfortably so, and there was a window in the corner. He crossed over to it and looked down. The Wrenwhistle estate stretched out before him, magnificent in the dusky light. He could see the garden from his window and his mind began churning with ideas to incorporate for the task at hand. As he turned to grab his notebook to write some ideas down, his eyes caught on two figures strolling towards the house. He smiled to himself and wondered briefly if Mr. Cricket had been assigned his own room.

CHAPTER 2

KEELAN

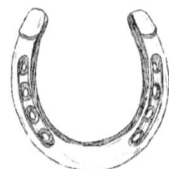

KEELAN CRICKET WOKE before the sun, as he usually did. His mornings in London were often marked with a simple breakfast of coffee and toast before he was dressed and out the door, though his list of responsibilities was remarkably short. Instead, his days were full of leisure activities. Everything from drinks and card games at the club on St. James's Street, to performances at the theater, to calling on friends—anything to keep him out of his family's townhouse.

After spending a couple of days in the country preparing for Emrys' wedding at his family's estate, Keelan had run out of things to do. The rest of the house was still sleeping and likely would be for several more hours considering how late the celebrations had gone the night before. He had already spent one morning wandering the gardens. The next, he had explored the house, quietly letting himself into any room that was not locked or otherwise occupied. There had been nothing nefarious about it; he'd simply been searching for anything to hold his attention and make his time alone a bit less...lonely.

On this third morning, he had decided to borrow some of Emrys' riding clothes and make for the stables. The Wrenwhistles kept beautiful horses, and if there was one thing that could always bring Keelan joy no matter where he was, it was a nice ride.

The groom saddled a stunning dark bay mare and instructed him on which trail would provide the best views of the surrounding land. He set out and was pleasantly surprised at just how much of a show the local flora decided to put on.

It was early spring, the perfect time for a wedding in the countryside. The weather was finally beginning to warm up enough to signal the grasses and plants to wake up and stretch after their long winter nap. The branches of the trees were starting to sprout bright green leaves; the river that cut across the property was flowing fast with runoff. It wasn't quite time for the little peeps and unsteady first steps of baby animals, but it would come soon enough. And, of course, the touch of fae magic made everything that much more magnificent.

Keelan had never cared for life in the country. It wasn't that he did not appreciate the beauty, because he did. He enjoyed the fresh air and abundant greenery that were not available in the city, but he had always found the time spent at his own family's country house during the summer months so very *boring*. Ever since he was a child, he'd spent every moment of his mother's months-long holiday from the Council longing to be back in the bustling city streets of London where he could always find something to divert his attention.

Keelan directed his borrowed mount along the well-kept path, looking out across the stretch of fields dotted with trees. They paused at the river so the mare could have a taste of the burbling, icy water. Keelan crouched and helped himself to a sip from his cupped hands before splashing a bit onto his face. Perhaps one small cup of coffee had not been enough to make up for the few hours of sleep he'd gotten.

He smiled to himself at the memory of the previous night's festivities. His best friend was getting married. Keelan still could not believe that Emrys had been capable of keeping his romance with Torquil a secret for nearly five years. He'd never been known for his discretion. After seeing the two of them together without the guise of society's expectations, however, it was clear that their connection was genuine, and Keelan could hardly blame him for keeping such a remarkable thing all to himself for a time.

With the promise of a hot, heavily-scented bath in his future before he was dressed in his official outfit for the day, Keelan decided to have some fun on his ride back to the stables. As he crested a slight hill, he urged the mare from a controlled trot all the way up to a full gallop, one hand with a grasp on the reins as he used the other to keep his hat from flying off. A burst of laughter escaped him. Even the most excellent of riders did not often find themselves in a position to let their horses run freely in the confines of the city.

"My compliments, indeed," he panted to the young groom when he dismounted outside the stables, offering the mare a solid couple of pats to her shoulder. "Though I expected nothing less at the Wrenwhistle estate."

A small part of him had hoped that the boy would accept the praise in such a way that they might strike up a conversation, but the groom only offered a quick bow of his head before leading the horse away. Keelan let out a soft sigh as he watched them go before he turned toward the house.

He could already feel the slight burn in his thigh muscles as he trudged across the manicured lawn toward the garden. He flipped the latch of the gate and let himself in between the tall hedges, crushed stone crunching under the riding boots that were just slightly too big for his feet. To his relief, the breeches fit well enough that he hadn't needed to worry about constantly fiddling with them as he walked, and the fabric had not migrated to any unmentionable places as he'd sat in the saddle.

As he rounded the corner of the hedgerow, Keelan was met with a flurry of activity that had replaced the silence he'd walked past when he left through the garden that morning. There were people everywhere, hurrying this way and that, most of them carrying something.

Large bouquets of flowers had been brought in, washing the ceremony space in a rainbow of every type of bloom imaginable. Keelan snorted out a laugh. Naturally, Emrys had insisted on not just one color, but *all* of the colors, mostly to see the look of distress on his mother's face. Lanterns were being fixed onto the branches of the surrounding trees, which would be mere accents among the thousands of fairy lights that would be released closer to time. A sea of benches had been arranged to face the spot under the archway made of woven branches and vines where Emrys and Torquil would say their vows, the most important part of the evening, save for the wedding spell.

A shout pulled Keelan's attention to where they would perform their fire spell to conclude the ceremony. The craftsmen they'd met the day before appeared to be well on their way to constructing a...*something* to contain the fire to keep everyone safe while still allowing the spectacle to happen. Keelan watched as one of them unloaded bricks from a cart pulled by two massive workhorses while the others used magic to mix a thick slurry and set the bricks into place.

"Some introduction that was," Keelan had teased Emrys after he'd caught up with him the night before. *"Not 'this is my* friend *Keelan Cricket' or anything! You made it sound as though I was your keeper or some nonsense."*

Emrys had given him a sidelong glance. *"I daresay you are for the course of the week. Regardless, it was a fine introduction. Or would you rather let them believe you are, in fact, my betrothed?"*

Emrys' playful wink had been met with a sly grin.

"Well, you did show me the ring first..." he'd chaffed.

Keelan wondered vaguely why the mason in the cart was not using magic to move the bricks. They looked rather heavy, if the flexing muscles and grunts of exertion were any indication. Keelan's quick stride slowed as the man straightened to swipe at the perspiration on his forehead with the rolled fabric of his shirtsleeve. His powerful forearms and broad shoulders indicated that he was clearly used to the strenuous work.

Keelan swallowed thickly.

Before he could be caught staring, he hurried toward the house, hopeful that quite literally anyone inside was finally awake for him to talk to.

MUCH TO HIS RELIEF, Keelan found Emrys not only awake but out of bed and somewhat clothed. He made a plate of food from the array of serving platters that had been brought up to Emrys' room and sat down to join him.

"I hope my clothes served you well," Emrys said tiredly, eyeing the boots and breeches he was still wearing.

"Very well," Keelan agreed with a sunny smile. "I must admit I was relieved when I came in to get them and found you alone. The last thing I need is you and Torquil breaking all sorts of traditions, tempting as it may be."

He'd been told by multiple people that one of his main responsibilities over the course of the celebrations was to keep the man in line. He wondered if anyone had ever fully succeeded in that task for a wedding in which fae were involved.

Emrys' response was a long, silent pause. Keelan looked up from his plate and was met with a rueful grin. He gasped and shook his head in feigned disappointment. "Your poor mother," he said with a chuckle. "Such disobedient children she has."

After breakfast, the rest of the afternoon went by with increasing momentum. Keelan was able to dip himself into a bath just long enough to wash away the stench of horse sweat and leather before he was dressed and assisting Emrys into the intricacies of his wedding outfit. The details were overwhelming. The thread used to stitch each garment together glittered with flashes of gold at the tiniest of movements. Delicate swirls of the same thread were spread across the entirety of Emrys' soft eggshell waistcoat, which was set beneath a deep green jacket with golden buttons. Keelan placed an emerald pin into Emrys' cravat and then stepped back so they could both admire the finished look in the full length mirror.

"Are you nervous?" Keelan asked.

Their eyes met in the reflection.

"Not in the slightest," Emrys told him with ease. "I've been waiting for this day for a very long time, and now it's finally arrived."

Keelan smiled and nodded. He gave his friend a once-over and realized they'd forgotten his hat. He stepped to where it was sitting on a chair and glanced out the window next to it. His attention snagged on the scene below. By the look of it, the masons had nearly finished constructing their masterpiece in the garden. Keelan could only see three of them. The man he'd been admiring and the horse cart were gone. His lips bunched into a small pout as he picked up the hat and brought it over for Emrys to take.

"Does your family know those craftsmen well?" he asked, trying at casual.

"Craftsmen?" Emrys asked vaguely as he set the hat on his head, still eyeing himself in the mirror.

"Yes, you know, the ones we encountered last evening," he explained. "The ones who are constructing the piece for your wedding spell?"

"Oh," Emrys said, his brow furrowing slightly. "Not that I'm aware of, no. My mother is the one who organized everything, as you well know, but I cannot recall seeing them before." He finally tore his attention away from perfecting the tilt of his hat and looked at Keelan. "Why do you ask?"

"Only curious," Keelan told him, eyes flicking toward the window again. Thankfully, Emrys did not notice. He shook the thought from his mind and clapped his hands together twice. "Come along then, Mr. Wrenwhistle, there's a party waiting for you downstairs." He wrapped an arm around Emrys' shoulders and began leading him toward the door. "And afterward I get to douse you with oil and sprinkle rosemary in your hair while chanting some ridiculous wedding incantation, isn't that correct?" he asked mischievously. "I only skimmed over the notes your grandmother gave me, I'm afraid."

Emrys laughed. "Something like that."

CHAPTER 3

SILAS

SILAS PULLED his pack of supplies from the cart before returning to the garden. They had constructed an elegant fire pit, with his siblings and father using the magic within the brick and the clay to bind it together more securely. Now, it was time for *his* magic work to start.

Silas could never determine if this part of the projects were his favorite or least favorite part. On one hand, he appreciated being necessary, employing magic that no one else in his family—other than his mother—could attempt. On the other hand, it always stung that his magic was fairly useless up until that point. He had stood on the sidelines as Briony extended the branches in the tree and used the magic in the ground to pull to the surface for more protection, as Quince spread the magic in the bricks to shield from within the pit, and as his father had connected all the bits of magic together into a cohesive blend. Meanwhile, Silas had hauled materials, taking the bulk of the heavy lifting, and finally moving the cart back to the stables and out of the way.

He opened his pack and pulled out a sheaf of spellpaper, as well as a pencil and an apothecary belt. The belt had been a gift from his father when he first joined the family business; it was handcrafted leather with small pouches and pockets all around it to hold his most used ingredients. He donned the belt, stuck the pencil behind his ear, and glanced up at the tree. He felt out with his sensing—the only form of fae magic he possessed—and noted the way Briony had instructed the breeze to loop outside of the branches, a precaution to keep the smoke and fire from catching onto the leaves. He spread a sheet of paper on the ground and wrote a few sigils onto it, then reached into his belt to pull out a couple of small jars, sprinkling powders into the written designs. The natural shade of the tree branch deepened and Silas sat back on his heels, pleased.

"A nice touch of drama," Quince commented.

"They seem the type to appreciate it," Silas said.

Quince snorted a laugh.

Next, Silas worked on the fire pit, adding to his brother's magic by incorporating a human protection spell. Finally, he created a new protection spell that fit into the space like a large bubble, encasing the fire pit. This spell would, hopefully, keep the fire magic within the bubble. If Mr. Wrenwhistle and his betrothed got carried away with their wedding spell, then the damage would stay enclosed.

Silas glanced up at his father, who nodded his approval. Relieved, Silas gathered up his supplies and followed his family toward the house to clean up. Their presence was required for the ceremony, in case something with the fire pit did not go as expected. Silas paused at the edge of the garden and felt out with his magic one last time, noting the way they had steeped the area with protection. It was practically dripping with magic now.

THE CEREMONY ITSELF WAS, IN SILAS' mind, a little dull. Fae weddings were so *involved*. He was intrigued by Mr. Wrenwhistle's betrothed, Torquil Pimpernel-Smith, the first fae-human member of the Council for Fae & Human Relations. Silas did not follow politics very closely, but he had been intrigued by the young writer's career. The previous year, Pimpernel-Smith had published a request for other fae-humans to submit descriptions of their own magic. Silas had done so, secretly, and had been inordinately pleased when Pimpernel-Smith had written him back. It had been nice to know his magic was not the only one that was strange. It made him feel a little less alone about it all. He wasn't sure if he'd have a chance to meet the writer, especially on their wedding day, but he quietly hoped he might find the opportunity.

He amused himself throughout the ceremony by observing the magic Mr. Wrenwhistle emitted, probably without realizing it. His joy was palpable. Silas allowed himself a small smile.

Aside from observing magic, Silas was properly distracted by Mr. Cricket, who stood at his friend's side. His suit, far more formal than what he'd been wearing the first time Silas had seen him, fit his figure beautifully. Silas' gaze roamed leisurely over the gentleman, content with the knowledge that no one was paying attention to his interest at the back of the crowd.

When it was finally time for the wedding spell, Silas held his breath, spooling his magic out before him, and feeling his family do the same. The wedding guests did the same—mostly the fae, but Silas noted that some humans tentatively felt out as well—although they were clearly doing so out of curiosity rather than professional concern.

Silas was grateful that so many precautions had been put in place. While Pimpernel-Smith's magic started out mildly, as soon as it brushed against Mr. Wrenwhistle's magic, the fire blazed higher. The couple's combined magic was extraordinary, filling the garden in gusts. Thankfully, the fire stayed within the bubble Silas had constructed. The pit stayed intact, held together by the blend of magic Silas and his family had placed. The shade spell was a particular triumph, however, as it provided a stark contrast to the fire spell, making it stand out even more. The couple standing next to it were shown to advantage, silhouetted against the dark of the shade, with the fire blazing bright in front of them.

As was typical of wedding spells, the newlyweds seemed too taken with each other to have eyes for their surroundings. Silas let out a long exhale of relief, pleased that he and his family had afforded the couple that blissful moment. The couple kissed, the fire grew, and then dramatically extinguished with a spark and a snap of magic. The audience gasped and applauded. The couple broke apart from their kiss, and the ceremony was complete.

As soon as the party moved indoors for cake and champagne, Silas and his family began taking down some of the spells they had set up.

"Enjoy the party," his father told them. "But stay out of trouble," he added with a wink. "We're leaving first thing in the morning."

Silas slipped into the crowd, eavesdropping on conversations about how sensational the wedding spell had been, as he sipped on fine wine. This was, arguably, the best part of any job—relaxing afterwards with some well-deserved treats. He cast an eye at the various guests, looking for one in particular. If he was lucky, he'd get several kinds of treats that evening.

As he wandered through the house, careful to stay out of the way and far from the expensive furnishings, he noted with some surprise how well the human guests were conversing with the fae guests. Despite living out in the country, he had heard about the wedding the previous fall between Mr. Wrenwhistle's younger brother and a human man. A high profile wedding of that kind had seemed impossible before, considering how Silas' own parents had had to shield Silas from bigotry for most of his childhood. Now, Mr. Wrenwhistle had married a fae-human, further cementing that idea of respectability.

Silas sat with the feeling for a long moment. The world was changing—slowly, but gradually. A feeling he couldn't entirely name filled his chest at the prospect of so much change. The feeling sharpened when it occurred to him that he was acting as witness to it.

He stepped away from the party and back out to the garden. Lanterns hung in the trees, accompanied by fairy lights that twinkled in the branches. Silas strode around the perimeter of the seating area, feeling the way the magic had mellowed since the wedding spell. He peeked into the fire pit, pleased with how the protection spells had stayed intact, even though the others had been taken down. He wondered if the Wrenwhistle family would use the firepit in the future. He hoped so.

"You are one of the craftsmen, are you not?" a voice said from behind.

He turned to see Torquil Pimpernel-Smith approaching. The young councilmember gave him a bright smile. "It was wonderful work."

Silas returned the smile and gave a small bow. "Congratulations, Councilmember. I'm Silas Rook-Worth."

Pimpernel-Smith paused and their expression turned shrewd. "Rook-Worth? Not the same Rook-Worth who responded to my column last year?"

Silas' grin widened. "The very same. I'm surprised you remembered."

"I remember all of those responses," they replied. They glanced back at the house for a moment. "I realize this is not the time or the place for such a discussion, but I'll be starting a new project when I return to London. The Council has agreed to devote some time and resources to the study of fae-human magic."

"That's wonderful," Silas said.

They beamed and bit their lip. "It's my first major Council project. I confess I'm torn between being relieved to be away from London for an entire month and being anxious about the delay."

"I'm sure you deserve a rest after all the work you've been doing," Silas assured them.

"That's what everyone keeps telling me," they chuckled. "At any rate, I plan to use some of my honeymoon writing to everyone who described their fae-human magic to me. I hope you don't mind."

"Not at all. I'm happy to help with your project in any way I can."

They looked delighted. "Oh, wonderful! In that case, perhaps I might—"

"Torquil?" Mr. Emrys Wrenwhistle said, walking towards them. "What are you doing out here?"

They cocked an eyebrow at their husband. "I'm discussing my Council project."

Mr. Wrenwhistle rolled his eyes. "Again?" He reached for his spouse's hand and dragged them closer. "Need I remind you that you're one of the reasons for this party?"

"But it's so crowded," they murmured.

Mr. Wrenwhistle tucked a finger under their chin and lifted it. "Do you need to leave? You know you've only to say the word."

They relaxed a little and then leaned up to kiss him. "Perhaps just a little longer."

Silas wanted to disappear into the shade of the tree and leave the couple alone, but then the councilmember turned back to him and said, "I'll be in touch Mr. Rook-Worth. It was a pleasure meeting you." Then Mr. Wrenwhistle tucked his spouse's hand around his arm and led them back inside.

Silas watched them go, feeling a twinge at the tenderness of the moment. Silas felt a little wistful at the sweet intensity of such a small interaction. He sighed and walked slowly back inside. He had learned over the years that the best cure for wistfulness was either drunkenness or intimacy. He couldn't get drunk at a wedding he was working at, so he would opt for the next choice. He grabbed a glass of wine, took a large sip, and then strode purposefully through the crowd, eyes peeled for a certain gentleman.

CHAPTER 4

KEELAN

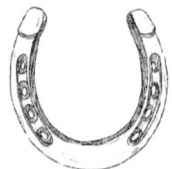

WITH HIS DUTIES for the evening fulfilled, Keelan wasted little time joining in on the party. There was an endless supply of serving trays being carried around with bites of food, dessert, and bubbling refreshments. After two glasses of champagne, the young lady with dark hair and plump lips he'd asked to dance became even more beautiful. After two more glasses, he found it quite amusing to be dancing at all.

His feet followed the steps he'd learned years before while he chuckled at the pleasing swell of the music from the corner of the room. His partner—another young lady with bright fae-green eyes and freckles hiding under the powder across her nose and cheeks—smiled demurely at him as they turned, close but not close enough to touch, as much as he would've liked for them to. He committed her face to memory in hopes that he could find her again later on in the evening.

Before he could entertain the idea of another dance, Keelan found himself swept up into the crowd. When a silver flask was placed in his hand, he did not question the contents as he brought it up to his lips. He was expecting the usual sort of liquor that was passed around at social events. When he swallowed, however, he discovered that whatever he'd been offered was a shatteringly strong herbaceous sort of spirit that he scarcely managed to keep down. He made a face and handed the flask away, his whole body shuddering violently in protest.

Keelan was not prone to overindulgence, but sometimes he did enjoy clearing his mind with a swig or two of liquid assistance. As isolated as he'd felt the previous few days, his return to London in the morning would not help very much, and he desperately did not want to think about it. Emrys would stay behind to enjoy his honeymoon, which he had every right to do, but it also meant that Keelan would be without his closest friend in the city. Consequently, he would have to get even more creative with filling his social calendar.

Unlike Emrys' mother, his own had little time to bother with such things on his behalf. She was far too busy focusing on her work with the Council or enjoying her own events to worry about what he was doing. His father was no help either, for he hardly ever left the house. He was too consumed by his odd hobbies and eccentric interests to care what was happening beyond the spot of property their townhouse sat upon. Unless Keelan wanted to spend an afternoon listening to the man recite poetry in foreign languages he did not understand, or discover exactly how much fabric it would take to reupholster an entire sitting room worth of furniture, he was better off avoiding him altogether.

As he lifted another glass of something more tame off a passing tray, Keelan spotted Emrys and Torquil standing together on the far side of the room. He was certain that he had never seen two people more in love.

Torquil's outfit was an impossibly perfect balance to the one he'd helped Emrys put on. They wore a dark green waistcoat cut in the most fashionable style. Over it was a cream colored jacket swirled with the same eye-catching gold thread. The fit was close at the top, but the satin fabric flowed all the way to the floor at the back, long enough to glide elegantly near their feet as they walked. Their dark, curly hair was set with an ornate golden comb covered in diamonds and emeralds, which was rivaled in its glistering splendor only by the ruby and fire opal ring on their finger.

The show of wealth had been expected. The Wrenwhistles were a very prominent fae family, and with Emrys set to inherit, a lavish wedding was all but guaranteed. More recently, Torquil had also come into their own fortune by reuniting with their grandmother, Mrs. Pimpernel, after the death of her husband. The man had kept their family broken for decades due to his antiquated enmity toward Torquil's mother for falling in love with and marrying a human. With that barrier finally removed, Mrs. Pimpernel promised to make up for lost time in every way that she possibly could, beginning with Torquil's official debut into society as a fae-human with affluence and status.

Keelan's mouth twitched into a small grin.

He knew none of it mattered to the couple. Emrys would've been just as happy to marry Torquil wearing burlap sacks in the middle of a muddy London street if it meant he could spend the rest of his life showering his beloved with affection. Their connection was undeniable. Their smiles were radiant, and they only had eyes for one another.

Keelan craved what they had with every fiber of his being. He wanted so badly for someone to look at him that way, and to have someone to look at in return. He longed to have a connection that lasted more than a single night. The advice he'd given Emrys about finding someone to share life's quiet moments with was his own silent wish, a dream he'd had since before he was old enough to begin properly court-ing. They sang about it at the opera, died for it at the theater, and wrote endlessly about it in his father's favorite books of poetry: love.

Keelan tossed his head back and drained the rest of his drink, swal-lowing it down before he moved a bit ungracefully toward the garden.

A few lungfuls of the fresh night air helped to clear his mind a bit. He thought briefly about sitting on one of the benches left behind in the ceremony space, but he found that his feet did not stop. Instead, he continued down the path between the hedges until he came to the gate that led to the stables. He let himself through as he recalled how thrilling his morning outing had been, the mare running full tilt until they were both out of breath—her from the exertion and himself from the effort of staying on her back.

"A little late for a ride, isn't it?" a voice said from somewhere in the dark. Keelan startled and spun around, blinking toward the figure he could now see a faint outline of thanks to the lantern they had in one hand.

"I–" Keelan began as he tried to formulate an answer. He found that his thoughts were rather wooly in his head now that he was attempting to do something other than drown them with alcohol. "I already had a ride earlier."

His reply was met with a soft hum of a laugh.

"Plenty of folks to choose from when you look like that, I suppose," the shadowy figure mused.

"I cannot see you," Keelan said, squinting against the lantern light. The stranger had come close enough that when he lifted his arm, his face was washed in a soft glow, and Keelan recognized him as the handsome mason he'd seen earlier moving the bricks from the back of the horse cart.

His eyes decided to betray him as they wandered over the man's strong shoulders and down his forearms which were, unfortunately, now covered by his shirtsleeves. Slung around his hips was a leather belt weighed down with what appeared to be tools of human magic.

It was his mouth's turn to be disloyal when he said, "You're significantly less sweaty now than when I saw you last." Keelan blinked again and met the man's gaze in the low light. He still looked as stoic as he had during their two previous encounters, but even this well-foxed, Keelan couldn't misunderstand the look of interest in his dark eyes.

"I apologize if I offended your *proper London sensibility*," the stranger said, playing at Keelan's accent that immediately gave him away as someone from the city. "Stonework is not exactly a delicate sort of occupation."

"Yes, I can see that," Keelan agreed a bit breathlessly. He found that his heart was beating harder than it should've been for someone standing still.

Even though he knew better, Keelan reached out with his magic and was instantly hit with a burst of everything the craftsman was sending his direction: intrigue, lust, desire. The emotions were inherently fae and entirely overwhelming, enough to force a soft gasp from Keelan. There was no confusion about what the man was after, and he could hardly deny his own feelings now that their magics had brushed there in the dark.

"I would hate to ruin your fine clothes," the man said, voice gruff as his eyes went pointedly to the front of Keelan's trousers.

"Then I suppose you should remove them," Keelan told him on an exhale as their reserve broke, both of them taking a step forward to close the distance so their mouths could crash together. Keelan moaned as the stranger used his free hand to grasp his backside, squeezing as he hauled him closer so that their bodies were flush. His body lit up at the show of strength and possession. It was something he was quite unaccustomed to while sharing a bed with those of a more feminine persuasion. Even sober, it would've taken more than a moment to recall the last time he'd been intimate with a man.

As they broke apart long enough to stumble toward a more private place, Keelan heard the whisper of his earlier thoughts. Genuine connection. Courtship and romance. Love. He felt the ache in his chest as he shoved it all away.

Someday, he thought, *but not tonight.*

He was unsurprised as a newly-familiar cart came into view when they made it to the area behind the stables. The stranger hung his lantern on a hook nearby and climbed expertly into the cart with little effort. As Keelan tried to determine how he should even attempt to follow, the man reached a hand down for him. He took it and allowed himself to be pulled up as though he weighed nothing at all. There was no time to offer a compliment on the man's strength before he was all but thrust down onto the dirty floorboards of the cart. So much for his fine clothes.

"You needn't rush," Keelan said with a lazy chuckle as he turned to look at the man, who was already working to remove his belt. "I will not run away."

The stranger only grunted in response and pushed his trousers down, settling onto his knees in one swift motion. Resigned, Keelan let out a sigh and got up onto his knees as well, pulling the man closer for another heated kiss. Keelan felt deft fingers unbuttoning him before his own trousers were shoved down, exposing him to the night air. The slight chill made him shiver.

"Turn around," the man said, guiding Keelan in that direction with a hand on his shoulder.

A wash of uncertainty mixed with the heat that had settled low in his stomach. "Wait," Keelan told him in a rush. "I haven't been on this...*end* of things in some time." He wasn't sure why admitting that embarrassed him so.

The man finally paused.

"Do you want to be?"

He asked this so confidently that Keelan felt a weakness in his wrists and elbows where they were holding him up off the floor of the cart. He let out a shaky breath and swallowed. He might not have been able to remember how long ago it was, but he knew he'd only been in this position twice before: once in a similar situation with a man he never saw again after a ball, and once with the man he'd just watched get married.

"Yes," Keelan murmured, nodding even though he doubted the man could see it. Callused fingers smoothed over his backside then, before the stranger's body was bent over his and a kiss was placed against the side of his neck.

"Then you've nothing to worry about," the man whispered.

More distracting kisses and a strong hand on his hip were enough to dissolve his reservations. It took hardly any time at all before Keelan wanted to demand that the man trade his slicked fingers for what they were both really after. The thought crossed his mind to make a teasing remark about being ready with the rose oil but lacking, at the very least, a blanket for him to kneel upon—another very *fae* thing to do—when the stranger finally took him by both hips and pressed in.

Keelan squeezed his eyes shut tight and grimaced at first with a huff, willing himself not to cry out. The man moved slowly, giving him a moment to breathe and adjust, before he settled on a careful rhythm. Keelan found a clear space to rest his forearm flat on the wooden boards beneath them and set his forehead against it, using his other hand to work himself.

As much as he wanted this for exactly what it was—a fleeting moment of unattached amusement that neither of them would remember with any great detail before long—Keelan couldn't escape his usual ponderings.

Would he ever see this person again? Unlikely.

Were they someone he could see a future with? Keelan hardly knew the man aside from his occupation and appearance. Not that he knew much about anyone else he'd been with for a single night either—but they'd usually shared a dance or a conversation over tea and biscuits beforehand, at least.

Was his partner looking for anything more than what they were doing at present? Though he participated dutifully, Keelan deeply disliked the fae habit of keeping casual lovers. It was near impossible to discern who was after a true courtship when the expectation was always...*this*.

If nothing else, Keelan wondered, was the man enjoying himself too?

In answer to his silent question, the stranger grunted and squeezed Keelan's hips, rocking his own with more enthusiasm.

"Your magic," he said through gritted teeth.

"P-pardon?" Keelan asked, clinging to his etiquette as his voice jounced along with his body.

"Magic," the man demanded, thrusting harder than he had before.

Keelan whimpered at the resulting mix of dull ache and delight and drew in a sharp breath so that he could do as he'd been told. His exhale caught in his throat as he did, for when their magics touched this time, gratification filled him near to the point of bursting.

"Stars *above!*" Keelan wailed, back curving as he pressed into the man behind him. All of his wandering thoughts vanished as his entire world narrowed to what was happening there in the cart, each thrust bringing more clarity than the last.

He almost shouted again in protest when the stranger pulled out, abandoning him so close to the edge. Forceful, stunted breaths ended in a groan and he felt himself marked with the man's release, which was all he needed to finish by his own hand. Keelan breathed through the diffusion of his pleasure and waited until they had both gone quiet to sit back on his heels.

Clean up. Get dressed. Offer thanks, if it seems appropriate. Leave.

Keelan knew the next steps, but he found that he could not bring himself to do them. He blinked several times, staring at the pile of unused bricks in the corner of the cart that his head had almost knocked into just minutes before. It all seemed a touch unceremonious for what he'd just experienced.

From everything he'd heard, Keelan always imagined finding magical compatibility with someone for the first time would be a trifle more romantic. He assumed that perhaps there would be a certain tenderness to the moment as understanding settled over them like a rich wine sauce being spooned over a hot meal. If not a confession of devotion, then at the very least some impassioned kisses or fond caresses. Something so significant deserved to be savored.

After finally finding it in himself to tug his shirt and waistcoat back into place so he could pull his trousers up and fasten them, he turned to discover that his rendezvous partner was already dressed and out of the cart, looking a strange mix of impatient and bewildered beneath the seriousness Keelan had seen before.

"That was..." Keelan finally tried as the man helped him back to the ground. *Extraordinary*, he wanted to say. *Sublime. Unforgettable.*

"Agreeable," the stranger finished laconically.

The word landed like a weight on Keelan's chest.

Had he not felt the same? Was the intensity entirely one-sided?

"Most agreeable," he said bravely with a tight nod, ignoring the surge of self-doubt that soured his stomach as best he could.

Their eyes met in passing before the mason tipped his chin up at the cart.

"I'd better clean this up. Last thing I want my family to find come morning."

Keelan knew a dismissal when he heard one. He hoped that the dim light from the flickering lantern helped to mask the way he flushed with embarrassment. The stranger was ready to be rid of him and the mess he'd left behind. He gave another short nod and walked away.

CHAPTER 5

SILAS

SILAS WAS NOT a man prone to regrets, particularly when it came to pleasure. But he was full of regrets as he watched Cricket walk around the stables. When Silas had deemed the encounter "acceptable," he'd watched the man's face fall instantly. Even worse was the way Cricket had attempted to look brave despite his obvious disappointment. The slump of his shoulders as he left nearly drove Silas to call for him to come back.

But he didn't.

He reasoned with himself as he put the cart to rights and cleaned up the mess. He hadn't offered anything more than what he'd given. There had been no false promises, no lies. So why did he feel as though he'd broken a heart?

He made his way up to his room, unsurprised to find it empty. He was relieved that Quince had not taken his own treat to their shared room. He undressed and climbed into bed, but sleep did not come to him as easily as it should after a day of hard work. He folded his arms behind his head and replayed the evening in his mind. He thought about the way Cricket's eyes had roamed greedily over his body. The *you're significantly less sweaty now than when I saw you last* that seemed to escape from his mouth unbidden. The idea that Cricket had been observing him from afar was a pleasing one and had removed any lingering doubts Silas had about the man's interest. Then he'd felt the gentle probe of magic and the final snap of Cricket's resolve.

Coming together had felt like a magnet slotting into position: natural, unavoidable, and right. Now, with the other man gone, Silas felt a keen lack—almost as if a necessary piece of him was now missing. He quickly brushed the thought away.

He closed his eyes. Cricket had been unexpectedly *perfect*. He'd been beautifully responsive, refreshingly honest, and it had felt so natural to hold him, to touch him, to guide him into place. Silas had an uncomfortable feeling that he'd be comparing all future encounters to this one, and an even worse feeling that they would all come up lacking. He wondered, briefly, what it might have been like to indulge in the softer side of such activities: curling around Cricket's body afterwards, stroking through his damp hair, feeling the man's breathing even out beside him.

Then there was their magic—the memory of it made his pulse pick up. The way their magics had blended was unlike anything Silas had experienced. It had felt wild and explosive, filling him up as if he might burst. And just like everything else about Cricket, it had all felt tantalizingly *right*.

He shook himself mentally. Cricket was a complete stranger—Silas realized he'd never even given the man his own name—and he was from a different world entirely. As fanciful as it had been to witness a wedding between a fae and a fae-human of lower rank, Silas was too practical to believe such a thing could happen to him. Torquil Pimpernel-Smith was from a wealthy fae family, no matter how common their father was. There was no doubt that their eligibility was markedly different from Silas' own. After all, Silas' parents were both of common country stock.

Fleeting thoughts of a pretty fae gentleman with the posh lilt of London in his voice and a gentle demeanor came unbidden to Silas' mind. He sighed, fluffed his pillow, and laid on his side. As he gradually drifted off to sleep, he told himself that this was the benefit of doing work that took him all over the English countryside: he got to meet and dally with all sorts of men. Never seeing them again was a decided benefit.

The thought did not comfort him as much as he thought it should, nor did it ease the feeling that Silas had dismissed what could best be described as a soulmate.

THE RIDE HOME felt longer than the ride to the Wrenwhistle estate had been. The Rooks were tired from a full day of work, followed by an evening of revelry that had gone late into morning. Silas' father was the only one who looked remotely bright-eyed and he cast an amused glance at his children, who were all slumped with fatigue.

Silas ought to have been just as alert, considering how early he'd gone to bed and how little he'd drunk by comparison. But he could not rid the images of Cricket from his mind. Everything from the way Cricket had shivered in the chilly air, to the way he'd arched back, to the look of defeat as he'd left, felt imprinted now. Silas was so distracted thinking about it, he didn't immediately notice that he was a topic of conversation.

"I take it your night was disappointing," Quince said.

"What makes you think that?"

"You were already asleep by the time I came to bed. And there was nothing to suggest you'd had a guest."

Silas raised an eyebrow. "I was not about to take someone into a shared room with you. Hardly considerate."

Quince laughed. "Much appreciated."

"Who did you take to bed?" Briony asked.

Silas rolled his eyes.

"The fellow we met when we arrived," Quince supplied. "The one who had been with the groom."

Briony gave a thoughtful hum. "Say what you want about Si," she mused, "he does have good taste."

"What do you say about me?" Silas said, without heat. The banter was well versed. Predictably, both of his siblings jumped in to supply him with descriptions.

"You're mulish."

"But hard working!"

"No-nonsense."

"A little too to the point, sometimes."

"You lack confidence, though," his father added.

"But what you lack in confidence, you make up for in vanity," Briony commented.

"Vanity?" Silas echoed. "I'm not vain."

"Oh, no?" she said with a grin. "Don't think we didn't catch the way you glance around when you've rolled up your sleeves during a job. You *know* the lads go wild for it."

Silas hid a smile, remembering the way Cricket's eyes had caught on his arms during their early perusal. "All right," he conceded. "A little vain. It's important to know one's attributes."

She snorted in response.

Silas pivoted the topic to ask about his siblings' conquests. Quince's was described with relish, much to everyone's annoyance, while Briony was more coy. In the end, it helped to distract Silas a little from his own niggling guilt.

Silas threw himself into work when he returned home. He helped his father organize the correspondence they'd received from potential clients, helped Quince with the mending and the washing, helped Briony fix and paint the fence around the house, and he repaired the kitchen table so his mother could knead bread without the rhythmic creaking.

When there was no work to be done, he went on long walks in the countryside. There was a spot on the family property that his father had reserved for him. Silas usually liked to go and sit under the tree overlooking the space and let it clear his thoughts. But now those thoughts were full of a sunshiny man, and Silas couldn't stop himself from picturing Cricket in the cottage he'd always imagined building, cheerfully chatting with his family, or sitting under that very tree at Silas' side.

A week later, he joined his father and siblings on a new job, working up a sweat as he heaved stones and bricks into place for the miniature house they were building for a wealthy family's children to play in.

Silas took charge more than usual, telling himself it was necessary since their clients were human. As he felt with his magic, reaching for Briony's fanciful casting, the bustle of Quince's, and the steady thrum of his father's, he pretended this was perfectly normal, that his mind wasn't working doubly hard to focus, that his magic wasn't searching for the pull of a particular man.

He could see the children watching them work from a distance, gasping whenever one of Silas' family members made the breeze billow, or the mud harden, or the earth settle around the new structure. He tried not to feel the familiar sting that his magic was not as extraordinary and awe-inspiring. Despite his best attempts, his thoughts continued to drift to the wedding. He thought about how both of the Wrenwhistle brothers had married outside of their social circle, heralding a change that Silas never thought possible. He thought about the children watching them and wondered if they would grow up to think his family's magic wild and dangerous and Silas himself an oddity, or if they would be part of a bright new future. And try as he did to avoid it, he thought of Cricket, wondering if the man was still disappointed and thinking ill of him, or if he had moved on to be as sunny as he'd seemed when Silas had first clapped eyes on him.

A week later, Silas was still thinking about Cricket, and getting increasingly more irritated about it. What right did the man have to wiggle into his thoughts so securely? Even if he *had* been the best knock Silas had ever had, he had no right to set up camp in Silas' mind. Even if everything about him had been perfect, he had no reason to make Silas *yearn*. Silas' irritation leaked out in a progressively grumpier attitude and dwindling patience. His family attempted to prod the truth out of him, but he remained tight-lipped on the matter, unwilling to admit that he was thinking about a stranger he'd never see again, and even less willing to admit that he might have been unkind.

When a letter arrived for him from Torquil Pimpernel-Smith, Silas felt an overwhelming sense of relief at the prospect of a real distraction. His relief faded, however, as he read the letter. It detailed the project that Pimpernel-Smith had mentioned, explaining that they wanted to gather various fae-humans in London to conduct a more thorough study of fae-human magic. They promised compensation, as well as food and lodging if desired. The duration of the project was predicted to be about two months.

Silas closed himself in his room and sank onto his bed. Two months in London? He'd never been to London. He'd never been that long apart from his family.

He knew they would be able to get by without his assistance. After all, they'd managed perfectly well without the aid of human spells until Silas was of age. But that was almost more worrying. He'd always felt as though he was barely pulling his own weight in the family business; to leave it altogether, even briefly, would prove that fear right.

Besides, his magic was hardly extraordinary. He could handle human spells adequately and had a passable ability to feel magic, but he couldn't manage fae spells at all. There were full-blooded humans who could do that much. His magic had never felt remotely exceptional— except once, and he'd been trying very hard not to think about the way Cricket's magic had blended so beautifully with his. He read the letter again, attempting to curb that final thought. He couldn't help but remember that he'd promised the councilmember he'd do anything they needed. He sighed and placed the letter on his bed before venturing back out of the room.

His mother was in the kitchen, arranging a freshly cut bouquet of flowers from their garden. "Everything all right, love?" she asked as he greeted her with a kiss on the cheek.

He grunted in response.

Her eyes narrowed. "I'd hoped that letter would ease this foul mood you've been in lately."

"What foul mood?"

She gave him a *look*.

"It's a letter from that writer in London, Torquil Pimpernel-Smith. Or Pimpernel-Smith-Wrenwhistle now, I believe. They…er…want me to come to London to help them with a project."

Her surprise was evident. "Really? What sort of project?"

"They're doing research on fae-human magic."

Her surprise transformed into delight. "That's wonderful!"

"You think I should go?"

"Of course! You've always been a bit uncomfortable with your magic." Silas balked at that. Not because he didn't agree with it, but because he hadn't been aware his discomfort had been so noticeable. "This will be a perfect opportunity for you. Besides, it would be good to see London and meet more people."

Like you hung in the air, unspoken but nevertheless present.

Silas tapped the kitchen table pensively.

Quince strode into the kitchen, a laundry basket propped on his hip. He stopped and gave Silas a once-over. "I guess the letter did the trick?"

"What do you mean?"

Quince flapped a hand at him. "This the calmest I've seen you since we left the Wrenwhistle place."

"Told you," his mother said, her back to them both. "Tell him what it said."

"It's from that Pimpernel-Smith person. They want me to come to London to help on a project for the Council for Fae and Human Magical Relations."

Quince brightened. "Just what you need! A change of scenery will do you good."

"Yes, it will," Briony said as she walked into the kitchen behind Quince, dumping an armful of soil-covered radishes and a head of lettuce onto the counter. "Where are you going?"

"London," Quince said before Silas could. Silas glared at his brother, annoyed at the way he was answering for him.

"Good," Briony said in a decisive tone, dusting off the front of her vest. "Excellent way to use up all of this frantic energy and general moodiness."

"Told you," Quince and Silas' mother said at the same time as Briony shuffled past them and out of the kitchen.

Silas groaned.

"What's the matter?" his father asked as he entered the room, ledger tucked under his arm as he poured himself a glass of springwater from the ewer. "Did the letter bring bad news?"

"No!" Silas all but shouted. "I'm going to London to help Pimpernel-Smith and the Council study fae-human magic and *apparently* it will cure my temper and everything else that's wrong with me."

Quince chuckled.

His father cocked his head after taking a sip from his cup, looking thoughtful. "That's a good idea. Your magic ought to be studied. It's extraordinary."

Before Silas could respond to that, his father walked back out of the kitchen.

That evening, Silas dragged his mother's old trunk from the attic and put his finest clothes, his notebook, and pencils inside. After some deliberation, he set his work belt inside too. He was fairly sure the Council was not the right place for such a plebian accessory. But, at the very least, having it handy would be a comfort—he suspected it would be a much needed one.

Perhaps going to London would provide him the right sort of distraction to get Cricket out of his head once and for all. Whether that distraction came in the form of this Council project or some new bedmates hardly mattered. And if he could discover whether his magic was truly extraordinary and how he'd need to wield it to truly earn his place within the family business, so much the better.

TORQUIL'S TRIBUNE

Greetings, romantic readers,

London is abuzz that Mr. Emrys Wrenwhistle and Councilmember Pimpernel-Smith are expected to return to town today. With such a whirlwind romance as theirs, many are anticipating the couple's return with relish.

Even the elopement of Lady Cynthia Proust with Lieutenant Rosethistle is not enough to overshadow something as arguably mundane as a married pair coming to their townhouse.

We look eagerly to the rest of society to see who will be next to enter nuptial bliss.

Will it be Mr. Benedict Brooks, a fae who has captured the attention of many gentlemen?

Or perhaps Mr. Keelan Cricket, the best friend of Mr. Wrenwhistle?

Mr. Sage Ravenwing continues to elude the wedding vow as he enchants the hearts of others.

Miss Lydia Stanton is entering her second Season and looks ready to take the *ton* by storm.

With Mx. Fern Hillcrest, Miss Harriet Thackeray, and Mr. Cyril Thompson always seen in each other's company, we anticipate a friendship continuing to blossom.

Mr. Gerald Irving has not returned to London this Season. Some say he is still in his library in the country. We wish him joy there.

Many are placing bets that Miss Aveline Wrenwhistle will finally join her brothers in her own trip to the altar, as her courtship with Mr. Arlen Buckthorn seems to be a promising one.

It has been hinted to this paper that a new Council project will soon steal our attention. We look forward to learning more. With the additions of Pimpernel-Smith, and Messrs. Wyndham and Roger Wrenwhistle, the Council may finally become more than a body of blustery politicians with little influence. Some have criticized the additions of new members who are related to existing members, but this writer believes that a little nepotism lacks the usual bite when incorporated into a figurehead committee. Let us hope these three additions prove their worth and move the Council for Fae and Human Magical Relations to an entity that oversees more than magical testing.

Your winsome writer,
Sal Bailey

CHAPTER 6

KEELAN

KEELAN HAD BEEN awake for hours by the time a footman delivered a copy of the *Tribune* to him in the sitting room where he'd decided to take a more leisurely breakfast. It was the only sort of entertainment that could keep him at home. He read it fervently, smiling through a bite of spiced honey cake at the biggest bit of news that he was already privy to: Emrys and Torquil were set to return to London that very afternoon. He could hardly contain his excitement.

At the familiar sound of paws scuttering across polished wood, he instinctively raised both the paper and his last bite of cake as his father's two spaniels came rushing across the room to greet him. The smaller one, Elodie, leapt onto his lap and snuffled around in the folds of his dressing robe for crumbs, while Alouetta licked his arm. Keelan was about to ask why they were so dreadfully *wet* when he caught sight of his father's equally damp and dirty clothes.

"It's a lovely morning to be out in the garden," he said cheerfully as he entered the room with just as much enthusiasm as the dogs, though his voice was as gentle as ever. "You really ought to join us."

Keelan's brows pinched as he looked out the window. "It's raining."

"Indeed," his father said, eyes wide. "It's when the soil is most alive." He untied the ribbon of his oversized bonnet and tossed it onto an empty chair along with his gloves as he sat heavily next to his son on the sofa. Keelan moved his feet to make more room on the cushion as Elodie clambered over his legs to reach her favorite person. He was glad to be rid of the acrid smell of her as he put the last bite of honey cake in his mouth.

"Emrys is coming home today," he said after he'd swallowed it down.

"Has it been a month already?" his father asked with genuine surprise as he leaned around Elodie to pour himself a cup of tea. "I daresay it doesn't seem possible."

"You should come to the party tonight," Keelan told him with tender encouragement. He hadn't come to the wedding or any of the other celebrations. He never did.

The man laughed dismissively. "Parties are not for me." Keelan noticed the dark lines of soil under his fingernails as he scratched at the shadow of a beard on his round cheek. He and his sister had both gotten their blond hair and light green eyes from him. "But please pass my congratulations on to the couple again."

"I will," Keelan promised.

His father took one large sip of tea before he set the cup down with a clatter and was back on his feet, collecting his things from the chair.

"Off we go, ladies," he announced to the overzealous spaniels, and the three of them left as quickly as they'd come. Keelan watched after them for a moment before he shook his head and went back to reading the *Tribune*.

WHEN IT CAME time to dress for the party, Keelan was hardly focused on what his valet, Marten, picked out for him. He trusted the man's judgment completely when it came to such things. That was why Keelan's sharp gasp of surprise startled both of them when he realized which waistcoat and jacket the valet had chosen.

"Sir, is something the matter?" Marten asked with genuine alarm, holding the waistcoat up to inspect as though he'd somehow missed the fact that it was covered in a massive stain or torn to shreds.

"No," Keelan said quickly, shaking his head. "It's nothing."

It was the same set he'd worn for Emrys and Torquil's wedding.

"Shall I pick something else?" He was already moving swiftly in the direction of the wardrobe. "Perhaps a different combination? You just look so well in plum."

"You needn't change it," Keelan told him.

"Very well," Marten responded in a tone that indicated he wasn't quite sure he believed him.

Keelan avoided looking at his reflection in the mirror as he was dressed. The waistcoat and jacket had made it through that night unscathed, but the trousers had met a more unfortunate fate.

A fresh wave of embarrassment came over Keelan as he remembered how terrible he felt when he'd made it back to his borrowed room at the estate. He was sore and covered in a fine layer of whatever dust coated the bottom of the cart. To make matters worse, both knees of his trousers had ripped on the rough floorboards. He'd sheepishly removed them and draped them over the back of a chair so he had something to glare at while he washed himself with the tepid water left over at the basin from earlier in the day.

As badly as he wanted to cling to the unpleasant parts of the experience to help soothe his wounded pride, he found that a month later, all he could remember was the thrill of the encounter. The memory of the alluring stranger's bruising grip on his hips and the sounds the man had made—the sounds they'd *both* made—after their magics touched had caused Keelan to go a little weak more times than he cared to admit.

That was in the past, he reminded himself as the valet slid the jacket up his arms to his shoulders. He knew that he would eventually forget about the craftsman if he tried. There were countless other people for him to put his focus on in London. Perhaps it was time for him to take better control of his future and begin seeking courtship. He was thirty-two, after all, and as eligible as anyone of his status might hope to be.

With this fresh mindset, Keelan went with his mother to the Wren-whistle townhouse. He was eager to be reunited with Emrys, despite knowing that all of the stories he'd have to share would be sickeningly romantic ones. Fortunately, Keelan had stories of his own. He'd been saving up every interesting thing that had happened while Emrys was in the country to share upon his return.

Keelan imagined that even Torquil might be impressed by the more dramatic bits. At least, he hoped they would be. They were London's most well-known former gossip columnist, after all. To impress Torquil with trifling tales of the *ton* would be comparable to presenting a scholar with new information on their subject of interest—nearly impossible, but boundlessly gratifying if one could manage it.

The arrival of their carriage in front of the townhouse rivaled that of royalty. Keelan pushed his way to the front of the crowd as politely as he could. There was a wave of applause as the door was opened and Emrys stepped out first. To everyone's surprise, rather than taking Torquil's hand to help them down, Emrys swept them up into his arms and spun them around once before setting them down with a kiss.

Torquil's smile was shy when they broke apart, and Emrys grinned as they hid their face against his neck for a moment before allowing him to lead them toward the front steps.

"Welcome home, lovebirds!" Keelan shouted, hands cupped around his mouth so that he could be heard over the rest of the people gathered there.

Emrys found him in the crowd immediately and they locked eyes. His smile grew, as did Keelan's, and Emrys waved his hand in invitation for him to join them as they went inside.

"You didn't write me any letters," Emrys scolded playfully as they climbed the steps. "I hoped I would hear from you."

"I didn't like the thought of you reading them naked," Keelan said, scrunching his nose.

Emrys laughed and rolled his eyes.

"I was not naked the *entire* time," he said.

"He was," Torquil amended from his other side.

Emrys gave his spouse an open-mouthed look of surprise before he laughed again and shrugged in admission.

"I suppose we will just have to catch up in person," he concluded.

That made Keelan's chest fill with warmth. It was exactly what he wanted.

CHAPTER 7

SILAS

SHORTLY AFTER SENDING HIS REPLY, Silas received a response from the councilmember, providing an address for him to report to, and a date to arrive by. He traveled by post to London, an experience and expense he was altogether unfamiliar with, and finally stepped in front of his destination.

The address he had been given was for a townhome which Silas guessed was fashionable and expensive, if the manicured trees, clean walkways, and bright paint were anything to go by. He double checked his letter and then strode to the door, disconcerted to be using the front entrance for once.

A liveried footman answered the door and then let him in after he'd given his name, which cleared some of his doubts. He was clearly expected. An elegant fae lady greeted him as he walked in. The footman provided her with his name and she smiled in response.

"Excellent," she said. "You are one of the first to arrive, Mr. Rook-Worth. Would you like to refresh and relax in your room or would you like some tea first?"

Silas accepted the offer of tea and soon his luggage was being carried away up the stairs and he was trailing in his hostess' wake toward a sunny sitting room.

"Forgive me," she said as she gestured for him to sit. "I haven't properly introduced myself. I am Leonora Pimpernel. My grandchild is Torquil Pimpernel-Smith. They only just arrived in London yesterday, so I offered to welcome all of the arrivals until Torquil had settled more comfortably."

"You live here then, I take it?" Silas asked.

"I do. And staying seemed like the simplest way for me to offer chaperonage while also acting as hostess. With all of you coming from out of town, we were sure it would be nice to have someone at home to offer directions and recommendations." She gave him a friendly smile.

The tea was brought in and Silas spared a moment to be surprised at the speed of service. As he accepted a cup from Mrs. Pimpernel, he reasoned that her staff was likely prepared for such requests, particularly if many arrivals were imminent.

"How many will be staying here?" he asked.

"A half dozen in total, I believe."

Silas attempted to hide his surprise as he sipped his tea. He had never encountered that many fae-humans in his life. Pimpernel-Smith had been the first fae-human he had ever spoken to, although he was dimly aware that others existed. He felt a small frisson of excitement run up his spine at the thought. He would be sharing space with others like him, with magic just as strange as his own. For the first time, he began to feel a little thrilled about this project.

His anticipation increased as another gentleman strode into the room. He was tall with tanned skin, broad shoulders, a chiseled jaw, and stunning blue-green eyes.

"Mr. Rook-Worth, may I introduce Mr. Hedge-Wyck," Mrs. Pimpernel said as Silas stood to greet the newcomer.

They both bowed and Mr. Hedge-Wyck gave Silas a once-over before taking a seat. "Where are you from, then?"

"Manchester." Silas answered. "You?"

"Cornwall. Came here as soon as I could after getting that Pimpernel-Smith person's letter. I wrote to them last year, thought it would be the end of it. But it seems they want to study my magic."

Silas blinked. "Yes…I received the same message."

Hedge-Wyck humphed. "So what's your magic like?"

"I am well versed in human spells but I've never managed any fae magic, aside from sensing."

Hedge-Wyck grinned and sat forward eagerly. "I can do both forms of magic. I've heard that Pimpernel-Smith can only do human magic to start, but I can do both."

Silas felt his stomach churn a little at the other man's words. "Oh," he managed. "Congratulations?"

Hedge-Wyck waved the compliment away. "Can't do sensing, though. Can't imagine it's very useful anyway."

Silas exchanged a look with Mrs. Pimpernel. Her small smirk spoke to his feelings succinctly: only someone who couldn't do something would dismiss it as unimportant. Silas decided not to take the bait. He addressed his next question to Mrs. Pimpernel. "Did you say we were among the first to arrive?"

"Yes, I believe we can expect a couple more today and the others should arrive tomorrow. Once everyone is here, provided there are no delays, of course, I'll see to it you get to the Council chambers to meet with Torquil."

"Perhaps I'll freshen up in my room after all, then."

She smiled knowingly. "Of course. I'll have one of the servants show you to your room. We serve dinner at eight, but if you need something to tide you over until then, just ask. I know you may not yet be used to London hours."

Silas thanked her and followed the servant out of the room. To his annoyance, Hedge-Wyck trailed behind.

"First time in London?"

"Yes," Silas said.

"It's quite a remarkable city, although a great many of the people are toffee nosed idiots."

Silas forebore commenting.

"Were you raised by both of your parents?"

Silas sighed. "Yes," he answered.

"Not me," the other man said. "My mother died just after I was born and my father raised me by himself. He had a local human family teach me how to do the spells he couldn't."

Silas wasn't sure if condolences or more congratulations were in order, so he said nothing.

"Thankfully," he went on, "it means that I've been raised in fae culture." He gave Silas a meaningful look that was best described as a leer. "This is my room," he added. "I'll see you around." He gave Silas a wink and disappeared behind the door.

Silas chuckled to himself after he was shown into his room and closed the door behind him. If nothing else, Hedge-Wyck would clearly be good for bedding. He supposed the man had to have something redeemable, other than good looks. Perhaps Silas would get the distractions he needed after all. With this cheerful thought, he took off his traveling clothes, sank onto the plush bed, and fell asleep.

CHAPTER 8

KEELAN

THE DAY AFTER THE PARTY, Keelan went for his customary morning ride in Hyde Park, hoping it would clear his mind the way it often did when something was troubling him. His family kept a liver chestnut gelding that he adored; the horse was steadfast in every way and made for a perfect companion. When even that failed to lift his spirits, he waited somewhat impatiently until a respectable hour later in the afternoon before he wrote a note to Emrys asking him to meet at the club they belonged to. He hoped that the newlyweds were settled enough by then for Torquil to allow it.

Keelan hadn't the faintest idea what their dynamic would look like now that they were married and living together. After their years-long romance had finally been revealed around the winter holidays and Emrys proposed, the couple had made quick work of trading in their secretive behavior and midnight visits for a very public courtship. Keelan had to wonder what Emrys would do with all of his time now that he was not so busy arranging for flower deliveries and special outings to finally show off his feelings for the person who had captured his heart.

As enjoyable as it had been to talk with Emrys the night before, the conversations they shared at social events were nothing like the ones they were able to have when it was just the two of them. Keelan always found that speaking with anyone away from others made for a more meaningful experience for both people involved. He had spilled some of the gossip that was guaranteed to earn a laugh or a look of surprise, but there was so much more he wanted to discuss, and some of it was not exactly fit for divulging in a room full of people.

He was so distracted by his own muddled thoughts that he did not notice Emrys approaching until he sat down in the chair next to his, casual yet confident and poised as always. His friend offered a familiar grin.

"It's good to see you," Emrys said into the quiet of their favorite little corner spot next to the fireplace. The late hour further emphasized the popping kindling and the soft *clink* of metal against glass as Emrys accepted the drink Keelan had waiting for him, his new gold band flashing on his finger in the firelight.

"I suspect you'd nearly forgotten what anyone aside from Torquil looks like," Keelan said, only half-joking.

"They are rather captivating," Emrys agreed in a dreamy tone, taking a sip of his drink before he turned his attention back to Keelan. "As per usual, your message sounded urgent, so here I am. I've come prepared to listen. I could tell by the way you spoke last night that something is heavy on your mind."

Keelan took a deep breath and sighed it out slowly, his bottom lip curving into a small pout. Was it so obvious? He'd considered how to approach the topic as tactfully as possible. After all, their own shared experience when they were much younger and still figuring out their friendship had also been frightfully unforgettable, though not at all in the same way. And after what had happened the night before, he was truly lost.

"I think I am broken," Keelan admitted at last.

Emrys gave him a puzzled look. "Broken?" He cast a glance over Keelan's body, searching for some sort of physical ailment. "You appear fine to me."

"Yes, I *appear* fine, but in truth I am…not myself."

"Has something happened?" Emrys' voice was laced with real concern. Keelan hesitated. He'd agonized over the topic for weeks, and he felt Emrys was the only one he could tell without any judgment, aside from his horse. He gave the man a pained look.

"Do you remember our conversation at the coffeehouse several months ago? About…" he lowered his voice to a whisper, "compatible magic during intimacy?"

Emrys' eyebrows rose sharply before his expression fell to something more sly. "Yes, I remember," he encouraged.

"Well, I might've…that is, I believe I've, you know…*found* it."

"And was I wrong?" Emrys asked smugly. "It's quite wonderful."

Keelan let out a small groan and rubbed a hand over his face.

"It was, but there's only one problem," he said, ignoring the fact that there were plenty more than just one. "It was with a stranger."

"You did not even ask her name?" Emrys chaffed.

"It was a man, and no, I'm afraid I did not get the opportunity." Keelan's face went hot. "The whole encounter was rather…unrestrained."

"My word." Emrys gave him a scrupulous look. "Keelan Cricket, the most respectable knock in all of London, has finally found the pleasure of a wild romp and it's *broken* him? I'm still not entirely sure what you mean."

"Oh, all right," Keelan grumbled, looking over his shoulder before he leaned more of his weight on his armrest in Emrys' direction and continued in a hushed tone. "To be perfectly honest with you, it was incredible, and I've not stopped thinking about it since. Naturally, the one person I find a connection with is someone I'll never see again. I decided to use last night as a way to try and rid myself of it—of *him*— for good, so I took a delightful young lady home from the party—"

"I wondered where you disappeared off to," Emrys mused.

" —and I took her to bed, and it was…it was…" he searched.

Emrys grimaced. "Oh dear, you couldn't keep it up?"

"Oh, confound it, Emrys, yes, but it was *fine!*"

They both sat in silence for a moment as Keelan's confession settled between them. It sounded so silly now that he'd said it out loud, and Emrys was quick to confirm this.

"Not every intimate encounter is going to be remarkable."

"I'm well aware of that," Keelan said a bit defensively. He knew

Emrys had far more experience with such things, but he'd certainly had his own fair share of mediocre encounters. "I was going to use my magic again, to see if I could recreate such a feeling. But when the moment came, I discovered that I couldn't bring myself to do it."

Severe lack of propriety aside, Keelan found that he'd been too nervous to carry out his plan for fear of disappointment. What if he was ruined forever? How could he hope to find the romance he'd always dreamed of if his greatest chance at love was off roaming anonymously across the countryside using his muscular arms and quick wit to woo other gentlemen into the back of his cart whose names were decidedly *not* Keelan Cricket?

Emrys hummed, drawing him away from his fretful thoughts. "How long ago did this happen? Perhaps you haven't given yourself enough time."

"A month," Keelan admitted with a slight cringe, catching his bottom lip between his teeth as he avoided eye contact. He knew Emrys was smart enough to make the connection there.

"Have you considered the possibility that your interest in intimate partners has shifted? I know you've always been fond of a more delicate sort of person. Was that not the case with your stranger?"

"Quite the opposite, actually." Keelan tried desperately not to think of the man's rough hands and solid body, nor the sultry way he'd spoken to him that had turned his insides to porridge.

"Well, there's your answer," Emrys said with confidence. "You only need to find another strapping gentleman to take you to bed and put all of your pieces back together again. That shouldn't be too difficult. You are very charming, you know."

"I'm not entirely certain that taking *more* people to bed is the answer to my problem," Keelan argued helplessly.

"Then we'll just have to find something else to occupy your mind." Emrys made a thoughtful face, before his expression brightened. "I've got it! Torquil has been talking endlessly about some new project for the Council. I haven't a clue what it's for—you know how my attention tends to wander when anyone speaks of magic in great detail—but they said something the other day about needing volunteers. That ought to keep you busy for at least a little while."

Keelan considered the offer. He was always searching for something interesting to do, and if Torquil was the one behind the project, then it might provide him with more opportunity to get to know them better.

"Are you going to volunteer, as well?"

Emrys shrugged. "I will do whatever Torquil requires of me."

There was a flicker of hope in Keelan's chest. Perhaps Emrys was right. He could use a good distraction.

"Yes, all right," he agreed. "I'll do it."

CHAPTER 9

SILAS

Silas woke up alone in bed. He had weighed the prospects of inviting Mr. Hedge-Wyck the previous night, but had ultimately decided that if he were to stay in London for a couple of months, he would do well to exercise some restraint—or at the very least, tread more carefully when it came to such encounters. He had no desire to repeat his offense from the Wrenwhistle wedding, although he had doubts that a man such as Hedge-Wyck was capable of remorse.

Silas dressed himself and went down to the dining room, surprised to find two additional people at the table. Mrs. Pimpernel introduced them as Mx. Ellery Badger-Thorp and Miss Anise Gloucester-Stone.

Mx. Badger-Thorp was an older person with light brown skin, silver hair, and round physique. They were soft-spoken—not in a way that suggested shyness, but rather mildness of temper. Silas liked them instantly.

Miss Gloucester-Stone was pale with pink cheeks, coiffed brown hair, and a shapely figure. She was chatty and energetic and barely ate in favor of talking about the upcoming project. "It is *so* delightful to have our magic be the focus of study, is it not?" she asked as she picked up a teacup, took barely a sip, and then placed it back down to continue. "I could hardly sleep on the carriage here. Granted, that might have been because it was frightfully uncomfortable. Have you ever slept in a carriage? How do you manage it? I never could. Then again, I don't travel very often as a rule, so that may account for it. Have you ever seen a house so grand? I cannot believe we shall be staying here for as much as two months? My parents couldn't *believe* it when I told them."

Mrs. Pimpernel and Mx. Badger-Thorp gave the young lady pleasant smiles and engaged her in conversation, which was a relief. Silas did not think he was equipped to handle such chattiness first thing in the morning.

Unfortunately, it did mean that he was left alone to entertain Mr. Hedge-Wyck, which was hardly a better option. Silas quickly decided he was not equipped to handle *that* either, so he asked the room at large if all of the participants had arrived.

"Not yet," Mrs. Pimpernel responded. "We are waiting on two more. I know that one will be late, but I expected the other by now."

"Do you know how we will be tested?" Miss Gloucester-Stone asked.

"I do not. But my grandchild is expecting you this morning, and they will explain everything."

"When do we go?" Miss Gloucester-Stone asked.

"Well," Mrs. Pimpernel said, reaching for a watch that hung on a chatelaine at her waist, "I had hoped to wait for the late arrival before sending you all in the carriage."

"Surely you can direct the late arrival when they finally arrive," Mr. Hedge-Wyck said. "There's no need for us to delay simply because of one person's tardiness."

"I don't mind waiting," Mx. Badger-Thorp said. "It would mean Councilmember Wrenwhistle will have to explain things fewer times."

It was decided that the group would wait another hour before heading for the Council chambers. But when the hour passed and the fifth person did not show up, they agreed to leave without them.

Just as they were prepared to step into the carriage, a harried-looking young man raced down the street, shouting, "Don't leave without me!" He paused at the carriage and caught his breath. "Is this the Pimpernel residence?"

"You must be Mr. Finkle-Finch," Mrs. Pimpernel said from the doorway. "What marvelous timing you have! They were heading to the Council chambers to meet my grandchild. Why don't you leave your things here and go with them?"

He gratefully handed his luggage to the footman and then climbed into the carriag. As the carriage started down the street, he apologized profusely for his tardiness, explaining the state of the roads, the difficulty in acquiring transportation, and a serious case of incorrect directions.

Silas took the opportunity to observe the fifth participant. Like both Silas and Mr. Hedge-Wyck, Mr. Finkle-Finch was tall and broad-shouldered, but with more roundness of figure than either of the other two. He had pale skin, tawny hair, and a broad face. Altogether, a very attractive gentleman. Silas felt his hopes rise. This London adventure was proving to be very promising indeed.

They arrived at the parliament buildings and were met by an aide who led them to the Council chambers. Their pace was slow, as everyone in the group dawdled to gawk at the architecture, the paintings, and the furniture. Silas had to refrain from professional commentary; after years of masonry, it was impossible to avoid looking at things with a critical eye. He had a feeling that such observations would hardly cast him in a positive light, so he kept his thoughts to himself. Thankfully, the aide seemed more amused than annoyed. Finally, they were led into a large room with a long table at one end and a podium in front. Councilmember Pimpernel-Smith was seated on the table, perched on the corner, with one leg hitched at an angle. They beamed as the group entered the room.

Hurrying forward, they shook everyone's hand and made introductions. "Thank you all very much for coming. I cannot tell you how much I appreciate it. Please do sit." They gestured at the long table and everyone hesitantly took their seats. "This is typically where the Council convenes," they explained, "but we were given permission to make use of the room this morning. Now." They leaned against the table, still standing. "I've explained this project a little in my letters. Essentially, we would like to fill the gap in understanding of fae-human magic. From what I've learned, every fae-human's magic manifests differently. Last year, two of my colleagues and I wrote out a rubric to use in testing magic in fae-human children. We intend to use that rubric with you all in the coming months, and adjust as needed.

"Each of you will be paired with a fae volunteer who will use their own fae magic sensing abilities to observe your magic use. If you have any difficulties with the fae you are paired with, either in terms of magical compatibility or personality compatibility, please do not hesitate to bring it to my attention. Any questions so far?"

There was silence for a long moment and then Mx. Badger-Thorp raised their hand. "I confess I'm very out of practice with my magic. I worry that I won't be as useful as I'd like."

Councilmember Pimpernel-Smith gave a warm smile in response. "Not at all. I was very out of practice, myself. I have found that the most important thing is to have an understanding and safe partner with which to perform magic."

Badger-Thorp nodded. "Thank you."

Mr. Finkle-Finch raised his hand nervously. "I'm afraid my magic is a bit of a…gamble. Will that be an issue?"

Pimpernel-Smith looked delighted. "Ah! I remember your letter. It won't be an issue at all. Think of all the children whose magic is similar to yours—it will be so helpful for us to have an understanding of what that magic might look like so they can be tested fairly."

Finkle-Finch relaxed with a relieved expression.

"Now, for the next part of the project, I've been working with Councilmembers Wyndham and Roger Wrenwhistle on an experiment of theirs in regards to raw materials. After we have a better understanding of what all of your magic is like, we'd love to see how that magic changes when working with raw ingredients."

"But isn't that dangerous?" Miss Gloucester-Stone asked.

"It can be," the councilmember admitted. "And I will not pressure anyone who does not feel comfortable. My own magic is very weak when I use treated materials, but when I use raw ones, my magic is at the level of many full-blooded magic practitioners. I'm keen to learn if that is the case for others. And please know that we will take every precaution to ensure everyone's safety. You don't have to decide now," they added hurriedly. "But I wanted you all to be aware of that part so you could consider it in the coming weeks."

"My magic is already quite powerful," Hedge-Wyck said. "But I'd be game to try."

"So would I!" Miss Gloucester-Stone said. "How thrilling it would be to use raw materials!"

"And to be as powerful as full-blooded people," Mr. Finkle-Finch said in an awed tone.

"I would be open to trying as well," Mx. Badger-Thorp said.

"And I," Silas said.

"Excellent!" the councilmember said, clapping their hands together. "If you change your mind, or have any concerns, don't hesitate to tell me. But I'm so grateful to you all for your assistance. You can call me Torquil." They paused for a long moment and then said, "If there are no other questions, I'll send for the fae volunteers."

CHAPTER 10

KEELAN

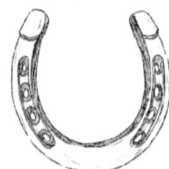

As Keelan peered around the compact office he and the other fae volunteers had been escorted to upon arrival, he couldn't help but feel the curl of nerves in his stomach. It was as though a publication of the *Tribune* had come to life before his very eyes.

He was seated in a chair by the window, as he'd been the first to arrive, and Councilmember Wrenwhistle—Roger—had told him to make himself comfortable. Next to him sat Emrys, who had sparked an easy conversation with Mx. Fern Hillcrest, sharing details he'd gathered from listening to Torquil while preparations were made for this project to begin. It wasn't much.

Mr. Arlen Buckthorn and Mr. Benedict Brooks were also conversing casually where they stood near the door, though neither of them seemed to be paying much attention to the other. Across the room, Emrys' sister Aveline was busy sending peeks of a coquettish grin to Mr. Buckthorn over the pages of her book. Keelan had not been aware that fluttering eyelashes could send such a strong message. Her beau was reciprocating with subtle glances and a curved grin of his own.

Mr. Brooks, on the other hand, was not subtle in the slightest as he leered openly at Emrys' brother, Wyndham. Brooks was the youngest of the group by several years, perhaps not yet twenty-five, and was apparently still learning that it was not the done thing to stare so wantonly at a married gentleman in a room full of people.

Wyndham was, admittedly, the most beautiful man Keelan had ever seen. He had known him since childhood, which meant he also knew the temper that simmered just below the surface of his cool exterior. On several occasions, he'd been witness to the way Wyndham's magic could easily go beyond what was socially acceptable, sudden and without warning. Keelan wasn't sure he could handle that sort of unpredictability in his life. Besides, one night with Wyndham never would have been worth finding out what Emrys' reaction would've been to him sleeping with his youngest sibling. Decidedly off-limits.

Wyndham and Roger were facing each other in private conversation, Wyndham wearing his familiar expression of vague disinterest as he seemed to be reassuring his much shorter and far more hospitable husband. Roger kept glancing at the open doorway and wringing his hands nervously in the space between them, which was doing nothing to ease Keelan's own uncertainty. He watched as Wyndham stooped to press a gentle kiss to Roger's forehead before he turned on the group and clasped his hands behind his back.

The room was suddenly at attention, save for Emrys, who continued what he'd been saying to Mx. Hillcrest with no sense of urgency. Keelan swatted at him with the back of his hand a couple of times. Emrys turned, eyebrows raised slightly, before he gave Wyndham a look that only someone with a younger sibling could probably decipher.

"Apologies," he said, smooth and charming. "Were you saying something?"

Wyndham gazed at him with a level expression for a moment before he took a breath and tilted his chin up slightly, making eye contact with everyone in the room before he began.

"As you're all aware, the Council for Fae-Human Magical Relations is going through some significant changes. With those changes, we are hopeful that we will also be able to make improvements to the way we serve and advocate for all members of society, both fae and human."

Roger appeared at his side then, hands still working uneasily in front of him, and Wyndham placed a reassuring touch on his lower back. Despite the kiss he'd seen before, the sweetness of the gesture took

Keelan by surprise. It seemed that married life looked as well on Wyndham as it did on Emrys.

"A-and not only those who are fae *or* human, but also those who are both," Roger explained. "Torquil, Wyn, and I have spent countless hours over the past several months learning more about the capabilities of fae-humans. But with only one subject to, er, *study*, of course, there is only so much we could do."

"What does that have to do with us?" Brooks asked, looking around at the group as if that alone proved his point. "We are all fae."

Wyndham rolled his eyes so hard it looked like it might've hurt.

"Torquil spent every spare moment of our honeymoon writing to other fae-humans across the country, inviting them to come and be a part of this new project," Emrys told him. He did not exactly sound bitter, but Keelan could tell by the tone in his voice that it had probably been a point of contention between them.

"That still does not explain why we are here," Brooks replied.

"For the purpose of our research, we need to have each fae-human work closely with someone who can observe their magic. Someone to take careful notes and help us compile the information," Roger said. "Yes, we might've been able to conduct the study on our own with one fae-human volunteer at a time, but I—that is, *we* believe it will be much more useful to collect particulars from multiple sources all at once."

"Fae-human magic can be similar to our own," Wyndham told them. "Or, it can be entirely different. From what we already understand, each person's magic is unique, and there is no way to know or predict what a fae-human is capable of."

"That's rather ominous," Mx. Hillcrest muttered, earning a chuckle from a few of the others.

"Not in a dangerous way," Emrys cut in, though he was smiling.

"Yes, you should know better than any of us, old chap," Buckthorn said.

Emrys' expression turned to something more clever, perhaps with a bit of pride at the fact that he knew something the rest of them likely did not. To his knowledge, Keelan had never interacted directly with a fae-human's magic before, and certainly not so *intimately* as that. From the sound of it, he supposed he was about to get his first opportunity rather soon.

"There is always a risk with anyone's magic." Wyndham directed the attention back to himself before they could get too far off topic. "We will use what we already know to ensure that this is done with caution in mind every step of the way."

"Are there any other questions?" Roger asked, looking hopeful. There were a couple of glances exchanged among the group, but none of them said anything.

Keelan did have questions, though he did not want to be the only one asking. How much would he be using his own magic during the project? Would it be anything beyond sensing? How often would they be meeting? Would there be any obligations outside of the work on the project?

"As you're all volunteering, you are free to change your mind about participation at any time," Roger assured them as he pushed his specta-cles up on his nose with a bent knuckle. "However, we do hope that you'll stay the course. We tried to be diverse in our selections, as Torquil has promised the same from their own group. You'll be meeting all sorts of lovely people from various places." He looked up at Wyndham in what looked like a reach for some reassurance of his own. "I believe each of them is from somewhere outside of London?"

Wyndham gave a short nod and then regarded the group.

"Shall we?" It wasn't a question, but a direct invitation to follow him. Keelan stood from his chair and fell into line beside Emrys, hopeful that situating himself there would give him a bit of an advan-tage if there was one to be had.

Once they had filed into the hallway, Keelan leaned forward and asked quietly in Roger's direction, "Have the assignments already been made for who will be working together?" They passed by his mother's closed office door as Roger turned to look at him.

"Yes," he said with a nod. "We tried to be thoughtful about it, though it's hard to say for sure who will work well together. We consid-ered letting all of you meet first and then assigning partners after, but… well, we felt that might lead to some, er, undesirable results," he added, color blooming on his tan cheeks as he fumbled over his answer.

It was clear that *undesirable* actually meant unprofessional and inappropriate. Keelan again considered the selection of London's most eligible or very recently married fae he was walking with. It seemed to him that it might've been wise to cast their net a little wider if they expected to have no concerns about such behavior. Then again, fae were not exactly known to let go of their proclivities simply because they had aged—or gotten married, for that matter.

When they arrived outside of the heavy double doors leading to the room where the Council met, an aide standing outside the door opened it just far enough to peer in, asking something in a low voice. Keelan touched two fingertips to his tongue and smoothed them over each of his full brows before he tugged at the bottom of his waistcoat.

Emrys snorted a laugh at him.

"You look as though you're preparing to meet the Prince Regent," he whispered loudly.

Keelan shoved an elbow into his side, pressing his lips together to hide his grin. "I want to make a good impression," he whispered back.

The aide turned around and nodded at Wyndham, who then whirled neatly on the group behind him. He considered each of them—Emrys for the longest. Emrys stared right back, still smirking.

"Be nice," Wyndham warned, placing subtle emphasis on both words.

The doors opened. Wyndham and Roger led them in, the air immediately swirling with piqued interest and the prickly feeling of outright assessment that only came with unfamiliarity.

In the hallway, Aveline had said something about the excitement of making new friends. He decided to focus on that. Keelan loved London, and he loved it even more when he had the rare opportunity to show someone new around. He knew the best places to eat, the most interesting shops, and *all* of the best forms of entertainment to be found. He also had little opportunity to use his magic, so to have a good excuse for letting it free was very tempting, indeed. Emrys had promised him a distraction, and he felt confident that he would find it in this new project.

Keelan was only able to glance briefly at the selection of fae-humans, who had risen to their feet on the opposite side of the long table, before his focus went to figuring out which chair he was meant to take. He waited for Emrys to stop at one before he looked behind him to see that Mx. Hillcrest also found their spot. Keelan offered them a polite grin before he raised his head to properly greet the newcomers.

Their clothes were not quite as fine, their features not nearly as pronounced as full-blooded fae, but they were still undeniably alluring. Keelan took them in one at a time, appreciating the novelty of them, until he got to the fifth chair and was struck with such violent surprise that he gasped hard enough to draw Emrys' attention.

There, directly across the table, was his stranger.

CHAPTER 11

SILAS

Silas did not expect to see Cricket ever again. Even less, did he expect to see the man as much at a disadvantage as he had left him. Well, perhaps less of a disadvantage. He had the opportunity to see the gentleman file through the door, observed his relaxed smile to the fae next to him, and his pleasant expression as he glanced around the table. Then he saw that pleasant expression swiftly shift to one of shock and—though Silas hated to admit it—horror. The man gasped so loudly that Mr. Emrys Wrenwhistle turned to stare at him.

"You look as if you've seen a ghost," Mr. Wrenwhistle muttered.

Cricket was indeed pale at the sight of Silas. He sank into his own seat without a word. Silas willed himself to look away. If the two of them stared at each other so obviously it would most certainly cause a scene. He glanced up to see Torquil watching him with a curious expression and he attempted to force his face into something bland and neutral.

Torquil's mouth quirked a little as they gestured to two of the men who had entered. "Allow me to introduce Councilmember Wyndham Wrenwhistle and Councilmember Roger Wrenwhistle. We will be working together for the whole of this project. If you have any questions, you will be free to ask any of us."

Although Silas had seen them at the wedding, he took a moment to observe the other two councilmembers. Councilmember Wyndham Wrenwhistle was a tall and slender fae with light brown hair that fell to his shoulders and was tucked behind his pointed ears. He had pale skin and sharp green eyes and was remarkably beautiful, even more than most of the fae in the room.

Councilmember Roger Wrenwhistle was a short and round human, with a handsome and friendly face. He had dark brown eyes, light brown skin, and curly dark brown hair. He wore a pair of spectacles that he pushed up his nose in what Silas could quickly tell was a nervous habit.

After the two councilmembers bowed to the rest of the group, Torquil held up a paper. "The Council has put together a list of the first pairings. Please keep in mind that if you need to change partners, you need only ask. We want to ensure this is a pleasant experience for all. We would like everyone to try and work with your assigned partner for the first four or five days, to give each pair an opportunity to become acquainted, both with each other and each other's magic."

"How often will we be meeting?" Miss Gloucester-Stone asked. "Every day?"

Though Silas tried not to notice, he couldn't help but observe that Cricket seemed to relax slightly at the question. He was no longer staring at Silas, but watching Torquil with determined focus.

Torquil smiled. "Very good question. Yes, we intend for everyone to meet most days, with a day or two off every week to rest. Ideally, we'd like you all to practice here in the Council chambers. We have some empty offices you can use, and this room can be sectioned off easily to accommodate a few groups. If anyone requires privacy, exceptions can be made, but we would prefer if everyone stayed here in case questions come up or if any councilmembers need to assist. The Council chambers seemed better suited to our project than the Pimpernel townhouse where you're all staying. We'd like you all to have a place to relax, without project detritus everywhere, and we have more offices here than there are sitting rooms in the townhouse." They paused. "Any other questions before I read out the groups?"

Torquil's husband raised his hand, causing Torquil to smile more broadly. "Yes, Emrys?"

"There don't seem to be enough fae-humans in the room? Do you intend to be part of the project too?"

Torquil chuckled. "Another good question. And, no I don't. We are still waiting on our last out-of-town guest. She did write that she would be a little late—some social obligation or other, I think—but I anticipate her arrival today."

Mr. Emrys Wrenwhistle looked pleased with himself for having asked a good question.

Torquil paused again and then said, "Now, our first pair will be: Mx. Badger-Thorp and Mr. Buckthorn."

The two stood up, looking a little uncertain. The two Wrenwhistle councilmembers ushered the pair to the door where an aide was ready to lead them down the hall.

"Next, Mr. Finkle-Finch and Mx. Hillcrest." These two were led out the door as well. "Miss Gloucester-Stone and Miss Wrenwhistle."

Silas attempted to school his expression of surprise as the two ladies exited the room. Just how many Wrenwhistles were involved in the Council?

"The last few pairs will be working in this room," Torquil explained. "The remaining offices all still have councilmembers using them. If this becomes too challenging for focus, we will reevaluate."

One quick look around the table and Silas felt dread coating his stomach. He was *not* about to be paired with Cricket. It was simply not possible. But how could he refuse without explaining the reason? He began trying to come up with some excuse. He glanced at the gentleman in question and quickly guessed that he was coming to the same conclusions. His face was bright red and he was staring at the table as if he hoped to be paired with *it*.

"Mr. Hedge-Wyck and Mr. Brooks, if you two will take that corner over there. Mr. Rook-Worth and—"

The door swung open and an aide held it for a young lady who strode in with an air of calm self-assurance. Her chin was tilted upward and her posture was impeccable. Silas was no judge of feminine beauty, but he supposed she was probably a pretty sort of person.

"Ah," Torquil said, beaming at her. "Miss Wilton-Reed?"

"The same," she said in posh tones.

"You have perfect timing. We were just getting to the assigned pairs. I'll finish the list and then explain everything you've missed."

She nodded and stayed standing. Silas couldn't tell if she had already reasoned that she'd have to get up from the table again or if she merely didn't want to deign to sit with them. He suspected it was the latter.

"Where was I? Ah, yes, Mr. Rook-Worth, sorry for the interruption. You will be paired with Mr. Emrys Wrenwhistle."

Silas barely avoided letting out a huge sigh of relief. He looked at Mr. Wrenwhistle, who gave him a friendly nod and indicated another corner of the room. Silas did not glance behind him to see Cricket's reaction, but he hoped the other man was just as relieved as he was.

He followed Mr. Wrenwhistle to the corner of the room and the gentleman rubbed his hands together with enthusiasm. "Truth to tell, I'm not entirely sure what we're to do," he said. "I expect Torquil will give us more instructions later."

"They said something about us using the rubric they created and going through that."

Mr. Wrenwhistle brightened. "Did they? That's good. I'm sure they've told me but I do tend to get a bit lost in all the explanations."

Silas did not like to hear that but he kept his expression carefully neutral.

"Is your magic like Torquil's, then?"

"From what I can tell, our magic is all quite different."

"What's yours like?"

"I can do human spells, but I've never managed fae spells. I can sense magic very well, though."

"Right," Mr. Wrenwhistle said. "Not at all like Torquil then. Well, this will be interesting."

Silas managed a grunt of acknowledgement.

One of the other Wrenwhistles hurried over, the shorter one, and one Silas hadn't met yet. "We don't have all the supplies prepared yet," he explained, pushing his spectacles up his nose in a nervous gesture. "So we thought today might be good for general acquaintanceship.

We'll start in earnest tomorrow morning." He bustled off again to tell another group.

Silas snuck a glance at the long table and saw Cricket now sitting across from his own partner. Torquil was clearly still explaining things to her.

"So," Mr. Wrenwhistle said and Silas returned his attention to him. "Tell me about yourself."

CHAPTER 12

KEELAN

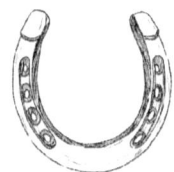

IF IT WEREN'T for the pressure to uphold his promise and help gain the favor of his best friend's new spouse, Keelan would have stayed as distant from the Council's chambers as possible for the next several months. He could find plenty to do away from the parliament buildings, away from the Thames, away from Mayfair if needed. Anywhere but in the same room as the man who'd become a source of discomfiture and fantasy in equal measure.

Worse yet, the fae-humans were boarding in a townhouse absurdly close to his family's own that had previously belonged to Torquil's grandmother, but now belonged to Torquil. Of course they would be so kind as to offer a place for the visitors to stay. He'd slept with his windows shut and curtains drawn in a ridiculous attempt to create any sort of additional distance between himself and one guest in particular.

With a fortifying breath, Keelan climbed the steps outside the massive limestone building and found his way to the meeting room they'd all gathered in the previous day. To his relief, it appeared he was the first to arrive again as the aide let him into the empty room. Rather than taking a seat, he wandered his nervous energy to the windows along the far wall and bent slightly at the waist to peer out one of them, hands still in his pockets.

It was a gray morning, the heavy clouds overhead reflected in the darker water of the river that he could see only a small part of from his vantage point. He'd dressed for rain just in case, but he was starting to regret it. The damp heat already gathering beneath his arms and within his high boots told him he had planned poorly for a day inside this stuffy room.

The low sound of voices on the other side of the doors caught his attention. He turned to find Torquil and Roger being let in, caught in a somewhat serious conversation judging by the tone of their words and the expression he could see on Roger's face. Though, to be fair, Roger often looked concerned without reason, dark brows pinched together and a slight frown on his mouth. He noticed Keelan and rallied instantly.

"Mr. Cricket!" he greeted, as Torquil gave him their attention as well with a far more subdued but kind grin. "You're here early."

"I always am," Keelan offered a bit sheepishly, stepping closer to them.

Torquil huffed out a hum of mild amusement. "I'm afraid the same cannot be said for either of our husbands, as you well know." Keelan did know. "It appears that the rest of our study group also prefers to keep London hours."

"Perhaps it is a novelty for those who are not used to it?" Keelan guessed. He was not sure what all of the fae-humans did with their time, but if they were of the working class, they would be expected to wake early. He briefly speculated about the habits of the craftsman in particular before he caught himself.

Torquil seemed to consider this answer and then made a thoughtful sound of what Keelan took to be agreement. He swallowed down the rush of pride he felt at their approval.

"Torquil and I were just discussing what we hope to get accomplished by the end of this week," Roger explained, welcoming Keelan into the conversation. "Our plan is to allow all of you several days to become better acquainted with what your partners are capable of magically before we begin applying it to the rubric. It seems unfair to begin the formal observations straight away."

Keelan hoped his face did not give too much of himself up as he thought more seriously about the project. Or rather, about his partner.

Melisande Wilton-Reed was the spirited sort of young lady who was easy to know, so long as you didn't mind listening to her talk about herself and little else.

Within the first quarter-hour of their meeting, Keelan learned she'd traveled from Bath, she had several sisters whose names also began with *M*, and that she was *very* fond of flowers. She'd described the manicured grounds at her family's home in great detail, naming several blooms he'd never even heard of. More than once, she proclaimed that she was singularly responsible for her family winning first place in the local gardening society's annual competition four years running. When Keelan offered his congratulations and praised her success, her smile was as radiant as any marigold or sunny columbine might hope to be.

When he attempted to share something about himself, however, she did not return his enthusiasm. Her responses were curt, her expression largely uninterested, and she kept glancing around him as though she would've preferred to speak with anyone else. After a while, he attributed it to her being distracted by the newness of London and all it had to offer. He could certainly appreciate that.

"Yes," Keelan finally agreed with an eager nod. "Some more time to get to know one another would be most helpful."

Slowly, the rest of the participants showed up. The ones who had been sent to work in the empty offices checked in before they disappeared again, while the same three groups as the previous day remained in the larger room. Keelan asked Emrys if he knew why they were so lucky as they both waited on their respective fae-humans to arrive.

"Neither Mr. Brooks nor Mr. Hedge-Wyck have reached majority," he explained in a hushed tone as they both looked over at the gentlemen. "Not that anyone in this assembly can be accused of standing on ceremony, but I do believe placing those two alone in a room would prove rather unproductive for the purposes of this project." By the lustful looks they were busy giving each other in their far corner of the room, Keelan guessed that was a fair assessment. "As for me, would you believe that Torquil does not trust my ability to report my findings accurately?" Emrys said this with such mock affront that it made them both chuckle. "I promised them I would be most thorough, but alas, here I am to be watched like an infant."

"And me?" Keelan asked with uncertainty.

Emrys raised an eyebrow at him.

"Are you looking to be left alone with your partner?"

"No," Keelan said, perhaps a bit too emphatically. "Certainly not." He'd already had relations with one fae-human volunteer. The last thing he needed was to earn a reputation by repeating his blunder with another.

Emrys gave him an amused look and tilted his chin up at where the trio of councilmembers was standing together off to one side.

"It was Torquil's idea, so that you and I could spend more time together. They're very appreciative that you decided to help with the project." He leaned closer. "As it turns out, they struggled to find enough people to even make the whole thing possible. But you did not hear that from me."

Keelan nodded his understanding and felt appreciation of his own welling in his chest. Perhaps earning Torquil's favor was not going to be as difficult as he'd thought.

"Speaking of partners," Emrys went on then with a devious smirk. "Mine seemed to get quite the reaction out of you yesterday. Care to explain yourself?"

Keelan opened his mouth to begin his defense just as the doors opened. Miss Wilton-Reed gave the room a sweeping look of assessment as she entered, smiling at those who noticed her, followed by Mr. Rook-Worth. At least Keelan finally knew his name.

"Later," Keelan promised as he stepped away from the corner that Emrys had been assigned to so he could greet his partner at the table. He pointedly took the long way around and did not spare a glance in Mr. Rook-Worth's direction.

"Good morning, Miss Wilton-Reed," he offered with a slight dip of his head and a friendly expression, neither of which she reciprocated. Just as the day before, her wardrobe was fashionable and very well put together, if not a bit overdone. The tiny flowers embroidered along the neckline of her dress seemed rather delicate for a day full of doing magic.

"Aren't the details lovely?" She swept her fingers over the little blossoms, clearly taking his attention on them as a compliment of some sort.

"Yes, quite. Did you do them yourself?"

Ms. Wilton-Reed's eyes went wide before she barked out a laugh.

"I assure you, Mr. Cricket, my talents are better put to use elsewhere. We employ our own seamstress for such tasks."

Roger approached with an armful of materials including a stack of paper, two well-worn reference books, and several jars of ingredients. He set them on the table, scrambling to fix one of the jars as it toppled over and began to roll away. He gave them an apologetic smile.

"Right," he began. "Today we would like for Miss Wilton-Reed to begin by showing a few examples of what she is most comfortable doing with her magic. We have provided some basic materials for her, and er…spellpaper that you can also use to write down your observations, Mr. Cricket."

"You may address me directly as well, Mr. Wrenwhistle. I am sitting right here." Miss Wilton-Reed reached for one of the jars. She unscrewed the lid and sighed down at the contents. "I hate to be a bother, but I have a negative reaction to peppercorns. You'll have to bring me something else."

"Oh," Roger said quickly, taking the jar and lid from her and holding them close to his chest. "I do apologize," he added before walking away.

Keelan blinked at the woman. What she lacked in stature, she certainly made up for with her presence.

"Anything in particular you would like to see first?" she asked, looking directly at him in what felt very much like a challenge. Her eyes were a deep brown to match the color of her hair, flecked with green and gold. "As I told you yesterday, I start most every casting with my natural magic and enhance it with a human spell."

"Natural magic," Keelan echoed.

She gave him a dubious look. "You know," she said, flicking her wrist in such a way that he wondered how it was not painful as the lids of the two remaining jars they'd been given unscrewed in a whirl of air and fell noisily onto the table. "Natural magic."

Keelan shuddered a little in his chair.

"Of course," he said, recovering. He leaned forward for a sheet of paper and the pencil, hastily sliding both across the smooth tabletop toward himself so that he could begin writing. Penmanship had never been a strength of his in school, so he could all but feel her critical eye on him as he wrote down what she'd said.

"Do you use your magic very often?" he asked when he finished.

Her answer was breezy and confident. "I take every opportunity I'm given to demonstrate my aptitude."

"Is that…often?" Keelan tried again, feeling smaller by the second.

"How would you define *often?*" she asked impatiently.

"Well, for example, here in the city I hardly ever use my magic," he tried to explain. "I suppose it's mostly because I have other people to do things for me. Servants and such. I used it far more when I was younger, but now it's…well, it's something I'm glad to have if needed."

"You do not appear to be very old now," Miss Wilton-Reed discerned, her eyes trailing down the front of him before returning to his face. "I turned thirty a fortnight ago," she offered with a well-pleased smirk. "This is my first time traveling alone. My first time in London."

"I hope you're enjoying it so far," Keelan told her, unable to stop his grin.

"Not really," she said plainly. His grin faded. "My father begged me to come here. After all the fancy business with Mx. Pimpernel-Smith being accepted back into society, my own family has been rushed into the center of everyone's attention back home. Father thought it essential that I make good use of this opportunity. He wants everyone to associate our names with *progress* and *forward-thinking.*" The last words came out thick and mocking. "I only agreed so that I might discover how the shops here compare to the ones in Bath."

"That's unfortunate," Keelan told her softly.

He understood how difficult it was to behave a certain way to appease a parent. Though in his situation, it was because his mother had been on the Council for most of his life. *Progress* and *forward-thinking* had been in his vocabulary for decades, alongside *etiquette* and *propriety.* Soon enough, he knew he'd be expected to do what society—and his mother—begged of him: stop dreaming of the perfect romance and find a spouse.

Ms. Wilton-Reed regarded him skeptically. "Why are you here?"

He considered his answer. He nearly peered over his shoulder at Emrys, but caught himself, remembering who else he would find.

"Helping a friend," he said in earnest.

To his astonishment, this was met with a bubble of laughter.

"Can you even do magic?" Miss Wilton-Reed goaded.

"Yes," he argued sharply, sounding more offended than he actually was. His sister was the one set to inherit, but his magic was still quite respectable. He poked his bottom lip out faintly as his eyes danced over the items on the table between them. He realized that someone who could do fae magic *and* human magic might not find his own magic impressive at all, but he had to prove that he was competent at the very least.

He decided to keep it simple. Emrys had far better control with liquids than he did, but this was a trick they'd been perfecting for over a decade. He picked up the open jar of oil between them and tipped it sideways over the stack of papers as though to dump it out. At the same time, they both looked up from the table to see that the syrupy contents of the jar had remained in place. He righted the jar and set it down with a satisfied little smile.

Seconds later, the jar tipped again, only this time it was directed at him. The oil spread across the paper he'd been taking notes on and only gained momentum as it neared the edge of the table. Keelan let out a ridiculous yelp as he pushed up out of his chair to avoid getting it on his clothes. With no lip to contain it, the oil flowed over the side onto the polished wooden seat of the chair he'd abandoned, and then dripped steadily from there onto the floor.

He shot a mortified look at his partner. She had started laughing again, this time with a hand securely over her mouth.

"It wasn't me!" she protested.

Then he heard the laughter from behind him. Keelan spun around toward Emrys, who offered a guilty shrug and a wink. Roger hurried over to see if everything was all right. Wyndham called out for an aide to bring some rags at once. If it had been another liquid, such as water or wine, the cleanup would've been simpler. But even magic was no match for paper drenched with oil.

"I'm sorry," Keelan muttered to Roger, who waved a hand at him.

"Nonsense," Roger reassured him. "We fully expected for there to be some mishaps. I'll get you some more, er...everything," he added, gesturing to the materials that had been ruined by the spill.

Miss Wilton-Reed collected herself and let out a sigh laced with satisfaction. "Perhaps I will enjoy my time in London, after all."

CHAPTER 13

SILAS

Silas couldn't take his eyes away from the sight of Mr. Cricket attempting to mop up the spilled oil. Part of the reason was because the man kept bending over in a very pleasing way. But the other reason was a little harder for Silas to understand—seeing Mr. Cricket blush and apologize to his partner, Councilmember Wrenwhistle, and the aide made Silas feel…protective? There was something so vulnerable about the gentleman. Vulnerability had never appealed to Silas before and he had no idea why it suddenly appealed now. Just as he had felt an inexplicable desire to follow after Cricket that memorable night, he felt a similar desire to hurry over and help the man now. Though what he might have done, he had no idea.

His own partner's laughter pulled his attention back to where it ought to be. Mr. Wrenwhistle met Silas' eye with an expression that anticipated matched amusement. Before Silas could determine how best to respond, Mr. Wrenwhistle's brother approached them.

The councilmember gave Mr. Wrenwhistle a stern look. "I believe I gave you very particular instructions."

"You gave a great many instructions. Do you really expect me to remember them all?" Mr. Wrenwhistle replied.

"I told you to be nice," Councilmember Wrenwhistle said. "You couldn't even manage that for two days."

Silas' partner rolled his eyes. "I'm being perfectly nice to my partner. Am I not, Mr. Rook-Worth?"

Silas was saved from having to answer as the councilmember leaned in and said in a low tone, "You have set a very poor example for the other fae volunteers. How is poor Keelan's partner going to look at him now? And how do you expect your partner to trust you with the way you're behaving?"

Mr. Wrenwhistle's expression turned slightly wary as he looked at Silas. Silas shrugged. "I know better than to trust you around an open bottle of oil."

Mr. Wrenwhistle grinned. "See? No harm done."

"I will not hesitate to remove you from this project. Remember that you're representing people other than yourself right now." He flicked a glance across the room to Mr. Wrenwhistle's spouse.

Now that the oil spill was cleared up, Torquil was busy talking to the pair and examining the ingredients remaining on the table. Mr. Wrenwhistle's expression softened. "Oh, very well," he muttered.

Councilmember Wrenwhistle gave Silas a curt bow, although Silas suspected the curtness was due to the gentleman's irritation with his brother, and strode away.

Mr. Wrenwhistle sighed. "Right, where were we?"

"I was explaining the human spells I'm most accustomed to."

"Ah, yes." Mr. Wrenwhistle frowned down at his notes. "You said you excel at levitation, fire spells, shade spells, fortifying spells, cleaning spells—I can't quite read that one so we'll skip it—and pouring spells?"

Silas chuckled. "I believe that's breeze spells. And I'm afraid 'excel' might be a bit too strong of a word. Let's say I'm proficient."

Mr. Wrenwhistle made a note next to the indecipherable writing. "What was that?" Before Silas couldn't reply, he said, "Oh, I think excel's a perfectly fine word. Confidence and all that. Should we give it a go? I don't know what ingredients you need or which spell you want to do first."

Silas looked through the ingredients again. "Levitation should do nicely, I think."

"Excellent." Mr. Wrenwhistle leaned back in his chair expectantly.

Silas liked his partner. He seemed an affable young man. He didn't strike Silas as particularly academic, but he found that a good deal less intimidating. Nevertheless, he was uniquely nervous to perform magic before a stranger. Considering how often he'd felt the magic of strangers in bed, it was odd to feel reticence now. Without the cover of nighttime, there was a sense of exposure that made him uncomfortable.

Still, he was here to work. He took off his coat, rolled up his sleeves, and pulled out a sheet of paper. He could feel his partner's eyes on him as he wrote out the memorized sigils and sprinkled the ingredients over the paper. Then he pulled out a handkerchief and placed it in the center of the paper before casting the spell. As the handkerchief glided upward, Silas felt out with his magic. Then he bent over the paper to add another sigil to increase the strength. He felt a brush of magic against his own—Mr. Wrenwhistle reaching out with his own magic to sense Silas'—not an uncomfortable feeling but an ill-fitting one. When he went to expand his spell, he found the sensation of Mr. Wrenwhistle's magic oddly *constricting*. The spell increased in power, but not nearly as much as Silas expected. Surprised, he let the spell drop and the handkerchief fluttered down to the paper.

Mr. Wrenwhistle pursed his lips. "What's the difference between that and a breeze spell?"

"It's a bit more specific. Breeze spells and wind spells are a little wilder. Levitation spells are more straightforward. You want the object to go up. Or you want the object moved to the top shelf. That sort of thing. That isn't to say you couldn't use a breeze spell to do that, but you might knock off the things on the shelf you're trying to move your object to."

"Hm," Mr. Wrenwhistle grunted.

"Any observations?"

His partner puffed out his cheeks on an exhale as he looked over his notes. "It was interesting the way you added power to it after it was already in motion."

"That was this sigil," Silas explained, pointing to it.

"It's the same as this one," Mr. Wrenwhistle said, pointing to another.

Silas smiled. "Yes. It indicates direction. I wanted the handkerchief to float higher up, so I added another sigil. Alternatively, I could have adjusted my calculations," he said, gesturing to another corner of the paper, "but those have never been my strongest suit. I prefer to go with something simpler."

"Thank goodness for that," Mr. Wrenwhistle muttered. He bent over his paper and began writing notes.

Silas snuck a glance at Cricket. He had recovered from the oil incident and was watching as Miss Wilton-Reed made one of the jar lids pinwheel across the table. As there was no spellpaper in front of her, it was evident she was using her fae magic. Silas wished, briefly, that he could sense her magic, but he worried that it might impact the project, especially considering how his own magic had reacted. There was something about her spell that seemed weak to him. He felt the corners of his mouth tug upwards at the thought. He hadn't cared for the way she'd laughed at Cricket. Not that he was in any place to judge anyone's treatment of the gentleman, but he felt Cricket deserved better. With a pang, he remembered that Cricket deserved better from him too. He turned back to his partner, who was still writing, and planned his next spell.

CHAPTER 14

KEELAN

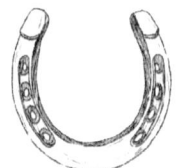

On his life, Keelan could not determine why he had agreed to subject himself to a dinner at the Wrenwhistle townhouse that evening. Not only was he exhausted from spending the entire day attempting to remember a thousand personal details his partner had shared about her various interests and assets, but the lingering tension between Emrys and Wyndham after the little mishap with the oil was so uncomfortable that he could hardly sit still in his chair. Everyone was eating in silence and looking at anything but one another.

It was Mrs. Wrenwhistle who eventually said something.

"Wynnie, dear, you could at least pretend to eat something," she chided. "You look thin. Do I need to send someone from our kitchen to offer guidance on your preferred meals?"

Wyndham's eyes slid shut. "Mother," he began tightly, before Roger put a hand on his arm and gave Mrs. Wrenwhistle a timid smile.

"It's been a trying couple of days," he explained, choosing his words carefully. "Wyn has put most of his attention toward our project. We all have." There were several nods and sounds of agreement from around the table, though it was really only Roger, Wyndham, and Torquil who could claim it in truth.

"You'd do well to still look after yourselves," Mrs. Wrenwhistle sniffed before she reached for her wine. "Certainly whatever you discover will be no use to anyone if you're all ravenous and sleep-deprived by the end of it."

Keelan did not think there was any chance of the Wrenwhistle siblings lacking sleep, but he kept that to himself. Instead, he took a generous bite of his meal and peeked at Emrys in the seat beside him, who was looking right back.

"Will you forgive me?" Emrys asked, looking piteous.

"Of course I forgive you," Keelan told him on an exhale. He couldn't stay upset with the man for very long. The dinner invitation had been the first part of his apology, and he'd already let go of his irritation by the time Emrys had asked him. The only thing that remained was his embarrassment.

"I was simply trying to lighten the mood," Emrys went on. "I could hear how beastly she was being from across the room, questioning your magic."

Keelan was suddenly aware of three more pairs of eyes on him.

"Miss Wilton-Reed?" Torquil asked. "Has she been unkind to you?"

"No," Keelan said, shaking his head. "I think...well, I think she's rather upset with her father, you see. It seems as though it wasn't entirely her idea to participate in this project." He stole a nervous glance at Torquil. "Though I'm certain she'll come around. She's incredibly talented by all accounts, magically and otherwise, and a fine conversationalist. I do believe she will provide a wealth of information to the Council."

His answer seemed to satisfy everyone, which was a relief.

"My partner is lovely," Aveline put in after a lull. "In another life, I think Miss Gloucester-Stone and I might've been sisters. She and I spent the entire day chattering about our favorite romantic novels and reticule collections. She only has one bag with her in London, but I've promised to bring a different style of mine along each day for her to see. She's as excited as I am about the latest trend in flashy spangles along the trim. We've so much in common!"

"Let us be grateful that siblings do not always share characteristics," Wyndham said pointedly over the rim of his wine glass.

Emrys did not look up from his plate as he huffed out a laugh, a smirk forming at the corner of his mouth. "You're right. It wouldn't do for more than one of us to be such an unimaginable prig."

The shift in the air was tangible. Keelan watched as something flashed across Wyndham's hard expression before the legs of his chair scraped against the floor as he got to his feet.

"Thank you for dinner, Mother," he said, jaw working. "Torquil, we'll see you in the morning." With that, Wyndham turned and walked out of the room with Roger close behind.

Another silence stretched out until the sound of their footsteps in the hallway had faded.

Mrs. Wrenwhistle sighed deeply.

"Why must you torment your brother so?" she asked Emrys without looking at him, sounding more tired than anything else. "It pains me to see you still squabbling after all these years."

When the meal was finally over, Emrys made no offer for Keelan to linger at the house for drinks or a game. Even if he had, Keelan was too ready for his bed to accept such a proposition. He had a sinking feeling that the next day was going to be equally as draining. Emrys escorted him to the foyer and remained there as Keelan was helped into his coat and hat. The skies had finally opened up and let go of the rain they'd been holding back earlier.

Keelan could tell what Emrys wanted to say by the look on his face alone.

"It's fine, Emrys, I promise," he said easily. "I'm not angry with you. I would have been if you'd ruined my clothes, but luckily for you it was only my dignity that was sullied." He finished with a grin to help prove his point. It earned him a sympathetic grimace.

"If it helps, Mr. Rook-Worth did not seem to care that you made a spectacle of yourself," Emrys told him. "I daresay he's not the excitable type."

Keelan's eyes went a bit wide as he looked down at his boots and cleared his throat. "Indeed," he managed.

"Which reminds me, we never finished our conversation from earlier." Emrys arched a brow. "How do you know him?"

Intimately, Keelan blurted in his mind.

He let out a small laugh and said, "Did the two of you not speak at all about yourselves yesterday?" He'd had the entire afternoon to come up with this response and hoped it was good enough to steer the topic away from himself. "I'm surprised that you do not remember him. He was one of the craftsmen who built the fire pit for your wedding spell."

Emrys was taken aback by this. "Not really?" Keelan nodded sagely, as though he wouldn't have also forgotten the man entirely by then had it not been for their ardent encounter behind the stables. "I suppose I was rather distracted at the time."

"Perhaps you should offer your thanks tomorrow. They really did a wonderful job with it."

After a moment, Emrys let out a long breath, apparently satisfied with the outcome of his extended apology. He clapped Keelan on the shoulder and took a couple of retreating steps toward the staircase behind him.

"Well, on to the next." His expression turned sly. "Earning Torquil's forgiveness is not so easy, but I am quite familiar with what usually works the best." Emrys had already charged halfway up the stairs before he called out over his shoulder for Keelan to wish him luck.

Keelan chuckled and stepped out the door after it was opened for him. He peered up into the rain, squinting against the drops that pattered softly on his cheeks, before he started down the front steps.

"Good luck, my friend."

CHAPTER 15

SILAS

The townhouse was filled with chatter as everyone sat down to dinner. Mrs. Pimpernel smiled around the table and asked how everyone's day was.

"Miss Wrenwhistle is lovely," Miss Gloucester-Stone gushed. "So sweet. We got on immediately. I'm sure we shall be great friends."

Mrs. Pimpernel beamed in response. "I'm delighted to hear it. Although I'm not surprised. The Wrenwhistles are a wonderful family. I've known them for years."

"There are quite a lot of them," Miss Gloucester-Stone remarked.

Mrs. Pimpernel chuckled. "That happens when so many of them get married. I know two of them are on the Council. I believe Torquil mentioned that their husband was assisting as well. Is that correct?"

Silas nodded. "He's my partner. Very friendly."

"Yes, quite," she said. "How is everyone else's partner?"

"Mine has been surprisingly patient, considering how out of practice I am," Mx. Badger-Thorp said as they took a sip of wine. "Mr. Buckthorn. He had a lot to say about your partner as well," they added with a grin at Miss Gloucester-Stone, who giggled.

"I'm sure," she replied. "Dear Miss Wrenwhistle mentioned him a great deal as well."

"My partner was also very understanding," Mr. Finkle-Finch said meekly. "It can't be easy dealing with my magic. It's so dashed unpredictable."

"Mine seemed quite impressed with my magic," Mr. Hedge-Wyck said, puffing his chest out. "Not that I'm surprised, mind you. He seemed duly…fascinated," he added with relish.

Silas resisted the laugh he felt bubbling up at that. He had a feeling Mr. Brooks was not entirely fascinated with Hedge-Wyck's magic, but he knew better than to say so.

"I'm not sure mine is the sharpest of men, but he's handsome, so it's not a total loss," Miss Wilton-Reed said with a wry smile.

Silas felt irritation rising at the slight against Cricket's intelligence. He hardly knew the man, though, so he said nothing.

The lady went on, unaware of his annoyance. "I cannot imagine this project will do very much anyway, in the grand scheme of things, so I wouldn't worry too greatly about what your partners think of your magic," she added in a soothing tone to Mr. Finkle-Finch and Mx. Badger-Thorpe. She patted Mr. Finkle-Finch's hand with a smile.

Mr. Finkle-Finch blushed under the attention and was so flustered that he dropped his spoon.

"What makes you think the project won't succeed?" Mrs. Pimpernel asked. The question was politely spoken, but Silas thought he caught a sharpness to the woman's voice. He wasn't surprised, considering the project was of particular importance to her grandchild.

"Oh, please don't misunderstand me, ma'am," Miss Wilton-Reed said with a flutter of her eyelashes. "I meant no offense. *Dear* Mx. Pimpernel-Smith seems very clever and very earnest. And I'm certain their heart is in the right place. But I confess I cannot imagine the change in society that they seem to be hoping for."

"It *is* difficult to believe," Miss Gloucester-Stone agreed quietly.

Mr. Finkle-Finch nodded his head somberly.

Miss Wilton-Reed sighed and the ruffles around the neckline of her dress billowed slightly at the whoosh of air. "It is indeed a sad state of affairs, is it not? We have all been the subjects of such dreadful prejudice and hate. Why, my family used to be one of the most celebrated in Bath. And after my parents married?" She snapped her fingers. "Poof! It was all gone! My father has worked *tirelessly* to move us up in society. That is why he encouraged me to write to Pimpernel-Smith about my magic and then attend this project. No amount of money, status, or good breeding can change people's minds. I don't see how a magic test will do any differently."

Silas' mind snagged on the term *good breeding* but as he glanced around the room, he noticed that everyone else seemed downcast by the lady's words, rather than critical of them. Although he thought Mrs. Pimpernel was overly preoccupied with straightening her rings.

"You truly think it is hopeless?" Mx. Badger-Thorpe asked.

Miss Wilton-Reed cast a pitying smile across the table. "I do not mean to bring a sense of gloom upon the proceedings. I agree with the essential tenets of the project: our magic is extraordinary and should be studied. And I shall, of course, give it my all for I could not *bear* to see it fail due to my pessimism."

"I agree," Mr. Hedge-Wyck said. "It's all very interesting, of course, but what power do they even have?"

"Very little, if the *Tribune* is to be believed," Miss Wilton-Reed said. "So take heart," she went on, giving Mr. Finkle-Finch's hand another pat. "It certainly takes the pressure off of you and dear Mx. Badger-Thorpe, does it not?"

"I suppose," Mx. Badger-Thorpe said in a dubious tone.

"It is interesting how you put it earlier," Mrs. Pimpernel said quietly. "That you cannot imagine the change that Torquil seeks. Surely that is the strength of the imagination, to believe in the seemingly impossible?"

Miss Wilton-Reed's answering smile didn't quite reach her eyes but it did show off her teeth. A very practiced sort of smile, Silas thought. "I confess I have always been a practical sort of creature. I leave the fanciful thoughts to the poets and the painters."

"I suppose your father is of a less practical mind?" Silas asked.

She chuckled and gave a delicate shrug. "*Papa* is ever the optimist. I daresay that is why he insisted on us having all of the advantages of an expensive education. Since we were not accepted into any schools and had no scores, he made sure we had French tutors, Italian tutors, instructors in both fae and human magic."

Mr. Hedge-Wyck brightened at that. "You as well? My father also made sure I was taught in both."

She flashed her smile at him. "A wonderful approach, was it not? And then of course we also learned all of the dances, how to draw, how to play, how to sing. We were given the most thorough education money can buy, the most beautiful gowns Bath had to offer, and what did it accomplish?"

"You are very elegant," Miss Gloucester-Stone said.

"Thank you, my dear. I do try." She gave another sad sort of sigh and the ruffles on her dress did another sad sort of dance. "But I intend to make the most of the experience, including enjoying the company of such lovely new friends."

Mr. Hedge-Wyck raised his glass. "I'll drink to that!"

The others all raised their glasses as well, seemingly cheered by the lady's words as swiftly as they'd been saddened by them. Silas raised his glass high enough to avoid notice but did not echo the sentiments. He noticed that Mrs. Pimpernel had done the same.

CHAPTER 16

KEELAN

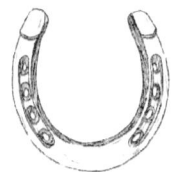

IF THE SHARED look of affection was any indication, it was safe to assume that Torquil had also accepted Emrys' apology. The two were gazing at each other where they stood near the far end of the long table, Emrys murmuring something just to make Torquil laugh, and Torquil trying halfheartedly to push him back in the direction of where he'd abandoned Mr. Rook-Worth.

It was late afternoon and the itch of restlessness in the air had Keelan's attention wandering. Emrys was clearly feeling it, as well. It was the third time he'd wandered away from his post in the span of an hour.

Keelan was startled back into focus when something tapped against the side of his face. With a small frown, he straightened from where he'd propped his chin in one hand and looked down at the piece of crumpled spellpaper resting by his other arm on the table. He desperately hoped it had not been one he'd used for his notes. He'd already had to redo the ones covered in oil.

"Which one of them are you in love with?" Miss Wilton-Reed asked flippantly from her seat across from him. She had a bright purple crocus pinned in her hair above a cluster of tight ringlets.

"I'm not in love with anyone," Keelan said, his frown deepening.

"Someone ought to tell your face," she told him with a giggle. "You've been staring at them for a quarter of an hour with a halfwitted little grin."

"They're my friends." Keelan glanced over just in time to watch Emrys steal a kiss before he strolled back to his partner. "They've just come back from their honeymoon. I'm happy for them, that's all."

He thought to apologize for his lack of concentration, but he could not quite bring himself to do it. In the time they'd spent together that day, Miss Wilton-Reed had only shown him one spell that involved little more than what she had done previously with the jar lids. She was able to use her fae magic to make them spin, slide, and roll across the table as she pleased. With the addition of a few ingredients and some lines on the spellpaper, Miss Wilton-Reed gained more control, sending them one after the other in a pattern of her choosing.

Keelan had written down as much of the process as he could. While he still wasn't entirely sure what he was meant to be recording, he took note of how the use of the human spell did not change the speed of the lids as they moved. When the lids came to a noisy stop, he made the mistake of asking her to do it again. He'd only wanted to make sure he had not missed anything worth taking note of, but Miss Wilton-Reed made a sound of frustration and told him it was not her fault that he had not been watching the first time.

They'd been sitting in uncomfortable silence since then, which was even worse than listening to her rather incessant talking the previous day. At least that gave Keelan something to do.

"Miss Wilton-Reed, Mr. Cricket," Torquil said calmly as they appeared at Keelan's side. Rather than taking a seat in the available chair, Torquil gripped the table and hoisted themself onto it far enough that the bend of their knees met the edge. They set a couple of finger-tips against the pages of notes in front of Keelan and met his gaze. "May I?"

"Of course." Keelan placed his hands in his lap. As Torquil picked up the stack of papers, Keelan bit back his confession that he'd only written on two of them so far. They would find out soon enough. He watched as their eyes moved over the words he'd written, as they tilted their head at the part he'd done a bit crooked, and as they moved to the second page that was mostly a few lines of rushed scribbles.

"Interesting approach to a motion spell," they said finally, setting the papers down with a grin. Keelan felt himself relax.

"Interesting?" Miss Wilton-Reed repeated. "What about it?"

Torquil seemed to think for a moment before they offered a response.

"Mr. Cricket indicated that you used a sigil for direction and balance, but not one for power."

Miss Wilton-Reed improved her already impeccable posture in her chair and said, "That's because I use my natural magic for power."

"Mr. Cricket also made a note that the speed of the lids did not change after you cast your human spell. So we can assume you were trying to keep it consistent throughout the demonstration?"

There was a slight shift in Miss Wilton-Reed's expression at this; a hint of wavering confidence. She glanced at the notes on Keelan's paper. Her lips pressed together primly before she provided an answer.

"I sometimes find that the strength of my natural magic is dampened with the addition of a spell." Even Keelan could feel how hard it was for her to admit this. "However, that does not mean my human magic is *weak*, only that I prefer to focus on accuracy."

"Not to worry," Torquil said as they pushed off the table smoothly back to their feet. "None of us here are questioning your strength, Miss Wilton-Reed. Keep up the good work." They cast a look in Emrys' direction and started that way, but turned to add, "Mr. Cricket, you might want to write all of that down."

It was said with encouragement rather than admonition, and Keelan felt himself uplifted as he reached for the pencil and a new sheet of paper.

THE FOLLOWING DAY, each pair was provided with a fresh supply of materials and a short list of tasks to complete. They were instructed to read over the list and determine if any of the simple activities might provide new insight that had not yet been observed between each set of partners.

Keelan wondered privately if the list had been created with Miss Wilton-Reed and himself in mind. From what he had seen and heard around them, the other pairs had hit it off splendidly, with magic and spells filling the air as easily as conversations between friends.

"We've got rosemary, dried hibiscus, and pine needles today," Keelan said as he read the labels on the jars they'd been given. He lifted his attention to Miss Wilton-Reed, who was reading over the list with vague interest. The purple crocus in her hair had been replaced with a thin, braided circlet of delicate primrose blooms. "Any ideas on what you'd like to do with them?"

"Rosemary is easy." She reached for the jar. "It can be used for just about anything in a pinch." Keelan wrote that down. When he looked up again, Miss Wilton-Reed looked positively devious. "Untie your cravat. Give it to me."

Keelan's hand went to the knot at his throat. It was a simple one, nothing above what was required for a morning out, but the silk fabric was finer than some others he had. "Will I get it back?" he asked warily as he set the pencil down and began loosening the knot until he was able to hand the strip of cloth across the table. Miss Wilton-Reed snatched it away from him.

"We shall see," was her simple reply.

Still uneasy, he watched carefully as Miss Wilton-Reed called on her magic, a breeze flowing in from one of the windows that was propped open to allow it. With the flick of her wrist, the fabric was swept up in it, making a lazy circle around them. It continued on as she picked up her own pencil, made a few marks on her paper, added the rosemary and a generous pile of the hibiscus petals, drew two more lines, closed her eyes, and took a sharp breath.

The dried hibiscus petals leapt off the paper into the air and were tangled up with Keelan's cravat in a whirl. The fabric twisted so tightly that it became a rope, snapped taut, and then fell to the desk. As soon as the air had settled, Keelan picked it up by a loose corner, pinched between his thumb and forefinger, and shook it gently to help it unfurl. The petals were gone, and the crisp white of his cravat had gone a deep, mottled shade of pink.

Miss Wilton-Reed chuckled from her seat.

"Now it matches your outfit," she said, clearly satisfied with herself.

"Thank you?" Keelan managed faintly. His waistcoat was, in fact, a similar shade of dark rose accented with thin stripes of gold. He put the strip of cloth around his neck, wondering how the blazes he was going to retie it himself without a mirror, when the doors opened and in walked the rest of the Council, including—

"Keelan!" his mother said as she approached, sounding warm enough but still surprised to see him. It was not unlike the greeting offered to an acquaintance in the street. He whipped the undone cravat from around his neck and hid it behind his back as he stood to greet her. The last thing he needed was for her to see him looking unraveled in her place of work.

"Mother. This is Miss Wilton-Reed. She is my partner for the project."

Councilmember Cricket gave her a polite nod at first, but seemed captured by the young lady as she paused to regard her more fully.

"Miss Wilton-Reed," she echoed, "a pleasure to meet you."

"You did not mention you have a parent on the Council," Miss Wilton-Reed directed at Keelan before she returned his mother's greeting with a broad smile. "A pleasure."

"It appears things are going well," Cricket said as she cast a critical eye around the room, her hands clasped neatly in front of her. "Nothing has been destroyed yet, from the look of it." She gave a haughty laugh. "I've no interest in this little endeavor costing the Council money *or* its reputation."

"I do not think you have to worry about that," Keelan told her, his stained cravat now fully hidden in his fisted hand behind his back. He squeezed it gingerly. "We are being very careful."

"And have you been allowed any time to socialize?" His mother's attention circled pointedly to Miss Wilton-Reed. "There must be a healthy balance, you know."

"Unfortunately, I have only had the pleasure of seeing the inside of this building and the townhouse where we are staying." Miss Wilton-Reed's mouth curved into a small pout, her dark brows bunching together to match. "I was so hoping to see more of the city while I was here."

Keelan thought it was a marvelous idea. The topic of magic did not seem to interest her overmuch, but he knew of a dozen gardens and shops that might. If he could only get to know her better, and help her feel more welcome, then perhaps their work on the project would come easier, too.

"You should mention it to our project leaders," Keelan offered to his mother enthusiastically. "They are all rather business-minded, as I'm sure you well know. It probably has not occurred to them to hold a social event for our visitors."

"I believe I will," Cricket mused. She looked at Miss Wilton-Reed again, eyes narrowed slightly in obvious assessment. "And you said you were from…"

"Bath," Miss Wilton-Reed filled in for her.

"Is this your first time in London?"

"It is. My father thought this an important experience for me."

"Indeed. You've no chaperone with you, I see. Are you eligible?"

Keelan's face blazed. "*Mother*—"

"I am now, thanks to Mx. Pimpernel-Smith." The faintly curved tips of Miss Wilton-Reed's ears had gone pink. "Although I must admit I have never had much interest in marriage, even with the recent rise in society's acceptance of people such as myself."

Councilmember Cricket's smile turned sympathetic. "Dear child. Marriage does not have to interest you to be in your best interest." She leveled a steady look at her son and bid them both good luck with the rest of their work.

Keelan couldn't help but notice that she made a direct path for Roger, Wyndham, and Torquil. He let out a heavy sigh and brought the hand not holding his cravat up to his forehead.

"I apologize," he started as he turned toward Miss Wilton-Reed, though he did not look up to meet her gaze. "She is very direct."

"I quite like her," was Miss Wilton-Reed's smug reply. Keelan managed to contain his surprise. He brought his fist from from behind his back, took in the variegated pinkish color of his cravat, and gave a small nod.

"Yes, I suppose you would," he said softly.

CHAPTER 17

SILAS

Silas was intrigued by Cricket's change in posture when the councilmembers entered the room. He shouldn't have had as much attention to spare for the gentleman, and yet, he managed it. In fact, he seemed to always find his gaze pulled to Cricket, like a moth that can't resist a flame.

It helped that his partner was only vaguely interested in the project at hand. Mr. Emrys Wrenwhistle had attempted to sound knowledgeable when the ingredients were dropped at their table that morning. But it had been clear that he had no idea how human magic worked.

Silas had used the pine needles to do a small, contained fire spell, using his sensing abilities to ensure it did not get out of hand. Then he had used the hibiscus petals for a freshness spell.

"That's remarkable," Mr. Wrenwhistle had commented. "I've never seen that one done before."

Silas shrugged. "It is often done when we're doing work that is not particularly pleasant-smelling. The convenience of a spell like that is that it is pretty adaptable to many different ingredients, provided they smell nice. I could use this rosemary to do the same thing if I liked. And the pine, for that matter."

Mr. Wrenwhistle belatedly realized he ought to be making notes and jotted some down. Silas privately suspected that their notes would be thoroughly unhelpful considering how little the man wrote.

Once the other councilmembers entered the room, everyone paused in their work. Silas met Councilmember Barnes, the father of one of the Wrenwhistles. Like Councilmember Roger Wrenwhistle, Councilmember Barnes was short, round, and handsome, with light brown skin, dark brown hair, and dark eyes. He seemed a pleasant fellow, if a bit carried away by academic interest in magic. Thankfully, Mr. Emrys Wrenwhistle had been so lost by the topic that the conversation had not lasted very long.

Then the lady who had been talking to Cricket wandered over. She greeted Mr. Wrenwhistle like he was an old friend. She had pale skin, short brown hair that showed off her pointed fae ears, and keen green eyes. Up close, Silas recognized some facial similarities between the woman and Cricket. This was confirmed when she asked Mr. Wrenwhistle how her son was faring, and they had both glanced at Cricket.

"I think he's doing well," Mr. Wrenwhistle had said in a diplomatic tone.

He opened his mouth to say more but she broke in, saying, "We have many high hopes for this project, you know. I confess, I am anticipating the project to have a significant benefit for Keelan."

Mr. Wrenwhistle's eyes went wide. "You mean a match?"

She nodded. "It was my idea that he be paired with Miss Wilton-Reed. The Reeds are a very influential family, you know. I've never met them, of course, but I've heard good things. And I'm sure Keelan would do very well in Bath. Now that I've met her, I'm feeling very positive about the prospect. It is so nice when business and pleasure mingle, isn't it?" Without waiting for a reply, she gave him a smile and walked away.

Mr. Wrenwhistle stared after her and then glanced at the couple at the long table.

"I suppose it is common for high society folk to be matched in such a way," Silas offered.

Mr. Wrenwhistle looked startled, as if he'd forgotten Silas was there. He gave a sheepish grin. "Sometimes, yes. Councilmember Cricket has always been rather old-fashioned. My mother too, in her—*ahem*— anyway, we ought to get back to work."

The final councilmember approached them shortly after, Councilmember Applewood. She was a lovely fae woman of medium height and build with dark brown skin and dark braided hair. She was a soft-spoken and kindly woman who Silas liked immediately. Her presence caused them to get back to work as she expressed an interest in seeing the magic in action. Thankfully, she had no judgment or commentary to add, merely a brief thanks to them both for their participation in the project and for indulging her curiosity, before leaving them to it.

They continued to work, but Silas was relieved he was not the only one unable to focus after the interruption. Both he and his partner kept glancing at the table at the back of the room. Miss Wilton-Reed seemed to speak constantly and poor Cricket seemed unable to get a word in edgewise. Every time Silas felt his chest ache at the sight, he reminded himself sternly that the gentleman was none of his concern.

THEY WERE FINALLY GIVEN the rubric the next day, with the request to pick one of the five skills to demonstrate with their partner. Silas was still reading through the rubric when he heard Miss Wilton-Reed complain from her side of the room. He glanced up to ensure Cricket was not being harmed in any way and then turned back to the paper.

"Wonder what the matter is," Mr. Wrenwhistle murmured.

"I would guess she doesn't care for this final bit about us showing how we combine our different magics," Silas said. "She has *views* on blending magic."

"How will that work for you, considering…"

"Considering I only use human magic? I imagine I will have to demonstrate how my sensing impacts my ability to cast spells. Fae sensing is a form of fae magic. Some humans can learn the skill, but that is rare. So I shall have to show that my magics blend together."

"You make it sound simple," Mr. Wrenwhistle said in a cheerful tone.

"Well, we're expecting children to do it, so I should be able to manage," Silas said with a small smile. "And anything that I can't do will be helpful anyway, as that means they'll need to adjust the rubric." He glanced over the paper again. "You've already seen my fire spell, so why don't we try a shrinking spell this time?"

"Excellent," Mr. Wrenwhistle said in a tone that suggested he hadn't really been listening.

Councilmember Wrenwhistle—the shorter one with spectacles—approached their table and asked if they had any questions.

"No questions, but we did decide which skill I'm going to try first."

"So soon," the young man said eagerly. "Wonderful! Which?"

"The shrinking spell."

The councilmember smiled. "I'm quite partial to that one, myself. I'll get you the ingredients for it. Do you have enough spellpaper? Ah, good."

He scampered off and Silas stood and stretched his arms above his head. He felt his partner's gaze on him and turned to meet his eyes with a questioning look.

"You know, you're rather attractive," Mr. Wrenwhistle mused. "Are you also hoping this project will be of personal benefit to you?"

Silas recognized the reference. He shook his head. "I have no such ambitions. And no interest in marriage, particularly not to someone in London."

The other man pretended offense. "What do you have against Londoners?"

"Nothing against the people here. But I don't care for the city. Doesn't make much sense to marry someone who lives here, does it?"

"I suppose not," he said.

"But I appreciate the compliment." Silas flashed him a grin. "I can't deny that London holds certain temptations that I don't mind partaking in."

Mr. Wrenwhistle returned the grin with a wide one of his own. "Ah, yes, the city is definitely good for that. I've been wondering if you lot are more in line with the human opinion of propriety or the fae form of indulgence, in that respect."

Silas chuckled. "Everyone's a little different, but the majority of the group leans towards the latter."

The other man glanced at the corner of the room where Mr. Hedge-Wyck and Mr. Brooks were talking, their heads bent close to each other. "I suspected as much," he mused. "Is Mrs. Pimpernel acting as chaperone still?"

"She is. Although, between you and me, I suspect she's rather lenient. Mr. Brooks has definitely spent a few nights there."

Mr. Wrenwhistle laughed. "None of that surprises me."

The councilmember returned with the supplies and Silas set everything up for a shrinking spell. Silas had begun doing his spells slowly, explaining each step as he went, something that was quickly becoming a habit in this project. So he laid out the spellpaper and opened up the ingredients.

"This is to indicate the item being shrunk. If it's a container filled with items, that needs to be accounted for. But there is a particular sigil and formula used to indicate a container as opposed to a single object."

"Why would that matter?"

"I might have a box full of items and I only need to shrink some of the items to make them fit into the box. Or I might need to shrink the entire box, plus the items inside. You need to be specific when it comes to magic—that is, human magic—because it doesn't always know what you want it to do. You have to tell it."

Mr. Wrenwhistle duly took notes. "Right. Different sigils for different types of items being shrunk."

It was not a very exact or accurate summation, but Silas let it pass. "And this is to specify how small I want it to be. Once I start sensing, I might add another sigil, or add a calculation here to put more power into the act of shrinking. If that makes sense. I'll also use my sensing to ensure I don't make the item *too* small. That's always a risk with this spell, but I've gotten pretty good at it. I use it a lot when my family is hauling things across the country for different jobs. We used it for your wedding, actually. Would have been quite a challenge getting all that brick and stone to your estate. Not very kind to the horses. So I placed a shrinking spell before we left our house and then undid it when we arrived."

"Huh," he hummed, twiddling the pencil in his hand and not writing anything. "That's fascinating."

"This," Silas continued, waving a bottle, "will be used to initiate the shrinking. And these will be used to control it. Fairly simple spell, all things considered."

Mr. Wrenwhistle cleared his throat and shifted in his seat. "Oh, yes, very simple."

Silas hid a smile and cast the spell. Just like all the previous times he had cast alongside Mr. Wrenwhistle, his magic felt constricted when met with the other man's sensing. He managed to shrink the rock to the size of a pebble, but it was not his best work.

He didn't think Mr. Wrenwhistle had noticed, as the gentleman picked up the rock and examined it with fascination. But then he said, "Is your magic always so…restrained?"

Silas blinked in surprise. "No," he admitted. "That only seems to be around you."

The gentleman lifted an eyebrow. "Ah." He made a note. "Magical compatibility is a damned nuisance sometimes."

"I've never had the issue with anyone in my family. And I've felt the magic of others before, but it's never felt so…inhibitive."

Mr. Wrenwhistle tapped his pencil against his paper, his face screwed in concentration. "Interesting," he said at last. "I'll ask Torquil about it later. Anyway, I'd say you passed that skill. If I were your examiner, I'd give you full marks."

Silas chuckled. "Very generous."

CHAPTER 18

KEELAN

"I DARESAY the entire place must be a shamble of closed doors and muffled sounds of pleasure," Emrys purred, giving Keelan a smug look from his saddle.

It was the first day off from the project, and they'd agreed to meet at the Park for a ride before joining the rest of the volunteers for an afternoon of shopping at New Bond Street. Keelan was, for a change, grateful for his mother's tenacious stance on being out in society as much as possible.

"Of course, I have not seen it for myself," Emrys went on. "My nights are well occupied. But even Mr. Rook-Worth said that he's seen Brooks there multiple times sneaking into his partner's room. They are directly across the hall from one another, apparently, so imagine all the things going on that he *hasn't* seen."

Keelan made an unsteady sound of acknowledgement as he repressed a groan. It was the fifth time Emrys had mentioned Mr. Rook-Worth since they'd left the stables. A small part of him wanted to ask if perhaps he could stop mentioning the man, but he knew it was a silly request. Emrys had been working with him for a week; of course he was going to come up in conversation.

"And what of your partner?" Emrys asked. "Do you think she's taking full advantage of her time here in London?" The implication was heavy in his voice.

"For all that she has to say about herself—and there is quite a lot—that is one topic she has not yet introduced. I suspect views on intimacy are even more staunch where she comes from than they are here."

Emrys snorted. "I have met several people from Bath and that is decidedly untrue."

"Miss Wilton-Reed has younger sisters," Keelan explained, "and they all look up to her a great deal. She says she is always doing what she can to set a good example for them as they come into their own. It only makes sense that she would maintain that integrity while she's away from them."

"And you find this admirable?"

"Why shouldn't I? If a lady such as herself or anyone else chooses to abstain, that is their decision to make without needing to justify it." Keelan paused. "I imagine she would be more than willing to explain her reasoning if asked, however. She seems to have a strong opinion on most subjects."

They both offered a nod and polite greeting to an acquaintance passing by before Emrys said, "Perhaps more importantly then, do any of your beliefs align? Or better yet, does she know what any of yours are?"

Keelan winced. "I admit, I have been listening more than speaking."

"Have you tried asking her to stop being so self-interested?"

He gave Emrys an anguished sort of look. "And how am I supposed to do that? Politely mention that it would likely benefit both of us if she were to attempt a two-sided conversation?"

"It's a fair start," Emrys offered.

Keelan let out the groan he'd held back before. He let his forearms rest against his thighs as he turned his attention to the stretch of water they were riding past. It carried him back to the morning of the wedding, when he'd taken his ride out on the estate alone, enjoying everything that early spring in the country had to offer. The season was in full effect now; songbirds whistling in their trees, flowers in bloom along the crushed stone path.

"What did Torquil think of the estate?" He turned back to Emrys. "You were there at the perfect time of year to do a bit of exploring."

"I confess we spent most of our time indoors," Emrys told him. Keelan shook his head and allowed himself to grin at their antics. "We did take a number of walks through the garden, though. And Torquil found great joy in the novelty of sleeping with each and every window open."

"I can imagine, after living in that press building for so many years," Keelan agreed with sympathy. He had never been inside before, but if the squalid exterior was any indication, it must've left much to be desired. "It's still surprising to me that you were able to foster any sort of romance under such conditions."

Emrys gave a tender laugh. "The conditions hardly matter when you are in the presence of the person you are meant to love."

Keelan responded with an overly dramatic sound of disgust. "Yes, all right, we know, you are the happiest man alive. Please consider the rest of us while you're busy spouting your merriment."

Emrys did not respond right away. Keelan's grin faded as he prepared to apologize. He hadn't actually meant for him to stop. After what the man had endured, the countless suitors and agony of working through his feelings for Torquil so that they were able to come out on the other side together, Keelan could not be happier to hear him go on about it.

When Emrys finally spoke, he said, "Have you given any thought to the idea of finding someone of your own?" His tone indicated that he was genuinely curious about the answer.

"I have, actually," Keelan told him matter-of-factly.

"But in all seriousness, Keelan. Not just the dreams of romance that always seem to be floating around that idealistic head of yours."

"I have," he urged with a short chuckle. Both men reined their horses onto a connecting path that would loop them back toward home. "Are you truly so worried about me?"

"Has your mother spoken to you about it?" Emrys asked.

"You've probably spoken to her more recently than I have." Keelan was still recovering from the last conversation they'd shared, when she harassed Miss Wilton-Reed with her blunt, impolite questions. His mouth curved into a slight frown. "She does seem to have a bold interest in the topic at the moment, now that you mention it. If you can believe it, she asked Miss Wilton-Reed if she is eligible right in front of me."

Emrys angled an imploring look at him.

"Does that not signify anything to you?"

"Why should it? You know she is apt to pry."

"In case you've forgotten, you are *also* eligible," Emrys said slowly.

"Yes," Keelan agreed, also dragging out the word. "What are you getting at?"

Emrys released the grip on his leather strap to pinch the bridge of his nose. His response came out flat. "Your meddling mother asked a young lady, in your presence, if she is seeking marriage."

Keelan felt his magic go cold in his chest as he realized what Emrys was trying to imply.

"You don't think…" he said on a whispered exhale.

"I do," Emrys said. "She said as much to me when we spoke last."

Keelan's jaw went slack. "And you did not think to tell me until now?" he cried out. "We've been riding for an hour!"

"I was not entirely sure how to broach the subject," Emrys admitted helplessly. "I was correct in assuming that you would react somewhat negatively."

Keelan gave an incredulous huff of a laugh. "Somewhat? You might've told me quite literally anything else and I would be less surprised."

"It's not as though any arrangements have been made yet."

"Yet!" Keelan repeated, followed by a feeble, wavering moan as he slouched in his saddle. "I take back what I said. That was worse." He thought back to the conversation his mother had with the lady, now that he could see it for what it really was. "Miss Wilton-Reed said she is not interested in marriage."

Emrys brightened. "There, you see?"

"Then my mother told her it does not matter if she wants to marry or not, as long as the outcome is preferable for both families involved."

Keelan had long suspected that his parents' marriage had been arranged in a similar way. Even as a child, he felt the strain between them; no shared affection, no common interests. Not once had they exchanged a look like the ones Emrys and Torquil seemed to have an endless supply of, with soft eyes and warm, private smiles that said more than words ever could.

"Beastly woman," Emrys muttered. "Such an outdated practice."

Emotion burned the back of Keelan's throat and nose as he fought back the prickling urge of tears. He felt ridiculous to be so upset over the trifling *idea* of marrying someone who did not—and likely would never—love him, but the thought was petrifying.

Deep down, he knew it was why he had never spent more than one night with someone. He could not bring himself to risk feeling more. It happened so easily as it was, even without the physical connection to bolster his propensity for swift affections.

"I am aware that this project is meant to help us better understand the subtle differences that exist in the fae-human community, but I find myself intrigued more by their similarities," Emrys said after a stretch of companionable silence, allowing time for Keelan to collect himself.

"How do you mean?" Keelan asked, his voice a bit raw. He sniffled.

"You said Miss Wilton-Reed has no interest in marriage. Mr. Rook-Worth told me the same. If I remember correctly, Torquil was of an equal opinion for many years. It only changed after they were certain of their feelings for me."

"You think all fae-humans are opposed to marriage?" Keelan tried very hard not to allow the words *Mr. Rook-Worth* and *marriage* to wander too close in his thoughts.

"Perhaps not all of them, but I do think it is interesting."

"Yes, I suppose it is."

"I will have to ask my next partner what their inclinations toward marriage are, as well."

Keelan looked over at Emrys in surprise. "Next partner?"

"I'm going to ask Torquil to pair Mr. Rook-Worth with someone else for the remainder of the project. Our magics are very poorly matched. It seems to be affecting his ability to perform his spells when I am sensing them."

"Affecting his ability?" Keelan asked, unable to help himself.

"The spells lack power," Emrys explained, but then made a face. "No, that's not fair. It feels like my magic is holding his back, in a way. Neither of us have been able to determine a cause, other than an issue of compatibility."

Keelan's face went warm. He thought of Mr. Rook-Worth's magic, his experience with it, and could not imagine anything about it being restrained. It had been wild and strong, commanding. His own magic sent a jolt down his spine at the memory of it, which he fought with a shaky breath.

"Everyone is already paired," Keelan said after he'd recovered.

"I'm hopeful the Council will allow for a switch. It does not make sense for us to continue on if he is unable to perform." Emrys directed his horse closer to Keelan and gave him a mischievous grin. "You might like him. He's quite easy to talk to, once you get him going. And he's even easier to look at. Shall I ask Torquil if we can trade?"

"That's not necessary," Keelan said quickly, stomach twisting.

"Let us see what the Council decides," Emrys concluded. "I am certain they will do what's best for everyone."

KEELAN HURRIED home to change in somewhat of a brown study, which was very unusual for him after a ride with Emrys. Thankfully, Marten made no comment on it and instead dressed him in one of his favorite waistcoats—a cheery vivid green—and sent him on his way.

He emerged just as the rest of the party was beginning to gather on the pavement in front of the Pimpernel residence a few houses down. The other volunteers lived nearer to where they'd be walking, so they agreed to convene at the Berkeley garden square. It was hardly notable compared to Hyde Park, but the London plane trees planted there a quarter-century earlier were a source of pride for the fae who called the city home, so he was pleased that the newcomers would get to see them at least once during their stay.

"The weather is fine for a stroll about town," he said in greeting after crossing the street to join them, which earned him several answering smiles and murmurs of agreement. With an odd twinge of not-quite-relief, he realized that one of them was missing. "Is Mr. Rook-Worth joining us?"

"He's a rather humble sort of fellow," Miss Gloucester-Stone said with a slight lift of her shoulders. "We all encouraged him to come along, but he said he'd prefer to stay indoors and rest while we explore."

"All the better for us to walk in an orderly queue," Miss Wilton-Reed cut in with a companionable smile. "Assuming you'll offer me your arm, Mr. Cricket."

Keelan stammered over his reply and did as she'd asked, the pair of them taking the lead as the other fae-humans fell into line behind them two by two.

Subsequent to his conversation with Emrys, Keelan found himself in a unique position. He'd had the pleasure of being in the company of various fanciable ladies since his first Season out, both in and out of the public eye, but he had never had an opportunity to escort one for an entire afternoon. Further, he'd never spent that time knowing there was potential for a future between them. Of course, he was hopeful, as romantics often are. His heart had fluttered after countless pretty faces and engaging talents.

But he wanted more.

For all the love he felt toward his city, there was even more to give for someone who could captivate him in mind, body, and magic, leaving absolutely no doubt that they were meant to be as one. He wanted passion, devotion, tenderness, joy, contentment. Just once, Keelan wanted to be someone's priority rather than an option.

As they walked, Miss Wilton-Reed spoke fondly of Bath, describing her extensive wardrobe she'd woefully left behind for the project, and how she attended at least one ball a week during the Season. She loved dancing and sampling various wines, which she was quite sure none of them had ever been fortunate enough to taste before. Her life was as dazzling as her smile. A glance over his shoulder told Keelan that the rest of the fae-humans were equally intrigued, listening intently—if not a touch enviously.

His attention fell to where her hand was curved around his arm. Over her white glove she wore two flashy rings; the gemstones caught in the sunlight as her fingers moved expressively while she talked. They were the sort of jewelry better suited for an evening event, but Keelan supposed that she'd not yet had the opportunity to wear them in London, so she was using the outing to her advantage.

Keelan's father had taken the name Cricket when his parents wed. His mother's family had more status and far more wealth, therefore it was the obvious decision. By her lifestyle alone, he could tell Miss Wilton-Reed's family held an enormous amount of both. If they were to marry, the expectation would be for him to take her name, as well.

The lady had moved on to the subject of carriages as he tossed the idea around in his head: *Mr. Keelan Wilton-Reed.*

That thought remained with him for the next several hours. He took delight in showing his companion into various shops, pointedly ignored the way Emrys looked at him teasingly as he carried all of Miss Wilton-Reed's purchases, and smiled to himself when he discovered they both liked millefruit biscuits when the party took afternoon tea together at Ollerton's. He was in the middle of imagining what it might be like to sit closer to his partner on a settee in a fine parlor they'd decorated together when he realized she'd said his name.

"Pardon?"

"I asked if you always take so long to drink your tea," Miss Wilton-Reed said mildly, though it was done with a coy smile.

"Oh." Keelan realized he'd been holding his cup the entire time, set it down, promptly picked it up again to take a hasty sip, and then set it down again. "Sometimes my focus tends to wander when I am preoccupied."

She hummed. "I've noticed. I hope you'll try not to embarrass me in front of Mx. Pimpernel-Smith again when our work resumes. I've heard talk of shuffling partners and I do not wish to be paired with anyone else."

Keelan's apology drifted away, replaced with something like wonder. It must've shown in his expression, for the lady went on.

"The others seem nice, but you are uncommonly sweet. I wish to continue improving our acquaintanceship. I believe we make a superior match, with my magical talent and your—" she hesitated "—ability to write. Don't you agree?"

"Yes," Keelan told her earnestly. "I would like it very much if we could remain as partners. And to learn more about you."

Miss Wilton-Reed's smile lit up her entire face. "Excellent."

FROM SILAS ROOK-WORTH TO RUTH ROOK

Dear Mother,

I am getting along well enough in London. I cannot honestly answer whether my mood has improved or not. I am certainly more distracted though. Before Quince reads over your shoulder and asks: I have not been distracted in *that* way—although you can assure him that there are certainly plenty of attractive people about.

The project is not what I expected, but I cannot tell you what I expected exactly. There are six of us here and we are all from out of town. You might wonder at the fact that all of the fae-humans present are from outside London. I certainly did. It would appear that we were the only ones in the country who responded to the Councilmember's query last winter. So while I'm sure there must be more fae-humans in the city, it would appear they are not inquisitive enough to have reached out. Or perhaps they simply do not read the *Tribune*. I'm sure I wouldn't have read it either if you and father hadn't pointed out the issue in question.

At any rate, all six of us are paired with a different fae volunteer. I have found it curious that there are no human volunteers but I suspect this is due to the nature of fae magic. A large aspect of this project is for the fae to feel our magic while we cast and very few humans would be able to do that. My partner is very amicable and we get along quite well, although his note-taking leaves much to be desired. My magic has not been reacting well to his. I have experienced a variety of magics in my time (pray do not inquire how), so I know this is not an impossible reaction. But my magic has felt restricted when I cast with him. In my other experiences, such restriction is short-lived and, thus, hardly exceptional. But in the context of this project, it is far from ideal.

The food is excellent, although very rich. I find myself yearning for your meals. The bread simply does not compare—or perhaps I am merely spoiled by you slicing off a piece of freshly baked bread and adding a dollop of honey to it. It is difficult to compare anything to that.

If Father asks, the city is simply teeming with magic. It's woven into the bricks and the cobblestones: protection, cooling, privacy. I've never experienced the like. I daresay you'll tell me it's simply the effect of being in a city for the first time, and I'm sure you'd be right. But I confess I find it disconcerting. The rest of the group went out to explore this morning, as well as do a bit of shopping. I did not join them. I much prefer the quiet of my room to the bustle of the streets. Even the quiet of the townhouse is preferable with everyone gone.

Please give everyone my love.

Affectionately,

Silas

CHAPTER 19

SILAS

W HEN S ILAS HEARD that they'd received a day off from the project, his first feeling was one of relief. It would be nice to have a day away from feeling like his magic was on some sort of leash.

His next feeling was one of listlessness. The rest of the group had decided to go on a shopping spree and better explore London but Silas declined the invitation to join them. He liked most of his fellow fae-humans well enough, but he had no interest in exploring the city, and even less interest in shopping.

He took advantage of the time alone to write to his mother. Then he wandered the house until he found Mrs. Pimpernel sitting in a little salon, taking tea with another fae lady. They beckoned him to join them.

"Mr. Rook-Worth, may I present Mrs. Iris Wrenwhistle," Mrs. Pimpernel said.

Silas bit back a comment about meeting *yet another* Wrenwhistle. Instead, he greeted her politely and took a seat, accepting his tea, and feeling a little out of place next to the fine ladies in their elegant clothes. Mrs. Wrenwhistle especially had an air about her that emitted sophistication. Her posture was excellent—Miss Wilton-Reed would have been jealous—and her diction was impeccable. Silas was frankly surprised by how warm and kind she seemed when she spoke to him. He was not accustomed to *warmth* from the upper classes.

"How is the project going?" she asked him.

"It's going well, I think," he hedged.

"I believe you are paired with one of my grandsons, Emrys. Is that correct?"

"Yes, ma'am."

"We all have high hopes for this project. It is the first of its kind, really."

"You mean to study fae-human magic?"

"I mean to study magic in such a social way. There are so many factors involved when multiple people do magic together. Wyndham and Roger have made several discoveries lately that have uncovered even more factors that we didn't know about. Granted, those discoveries primarily supported the notion of performing magic in tandem." She gave a little laugh. "I suppose it's just as well that the Council changed when it did. I'm not sure the previous group would have permitted so much experimentation."

"The previous group?"

"Several members of the Council recently stepped down, myself included. Although I would have certainly been supportive of this project. But Williams, the previous Head of Council for the human side, was notoriously against change. As was Gibbs, one of the other human members."

"I didn't realize there had been such upheaval. Will they be expanding again?"

"I don't know," she said in a musing tone. "I expect they'll work to bring all three factions to three members, at the very least. Although I'm not sure they will do more. Roger has pointed out in the past that having an even number is foolish, and I have to say I agree with him. So if they can recruit one more human and two more fae-humans, I'd say they'd be in good shape to move forward."

"Does that pique your interest, Mr. Rook-Worth?" Mrs. Pimpernel said with a grin.

He shook his head. "I'm afraid not. I'm really doing all of this as a favor to Torquil—or perhaps I should say Councilmember Pimpernel-

Smith. I don't care for London and I'm not sure I'm cut out for this sort of work as a rule."

"Is that why you did not join the others?" Mrs. Pimpernel asked.

He nodded. "I have little interest in sight-seeing or shopping. A quiet afternoon is far more enjoyable for me."

She laughed. "Well, if you are not opposed to spending time with two old biddies, you are always welcome to have tea with us. I don't think either of us are up to showing the city to an energetic group of young people. Much better to leave that to their peers, who might benefit more from the society."

"I'm certainly not opposed," Silas assured her with a smile. "And thank you."

"You said you are not cut out for this sort of work," Mrs. Wrenwhistle said. "What sort of work are you cut out for?"

Silas launched into an explanation of his family business and the sort of work they do. She recognized his description of the fire pit in the recent wedding, and was full of compliments, which was gratifying.

"I believe a number of the fae volunteering for this project were at the wedding. Has that helped at all towards making you feel more comfortable?"

He considered deflecting on the topic, but was sure that would reflect poorly if Cricket did not do the same. Instead, he shrugged and said, "As I'm sure you can understand, ma'am, a craftsman like myself is not likely to attract the same sort of relationship as a partner in a project. There have been some familiar faces, but none of them are ones I'd call acquaintances."

Mrs. Wrenwhistle hummed thoughtfully at this.

"Which faces were familiar?" Mrs. Pimpernel asked.

"Mr. Emrys Wrenwhistle and Councilmember Pimpernel-Smith. And we met Mr. Cricket briefly when we were introduced to Mr. Wrenwhistle."

Mrs. Wrenwhistle's eyebrows went up at that. "I know the Crickets quite well. Keelan is such a sweet boy. He is close friends with my grandson, Emrys. Keelan's mother is a member of the Council, which I'm sure you know. She is a reasonable woman, all things considered, but not particularly warm. Keelan's father lives at home. Their marriage was arranged and was deemed a very good match. He had quite a bit of wealth and she had a great deal of connections. The family lives in London, primarily, what with the mother's work. Keelan's sister spends most of her time at the family estate. Very clever girl. The heiress to the family fortune. Rather like her mother in temperament."

Silas remembered how Councilmember Cricket had been when he'd met her, so matter-of-fact and businesslike, so unlike her son. Silas was no expert on Cricket's character, but their brief encounter together had suggested the man had a gentle spirit. Everything he'd seen in the past week at the Council chambers had confirmed his suspicions. Anyone else would have lost patience with someone like Miss Wilton-Reed. But Cricket had withstood her barbs with what Silas could only describe as superhuman perseverance. He thought of the way Cricket seemed more beaten down after every passing day and he felt a pang of sympathy that the poor man was stuck with a family that didn't seem all suited to him.

"What is the father like?" he asked, surprising himself. He was sure it was absurd for him to express any amount of curiosity about the family. When he caught a small grin on Mrs. Pimpernel's face, he was sure she found his interest exceptional.

Mrs. Wrenwhistle seemed to consider her answer. "He has a good heart. But he tends to spend most of his attention on his various hobbies and projects. He never comes out into society. I daresay young Keelan has been left to his own devices for most of his life."

Silas' sympathy for Cricket sharpened. He thought back to the way they'd left off before—his casual dismissal and Cricket's crestfallen expression. With an eccentric father, a cold and busy mother, and an absent sister, did Cricket have anyone who treated him like he mattered? He held back a wince at the memory that *he* certainly hadn't. Impulsively, he wished he could try the whole evening over again, knowing what he knew now. "That is unfortunate," he managed at last.

Mrs. Wrenwhistle's expression was thoughtful. "It is. But I suspect many people underestimate young Keelan, his mother included. People often mistake gentleness for weakness. He is kind, but I suspect there's a strength in him that goes unnoticed."

Silas thought of the way Cricket had lifted his chin as he walked away from him that night and privately agreed with her assessment.

Mrs. Wrenwhistle turned to her friend. "Do you know, I wonder if we ought to turn our attention to the young man. You and I are old hats at navigating the machinations of the *ton*. And I have a *very* empty calendar now that my work on the Council is over." She grinned in a way that would have looked wicked on anyone less elegant. "So I imagine a dash of matchmaking wouldn't go amiss."

Mrs. Pimpernel laughed. "It certainly wouldn't."

"Good. It shall be nice to have something to work on. With most of my grandchildren involved in this project, I have been quite bereft of entertainment. Well," she said, standing. "I'd best go home and make sure everything is ready for tonight. It was lovely to meet you, Mr. Rook-Worth. I look forward to seeing you again. I'm sure you'll enjoy this evening's festivities."

"This evening?"

"Oh, dear, didn't I tell you?" Mrs. Pimpernel said. "We're all going to a dinner party at Iris' townhouse tonight. To officially welcome all of you to London."

Mrs. Wrenwhistle bestowed a regal bow of her head and sailed out of the room. Silas thanked his hostess for tea and then returned to his own room, to see if he had packed anything remotely suitable for a dinner party with such a grand lady.

Silas was not mistaken in anticipating grandeur. Mrs. Wrenwhistle's home was large and immaculately decorated. Thankfully, she resided on the same street as Mrs. Pimpernel so their little group had been able to walk to the event. Silas was relieved that it meant he'd easily be able to leave if he tired of the social niceties.

All of the fae volunteers were there, as well as all of the members of the Council, and, Silas learned, assorted family members of each. It made him wonder briefly what his own family might have thought of such an event. He was sure his mother would be wandering into the kitchen to ask the cook for recipes, Briony would inspect the furniture with interest, and Quince would marvel at the upholstery. He could easily imagine his father feeling out with his magic to determine what spells had been cast about the place.

Silas did so himself, out of a strange sort of kindred feeling with his father. He noted that Mr. Emrys Wrenwhistle and Mr. Wyndham Wren-whistle both seemed to spool their magic towards their respective spouses, as if to assure themselves of their loved ones' wellbeing. He observed that none of the other fae-humans felt out with their magic, except Mr. Finkle-Finch, who seemed to do so involuntarily. His magic snapped sporadically around him like the fizzles on champagne—not dangerous in any way, but with a small feeling of wildness to it. Silas realized that Mrs. Iris Wrenwhistle was watching him. She gave him a small smile and a nod, the barest acknowledgement that she was aware of his sensing.

They were served wine as they waited for dinner to be ready and were encouraged to mingle. Silas was not one for mingling, so he stood at the wall and observed, noting with interest who gravitated towards who. Mr. Hedge-Wyck and Mr. Brooks were, predictably, talking together, with their heads bent close. Surprisingly, they invited Mr. Finkle-Finch into their conversation, although the man looked nervous to be there. Miss Wrenwhistle was standing next to her beau, as expected, but the couple was talking happily with Miss Gloucester-Stone and Mx. Badger-Thorp. Mx. Hillcrest joined the group as soon as they arrived. Silas' partner, Mr. Emrys Wrenwhistle, was speaking with Cricket—not surprising considering Mrs. Wrenwhistle's recent explana-tion that they were close friends. Mr. Wrenwhistle had his arm around Torquil's waist, although Torquil seemed distracted by glancing around the room at the various groups, no doubt worrying whether they were all getting along. Cricket kept glancing at Torquil as he spoke to his friend, his face lightly flushed. Silas wondered if he was pining for his friend's spouse. An unidentifiable feeling flared in his chest at the thought. Miss Wilton-Reed spoke to Councilmember Cricket and the two women seemed to get along very well. An observation that made Silas uneasy, although he couldn't determine why.

He managed to stay on his own for a little under a quarter of an hour before Torquil strolled over to him. "How are you doing?"

Silas shrugged. "I am well. Not one for these sorts of gatherings, I'm afraid."

Torquil smiled. "I understand. Neither am I, if you want the truth. There will be more socializing after dinner. I might hint that Wyndham and Roger typically sit to the side as well. If you're looking for safe harbor in social seas, they are both rather good for that."

Silas smiled. "I appreciate the hint. I'll remember it."

"Good." They were silent for a moment and Silas began to think that they were merely going to maintain a companionable silence— something that he found he might actually like—when they spoke again, "How would you feel about being paired with a new partner?"

He blinked at them in surprise. "I wouldn't be opposed, if you think it necessary. Although I'm getting along very well with your husband."

They flashed him a smile. "I'm glad to hear that. But Emrys did mention that he's noticed your magic feels a bit…restrained mixed with his."

Silas took a sip of wine as he considered the right response. Finally, he said, "I confess that is an accurate observation."

"Am I correct in guessing that it is an unusual reaction for your magic?"

"It is."

"I don't want you to be at a disadvantage. Magical compatibility is very unpredictable. But we have a number of fae volunteers, so I think it might be best to find someone better suited."

Silas thought of Cricket when he had released his magic the night of the wedding. Together, their magic had felt wild and warm, the opposite of the leashed feeling he had working with Mr. Wrenwhistle. "That makes sense," he said at last.

Torquil breathed out and Silas suspected it was out of relief. "We'll pair you with someone different tomorrow. You weren't the only pair to experience some incompatibility. So a number of the pairs will be mixed up for the next round of exercises."

"Glad to hear it isn't just me," Silas said with a small grin.

"Even if it were, that wouldn't be a problem. I'm determined to make this project succeed. And that includes finding someone who works well with your magic."

The conversation was abruptly cut off when they were called in to dinner. Once again, Silas was intrigued by who was seated next to whom. He was relieved when Miss Wilton-Reed was not seated next to Cricket. Although that relief quickly dissipated when he realized that *he* was seated next to Cricket instead.

CHAPTER 20

KEELAN

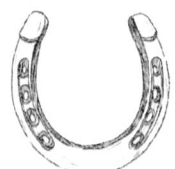

By the time dinner was announced, Keelan was exhausted from being acutely aware of the presence of too many people in the room. He'd attempted to share in the conversation with Emrys and Torquil, sipping his wine and basking in their ethereal glow. For the duration, he'd been turned deliberately away from a certain fae-human standing alone near the windows. It was the only way he could prevent himself from stealing glances at the man and his evening outfit of choice, which was modest like the rest of his clothes, but suited him *very* well.

He'd also made every effort to not overthink the way his mother and Miss Wilton-Reed had immediately found each other in the crowd, chattering on like old friends ever since. It would have provided some small relief if his mother's occasional laughter sounded like her typical parody of genuine amusement, but instead she seemed delighted by his partner, which burned more than he cared to admit. Keelan had never been able to speak with his mother in such a way, the conversation rebounding easily with no heavy implications of disappointment or disinterest. However, he supposed that if there was anyone he wished for his parents to approve of, it was the person who would someday become his spouse.

His mother waved him over to escort Miss Wilton-Reed into the dining room and he obliged, offering the lady his arm as he'd done for most of the day. He fully expected that they would be seated together at the table, as well. If his mother was known for anything, it was her skill of persuasion, not to mention that their hostess was a friend of the family. But before Keelan could locate two open chairs for them, Mrs. Iris Wrenwhistle got his attention.

"Mr. Cricket, do take the seat beside Emrys," she said warmly. "I've a place for Miss Wilton-Reed here beside me at the head of the table."

With the rate at which Miss Wilton-Reed abandoned him for the honor she'd been given, Keelan was surprised that the small bouquet of red rosebuds pinned into her hair remained in place.

"Stars above," Emrys said with a low chuckle as he readied Torquil's chair for them, "you'd think she's never shared a meal with an old lady before."

"Be kind to your grandmother," Keelan scolded under his breath with a crooked grin. "She may be old, but she is kind and most considerate."

"Allow me."

The deep voice startled Keelan into turning around, but not fast enough to prevent him from placing his hand atop the one Mr. Rook-Worth had already used to pull his chair out from the table.

Keelan snatched his hand away, covering his mouth in a late attempt to hide the gasp he'd let out. He squeezed his eyes shut for the briefest moment, silently cursing himself for the reaction as he felt his entire body go hot, before he let his hand fall to his side.

"Thank you." Keelan took the offered seat and stared intently at the table as Mr. Rook-Worth sat in the chair beside him. As grateful as he was for the reprieve their hostess had given him, he wondered if it was possible that this arrangement could very well be more difficult than sharing a meal with Miss Wilton-Reed.

Emrys' partner had arrived alone and remained that way until shortly before dinner was called, when Torquil excused themself to go and speak to him. *The way a normal, respectable person should*, Keelan told himself. He had no doubt that what Emrys said was true. Mr. Rook-Worth was probably quite nice to speak with. Even what he could recall of the short interaction they'd shared the night of the wedding had been pleasant enough, before…well, *before*.

"Ah, Mr. Rook-Worth." Emrys was leaned forward in his seat, looking back and forth between them with a satisfied smile. "I told my grandmother I thought the two of you would get on splendidly. I'm glad she took my suggestion into consideration while making the seating arrangements for tonight."

Keelan pinched his lips together, eyes widening at Emrys as he held back a strangled cry of outrage. It escaped instead as a high, thin whimper in his throat.

"Most thoughtful of you, Mr. Wrenwhistle," Mr. Rook-Worth said from Keelan's other side with as much enthusiasm as someone who'd just been gifted a pair of dirty stockings with holes already worn into them. He had his answer. This was decidedly worse.

Dinner was well into its second course before Keelan worked up the courage to speak to the man. He knew he was being absurd. His silence was more of a punishment to himself than anyone else. Besides, it was not as though Keelan had been the one to react oddly when their romp was over. He'd walked his merry self back to the estate and washed away the evidence of *both* their pleasure, not just his own. It should have been another encounter to look back on fondly, not wishing it had never happened in the first place. If he'd been capable of it with Emrys, then certainly he was capable of it with his stranger.

The first step was to not be strangers anymore.

"Do you miss your family?"

It took a moment for Mr. Rook-Worth to acknowledge that Keelan was speaking to him. He swallowed his bite of food and regarded Keelan with a cool, intense gaze. It was enough that Keelan had to look away. He went on before he got a reply.

"It just appeared that you all are rather close. I could never imagine working alongside my family at anything, really, but it seemed as though you did." He paused long enough to realize what he'd said hardly made sense. "I mean to say that it seemed you were able to work well with them." His brows bunched together with a slight grimace, still unsure if it had come out as he'd intended.

"It's a family business," Mr. Rook-Worth said finally as he collected another mouthful of food onto his fork. "That's generally the idea."

"Yes, right, of course." Keelan nodded tersely as he reached for the piece of bread on his plate so that he could force as much of it into his mouth as necessary to keep him from ever speaking again. He stared down at what remained of the soft roll as he chewed and wondered if it was too late to throw the rest of it at Emrys' head.

When the dessert course was finally set out on the table, Keelan made sure to soothe himself with a generous helping of the cheese and cut fruit.

"You're the first person to ask about my family."

Keelan paused in bringing another hunk of the striated Stilton to his mouth and turned his attention to his dinner partner. Mr. Rook-Worth was watching him again. He set the bite of cheese down on his plate and moved both hands to his lap, giving the man his full attention.

"Everyone else has asked about the project or how I'm enjoying London." Mr. Rook-Worth looked away first this time, his gaze shifting slowly over the rest of the guests seated around the table. "It seems that most of society is exactly what I expected them to be."

Keelan's mouth twitched into an uncertain grin. "A mite preoccupied with one's own affairs?"

Their eyes met again. Keelan forced himself not to avoid the contact. Mr. Rook-Worth's expression softened in the slightest way, before he huffed out a humorless laugh.

"Among other things," he said.

There was no time for him to elaborate on what other ways the people of London had disappointed him thus far. The rest of the party had risen from their chairs and were moving back toward the connecting room to allow the evening to find its natural end after a few more rounds of drinks. By the time Keelan had gone back for his last piece of cheese and stood to follow the group, Mr. Rook-Worth had found Mrs. Wrenwhistle to offer his thanks and was gone.

After collecting only a glass of water for himself, Keelan found a chair along the edge of the room and slumped into it with a long sigh.

"Oh dear. Is something the matter, Mr. Cricket?"

Keelan had failed to notice the two gentlemen sitting on the sofa nearby. He took in the way they were sitting so closely; Wyndham with his hand resting comfortably on Roger's thigh, their shoulders touching. If it had been Emrys and Torquil, he might've thought he was interrupting something. All the same, he got up to leave them to their quiet moment.

"Apologies," he said, "I did not see you there."

"Please, sit." Roger gestured to the chair with the wave of his hand. "You're not bothering us."

Keelan sat again, this time with better posture, and held his glass with both hands. A short silence stretched between them. Roger's attention had returned to his drink, but Wyndham arched a brow at him, foot bouncing lightly on the leg that was so neatly crossed over his opposite knee.

"I trust you've already heard we will be making some changes to the pairings next week," Wyndham said.

Keelan nodded. "Yes, I heard."

"Yours will not be one of them. Some issues of incompatibility have arisen, and we cannot afford to lose the pairs whose magics are suitable enough, as well."

"I understand," Keelan told him with a flash of a grin.

It was a fair assessment. Aside from the overall lack of observations he'd been able to make notes about, he had no difficulty sensing Miss Wilton-Reed's magic when she performed her spells. It was nothing like what Emrys had described between himself and Mr. Rook-Worth. Admittedly, he was not certain if it was more of a relief or a disappointment that the chance to make the man less of a stranger had gone away, but for the sake of the project, he hoped another fair match could be made.

"Thank you for telling me." Keelan glanced over his shoulder at the rest of the party and then pointed in the same direction with his thumb. "I think I'll go and find Emrys now." He stood and offered the gentlemen a nod. Wyndham returned the gesture, while his husband gave a warm smile and a little wave.

Finding Emrys at a party was not usually a difficult task. More often than not he was somewhere near the center of it, and that seemed to be even more true now that he had Torquil on his arm. Everyone wanted their chance to speak with them, or simply to be around them. After wandering through the adjoining rooms and asking around, however, it seemed they had disappeared.

Keelan could think of few things less stimulating than taking someone behind closed doors at his grandmother's home of all places, but he supposed they were as entitled as anyone to take advantage of a situation.

"Needs must," he muttered to himself as he returned to the main room where most of the party had settled down for a round of cards. Miss Wilton-Reed was situated in such a way that she could see everyone else, her back to the wall with a fiendish smile on her painted lips. At least she could write to her father and tell him she was finally starting to enjoy her time in London.

A flutter of motion in the black of the windows caught Keelan's attention. The sun had set more than an hour before, making it difficult to see anything outside. He stepped closer to one of the windows, near enough to the glass so that he could see out into the garden. Iris Wrenwhistle kept some of the most beautiful gardens in the city. It would be no surprise if someone had stepped out to enjoy them on such a mild, pleasant night.

Without meaning to, Keelan leaned close enough that his cheek pressed against the cool glass. His magic lifted in his chest, swirling delicately as a soft grin tilted at the corner of his lips. Emrys and Torquil had taken to the garden for a private moment after all, but not the kind he had assumed. They were on one of the paths laid with flat stones, mixed in with the flowers, holding each other and swaying to a song only they could hear.

The first time Keelan had found them this way, it had been shocking. Their love affair was still a secret at the time, though some had their suspicions, but Keelan had seen the connection between them and there was no denying it. The passionate kiss they'd shared at the end of their dance had been rather telling, as well. He had little interest in a repeat of witnessing that.

Keelan turned and leaned his back against the frame of the window instead, realizing then that he was standing in the very spot Mr. Rook-

Worth had occupied until dinner was called. Something sharp twisted in his chest and he had to swallow against the sudden rush of emotion.

Suitable enough, Wyndham had said. Suitable enough for what? A simple project, perhaps. Sensing magic and taking notes. But what sort of marriage could possibly be borne of magic that was suitable enough and nothing more? Could there also be romance? Passion? Love?

Emrys and Torquil were not just suitable, they were *extraordinary*. Their magics were destined to intermingle, fueling not only their wedding spell but every other connection they made. Such was the case for countless others who had been fortunate enough to find their perfect match. But Keelan was not so ignorant as to believe that magic was the only key to a successful marriage. There was also compromise, and sacrifice, and learning how to best support one another. Those were things that could develop over time. Things he believed he could develop with Miss Wilton-Reed, given the chance.

He only had to forget what it was to experience the all-consuming brush of a handsome stranger's compatible magic first.

CHAPTER 21

SILAS

SILAS APPROACHED the Council chamber the next morning with an unexpected feeling of uneasiness. He understood the sense in moving partners around for better compatibility; he only wished *he* had not been affected. He liked Mr. Emrys Wrenwhistle well enough. What if he was paired with someone he liked less? He was not particularly eager to have to explain his magic to someone new. Still, he had signed on to this project voluntarily; he would see it through.

When he followed his fellow fae-humans into the large room, his eyes immediately fell to Cricket, already seated at his usual table, waiting patiently for his partner. Silas held back a wince at the memory of their conversation the previous evening. He had been so determined to be kind to the man, especially after knowing more about him. And yet, when the gentleman had inquired about his family, a topic that Silas, admittedly, could usually speak on with some level of enthusiasm, Silas' first response had been dismissive. It had taken him until the dessert course to attempt to rectify the situation. He still remembered the way Cricket had immediately given him his full attention, the small quirk of the other man's mouth. He ought to have spoken longer, asked after the man's family. Instead, he had kept the conversation brief and left as soon as he was able, relishing the relative quiet of the Pimpernel townhouse.

Before he could do something foolish, like approach Cricket and startle the man with more conversation, Torquil greeted him and walked up with a stack of notes.

"Good morning, Mr. Rook-Worth," they said. "I hope you are doing well."

"Well enough."

"I have taken the liberty of compiling Emrys' notes on your magic. You'll be working with Mx. Hillcrest today in one of the empty offices. Emrys' notes could be better," they added with a small grin, "but they are still preferable to making you repeat everything you told him, or recast all of the spells you did last week."

"I appreciate that," Silas said feelingly.

"As it turns out," Torquil said, turning and gesturing for Silas to follow, "we are moving around half of our pairs this week. I'll be eager to see whether this improves things."

"Which pairs?"

"You, Mr. Finkle-Finch, and Mx. Badger-Thorp."

Silas supposed the other two made sense, considering how nervous they had been at the start of the project that their magic wasn't up to scratch. Silas had spent years feeling as though his magic paled in comparison to his family's. He was not particularly fond of that feeling resurfacing during this project.

He was led into an empty office.

"Mx. Hillcrest will be here shortly. Roger, Wyndham, and I will be making our rounds, like usual. But if you need any of us, our office is the last one down the hall and to the right."

They put the notes on a desk, giving the pile a little tap, and then left the room. Silas sat back in his chair and picked up the notes, reading through what Mr. Wrenwhistle had written.

His new partner showed up around ten minutes later, looking chipper and unbothered by having Silas instead. "Good morning," they said, taking a seat opposite him. "Mr. Rook-Worth, isn't it?"

"That's correct. Here are the notes Mr. Wrenwhistle took last week.

If you need any additional explanations about anything before we start, do let me know."

They smiled and took the papers. Mx. Hillcrest was an attractive sort of person, with an evidently cheerful disposition. They had dark, straight hair that fell neatly around their pointed ears, angular dark green eyes, tan skin, and a full mouth. As Silas would expect with a fae, their movements were graceful and fluid.

He waited as they read through the notes. They asked the questions Silas had anticipated, which was a good sign, as it meant they were thinking along the same lines he was. Finally, they set the stack down and pulled a bunch of ingredients forward.

"I think that is enough to give me a basic understanding. Do you mind casting once before we officially begin so I can get a sense of your magic?"

"Not at all. Anything in particular you'd like to see?"

They shook their head, beaming at him. "Whatever you like."

He sorted through the jars on the desk and decided to do a pouring spell. Pulling out a fresh sheet of spellpaper, he wrote out the necessary sigils, then laid some dried valerian petals, orange pips, and powdered hickory root into the appropriate spaces. He set a jar of peppercorns in the center of the paper and then cast the spell.

He could tell the difference with Mx. Hillcrest instantly. His magic was not only restrained, it was almost completely constricted. He hastily added a sigil to boost power and grimaced as he felt his magic scraping to get free. The jar of peppercorns wobbled on the desk. He added another sigil, attempting to ignore the discomfort. The jar wobbled again, and finally fell to its side with a clatter. He sank back into his chair, feeling his heart hammering in his chest.

Mx. Hillcrest's smile had dropped completely. "Oh, dear," they murmured. "I'm guessing it isn't usually like that."

"Not at all."

"It felt as though your magic was straining to work. Is that how it felt to you?"

He nodded. "It was…painful, really."

Their brow furrowed. "I'd better write all this down." They bent their head and wrote out notes in a small and tidy script. "I will say," they said after they finished, "that I was impressed that you managed to eke out the amount of power you needed, despite the challenge. That last sigil gave quite a boost."

He rubbed his temple. "I don't normally use that one. It can be a bit too much."

They hummed and wrote some more. "Well, we certainly don't want you in pain when you cast magic. Perhaps I should tell Torquil?" They set the papers aside and started to stand.

"No," Silas said hastily. He winced a little at how loudly the word had come out. "Not just yet. We can...we can at least discuss some things more. Perhaps fill in some of the details that Mr. Wrenwhistle left out in his notes first. Maybe it's simply fatigue that's affecting my magic this way. I wouldn't want to put them to the trouble of rearranging us for nothing."

He knew it wasn't fatigue, but the idea of having to be paired with another partner in the short span of a single morning made him feel ill. He liked Mx. Hillcrest. They seemed good-hearted and patient. Their questions had suggested intelligence and capability.

They looked doubtful. "I can certainly see the benefit in taking more notes. It would help your next partner, if nothing else. Emrys is charming, of course, but his notes are sadly lacking." They pulled the notes closer again and started a new page. "However," they added, glancing up at him and pointing their pen at his face. "I think it would be a good idea to report how it felt so they can be prepared to find you someone new. I have never seen fatigue make magic that painful."

Silas sighed, conceding the point. "Very well. I'll go find Torquil."

A quick glance into the big room proved that Torquil was not there, so Silas turned back to the hallway, following their directions from earlier. He passed an office with Miss Gloucester-Stone and Miss Wrenwhistle, and reached the last office on the right. It was pulled close but not latched, so he rapped his knuckles on the door and pushed it open.

He found Torquil on their back on top of a desk covered in papers, with Mr. Wrenwhistle kissing them into the furniture. Their legs were curled around their spouse's back and it was very plain that neither of them had heard Silas knock. He considered leaving quietly but didn't want to have to explain to Mx. Hillcrest that he hadn't told anyone, so he cleared his throat.

The two broke apart but, to Silas's relief, they did not seem too embarrassed at being caught. Torquil flashed him a grin and said, a little breathlessly, "Apologies for that, Mr. Rook-Worth. Did you need me?"

Silas saw them attempt to shove their husband away. Instead, Mr. Wrenwhistle pivoted a little so his hip was against the desk, still partially hovering over Torquil.

"It's nothing urgent. I just wanted to tell you that if you wind up moving partners around again, I will probably need someone new as well."

Torquil's grin dropped. "Oh, dear. Did something happen?"

"My magic seems even less compatible with Mx. Hillcrest than it was with Mr. Wrenwhistle. Which is a shame, because they seem very pleasant."

"They are," Torquil said, almost absently. "That is most unfortunate."

"But Mx. Hillcrest and I agreed to discuss my magic in more detail until you found more partners that needed changing."

"Thank you," Torquil said.

"I'll leave you to it," Silas said, giving Mr. Wrenwhistle a knowing look and closing the door again. He heard the desk squeak as he walked away. At least Torquil had found a way to relieve some of the stress this project had brought on.

CHAPTER 22

KEELAN

As much as Keelan did not want to admit it, the absence of Mr. Rook-Worth allowed him to breathe a little easier. Torquil had collected him as soon as he arrived and directed him out to an empty office to meet with his new partner. When his own arrived, he stood to greet her.

"Good morning, Miss Wilton-Reed," he said, expecting a mild response like he'd received all the mornings before.

"Isn't it?" the lady offered instead. She did not take her usual spot across the table. Keelan watched her round the far end before coming to his side with her distinct air of confidence. "Get my chair, won't you?"

He hurried to do as she'd asked with a faltering, "Of—of course."

Miss Wilton-Reed adjusted her full skirts around herself with care, as though she were settling in for tea with someone important rather than preparing for an afternoon of magic with him. Keelan sat beside her and noted that she was not wearing her typical flowers, but a braided circlet of leaves and vines settled on her dark hair like a crown.

"I had such a lovely time speaking with your mother last night," she gushed, placing her hand on his arm as she said it before gesturing arbitrarily. "She is so bold and sure of herself. What I would've given to grow up with such a formidable person to emulate."

Keelan blinked at her in surprise, still acclimating to her closeness. "I am glad you had such an enjoyable evening."

Not only had she been offered a prominent seat beside Mrs. Iris Wrenwhistle—and his mother—for the meal, but she'd also won both games of cards the party played before everyone took their leave. She was undoubtedly the shining star of the dinner. If her father had seen, he would've been proud.

"I certainly did." Their eyes met before she adopted a sweet tone to add, "It was a rather perfect way to end the evening after our successful shopping excursion, wouldn't you agree?"

His magic swirled pleasantly in his chest at the words, grin stretching a little wider. She'd enjoyed her time with him, after all?

"I'm happy you feel the same," he admitted quietly.

"Now," she said with purpose, inspecting the materials Roger had delivered to the table before she arrived. "What are we tasked with today?"

Keelan shook his thoughts and attempted to focus.

"I believe we're meant to begin working with the rubric."

When Roger had given him the supplies, he'd also provided an outline of the rubric that he, Wyndham, and Torquil had crafted for the testing of fae-human children. It was rather overwhelming at first glance, but Roger had been kind enough to explain it to him in a way that made it easier to understand.

There were five criteria: power, focus, control, understanding, and intuition. As each fae-human's magic presented itself uniquely, the rubric was to serve more as a guide than anything, especially as they were still testing it.

Keelan recalled the screening for his own magical aptitude and wondered if he might've scored better had it not been so terrifyingly strict. Twenty years later, he could still remember how nervous he'd been that morning. There was never any question that his older sister was the one who would inherit, but perhaps if the exam had been better suited to his own strengths, he would've at least earned more than his mother's vague approval at his results.

Miss Wilton-Reed picked up one of the jars by the lid and whirled her wrist in a circle several times, stirring up whatever it was that had settled at the bottom of the purplish liquid inside.

"Lavender oil," she mused. "I can do a great many things with this."

Keelan smoothed a hand over the knot of his cream-colored cravat protectively. "Indeed?"

Miss Wilton-Reed gave the rubric a cursory glance. "Since you've already made your disparaging little notes about my power, perhaps we can move on to something else. Shall I impress you? I could shrink your chair to the size of an acorn, or spell everyone in this room into a peaceful half-hour slumber. What do you think your mother would like best?"

Keelan let out an uncertain huff of a laugh. He glanced over his shoulder to see what Emrys and Mx. Badger-Thorp were doing to provide a more tame example. To his dismay, Emrys had already left his new partner alone.

"I do not think the expectation is for you to do such, er...*complicated* demonstrations each time." He leaned over the rubric again. "This says a drying spell would do nicely, or a cleaning spell."

His partner removed the lid on the jar of lavender oil and wafted the scent toward herself. She breathed it in and sighed out her evident approval. Miss Wilton-Reed lowered her middle and ring fingers to the surface of the oil before drawing them out carefully. With no urgency, she touched her fingertips to the dip at the base of her throat, behind both ears, and finally to her opposite wrist.

"Pick a number, Mr. Cricket," she purred, rubbing her wrists together.

It took him several seconds to remember what numbers were in the haze of lavender surrounding them.

"Three?" he managed around his heavy pulse.

Miss Wilton-Reed rolled her eyes. "Something larger, if you don't mind." She reached forward and slid one of the reference books closer to herself. "A page number, specifically."

The book was fairly thick, but not so large as to call for a number encroaching on one thousand like some others he'd seen. "Two hundred and eighty-seven," he decided.

A breeze picked up around them as Miss Wilton-Reed's fae magic came to life. With a few more drops of the purple oil, a sprinkle of dried peppermint leaves, and exactly four coffee beans, she marked up a fresh sheet of spellpaper with sigils, closed her eyes, and cast. The front cover of the book flipped open against the tabletop, followed by a quick cascading of pages from first to last. With more precision, the shuffling began in the opposite direction, steady until the action slowed toward the center of the book. When the final few pages turned and settled, Keelan's eyes darted to the small set of numbers printed in the corner.

"Two hundred and eighty-seven," Miss Wilton-Reed echoed with a satisfied expression as she opened her eyes.

"Splendid," Keelan breathed. He scrambled to collect his paper and pencil. "Would you say that was for control or focus?" It seemed to him that it was equal parts of both.

"Why specify?" Miss Wilton-Reed asked breezily. "Make of it what you will, so long as you note my accomplishment of the task."

Keelan wasn't entirely sure that helped with his notes pertaining to the rubric, but he wrote down as much as he could of what he'd observed. As he did, his mind began to wander. The lady beside him was elegant, beautiful, and clearly very capable with her magic. She was a little proud, but so was Emrys, and he decided she had every right to be. There was no doubt in his mind that if she'd been allowed to take her exam as a fae-human, she would be the one set to inherit her family's title and everything that came with it.

"Would you care to go riding with me?" he asked buoyantly. The outing the day before had gone so well. He could only imagine how pleasant it would be to share another of his greatest passions with her. "I'm at the Park nearly every morning. I would be delighted to have your company."

There was a brief wash of aversion on Miss Wilton-Reed's face before it was replaced with a smile. It looked frightfully similar to the one she'd worn while playing cards the night before, subtle but calculating. His stomach dipped with uncertainty, but then she placed her hand on his arm again and nodded.

"I would be more than happy to join you, Mr. Cricket."

CHAPTER 23

SILAS

THE NEXT MORNING, Silas walked into the Council chambers with even more foreboding than the day before. It felt like a failure on his part to be unable to perform magic simply because one fae or another was observing him. It hardly seemed fair, considering no one else was having such problems.

He had been so upset the previous evening, he had very nearly asked to join Hedge-Wyck and Brooks in their regular evening activities. He hadn't, in the end, choosing instead to borrow one of Mrs. Pimpernel's three-volume novels to take his mind off of things. When he saw Cricket sitting in his usual seat in the chambers, looking as unsettled as Silas felt, he was cheered by his decision to read in bed. Though he hardly knew why it mattered.

He went into the hallway and strode toward the office he used before, hoping to get another day of notes with Mx. Hillcrest instead of being shuffled around right away. His partner showed up shortly after, cheerful as ever.

"I just talked to Torquil," they said. "We're going to see how everyone works today and then they're going to see about rearranging us again. I was thinking about trying to watch you do magic without sensing it. It won't be as helpful, of course, but it would give you the opportunity to work through the rubric a little. What do you think?"

"That sounds perfect," Silas said gratefully.

He was in the process of writing out the sigils for a breeze spell when a loud *bang* came from the office next door. He and Hillcrest exchanged a look and then wordlessly hurried out of the room. The office door was open and the room was a mess: there were shards of glass and peppercorns everywhere. Paper debris was still floating down from the explosion like confetti. Thankfully, no one was injured, but Mr. Finkle-Finch was frantically trying to catch the falling paper.

"I'm so sorry," he babbled. "I did tell you my magic is unpredictable. I don't know what could have happened. I'm sure I got the sigils right. It is *so* embarrassing."

Meanwhile, Mr. Buckthorn was trying to pull the other man away from the mess. "For goodness' sake, my dear fellow, you'll get yourself injured. As I said, there's no harm done, but there will be if you cut yourself on the glass."

Councilmember Wyndham Wrenwhistle shouldered through the growing crowd and ushered both men out of the room before they could get hurt. Then he shepherded the entire group back to the large room. "Wait in here, if you please," he said in a tone that brooked no argument.

Mr. Finkle-Finch was led to a chair and plied with cups of water as he recounted what had happened to Councilmember Roger Wrenwhistle. Miss Aveline Wrenwhistle fussed over Mr. Buckthorn who, despite being quite obviously fine, seemed to enjoy the attention. Silas sank into a seat and watched the scene before him, already preparing himself mentally for being paired with Mr. Buckthorn next.

At length, Torquil and Councilmember Wyndham Wrenwhistle joined the group. Torquil's face was pale but Councilmember Wrenwhistle looked no more perturbed than usual, which Silas counted as positive.

"First things first," Torquil said, "is everyone all right?" When everyone nodded, they continued, "I sincerely apologize for what happened. Wyndham, Roger, and I will ensure that protection spells are reapplied before we start again. We were concerned about the impact our magic might have on yours but…your safety comes first."

"It isn't your fault," Mr. Finkle-Finch cut in. "It's my blasted magic. I knew it was temperamental and yet—"

"Your magic is extraordinary, Mr. Finkle-Finch," Torquil said gently. "Wyndham examined the office and we suspect your and Mr. Buckthorn's magics are highly incompatible."

"More like combustible," Councilmember Wrenwhistle muttered.

"So we will prepare better for our next castings in case any other pairings are equally…dangerous," they said. They took a deep breath and let it out slowly. "We have also come to the conclusion that after such an alarming experience, everyone might need another break. We would like to take everyone to the opera tonight—at least, anyone who is interested. We will make use of the Wrenwhistle family box and the Pimpernel family box to accommodate everyone."

"And then," Councilmember Wrenwhistle added, "we will start at midday tomorrow to give everyone the morning off."

"Will we be grouped with the same pairs tomorrow?" Mr. Buckthorn said.

Silas wanted to roll his eyes at the foolish question but refrained.

Torquil gave him a kind smile. "No. As it happens, there was another pair finding some incompatibility, so we will be swapping you and Mr. Finkle-Finch with Mr. Rook-Worth and Mx. Hillcrest."

Mr. Buckthorn's expression cleared. "Ah. Capital idea." He beamed at Silas, clearly relieved.

Silas could not find it in him to return the smile. He was about to get his second partner in as many days. He almost would have preferred it if his magic had reacted in such a violent way. As it was, he just felt incompetent and weak. He was beginning to wonder if he was even bringing much value to the project at all. Was his presence more of a burden than a help?

"Are you sure I should continue on?" Mr. Finkle-Finch asked, inadvertently echoing Silas' own thoughts. "After all that?"

Silas glanced at Mx. Hillcrest, who seemed unperturbed to be paired with someone whose magic had such explosive potential. They patted Mr. Finkle-Finch's shoulder. "Like the councilmembers said, we will take precautions."

Finkle-Finch looked doubtful, but couldn't argue in the face of his new partner's relaxed attitude.

Torquil clapped their hands together. "If no one has any questions, then we can end early today. Fae volunteers, if you would like to meet us at the opera, there will be seats available to you. We will pick up our out-of-town guests at half past seven."

CHAPTER 24

KEELAN

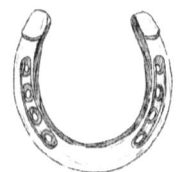

THE RIDE in the Park was meant to allow Keelan an opportunity to demonstrate his horsemanship, which was a source of pride he'd hoped might excite Miss Wilton-Reed the way her display of magic the previous afternoon had excited him. Unfortunately, she arrived in something as far from a riding habit as she possibly could have and insisted that a stroll was far more conducive to making acquaintances. Keelan swallowed his disappointment and handed the reins of his horse back to the groom, offering his arm instead.

Before long, he understood more fully what she'd meant by *making acquaintances*. Miss Wilton-Reed requested an introduction to every member of the *ton* they encountered, necessitating that Keelan present her again and again so that she could have the same short, hollow conversation with each of them. By the end of their promenade, he'd said her name so many times that it was echoing inside his head like a shout into an empty well.

His only reprieve came when they'd passed by one of the more impressive flower beds near the Cumberland Gate. Miss Wilton-Reed was swift to identify all of the blooms for him, using far more detail than he would ever be able to remember. Even quicker was her criticism over planting bellflowers in full sun.

"I believe this allotment in particular is meant to attract the bees," Keelan said wisely, recalling something he'd overheard Wyndham say once. "It's amusing to think of such tiny creatures also seeking the beauty of a flower, and then providing us with a gift such as honey for all their trouble, don't you think?"

"Bees make honey as food for themselves, not for us," Miss Wilton-Reed corrected in a condescending manner. "Though I suppose we ought to be thanked for our efforts of planting the flowers to begin with."

Keelan offered to walk Miss Wilton-Reed back to the Pimpernel townhouse, which she accepted. There was another hour or so before they were expected at the Council's chambers. When they paused outside the front door, Keelan raised her fingers to his lips and thanked her for her company. That finally earned him a smile from the lady.

It turned out to be a trying day for other members of the project, as well. Poor Mr. Finkle-Finch discovered a most impressive way to prove his magical incompatibility with his new partner, Mr. Buckthorn; fortunately no real harm was done. Instead, the mishap earned everyone a night out.

"Shall I see you at the opera this evening?" Miss Wilton-Reed asked upon hearing Torquil's announcement.

"I wouldn't miss it," Keelan promised. It would've been his answer regardless of who wanted to know.

"I'll be wearing azaleas. Do try not to clash."

Upon returning home, Keelan asked Marten to ready something that would go well with pink and collapsed onto his bed. He dragged his pillow over his face in an attempt to smother the way he felt as empty as Miss Wilton-Reed's countless conversations had been that morning. Or perhaps more like the bees, drained after working hard to create something that another seemed to easily take for granted. He silently vowed to never waste another drop of honey.

Keelan had never felt anxious about attending the opera before. He enjoyed most forms of entertainment in London, but live performances had always been a favorite. Many viewed an evening at the opera house as yet another opportunity to socialize and glean the latest gossip about the members of the *ton*, of which there was always plenty. Keelan was not unaffected by the whispers—after all, he liked a bit of intrigue as much as the next person. But the opera also provided him an excuse to sink into a beautiful, tragic, funny, and often deeply romantic story for a couple of hours.

Dressed and ready far too early, Keelan reluctantly decided to join his father for a late tea. The sitting room toward the back of the house had long since been taken over by his father's varied interests and always smelled vaguely of overturned soil and wet dog. At present, it was impossible to locate a place to sit that was not covered with various lengths and rolls of fabric.

"Here, come and sit in this chair." Elodie leapt off his father's lap as he got up and began clearing away another seat for himself nearby. "You look very nice," his father added after giving him a once-over. "Plans this evening?"

"The opera," Keelan told him. Alouetta was suddenly at his side, licking his fingers until he patted her between the ears. Her rear end wriggled when he relented.

His father sat and prepared a cup for Keelan before making another for himself. "With someone special, I wonder? You seem nervous."

"Do I?" The soaring pitch of his voice gave him away if it hadn't been obvious before. He drained his tea in a few swallows and returned the cup to the tray, waving off his father's motion to refill it. "All of the project volunteers received an invitation."

"How lovely," his father said with a gentle smile. He only just seemed to notice the strip of striped fabric still resting over his shoulder; he chuckled as he pulled it off and tossed it to the place he'd moved the rest of the materials.

Keelan studied the pile. "What are you making?"

"Oh," his father hedged. "A little of this, a little of that. I was looking for something to make new curtains for the windows in this room, but then I found a stunning thin cotton with the most delicate flowers on it that I'd forgotten I have." He gestured to the fabric he was speaking about. "I thought perhaps I could make myself something new for late spring. Have you any interest in a new waistcoat?" The hope in his father's voice was too sweet to deny.

"Of course, Papa. I would love it."

For all the man's eccentricities, he was quite talented with a needle and thread. Keelan had several pieces he did not mind wearing out. His father gave a satisfied nod and then narrowed an eye.

"You never did answer my question," he tried again.

Keelan's gaze fell to his hands in his lap. He sighed and began picking white spaniel hairs off his dark trousers. His emotions about the evening felt far more complicated than what he could sort out in one conversation at tea. The relationship he had with his father had never been the type that made him comfortable enough to reveal his worries, either. However, if anyone could understand what he was going through, it was probably his father.

"I believe Mother is seeking a match for me with one of the other participants in the study," he began, choosing his words carefully. "The lady is actually my partner. We did not get on well at first, as she wasn't exactly thrilled to be here. But I have made an attempt to know her better. We spent an afternoon on New Bond Street with several of the other volunteers, and this morning we went for a stroll in the Park together."

"My." His father cradled his tea in his hands. "It sounds as though you are being perfectly honorable about it. Has she reciprocated your interest?"

Keelan huffed, his brows pinching. "That's the mess of it. I fear I become more confused about the situation—about her true feelings for me—with each interaction we share. I wish someone had told me before now that courtship could be so thoroughly bewildering."

There was a heavy pause between them. Keelan couldn't help but feel that his father wanted to say something, but then decided against it as he took the final sip of his tea.

"I'm sure your mother is just trying to do what's best for your future," is what he settled on, with little emotion in his voice. He leaned forward around Elodie to set his cup on the tray and remained there for a moment before he continued in a hushed tone, switching to his native French. "Whatever happens, my darling son, you can still live your life however makes you the happiest."

He remained in place until Keelan nodded his understanding; he'd been nearly as fluent as his father when he was a child, but he'd since lost the ability through lack of practice. His mother, on the other hand, had never learned.

Keelan swallowed thickly against the swell of emotions at his father's private message. It was more confirmation of what he'd always suspected about his parents' marriage. He nodded again as he stood from his chair, brushing a hand against the seat of his trousers in an attempt to remove more dog hair.

"*Merci*, Papa," he whispered, not trusting his voice to speak any louder, before he hurried out of the room.

THANKS to his decades-long friendship with Emrys, Keelan had joined the Wrenwhistles in their box several times before, and he was pleased to discover that the Pimpernel box was situated a short distance away, only one row below. Not for the first time, he wondered how much sooner Emrys would have announced his perfect match if Torquil had been out in society all along rather than existing in the shadows due to their parentage. Or rather, due to the way they had been treated as a result of said parentage.

The couple was seated at the front and center, just behind the low wall that faced the stage, already leaning in toward one another with their hands clasped. It was too far for Keelan to read lips, but the sly grin that curved at the corner of Emrys' mouth was telling enough. Perfectly incorrigible, the both of them.

Miss Wilton-Reed had selected the seat to Keelan's left, which seemed promising, but soon after, her focus turned solely to the spectacle that was the inside of the opera house. He did not take it personally. The seductive red of the seats and curtains combined with the glinting, gilded accents that caught the light from the candles had always been inviting in a way that was difficult to describe. Not to mention the hundreds of society members gathered into one large room wearing their finest evening clothes and sparkling jewels to match.

His partner's presence also meant that the rest of the fae-humans had arrived to fill in the seats waiting for them. Mr. Hedge-Wyck and Mr. Brooks settled themselves together in the back row of the box behind Keelan. He wondered how long it would take for their hands to begin wandering after the lights dimmed. Aveline Wrenwhistle was the epitome of joy in her position between Mr. Buckthorn and her new friend Miss Gloucester-Stone. The open seats on the other side of Miss Wilton-Reed were claimed by Wyndham and Roger, the latter of whom looked far more delighted than his husband to be in attendance.

The remainder of the volunteers were scattered behind Emrys and Torquil in the Pimpernel box. Cautiously, Keelan's gaze slid to the man seated in the back row. Mr. Rook-Worth sat with his arms crossed, and Keelan couldn't help the faint grin that tugged at the corner of his mouth. Of course this rugged man from the country could not be bothered to put on an act of propriety for the people in a city that meant nothing to him. Keelan was in the process of appreciating his evening attire once again when the lights dimmed and the overture he could hum by memory began.

It became evident almost immediately that Miss Wilton-Reed did not appreciate the opera for the performance. She began asking Keelan what the songs were about, and he attempted to whisper an explanation back each time, but his replies were only met with more criticisms about the production.

All the while, Mr. Hedge-Wyck and Mr. Brooks were making very little attempt to be silent. Nobody else in the box seemed to be bothered by it, so Keelan tried his best to focus on the music. A breathy moan in a quieter moment had him bringing a hand up to scratch uncomfortably at his eyebrow. He glanced at the Pimpernel box and found that his vantage point did not serve him well in that regard, either. Emrys had abandoned his grip on Torquil's hand and was instead stroking the inside of their thigh in a way that could not be mistaken for anything casual.

Hugging his middle with his other arm, Keelan moved his hand to fully cover his eyes for a moment. He had run out of places to focus his attention; the performance had reached a point of intense passion, and apparently those in the audience so inclined were feeling inspired, as well.

He could not explain why, but Keelan parted his fingers just enough to look at Mr. Rook-Worth. The humiliation he'd felt at the man's dismissal could not quash the truth of their encounter. Keelan had never experienced anything half as pleasurable, and the way Mr. Rook-Worth had stared at him after *had* to mean something. He was sure of it.

The look of mild irritation on Mr. Rook-Worth's face had grown into something far worse as the night progressed. Keelan dropped his hand as he restrained the sudden urge he felt to reach out with his magic and see why the man appeared ready to destroy one of the empty chairs around him.

Several things happened at once just as the performance reached one of its biggest crescendos. Keelan felt a hand on his arm as everyone began to clap, likely Miss Wilton-Reed leaning in to offer another comment of disapproval or to describe how they might've done it better on a stage in Bath. But he found that he could not look away as Mr. Rook-Worth stood from his chair and swiftly exited the box. Keelan pulled away from Miss Wilton-Reed's touch as he also got to his feet.

"Pardon me," he muttered, hardly loud enough for her to hear over the applause, and not even in her direction, as he hastened to follow the man who still held far too much of his attention.

Once outside, Keelan paused on the pavement, turning in a tight circle as he searched for a glimpse of short, dark hair and broad shoulders in the crowd. Blast all the fashion plates for indicating that navy and gray and black were the only acceptable colors for a night out! Keelan stretched up onto his toes, worried that he had missed Mr. Rook-Worth completely.

A carriage pulling away farther down the sidewalk caught his eye. The whole group had probably arrived in one, of course. Keelan began walking at a brisk pace to see if he could find one that looked even vaguely familiar, peering inelegantly around the hats and shoulders of the people surrounding him, then straightened when he saw something he recognized without question.

"Mr. Rook-Worth," he tried not to shout as he jogged up to the man.

Mr. Rook-Worth's expression remained mostly neutral as he looked down at Keelan. "Why did you leave the performance?" His long stride did not slow, so Keelan matched his steps to keep up. "You'll miss the ending."

"I've seen it before," Keelan admitted, somewhat short-winded. He scarcely managed to hold back on giving a summary of the last act in case Mr. Rook-Worth ever went back to watch it again. It really was a beautiful story. "You looked upset," he went on instead, stepping around a gentleman helping a lady into a carriage before resuming his position at the mason's side. "I wanted to make sure you were all right."

"I appreciate the councilmembers' efforts in allowing us extra time to recover from the project, but when I am fatigued, I prefer to regain my strength while *asleep*."

The harsh inflection Mr. Rook-Worth placed on the last word left Keelan wondering if it was indeed the whole truth, but he decided to give a nod of understanding rather than push the matter.

"Do you know whose carriage you arrived in? I might be able to help you find it easier if you remember what it looks like."

"I've no issue returning on foot," Mr. Rook-Worth said.

Keelan's brows went up. "You mean to walk?"

"What's wrong with that?"

"Er, well, it's not that anything is *wrong*, necessarily. But the town-house you're staying in is not exactly close by." Keelan winced before he added, "and you're also going the wrong direction."

Mr. Rook-Worth slowed to a stop on the pavement, suddenly looking every bit as tired as he had proclaimed. His eyes slid shut as he took a deep breath and sighed it out with feeling. Keelan thought that was exactly the type of breath he needed to take after what he'd left behind inside the opera house, but he'd been too focused on finding his stranger to breathe normally, let alone resettle himself.

When Mr. Rook-Worth turned to begin walking back the way they'd come, Keelan impulsively reached out and grabbed his arm to stop him.

Even through the layers of the shirt and jacket he had on, Keelan could still feel the tight curve of muscles beneath the fabric. He let go.

"Allow me to take you home," he said. When he realized how it sounded, he quickly amended it. "Back to your townhouse, that is! I-I mean the Pimpernel townhouse, where you are staying." He squeezed his eyes shut for a second as he looked down at his shoes, before meeting Mr. Rook-Worth's gaze again with a forced grin. "I live on the same street, you see. Only a couple of houses down. It'll be no trouble at all."

Mr. Rook-Worth did not respond at first, giving Keelan plenty of time to silently scold himself for being so bold. Of course the man did not want his help. He could hardly stand being in the same room, let alone share a carriage for a ride across town. Just as Keelan was about to apologize and excuse himself to go lie down in the street and wait for a team of horses to run him over, Mr. Rook-Worth gave a grunt of what revealed itself to be acquiescence.

"Very well. Thank you, Mr. Cricket."

CHAPTER 25

SILAS

Silas knew it was a mistake to accept Cricket's generosity, but he was finding it increasingly difficult to resist the man's attempts at friendliness. There was something about Cricket, despite the differences between them, that gave Silas a sense of rightness. And he certainly needed that feeling. The opera had put him more out of sorts than usual. Sitting in plush velvet seats and feeling darted glances and curious tendrils of magic sent in his direction had made him feel like an animal at a zoo, as much a spectacle as the performers on stage. The performance itself had been too long and too drawn out to hold Silas' attention. He didn't understand what was being sung and observing the laughter, sighs, and gasps around him suggested that he was in the minority in that regard. The week had been challenging enough, what with his magic proving incompatible with his assorted partners. He'd already questioned whether or not he belonged in London and the project, he didn't need added reminders that he was out of place.

By all rights, accepting a ride home from Cricket ought to have contributed to his unease, but it didn't. He'd felt a magnetic pull towards the man since he'd first laid eyes on him, and that feeling hadn't gone away during their time in London. Standing close to him was like two magnets clicking into place. Cricket had every reason to hate Silas after being brushed aside at the wedding party. And yet, the gentleman had been kind. Even now, he had left the opera to see if Silas was all right. Perhaps Cricket felt the same pull Silas did. Perhaps he'd offered Silas a ride home for the same reasons Silas had accepted it. At any rate, he followed Cricket to a waiting carriage and, before he could think better of it, offered his hand to help the other man step inside.

Cricket gave him a tentative smile that made Silas' chest ache. "Thank you."

Silas climbed in after him and the carriage lurched into movement. He was now accustomed to traveling in a carriage packed with other people, so he braced his hands on either side of himself as the carriage rocked down the street.

"Sorry," Cricket mumbled.

Silas frowned at him. "Are you responsible for the state of the roads?"

It was too dark to tell but Silas would have bet money that the other man blushed. "No."

"Then you have nothing to apologize for. I dislike carriages, but that is not your doing."

Cricket clutched his hands together in his lap. "I see," he managed.

Silas sighed. Once again, he was being too harsh with the poor man. "It was kind of you to offer me a ride. I am still getting accustomed to London. I do not understand how a place can make me feel overly cramped and also overly small at the same time."

Cricket, it seemed, had nothing to say in response to that. A long silence followed and Silas began to wonder if the rest of the carriage ride would proceed in silence. He almost hoped it would.

"I find," Cricket began, his voice sounding strained. He cleared his throat. "I find," he tried again, "that the country makes *me* feel small. London has always felt more like home to me."

Silas grunted. "At least in the country, my smallness makes sense. There is a vastness to the countryside. I can breathe more easily. I can walk and know I'm going in the right direction. London is…London is not for me."

"So you will return when the project is over then?"

"As quickly as I can."

Another awkward silence ensued. Cricket stared into his lap as if it held the answers he needed, or perhaps his next conversation topic. Silas felt guilt creep over him once again. The gentleman had been kind, offering him a ride home, cutting his own evening short for his sake. The very least Silas could do was let him know it was appreciated. He spent another block of silence trying to determine what to say.

"I appreciate you coming to find me," he said at last. "This week has been…trying. And I found myself losing patience at the opera."

"Did the story not capture your attention?"

Silas chuckled. "Not really, but it was more than that. I am not a person who sits in velvet seats amidst a crowd of jeweled onlookers. I don't belong in that sort of space." He paused. "It felt like the conclusion to a feeling I've had all week, that I don't belong here in London at all."

"Because you miss your family?"

"That is certainly a large part of it," he admitted, and there was a strange relief in the admission. "But…I hate being grouped with a different partner nearly every day. My magic is not behaving as it should. It's coming out as weak or constrained."

"But your magic is anything but weak or constrain—" Cricket broke off and sat back in his seat.

Silas thought back to their night together, the heat between them, the spark of their magics colliding. "No," he said after a long moment. "But I suppose my magic is simply better suited to the country."

It was an easier thing to say than that his magic was simply better suited to Cricket, for that truth was far less comfortable and convenient.

They spent the rest of the trip in silence. When they finally pulled in front of the Pimpernel townhouse, Silas was ready to bolt out of the carriage and the awkwardness of their stilted conversation. He willed himself to get out at a reasonable pace—Cricket deserved that consideration at least—and thanked him again for the ride.

Before he could close the carriage door, Cricket said, "I know what it's like to feel alone in this city. If…that is…if you need anything…if there's anything I can do…well, I hope you know that you have a friend in me, if you need it."

Silas stared at him for a long time, trying to decide the right response. How did the man keep getting under his defenses in such a way? Silas had never been treated with such sweetness, and he was quite certain he didn't deserve it. When he noticed Cricket fidgeting again, he realized that he had left the poor man in suspense for too long.

"That is very kind of you, Mr. Cricket. I'll remember that." Then he shut the door and went inside.

THE NEXT MORNING, Silas dressed in his usual attire and went down to breakfast. He was surprised to see a pile of luggage at the foot of the staircase and when he strode into the breakfast room, Mr. Hedge-Wyck was dressed in a traveling cloak.

"You're leaving?" he asked without preamble.

Mr. Hedge-Wyck turned in the act of eating a sausage roll off the serving plate. "Yes," he said before popping the food in his mouth.

"Did the accident yesterday put you off?"

Hedge-Wyck rolled his eyes. He swallowed his mouthful and said, "Nothing of the sort. But I've grown tired of this exercise. The councilmembers in charge clearly have no idea what they're doing. And they have no real appreciation for the talent in their midst."

Silas arched an eyebrow.

Hedge-Wyck plucked another sausage roll off the serving dish. "I won't deny I've had an enjoyable time, of course. London is full of diversions. But Brooks, as delightful as he is in bed, is a poor conversationalist. I'm almost as bored of him as I am of the whole project." He popped the second roll into his mouth and wiped his fingers together. "If you're ever in Cornwall—"

"I won't be. Have a safe trip."

Hedge-Wyck gave a snort in response and left the room.

Silas watched him leave and then helped himself to breakfast. Mrs. Pimpernel came in as he sat down and then the rest of the volunteers began to trickle in. Their conversation was full of talk about the opera the previous night. Most of the group was full of compliments about the performance, the grandeur of the building, and the elegance of the other guests. Notably, Miss Wilton-Reed was full of criticisms.

"Did you not enjoy your evening, Miss Wilton-Reed?" Mrs. Pimpernel asked.

The lady sniffed. "I prefer the opera houses in Bath," she replied. "And my companion abandoned the performance before it was complete."

Silas hid a smile. He thought of Cricket's parting words from the night before: *I hope you know that you have a friend in me, if you need it.* Silas had little experience with befriending those he'd bedded. But he supposed if he could manage it with any of them, it would be someone like Cricket.

"Mr. Rook-Worth left early too," Mr. Finkle-Finch said. "Did you dislike the performance as well?"

"I was tired from the day's work," Silas replied.

Mr. Finkle-Finch nodded sympathetically. "Yesterday was indeed exhausting."

Miss Wilton-Reed gave a small titter. "I daresay it *would* be exhausting trying to perform magic when you have such little power to perform it with." She shrugged. "I find magic exhilarating, personally."

Silas had heard her complain from across the room about having to do spells over and exhausting herself, so he knew this to be a complete lie. Instead he said, "How happy for you."

"I wonder where Mr. Hedge-Wyck is," Mrs. Pimpernel said, more loudly than necessary. "I don't think he's usually this late to the breakfast table."

"He left this morning," Silas supplied. "He was disappointed by the collective lack of appreciation for his talent."

Everyone chuckled at this.

"Such a pity," Miss Gloucester-Stone said in a cheerful voice.

Miss Wilton-Reed smirked. "Indeed. I am pleased that the rest of us are more forward-thinking than Mr. Hedge-Wyck." She turned her gaze to Silas. "But I wouldn't blame you at all if you decided to abandon the project, Mr. Rook-Worth. After all, you're hardly contributing much."

Silas did not reply, merely giving her a long and steady look in response. She smirked and looked away, stirring her tea with exaggerated elegance. Silas waited for the conversation to change (thankfully it did rather quickly as Mrs. Pimpernel was always quick to divert any awkwardness) and then left the table. He strode up to his room, knowing that with the promised late start, it would be hours before they had to leave the townhouse again.

He paced the length of his room, irritated—not by Miss Wilton-Reed's words—but the fact that she had spoken the very things he had thought the night before. It was grating to agree with her on any topic, much less a topic of his own worth. He sat down in his bed and picked up his notebook. He had packed it in case he needed to write down ideas for spells, but since the project had been so particularly organized, there had been little room for his own creativity. He leafed through the pages, feeling a little cheered by the reminder that he *was* good at magic. He had combined spells to improve his family's work, he had pitched solutions to problems that had stumped his own father, and he performed a magic that no one else in the family business could do; he was integral. He sighed and let the notebook fall to his lap. He was uncomfortable with how inconsequential he felt now.

After a long moment, he picked the notebook back up again, pulled a pencil off his bedside table, and began writing a fresh page of notes. He'd read the rubric several times now. The whole idea of this project was to learn more about fae-human magic, was it not? Well, perhaps it was time—past time—for Silas to add his own contribution. He spent the next hour scribbling notes and ideas.

When he heard the other volunteers congregating in the foyer, he stood and pocketed his notebook. As he crossed to the door, he hesitated. Torquil had invited him to London, not because he was a magical scholar, not because he was a gentleman, and not because of some impressive family name. Torquil had invited him because they wanted his assistance, they wanted his magic, they wanted him. With sudden decisiveness, he opened up his trunk and pulled out his work belt. The feeling of rightness as he put it on validated his decision.

He strode down the stairs and hid a smile as four pairs of eyes looked up and then appreciatively down. He was quite aware of the effect the belt had on his overall appearance. It was nice to head to the Council chambers feeling confident for once.

TORQUIL'S TRIBUNE

SATURDAY 7 MAY, 1814

Greetings, regal readers,

London has welcomed a delightful crowd of newcomers to its midst. The Council for Fae & Human Magical Relations has invited a half dozen fae-humans to better facilitate the study of fae-human magic. A source close to the Council has confided that their project has already provided ample validation for further research. Each volunteer has a richly unique approach to magic. This writer wonders how the Council will narrow down their testing rubric if this is the case. Nevertheless, we are pleased to see a more open-minded view of magic, especially of the fae-human variety.

Many of our readers may have already encountered these visitors as they have explored London. They have been reported to shop on Bond Street, wander through Hyde Park, attend dinner parties, and even go to the opera last evening. The Pimpernel and Wrenwhistle boxes were stuffed full to capacity as both the fae-human and the fae volunteers ventured out. Reports suggest that the group in question is a handsome one. We wonder if London will provide opportunities for romance as well as research and entertainment. Our fair city could certainly use the diversion.

Others were also seen at the opera. Councilmembers Wyndham and

Roger Wrenwhistle were notably cozy, as seems to be their wont when they attend performances. Councilmember Pimpernel-Smith and Mr. Emrys Wrenwhistle were also clearly taken with the amorous mood. Mr. Arlen Buckthorn and Miss Aveline Wrenwhistle made a beautiful couple, although they had little attention to spare for the performance as their eyes seemed to be only for each other. Reports suggest that Mr. Benedict Brooks has been very friendly with the fae-human newcomers, as has Mr. Keelan Cricket.

Mx. Fern Hillcrest was seen to engage amicably with the councilmembers and other volunteers, although they chose to sit with Mr. Cyril Thompson and Miss Harriet Thackeray. Few will be surprised to learn this.

The Ladies Fitzhugh, freshly returned from their honeymoon, were also among the audience members. We are sure our readers will be pleased that these two lovely lovebirds have returned at last.

Mr. Sage Ravenwing was in attendance as well, although sources say he was more intrigued by the Wrenwhistle box than the performance, or his guest.

We are hopeful that this small crowd of visitors will provide us with more gossip to relay. In the meantime, we remain,

Your winsome writer,

Sal Bailey

CHAPTER 26

KEELAN

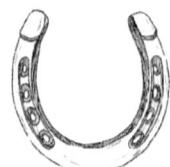

THE MOMENT the carriage had pulled away from the Pimpernel townhouse the night before, Keelan had collapsed onto his side along the bench seat with a groan. How was it possible for one man to leave him feeling so terribly rattled? He had less than one minute to collect himself before he arrived home, and as he sat up to drag himself out of the carriage, he found that his hands were a bit shaky. Keelan squeezed them both into fists as he was let into his house and made directly for his bedroom so that he would not have to speak to anyone about how his evening had gone.

A late start the next day was truly the last thing Keelan needed. It gave him far too much time to think about how his latest interaction with Mr. Rook-Worth had gone. He was so absorbed in his pensive state that he couldn't bring himself to dress for his usual morning ride.

"I hope you know that you have a friend in me, if you need it," he mocked himself out loud before he stuffed a piece of buttered toast into his mouth at breakfast, which he'd taken alone in his room. Mr. Rook-Worth had called his offer *kind.* "More like foolishly altruistic," he moaned around his mouthful. He'd been accused of having a tender heart on plenty of occasions, but rarely had it done him such a disservice as it had in the last several days.

This thought brought an entirely new wave of trepidation. How angry was Miss Wilton-Reed going to be that he'd left her at the opera without so much as a farewell? She was not alone, at least—the rest of the party had remained, as far as he knew. But the vague memory of her touch on his arm was a clear enough message that she'd thought of them as being *together* at the event, which meant his abrupt departure had been awfully rude.

A small part of him wondered why it mattered so much. In truth, the dynamic between Miss Wilton-Reed and himself was, at best, frustrating. With each interaction they shared, Keelan was left to wonder what sort of response she might have to everything he said or did. The uncertainty was maddening.

Keelan's magic wilted in his chest at his next thought. Was this how his father had felt at the outset of his courtship with Mother? Had his interests and talents also been pushed aside by an equally boastful, domineering lady with whom he was matched? Were those moments the first glimpses into the lifetime of isolation he'd eventually settled for?

After giving some serious thought to writing a note to the Council to inform them that he was terribly sorry but he was too ill to work, he pushed it all aside and allowed Marten to dress him for the day.

KEELAN WAS one of the first to arrive at the Council's chambers, but he could've cried at the relief he felt in seeing that Emrys was there, as well. He already had an idea of what Emrys was going to say to him—something teasing, no doubt. Whatever it was, though, it was worth the solace he needed in the company of his closest friend.

Emrys excused himself from the conversation he was having with Torquil and Roger when he noticed Keelan walking his way. Something about him, perhaps the look of distress on his face, was enough for Emrys to understand what he needed, and he gestured with one hand for Keelan to join him near the table in the corner of the room.

"Is something the matter?" Emrys brought his hand up to touch the back of his fingers to Keelan's cheek. "You look unwell. Is that why you left early last night?"

Keelan slapped his hand away and glanced over his shoulder to see if any of the councilmembers had noticed. Despite his earlier thoughts on dispatching a note, he really did not want to be sent home in front of everyone like a child.

"I'm surprised you even noticed," Keelan said, already feeling more himself in Emrys' presence. He let out a breath and felt his shoulders relax. "You seemed thoroughly distracted the last time I saw you."

Emrys smirked. "I am rather keen on fondling at the opera."

"Yes, and you are not the only one," Keelan muttered, wrinkling his nose. "I could hardly focus over the noises coming from the back row of my box."

"Roger was just telling Torquil as much," Emrys said, tilting his chin up at them. "Apparently Wyndham turned around and said something smart to the gentlemen just as Brooks was, well…you know."

A sharp laugh escaped Keelan, despite himself. He covered his mouth with his hand to hide his grin. "Oh, how embarrassing. You must've seen the way Brooks looks at him. I rather wonder if his *conclusion* was a direct result of Wyndham's attention, not just poor timing."

"Perhaps, but I'd prefer not to think of men reaching climax at the mere sight of my brother, if you don't mind."

Keelan chuckled and gave a small shrug. "I think you'd struggle to find anyone of his persuasion that hasn't thought of Wyndham in a private moment at least once in his life." Keelan was no exception to that rule.

Emrys' face twisted in an exaggerated grimace. "Are you trying to ruin my day? Let's discuss what's really important here: you and Mr. Rook-Worth both disappeared last night without a word to anyone. I have it on good authority that your family's carriage departed the opera house with two passengers." His expression turned sly. "What do you have to say for yourself?"

"He—!" Keelan looked over his shoulder again before he leaned closer to Emrys and lowered his voice. "He was upset. I just happened to glance over when he stormed out of your box, and I wanted to check on him." The excuse sounded thinner than a sheet of spellpaper as the words came out of his mouth, but he was determined to hold to his story. It was the truth. Mostly.

Emrys looked suddenly proud. "I knew the two of you would get on."

"You really are a hero," Keelan said dryly, words dripping with sarcasm. "What would I do without you?"

"You said you needed a strong, attractive man to help you forget about your stranger, did you not? And here I found you one."

Keelan gaped at him, stammering. "Y-you said that, not me!"

"It hardly matters who said it," Emrys argued flippantly. "What's principal is the outcome. Do tell all, Keelan. Did a night with Mr. Rook-Worth surpass the memory of your glorious romp in the country?"

Keelan was stunned into silence. The absurdity of this conversation was beyond anything he had ever experienced. Was it not a cruel enough twist of fate that Keelan had been forced to see the man who rejected him every day? Now, thanks to the single time in his life that he had not been entirely forthcoming with his best friend, Emrys had all but set him up with Mr. Rook-Worth in an attempt to help him forget about the very man himself.

Keelan could feel that he had gone very pale again. His late breakfast churned in his stomach. He really should have stayed in bed.

"He allowed me to give him a ride home, Emrys. Nothing more."

Emrys' air of confidence faltered a bit as he uncrossed his arms, his hands settling on his hips instead.

"Not really?"

Keelan managed a small nod.

"Drat. I was certain I'd read that correctly." He reached up to clap Keelan on the shoulder and was about to say something else, but the sound of the door opening at the front of the room caught his attention.

Keelan steeled himself to face Miss Wilton-Reed. With any luck at all, she would be understanding after he explained himself. He was willing to compromise on many things, but caring for others when they needed a friend was not one of them, no matter the circumstance. Finally, he turned to join the lady at their designated seats, but what he found instead compelled him to stop entirely.

Mr. Rook-Worth entered the room with a cool confidence in his stride that made Keelan draw in a silent, wavering gasp. The man was not dressed so differently than usual; he had given up wearing a jacket on the second or third day of the project. However, just as Keelan remembered him from that night behind the stables, his shirtsleeves were rolled to his elbows, exposing his thick forearms for all to see.

Having lost all control, Keelan's eyes dipped lower.

He could still recall the man's dark skin glistening in the midday sun as he moved the heavy bricks from the cart with that leather work belt slung low on his hips. He could still hear the sound of that same belt landing on the dusty floor of the horse cart where Mr. Rook-Worth had tossed it aside just before they came together for a scorching kiss that had taken his breath away.

Keelan thought absently that, perhaps, he had not yet regained it.

Emrys' chuckle at his back was what finally shook him from his stupor.

"You'd better go and speak to Miss Wilton-Reed," he said discreetly next to Keelan's ear. "That'll be the fastest way to attenuate any *hard* feelings you may be having at the moment."

Heat flashed up Keelan's neck to his cheeks. If he'd been ten years younger, he very well might've been sporting something to blush over, but instead he only shoved his elbow at Emrys and silently thanked his body for not betraying him. Sometimes it really was a bother to have a friend who had known you since your embarrassing pubescence.

Emrys laughed again as Keelan walked away and promised, "I won't give up on him if you don't."

Keelan glanced covertly around the room as things slowly fell back into motion around him. He had the distinct feeling that he was not the only one whose world had slowed at the sight of Mr. Rook-Worth.

A soft grin crept onto his lips. He had to wonder if their conversation the night before had anything to do with this shift in him. If Mr. Rook-Worth could not yet return to the country, where he felt most like himself, then maybe he had decided to bring more of himself to the city instead.

"Do hurry up, Mr. Cricket!" Miss Wilton-Reed's voice cut through the fluttery feeling that had formed in his chest like a blade. He hadn't even noticed her arrival. Keelan readied his apology to the lady, holding on tight to the frayed edges of whatever warm feeling he'd just had. Maybe he'd done more than give Mr. Rook-Worth a ride home, after all.

CHAPTER 27

SILAS

SILAS LIFTED his chin as he walked through the room. He could feel everyone's eyes on him. Perhaps his siblings were right; maybe he was a little vain. But if vanity got him through this ordeal, he was all right with that.

Cricket had hurried past him to go and speak to Miss Wilton-Reed. Silas noticed that the gentleman's face was worryingly pale. He also noticed that Cricket's gaze flicked occasionally to him amidst Miss Wilton-Reed's unceasing chatter as he escorted the lady to their usual table. Silas allowed himself a small smile. If he could provide a welcome distraction for the other man, it would be no bad thing.

Torquil approached him as he reached the back of the room. "Are you feeling well, Mr. Rook-Worth? You left the opera quite early."

"Yes, thank you. I was simply tired."

"I hope you're feeling better today," Torquil said, with an amused glance at Silas's belt.

Silas hooked his thumbs behind the belt and grinned. "Much better."

Torquil flashed a smile. "Excellent. If I were still writing the *Tribune*, you all would have made appearances by now. I can just imagine how I would describe this look." They winked and then switched swiftly into a more formal tone. "You will be working with Mr. Buckthorn today. We've cleaned up the offices and applied some protection spells—these spells should not interfere with your magic, but do let me know if you notice any impact. You will be working in the room Mr. Buckthorn has been utilizing. Although I'm sure everyone here will be most annoyed with me for depriving them of a pleasant sight."

Silas huffed a laugh in response and walked leisurely to the office. Mr. Buckthorn was exactly as Silas had anticipated: pleasant but a little vapid. His gaze took in Silas's belt and he went a little pink around the ears, but otherwise ignored it. If he hadn't seen the gentleman mooning over Miss Wrenwhistle, Silas would have been disappointed.

He dutifully began setting up a shrinking spell for the rubric. He felt Mr. Buckthorn's magic spooling out around them before he'd even started the spell. When he cast, he felt as though Buckthorn's magic was disrupting his own—as if his magic was a boat on a pool of water and Buckthorn's magic was ripples along the surface, rocking the boat haphazardly. The shrinking spell worked, but it did so in spurts.

Mr. Buckthorn frowned and leaned closer to look at the pencil that had been shrunk. "Is it usually so…"

"No," Silas said. He ran a hand over his face. "It's usually much smoother." *When I'm not in London*, he thought. *When I don't feel as if I'm letting an entire project down.* At least it wasn't painful now. "I'll cast again. Maybe it was just my magic getting accustomed to yours."

Buckthorn's expression cleared and he relaxed in his seat, hand poised to take notes. But when Silas cast again, it was the same.

"Perhaps I should tell Torquil," Buckthorn said dubiously, picking up the pencil to examine it.

"No," Silas said, more sharply than he intended. "Let's just try something else."

"All right. What else should we do? How about a levitation spell?"

They worked for the rest of the afternoon, trying each spell on the rubric multiple times, each with the same strange result. Before he left, Silas urged his partner not to report it yet, convincing him to give it one more day. The next day, Silas came armed with his belt and a notebook page full of ideas. He arrived in the office before Buckthorn and began setting up for a spell. He was grateful that they had been supplied with so many magical ingredients. Buckthorn strolled in while he was consulting with his notebook for the right sigil combination.

"Good morning," he said airily. "Ready to work I see!"

Silas closed his notebook and turned his attention to his partner. "How would you feel about trying something different today?"

"What do you mean? Different ingredients?"

"A different spell. Something not on the rubric."

Buckthorn shifted uneasily in his chair. "I don't know," he said uncertainly. "Isn't this whole exercise intended to work through the rubric?"

"In part. But this entire project is intended to better understand fae-human magic, my magic. And my magic has been acting strangely with every person I've met here." *Except for Cricket,* he thought privately. "So I'd like to try some spells that I've done more frequently, see if that changes things."

"Perhaps we should ask Torquil. I'd hate for Aveline to think that I'm doing a poor job of this."

"Torquil won't mind. And if I can get my magic to do what it normally does, you'll be doing a very fine job indeed."

Buckthorn looked pleased at this. "I would?"

"Definitely."

He smacked the desk. "All right. Let's do it." He paused and lowered his voice. "It's not really breaking the rules, or anything, is it?"

"There are no rules saying we *can't* do it this way. Besides, if the rules are keeping us from reaching our full potential then they're not good rules anyway."

Buckthorn's eyes widened. "Oh," he whispered.

Silas rolled up his sleeves an additional turn—more out of nervous energy than anything. "This is a shade spell. So the room will get a little dark." He cast, trying to imagine he was just performing a regular spell in the country, surrounded by his family. The room darkened.

Unfortunately, it darkened in stops and spurts. He sighed. "Damn," he whispered.

"I've never seen this one," Buckthorn remarked. "What would you even use it for?"

"There are a number of uses," Silas said curtly as he cleaned up the spell and the room brightened again. "It can make an afternoon in the sun more comfortable. It can allow for rest during a midday nap."

"I think it felt a *little* stronger than the spells yesterday."

Silas was absolutely certain the man was just being kind. But if it meant avoiding the inevitable shuffling around to a new partner, he would take it. "Excellent," he said, with forced cheerfulness. "Let's try another one."

He managed to keep Buckthorn from reporting on their incompatibility for several days. But eventually, he had to concede that it was better for the project if Torquil knew. He tried not to show his irritation as Buckthorn explained to Torquil the strange behavior of his magic.

Torquil had perched on the arm of an empty desk chair, one leg hooked around the front of the seat. They listened to Buckthorn's description, thanked him, and told him that he was free to leave for the day. After Buckthorn exited the room, Torquil turned their gaze to Silas.

"I would ask if this is abnormal behavior for your magic, but considering the fact that your magic has reacted uniquely to each person you've worked with, I think that's fairly obvious."

Silas ran a hand over his hair. "I don't understand it. It's never been like this before."

"Have you performed magic with such a variety of partners before? And all strangers?"

Silas thought back to his past intimate encounters—he'd always enjoyed experiencing the way his partners' magic felt against his own. None of them had felt this strange. But then again, until Cricket, he'd never experienced the explosion of power he'd felt in that cart. He considered his words carefully before speaking. "I've never had this much incompatibility before. I've experienced the magic of others many times, but it has never been this odd."

"Were you performing human spells?"

"No, just sensing."

"Perhaps that's the answer then."

Silas had a hard time imagining his magic behaving in such a way with Cricket as his partner, but instead he said, "Perhaps."

"I know you dislike being shuffled around, and I can certainly understand it. But it's not entirely a bad thing from the perspective of our project. We've just barely scratched the surface of what magical compatibility can look like, especially between the unique facets of our society. Roger and Wyndham learned only last year how well fae and humans can perform magic together. No one had tried it to that extent before. And, as I'm sure you understand, precious few people were interested in performing magic with me. Wyndham's magic was neutral when cast with mine. Emrys' was…explosive. Though not in the way of Finkle-Finch and Buckthorn," they added hastily with a small smile.

They went on, "I know you have experience performing magic with every member of your family, who are all fae, and all have their own unique magical personality. I'm not worried about your ability to perform magic with others. But I am eager to find the right partner for you so that we can see what your magic is capable of."

Silas felt some of the tightness in his chest loosen at Torquil's words. He could only nod in response.

Torquil slid off the chair arm. "We'll pair you with someone else after our rest day tomorrow." They paused at the door and glanced down at his belt. "Does that usually hold magical materials?"

"Yes. I use it for my work."

"If you want a replenishment of anything, give me a list and I'll see that you get what you need."

CHAPTER 28

KEELAN

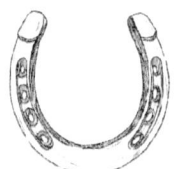

THE CLUB ON ST. James's Street was brimming with patrons at the end of the day, all seeking their preferred sort of respite from the world, if only for a little while. Some were there to play a spirited round or two of cards, while others had enjoyed a meal downstairs before migrating to one of the quieter areas to finish the evening with a drink.

For Keelan, it was one of the precious few places he could hide from his problems with the guarantee that he would not be disturbed, save for the one person he was always waiting on.

"Darling," Emrys began as he sat in the chair beside Keelan in their small alcove with the fireplace and many shelves of books. "Now that I am a married man, I must insist that your notes not be so vague and mysterious. Torquil was thoroughly convinced I was about to sneak out and meet someone."

"You're not serious?" Keelan's brows pinched in concern. His message had been written exactly the same as always, short and to the point.

Emrys chuckled and accepted the drink Keelan offered him.

"I'm only teasing," he said after taking a long sip. "But they did mention something about us making this more of a routine event. No need for a written request type of thing."

"That's very thoughtful of them." Keelan took a pull of his drink to hide the flush on his cheeks. "You could bring them along sometime, you know?"

Emrys made a gruff sort of dismissive sound. "Torquil would hate this place. Too many people." He turned a grin on Keelan. "Besides, we've only two chairs here in our corner."

"Yes, I suppose that's true." Keelan could do nothing to fight his own grin at the mention of *their* corner. It really had become theirs over the years, along with the custom of meeting, sharing a drink, and speaking in a way that only close friends could.

"However, if there was any night Torquil might've wished for an excuse to get away from the townhouse, it would be this one." Emrys drained his drink and breathed out sharply against the burn of the alcohol as he let the empty glass rest on his knee. "Mother has been crying uncontrollably for hours, even through dinner."

Keelan frowned at that. "What's happened?" Mrs. Wrenwhistle was known for her wild emotions, but that was not usually one of them.

"Yours was not the only exciting letter to arrive this evening," Emrys divulged with an arched brow. "It seems that the Wrenwhistle family will be growing yet again come fall. Auberon has written to share the good news and let us know that Rose is doing quite well, indeed."

"Oh, that's wonderful, Emrys," Keelan said with a smile. "Congratulations."

"It will be even more wonderful when Mother decides she must go and stay with them to help prepare for the baby to arrive," Emrys said, a flash of mischief in his eyes. "And after, of course, to help attend to the new mother and child. After all, she's got plenty of experience. Where better to use it than with the birth of her first grandchild?"

Keelan chuckled and shook his head affectionately. "Are we certain you're mature enough to handle the townhouse while she's away?"

Emrys scoffed as he brought his free hand up to press flat against his chest.

"Have you no faith in me, friend? Or in Torquil, I should say. The house will be more their responsibility than mine, when the time comes."

Something in this statement made Keelan's chest tighten to the point of breathlessness. He swallowed and turned his focus to the low flames on the hearth in front of them.

"Perhaps I should ask them for any advice they would be willing to share," he said, unable to mask the sudden shift in his mood. "It seems I will be in much the same position before long."

After the night at the opera, the situation with Miss Wilton-Reed had only gotten worse—in more ways than one. The lady had grown progressively more unbound in her behavior during their work on the project. Not only was she seemingly determined to perform magic that drew attention to herself from others in the room, she'd also begun gossiping about them. Keelan was a loyal reader of the *Tribune*, but the difference was that Torquil, and now Sal, never wrote to belittle others as Miss Wilton-Reed seemed to prefer.

She fussed over the temperature at which Mrs. Pimpernel kept the townhouse, surmising that she and her frequent visitor, Mrs. Iris Wren-whistle, needed to keep warm due to their *thinning, elderly skin*. Miss Gloucester-Stone was another favorite topic of conversation, as their bedrooms shared a wall, and Miss Wilton-Reed had no shortage of complaints about the noise the other lady made whilst dressing in the morning or readying herself for bed.

"I suppose I would need to hum constantly, as well," Miss Wilton-Reed had remarked over the flame of a fire spell, "if my brain were equally as vacant. All that empty space needs to be filled with something."

Mr. Finkle-Finch was tiresome and oafish; Mx. Badger-Thorp was meek and put too much sugar in their tea. She was relieved to have Mr. Hedge-Wyck out of the house, for his rakish behavior had brought with it the insecurity of strangers coming and going during the night, which greatly affected her ability to sleep restfully. And as for Mr. Rook-Worth, he was the greatest problem of them all. He was boorish and unrefined with an obvious lack of respect for his superiors. Everything about him, from his manner of dress to the way he spent his time of leisure, was entirely unacceptable.

"I'm quite certain I've never met someone less suited to life in high society," she'd said with a scowl after emptying the jar of powdered citrus peel they'd been given onto a sheet of spellpaper. "The man is simply feral."

The moment to nearly do him in had happened that very afternoon, just as everyone was working on their last spell of the day. A surprise visit from the rest of the Council had everyone a little more alert than they'd been previously. Even Keelan leaned in closer to his paper as he recorded his final notes on the motion spell Miss Wilton-Reed had placed on a reference book they'd been given.

"Keelan," his mother had said in an overexaggerated way as she placed a hand on his shoulder, peering down at his work. "Such a treat to see you focused on something worthwhile." Her smile had little emotion behind it, and the faint grin he gave her in return was much the same.

"I daresay he's become thoroughly engrossed with his note-taking, Councilmember Cricket," Miss Wilton-Reed said sweetly at his side. The book, which was previously turning end over end in the air, had settled on the table between them. "Such an improvement from how he was when this whole project began."

His mother gave a laugh. "Keelan was never a very good student. I have to think it must be your influence that's had such a positive effect on him."

"Perhaps he simply never had a subject he found interesting enough to hold his attention until now."

Keelan knew the irritation was plain on his face as he looked up from his notes and leveled it at his partner. The look of adoration she gave back was so terrifyingly real that even he had to pause and remind himself that she was only putting on an act for their present company.

Unfortunately, it was one that his mother seemed to be falling for harder with each interaction. She moved her hand from his shoulder and grasped his chin between her finger and thumb in what she probably thought was an affectionate gesture. He wanted so badly to pull away from his mother's touch, but he allowed her to tilt his face up toward hers instead.

"Keelan has always wanted to be married." It came out in the most painfully patronizing way. "Ever since he was a boy, he would go on and on about finding the right person to spend his life with."

Since he could not look away, Keelan closed his eyes instead. His mother revealing this to Miss Wilton-Reed felt more like betrayal than anything else she could've shared from his childhood.

"We all thought he would've found someone by now," his mother went on. "The trouble is, I think he is so concerned with the fairytale idea of love that he has overlooked many perfect opportunities." She finally let go of his chin and patted his cheek a couple of times. "I cannot tell you how encouraging it is to know that someone has *finally* held his attention."

Emrys' firm grip landing on his arm finally shook Keelan from the awful memory. "You must tell your mother how you feel."

Keelan blinked hard several times. Staring at the fire had left his eyes strained. He met Emrys' gaze, his bottom lip curved into a slight frown.

"My mother always gets what she wants, Emrys. I'm afraid this situation will be no different. I'm even more afraid that she and Miss Wilton-Reed are the same in that regard. It is entirely possible that I could plead my case and still go unheard because the lady is on her side."

Emrys knew better than to argue a point too hard when Keelan was in such a state. Keelan was endlessly grateful that the man understood when a change of subject was exactly what he needed. However, the subject he picked was not always so helpful.

"Torquil informed me on our way home that they'll be finding yet another new partner for Mr. Rook-Worth. Apparently his time with Aveline's beau has proven even less productive than the rest."

"That's dreadful," Keelan said, his concern over his own affairs fading as he thought of how Mr. Rook-Worth must've been feeling. "Does he already know?"

"Yes, Torquil said they spoke about it at length this afternoon." Emrys drew in a breath and huffed it out in mild irritation. "I really believe they should allow you to switch and be his new partner, but Torquil said there are reasons beyond their control for why they cannot. Whatever that means."

Keelan groaned and slumped in his chair, his head falling dramatically against the high back of it. He gave a wide berth to the idea of being Mr. Rook-Worth's partner and instead voiced the obvious reason for why Torquil could not approve it. "My mother."

FROM SILAS ROOK-WORTH TO ALBION ROOK

12 May 1814

Dear Father,

London has been keeping me suitably occupied. Although in regards to everyone's pointed questions about whether or not it has been improving my mood, I fear I cannot provide the answer you all are hoping for.

I joined this project in the hopes that it would help me understand my magic better and help me understand what other fae-human magic is like, as well as help Councilmember Pimpernel-Smith create a rubric for fae-human children. But I find that none of these aims have been accomplished since my arrival. I wish I could blame the councilmembers, or even my own self. For then at least there'd be the solace in placing blame on someone. Unfortunately, there is no one to blame for there is nothing productive to be done about it.

My magic has not behaved as it ought ever since I came to town. I have now been paired with three different fae and my magic has gone awry with each, albeit in a different manner. It has been sluggish, scraping, restricted, even sometimes downright painful. The councilmembers tell me this is a good thing, that it is beneficial to see a fae-human's magic combine poorly with another's so they can better prepare. While I do see their reasoning, I wish my magic was not quite so good an example. I feel as if I understand my magic less than I did before I came. At least with you, Quince, and Briony, my magic behaves normally. I can anticipate its strength and I never feel weary or pained after using it. It reacts differently to each of you, but it is a familiar difference. I feel as if my magic knows my family's magic and reacts accordingly. Perhaps my magic likes the city as little as I do.

There have been some fae-human volunteers whose magic has also reacted unfavorably with others. But mine has definitely been the most volatile. Well, perhaps I should say, it has been the most unpredictable. And to that end, I feel as if I still understand other fae-human magic as little as I did before. I daresay I know your response: perhaps that is the point of this entire scheme, to prove to everyone how little we know of fae-human magic. You'd probably be right. I will say it has been interesting to see the myriad combinations of magic in my fellow volunteers.

If nothing else, I have found my magic is uniquely perfect for my line of work. If I could not sense magic, as some of the other fae-humans cannot, I would not be able to work as easily with you all. And if I could not perform human spells, as some of the fae-humans here cannot, then I would not provide a form of magic that you and my siblings cannot offer. Some of the other volunteers barely practice magic as they are uncomfortable with the strangeness of it. So I confess I am grateful that despite all of my self-consciousness of my unique magic and that you and Mother have always encouraged me to practice it regularly. You needn't say you told me so. I can already hear the words from your lips.

If it were not for this constant shuffling around of partners, I might be encouraged by this trip. After reading over what I've written, I'm surprised I'm not more encouraged. But it is trying to be unable to demonstrate what my magic can do. I know it can do more, I know it can *be* more. And yet, I keep having to prove myself over and over and over again, and always come out wanting.

You need not fear that my discouragement will cause me to abandon the project. I intend to see it to its end. I am not one to go back on my word, as you well know. I am sorry I missed the task with the bridge, for you know how much I love that sort of work. I am sure there will be others like it when I return.

I miss you all greatly,
Silas

CHAPTER 29

SILAS

Silas took advantage of the day off from the project to catch up on his correspondences. He had been putting it off for days, unsure of what to say and how much to include. It had been too discouraging to admit that he was unable to perform magic with anyone in London. But after his conversation with Torquil, Silas felt encouraged enough to be honest. He told his mother about the townhouse, the furnishings, and Mrs. Pimpernel. He told his father about his frustrations over being unable to find a good partner, describing the behavior of his magic in detail. He told Quince about all the attractive men he'd met. He told Briony about the opera, although he left out the bit about leaving early, and about the food. By the time he was done writing everything, his hand ached and hours had passed since he'd left the breakfast room.

He stacked the letters into a neat pile and took them to the foyer to be sent out. He ran into Miss Wilton-Reed as she was putting on a bonnet. She glanced over her shoulder at him, eyeing the stack of letters.

"Homesick, Mr. Rook-Worth?" He didn't reply. She didn't seem to require an answer as she continued. "I'm surprised you've lasted this long, if I'm honest. I was sure Mr. Hedge-Wyck's departure would give you permission to leave as well."

"Funny," Silas said, "I thought the same thing about you."

She trilled a laugh as she took her gloves from the waiting maid. "This trip has been surprisingly fruitful, far beyond my expectations."

"How nice for you."

"I certainly didn't come here with a plan to find a spouse, but I can't deny I'm pleased with my progress to that end." She tugged the gloves on. "I'm having tea with his mother today. I quite like her."

Silas did not give her the satisfaction of asking whose mother.

"He will not be the cleverest of spouses, but I think that will suit me quite well. And he will certainly be decorative." She gave a satisfied sigh. "What a surprise it will be to return to Bath with a pretty little husband on my arm."

Silas had little difficulty putting the pieces together. It was a long moment before he trusted himself to speak. "You intend to marry Mr. Cricket?"

She hummed in response as she took her parasol. "If this tea goes as well as I expect, I shall be engaged within the week." She flashed him a smirk and left.

Silas stood in the empty foyer, filled with a frustration he couldn't entirely understand. He had no claim on Cricket; he barely knew the man. But he was overwhelmed by the injustice of such a gentle soul being entrapped by such a duplicitous creature. Underneath his frustration was a feeling as though something was being ripped away from him; although he knew that Cricket did not belong to him, and was hardly a *thing*. He thought of Mrs. Wrenwhistle saying that Cricket's gentleness belied a strength underneath. He hoped that to be true. The poor man would certainly need all the strength he could get.

As soon as the door clicked shut behind Miss Wilton-Reed, Mrs. Pimpernel and Mrs. Iris Wrenwhistle emerged from the sitting room. He saw them glance over his shoulder and then relax.

"How are you doing, Mr. Rook-Worth?" Mrs. Pimpernel greeted him cheerily.

"Doing well, thank you. I'm sorry I haven't been as social this morning. I had some catching up to do."

"Yes, your family certainly likes to keep in touch. I believe you and

Miss Wilton-Reed receive the most mail out of anyone else in the house."

He chuckled. "That's my family for you."

"We were just thinking what a lovely day it is for a promenade in the park," Mrs. Wrenwhistle said. "Won't you join us?"

"Yes!" Mrs. Pimpernel said. "Then you can tell us all about your family. I'm a strong correspondent myself, so I've been filled with curiosity every time I see your letters come in."

Silas agreed and his coat was fetched, along with the ladies' bonnets and Spencer jackets. He offered each of them his arm and they directed him to the Park.

As they walked, he answered the ladies' questions about his family. He described his mother's freshly baked bread, the way Briony had found a way to keep the squirrels from eating the strawberries in their garden, how Quince managed to repair clothing in such a way as to always make it better than it started, and how his father had built up the family business. It made him frightfully homesick to talk about them. The letters from home had never stopped coming, despite his infrequent replies. His family hadn't seemed surprised by it—their messages were full of certainty that he was having a grand time in London and prodding questions about whether he had gotten any less cranky on the trip.

As he led the two older ladies through the Park, satisfying their curiosity about the Rook family, he found himself wondering if he *had* gotten any less cranky. He thought about this irritation from constantly being paired with new partners, with the way he barely spoke at meals, and how abrupt he always was with Cricket. While he could easily chalk up his irritation to the circumstances and his lack of chatter as characteristic, he felt the same sense of shame at how poorly he always seemed to treat Cricket.

"Are you all right, Mr. Rook-Worth?" Mrs. Wrenwhistle asked. "You have not said a word in several minutes."

"My apologies."

"Our Mr. Rook-Worth is not the chatty type," Mrs. Pimpernel said. "I believe this is the most I've heard you speak since you arrived."

"Most likely," he said with a laugh. "On the subject of my family, I am more prone than usual to have something to say."

"I suspect your lapse in conversation just now was less due to a lack of thought, but rather an abundance of thought. Is that not so?" Mrs. Wrenwhistle asked.

He frowned at the question and was about to ask for clarification when he noticed a mischievous glint in her eye. He quirked an eyebrow. "Is there a particular thought you accuse me of, ma'am?"

"Oh, just curious if your family are the only ones to fill your mind of late."

"What makes you think so?"

"Leonora told me of the belt you've begun wearing."

He was surprised into a laugh. "That is merely the belt I use for work."

"And a very comely look too, from the sound of it. Are you sure there isn't someone on the project you are trying to impress?"

"I do not seek to impress anyone as a rule. Except, I suppose, my father, upon occasion. But he is not here to assess me. Nor does he care about my belt."

"That is one thing I like about you, Mr. Rook-Worth," Mrs. Pimpernel said. "You do not seem to crave admiration. It is a good trait."

"You interrupted my inquisition, Leonora."

"He isn't accustomed to you yet. Give him time."

Mrs. Wrenwhistle huffed. "Spoilsport."

Silas had to hide his amusement at the exchange. The ladies' banter made him feel as if he was back at home.

"As I was saying, I quite like how *you* do not seem to pursue the attention of the rest of the group."

"Ah. Is that why *I* was invited on this little jaunt and not… others?"

"I'm sure I don't know what you mean, Mr. Rook-Worth."

"I fear I've spoken as much about myself as others might have."

"Yes, well in you it's refreshing."

"Glad to hear it," he said with a grin.

He found them a bench in the shade to rest for a bit and observe the rest of the promenaders.

Mrs. Wrenwhistle fanned herself for a moment before she spoke again. "It is a sore trial to have all of one's grandchildren properly paired off. What is one to do with their time?"

"Match other people's grandchildren, naturally," Mrs. Pimpernel replied.

Silas leaned against a tree and settled in to listen to the ladies gossip. They pointed out different people walking or riding, discussing prospects.

"Now there's a pretty fellow who ought to be married," one of them would say. "I've always thought Andromeda Grebe might be a suitable match."

"Ah, my dear, but she's so reclusive."

"Exactly. She needs to be drawn out of her shell."

"Not that much out of her shell, surely."

"Very well, then who do you suggest?"

"I rather think Mr. Ravenwing might suit—"

"Oh, goodness me, no. That poor boy is nursing a broken heart in the worst possible way."

"Would a good romance not mend it?"

"Yes, but not with *him*."

"Well, you're just never satisfied."

A horse cantered down the path, nimbly navigating around carriages and pedestrians. Silas felt his eyes drawn to the horse's rider as if they'd been snapped into place: Cricket. The man was rising in the saddle with an ease that bespoke training and experience. Silas couldn't resist admiring the man's calves in his well-fitting riding breeches. On the horse, Cricket looked relaxed, at peace, one might say blissful. Silas hadn't seen that expression on the man's face since—well, since he'd shattered the moment with his own callousness.

"Ah, there's Mr. Cricket," Mrs. Pimpernel said. "Another young man who needs a good marriage."

"By all accounts, he practically has one," Mrs. Wrenwhistle replied.

"Oh, I know. And isn't it too dreadful? She's all wrong for him, you know."

"She is, but you know Terra. She will have her way."

Mrs. Pimpernel tsked. "Such a pity. He's such a sweet boy. Don't you agree, Mr. Rook-Worth?"

Silas dragged his gaze from the man across the park. "I beg your pardon?"

Mrs. Pimpernel's mouth quirked. "I said don't you agree that Mr. Cricket is a sweet young man? I believe you're acquainted with him."

"A little. He does seem very kind."

"Mm," Mrs. Wrenwhistle said, her shrewd eyes on him. "And so gentle in spirit too. Not to mention lively."

Mrs. Pimpernel turned back to her friend. "Oh, I agree. And wouldn't he do nicely with a solid type of husband? One who could provide security?"

"And a warm and loving family?"

"Oh, how the mind reels with possibilities."

Silas rolled his eyes good naturedly. "Far be it from me to curb any reeling possibilities, but as Mrs. Wrenwhistle only just mentioned, I do believe the gentleman is all but spoken for."

"You didn't say you don't find him appealing," Mrs. Pimpernel pointed out.

"That is interesting," Mrs. Wrenwhistle said.

"What are the odds that I would leave my nosy family to come to London, and discover that my family is, as it turns out, frightful amateurs when it comes to meddling?"

Mrs. Pimpernel laughed. "We must make you feel right at home then."

Silas grinned and shook his head, but said nothing in reply. She was, after all, correct. And he suspected she knew it.

THE FOLLOWING MORNING, he was relieved that Miss Wilton-Reed did not stride into the breakfast room with an engagement band on her finger. And when they all arrived at the Council chambers, Cricket looked in much the same mood as he always was, which suggested that he was probably unaware of his impending betrothal. Or perhaps he was simply resigned to it.

This time, Torquil introduced Silas to Miss Wrenwhistle. He had been returned to his first table in the large room. He suspected it was so the three organizers could keep an eye on his situation. The thought rankled as much as it relieved him. However, when Torquil asked if he'd brought a list of supplies he needed, he felt somewhat cheered in being able to rip a page out of his notebook and hand it over.

Torquil looked over the list. "I can't imagine we'll have any difficulty acquiring these." They walked away, hailing an aide from across the room.

Miss Wrenwhistle had the same ethereal beauty that Silas had come to expect from fae, and she was every bit as chipper as Miss Gloucester-Stone. Silas had come to appreciate the other woman's chattiness and forthright nature; it had saved many an awkward moment. But he found Miss Wrenwhistle's cheery disposition more irritating than he might have expected. He couldn't be sure if it was due to her, or due to the fact that he had grown weary of being paired up with new people.

"It's a shame you didn't get on with Arlen, Mr. Rook-Worth," she said as she dipped her pen in an inkwell and began writing notes. "He is so lovely."

"I liked him quite well, but I'm afraid my magic was less than fond."

"Didn't you find Arlen to be the sweetest creature?" she sighed happily. "And so considerate. And patient…"

Silas allowed her to continue in this vein for a quarter of an hour. But when Torquil approached and asked how things were going, he could no longer delay the inevitable. "I was just telling Miss Wrenwhistle about my magic."

Miss Wrenwhistle cleared her throat and bent over her paper. "Yes, it's very interesting."

Torquil chuckled and walked away.

"Thank you," Miss Wrenwhistle said. "It was kind of you not to tell them how chatty I've been."

"I didn't mind it."

She smiled. "I've spent this whole time with Miss Gloucester-Stone and we've been talking like old friends ever since we met. I'm afraid it will take me some time to get used to being more formal."

"I have little need for formality."

Her smile broadened. "Excellent! Now, perhaps we really *ought* to get started. Did you say you use human spells to get started or was it the other way around?"

"No, that's correct. Human spells to start, and then I use my fae sensing skills to build on it." He began to describe that in more detail.

As she bent her head to write all the notes, he snuck a glance at the long table at the back of the room. Miss Wilton-Reed was in the act of pouring a jar of beans onto the table in such a way that they spilled all over the floor. He watched as she then flicked her hand in a gesture clearly meant to tell Cricket to clean up the mess. He didn't miss the way her eyes roamed over the gentleman's body as he did what she asked. *He will certainly be decorative.* He ground his teeth together and turned his attention back to his partner.

When they were finally ready for Silas to perform a spell, he had worked himself into a state of uncharacteristic nervousness. He decided to perform a breeze spell, going back to the rubric. Once again, his magic reacted strongly to his partner's sensing his spell. Silas was no longer surprised by it. It was not painful like it had been with Mx. Hillcrest, nor as unsteady as it had been with Mr. Buckthorn. Now instead of feeling like a boat on a rocky sea, it felt as though his magic had been plunged beneath the water. It moved agonizingly slowly. The breeze spell did activate, but it ruffled the sheaf of paper Silas had used as a focus before subsiding.

Silas sighed and pinched the bridge of his nose.

Miss Wrenwhistle bit her lip and looked at her notes. "Would you mind doing that again, Mr. Rook-Worth?"

He did as she asked, adding a significant boost with a sigil that he only used when absolutely necessary. This time, the breeze spell lifted the paper off the desk and carried it lazily around the table, losing power halfway through its circuit. His heart sank as the paper did.

Councilmember Wyndham Wrenwhistle approached. "Aveline," he said to his sister, "perhaps we ought to try *not* sensing Mr. Rook-Worth with magic."

She frowned. "Is that not what I'm supposed to do?"

"It is. But I'd like to see if his magic changes when it's not conflicting with another person's magic. Do you mind?" he added to Silas.

Silas picked up the paper, returning it to the table, and started a fresh sheet of spellpaper to try again. This time, when he felt out with his magic, it felt free, strong, *normal*. He sent the spell in a circle around the table and then added another sigil to send it all the way around the room. Both Miss Wrenwhistle and Councilmember Wrenwhistle watched, but Silas noticed that neither reached out with their magic. He was impressed with their restraint.

That is, until the councilmember tapped his sister's shoulder and said, "Try feeling his magic now."

He knew the moment her magic collided with his. The breeze slowed dramatically and the paper flopped to the ground with a sad *shhh*. He looked up at the councilmember who was staring at the fallen paper, his brow furrowed in concentration.

Finally, he said, "Well, that clearly tells us that your magic is most certainly far from weak. Perhaps we ought to continue in that manner, at least for the time being. We'll pair you with Brooks after a few days. That should give you plenty of time to complete the entire rubric." He turned back to his sister. "I know it isn't ideal, but do your best to control your magic until then."

She sighed heavily as he walked away.

"Sorry," Silas said. He felt a breeze at the back of his neck and looked up to see Councilmember Wrenwhistle sending the paper back to the table with a flick of his hand.

"It isn't your fault," she mumbled, giving her brother an irritated look, even though Silas was quite sure the man was no longer facing them to see it. "I can see how different your magic was when I wasn't sensing."

Silas set about putting together a pouring spell. It was not ideal, but at least he finally had the ability to perform his magic without restraint or pain. It was blessedly freeing. The next few days that passed were the best he had ever experienced since coming to London.

CHAPTER 30

KEELAN

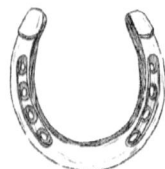

AFTER WATCHING Miss Wilton-Reed exit the room for a short break to take care of some personal matters, Keelan let out a slow sigh of relief as he crossed his arms on the table and buried his face in them. If possible, the last couple of days had been the worst since the entire project began. There had been no issues of great importance, only more of the same deceitful conduct from his partner, but it worried Keelan that he was starting to wish that something *would* happen so that he might finally find a reasonable excuse to be free of her.

The best he'd thought up was some sort of interference with her magic. He was just as capable with his own, after all, and he'd had plenty of practice doing mischievous things with it in his youth. It would be easy to go past his sensing and interject on one of her spells—nothing harmful, of course, but perhaps give her a taste of what she'd been doing from the start. If he could manage it in front of his mother, then she might finally see that the lady was not as pretty as the flowers adorning her hair each day.

The trouble was that it would take a lot of focus, and Keelan found that he'd been struggling with that nearly as much as he'd been struggling with Miss Wilton-Reed's behavior.

Mr. Rook-Worth had returned to the main room after changing

partners again. It appeared that he and Aveline had found great success, because the man had been showing off his aptitude with fervor. It was terribly distracting. Nothing as bad as that blasted belt, but enough that Keelan was doubly grateful to have his back to him as they worked.

The sound of someone clapping their hands for attention forced Keelan to sit upright in his chair. Torquil, Roger, and Wyndham were standing together looking every bit as weary as the rest of the volunteers, though they were trying hard not to let it show. They must've sent aides to collect everyone else, because the doors opened to let them in just as Torquil began to speak.

"We will be ending the session early today." The grin they gave did not quite reach their eyes; Keelan noticed for the first time there were faint shadows beneath them. They gestured to Wyndham and Roger with an open hand. "My colleagues and I have decided that another evening out has been well earned by all." Torquil's grin pinched to one side. "Despite the rather shocking cost of this project, we've found room in our stipend to reserve a dinner box at Vauxhall for everyone who wishes to join us."

The reaction to this announcement was mixed; most of those from out of town looked to the Londoners for what the appropriate response should be. Aveline Wrenwhistle's shriek of excitement was the first to break through the air.

"How wonderful!" she cried as she laced her fingers together beneath her chin, her entire body bouncing in place. Keelan risked a glance at Mr. Rook-Worth beside her. His expression gave nothing away. "There's to be some royal revelry in the city tonight, as well. Perhaps we will be able to see the fireworks display from across the river!"

A low murmur picked up around the room as everyone began sharing their thoughts on the invitation. It seemed that most everyone was in favor.

"Father always said Vauxhall Gardens was one of the most beautiful places in London." Miss Wilton-Reed's hand found Keelan's arm. "And romantic. Have you been?"

"Yes, many times," Keelan admitted, though he'd never participated in the amorous behavior it was infamous for. He found most ladies to be in favor of sharing a private kiss or two, especially after a few glasses of arrack punch, but rarely had he encountered one that wanted to do anything more outdoors. That was saved for a room with a bed.

Miss Wilton-Reed chuckled and raised her hand to gently tap her fingertip on the end of his nose.

"Then I expect I shall have a perfect evening with you on my arm."

KEELAN PAIRED the new waistcoat his father made him with a dark blue jacket and trousers to match. It was a fair balance to the creamy yellow color of the fabric dotted with a pattern of tiny, simple flowers. His valet had chosen a cravat pin with a bright yellow jewel to go with it. Miss Wilton-Reed would love it, and he hoped that maybe if he wore something that pleased her, she would be nicer to him.

The streets were crowded thanks to the various events going on across the city. Even after crossing the bridge, Keelan worried about arriving on time to avoid finding the dinner box alone. It had not occurred to him to offer the open seats in his carriage to anyone staying at the Pimpernel townhouse until it was too late to turn back. He fidgeted with the bottom button of his waistcoat as he wondered if Miss Wilton-Reed would be angry that he did not escort her himself.

Upon his arrival at the gardens, Keelan only had to take one glance around to find a familiar face. He moved through the stream of people and called out a greeting as Wyndham helped Roger from their carriage. The gentlemen both offered a greeting in return; a nod from Wyndham and a bright smile from Roger.

"Do you know if Emrys has arrived yet?" Keelan asked.

"Of all the people we are meeting here tonight, Emrys is the lowest of my concern," Wyndham said flatly. "And you can clearly see that we have only just arrived ourselves."

"Wyn," Roger said in a hushed, warning tone as he took his husband's offered arm. His cheerful demeanor returned as he gave Keelan another smile. "We tend to make a habit of being the last ones to make an appearance, I'm afraid. Let us walk together and we shall find out."

Roger had been correct in his estimation. The reserved table was full and already covered with food and drink. Only three seats remained open, and naturally the single one was next to Miss Wilton-Reed. Keelan met eyes with Emrys across the table as he was helped into his chair. Emrys raised his glass to him in solidarity before he took a sip.

"You look dashing this evening," Miss Wilton-Reed said, her gaze lingering on the new waistcoat. The compliment was not offered with any sort of affection, the way it might've been from a lover or soon-to-be spouse, but rather like a connoisseur admiring a piece of artwork they'd very much enjoy adding to their collection. Keelan reached for his own drink before he replied.

"Very kind of you to say, Miss Wilton-Reed. You also look well."

"Which shop did this come from?" She leaned closer to inspect the pattern of tiny flowers. "I shall have to go there and see if they've any of this pattern left."

"You would likely want to find something from this Season instead," Keelan told her in earnest. "I've no idea how old the fabric is. My father made it for me, and his collection of material is rather extensive."

What looked to be genuine surprise was quickly masked with a small, dismissive laugh.

"And do you have any such menial talents?"

Keelan bristled at her question. Not only was it meant to belittle his father's work, but it was also her way of asking something that a suitor might wish to know. He wasn't sure which was more upsetting.

"I can write," he said plainly. When he did not continue beyond what she already knew about him, Miss Wilton-Reed scoffed and turned away. He took his opportunity to fill his plate and try to enjoy his dinner.

The food was delicious and the punch was strong, which meant the end of their long meal was marked by members of the party slowly peeling away toward the dance floor.

Aveline and Mr. Buckthorn were the first, immediately putting everyone to shame with the chemistry they shared. Gloucester-Stone and Hillcrest were next, followed by a shy Mr. Finkle-Finch offering his hand to Mx. Badger-Thorp, which they readily accepted.

The pressure Keelan felt to ask Miss Wilton-Reed to dance had built slowly at first, but with the table nearly empty, it sat between them in a way that was impossible to ignore. Even Roger managed to pull Wyndham from his chair. Keelan wondered if anyone else had noticed the lingering kiss Wyndham pressed to Roger's knuckles as they'd made their way to the floor.

"Keelan!" Emrys' voice cut through the night air. Keelan's brows went up as he took in the mirthful look on his friend's face. What he said next came as no surprise. "I'm afraid six glasses of punch was too many." A loose smile formed on his lips. "Do me a favor and dance with Torquil."

Keelan's amusement washed away at the request.

"Dance with Torquil?" he repeated.

Emrys unwrapped his arm from around their waist and gently encouraged them up from where they'd been sitting comfortably on his lap. After staring at how elegant Torquil looked in their evening ensemble for far too long, Keelan scrambled up out of his chair.

"Er, yes, of course." He hurried around the table to offer his arm, forgetting all about Miss Wilton-Reed until Emrys gave him a subtle— and surprisingly sober—wink over the rim of his glass.

He really did love that man.

The dance they joined was an easy one. The steps took up a lot of space, which meant that there was little pressure to talk. Keelan was able to recognize fairly quickly that Torquil had not actually wanted to dance. They seemed distracted and looked back at their table more than once, where Emrys sat watching them.

"I am sorry he asked you to do this," Keelan said quietly when it was their turn to stand beside one another as the other dancers moved around them.

Torquil offered a small grin. "I do not enjoy dancing in public. But I do enjoy making my husband happy." There was a slight pause. "And I enjoy helping a friend."

Keelan let those last few words settle around him like a heated bed in winter. He had to turn his head away to hide his grin, pressing the corner of his mouth against his shoulder until he could control himself.

"Fortunate for you that a great many things make him happy," Keelan finally managed. "Namely the life you've built together."

Torquil gave a single, slow nod. "I am very fortunate, indeed."

Keelan's mood dimmed as his thoughts shifted to something else he felt he needed to apologize for.

"I do not know what my mother has been saying to you about my partnership with Miss Wilton-Reed, but I'm certain it's been awful. I hope you'll forgive me for putting you in the middle of it. You've got so much else to be worrying about, the last thing you need is—"

"I'm well aware that you've played no part in this arrangement," Torquil cut in gently. The final steps of the dance broke them apart before bringing them together again. "Emrys has told me some of it, but you're rather expressive with your emotions. It is not hard to see how it's affecting you."

Keelan and Torquil both joined in the applause at the end of the dance, each offering a slight bow. He expected Torquil to take their leave of the floor immediately after, but instead, they tilted their head to one side and searched his eyes with a somewhat sad expression.

"It's most unfortunate that our parents are often misguided when they try to do what they think is best for us, especially when it is done without our consent. I lost years of connection with my grandmother because of it. And while I can appreciate the reasoning behind the choices that were made, it still does not change the fact that I was never given the opportunity to speak and decide for myself." Their soft grin returned. "You've not yet lost the ability to be heard."

With that, they gave another departing nod and left Keelan to watch after them. How could he be so lucky to have one of London's most acclaimed writers giving him advice? Calling him their friend? He needed someone to shake him.

Unfortunately, it was Miss Wilton-Reed who stepped in to do it.

"I'll have your next dance," the lady said through clenched teeth as she gave a sharp but subtle tug on his arm. "In the future, I trust you shall remember yourself while we attend events such as this. At the very least, you will seek my permission to dance." A tight smile took over her previous expression. "We cannot have you embarrassing me in public, now can we?"

She made good on her promise. Keelan moved through the steps with her, his focus wandering all the while. Torquil had returned to Emrys' side, and it looked like more members of the party had found their way back to the table to have another drink or simply catch their breath from dancing. A few others, including Mr. Rook-Worth, had disappeared into the gardens.

The moment the music ended, Miss Wilton-Reed wrapped her fingers tight around the bend of Keelan's elbow and began dragging him toward one of the many footpaths that diverged from the main lawn. The trees were bright overhead with lanterns and fairy lights; flowers crowded the path on both sides.

"Where are we going?" Keelan asked, too weak to sound demanding.

"You're going to show me the gardens, of course. Since you've been here so many times before, who better to know where all the best hidden gems are?"

Keelan was not so ignorant as to believe she wished for him to take her to the fountains or one of the stages set for entertainment. He'd been guided with such intent several times before, usually away from a fae party in the early hours of the morning, and it was always with the same purpose in mind. His magic flared with apprehension in his chest as he dug his heels into the crushed stone of the path.

"Miss Wilton-Reed, are you certain that is what you want?"

The lady whirled on him now that she could not move him.

"You know precisely what I want," she argued. "And I've very nearly got it, if it would stop resisting!" With a puff of an exhale, Miss Wilton-Reed collected herself and let go of his arm to reach for his hand instead. "I believe my intentions have been made very clear, but because you seem to require such alterations for simple understanding, I will put it plainly. I find joy in your company, Mr. Cricket. I adore the ease with which I am able to speak to you. I cannot deny that yours is the only presence I have grown to take pleasure in during my time in London."

Keelan's brow furrowed with doubt. "What about my mother?"

Miss Wilton-Reed let out a trill of laughter. "Yes, her too." The lady's smile became subtly more alluring as she added, "but she is not the one I am here with in the pleasure gardens tonight."

Despite his hesitation in taking anything she'd said for the truth, there was a small part of Keelan that had already attached to her words. He'd dreamed so long of finding someone to share life's quiet moments with. Effortless conversations and undemanding time spent together were both very high on that list. After all, he was a good listener and a simple sort of man. To be included at all was better than nothing, and to hear that Miss Wilton-Reed already liked sharing those things with him was a promising start.

With his free hand, Keelan brushed the backs of his fingers gently across the lady's soft cheek and nodded. "Very well."

It did not take long for him to locate a private spot for the two of them behind a trellis covered with fragrant honeysuckles just starting to bloom. To his relief, Miss Wilton-Reed did not voice any objections over his selection. Her only answer was to reach up and place a gloved hand on the back of his neck, pulling him down for a kiss.

After sensing Miss Wilton-Reed's fae magic for several weeks, he was not surprised to feel the tickle of it there under the dim glow of fairy lights bobbing along from branch to branch. He held her closer by the waist and reached out with his own magic in answer. The sensation was exactly as he expected, similar to placing one's hand into calm water the same temperature as the surrounding air. You know it's happening, but you can hardly feel it.

Kissing her was exactly the same.

Suitable enough. The words echoed between his ears like a warning.

With a gasp, Keelan pulled away, his pulse racing for all the wrong reasons. Miss Wilton-Reed opened her eyes, searching his face for an explanation that he was certain he could not give without being reprimanded.

"I apologize," he whispered. "If you'll excuse me."

Without another word, Keelan left Miss Wilton-Reed behind the trellis with little care for who saw him emerge and began to run.

CHAPTER 31

SILAS

THE NIGHT at Vauxhall had started off far more promising than the opera. While it was certainly just as opulent, Silas preferred being in an opulent garden than operahouse. The arrack punch was strong, the food was delicious, and almost everyone in the group was relaxed and happy. Silas was almost enjoying himself.

True, he had a difficult time looking away when Miss Wilton-Reed had leaned in close to Cricket. But what made the evening truly terrible was when Torquil left to dance with Cricket and Councilmembers Wyndham and Roger Wrenwhistle returned to the table. Wyndham poured a single glass of punch and handed it to his husband before turning a beady eye on Silas.

Silas had a sinking feeling that he knew what was coming.

"We're going to pair you with someone new tomorrow afternoon."

Silas couldn't resist the groan that escaped him. "I was afraid you were going to say that. Is there even anyone left?"

Wyndham had the grace to look apologetic. "Brooks hasn't worked with you yet." He glanced at Miss Wilton-Reed, but she was thankfully busy glaring at Cricket on the dance floor. "And if that doesn't work, then I'll be your partner."

"I'm sure it doesn't look so from your side, Mr. Rook-Worth," Councilmember Roger Wrenwhistle piped in, "but it really is a good thing that we're coming up to this challenge now."

Silas took a swig of punch. "Is it?"

"Well, if we roll out the rubric and a fae-human child has a similar reaction to their fae examiner, it would be best to be prepared for such a scenario. We want to give them as great a chance for success as we can."

"I was not tested as a child."

Councilmember Wyndham Wrenwhistle grimaced. "Torquil said the same thing. But that is exactly what we aim to resolve. And it will hardly help things if, as Roger said, we roll out a new rubric and examiners come back saying that the fae-human children's magic seemed too constrained to be properly measured."

"Exactly," Councilmember Roger Wrenwhistle said. "You are integral to the success of this entire project."

Silas sighed. It had been so nice being able to use his magic properly for a brief time, but he could see the logic in their argument.

"And," Councilmember Wyndham Wrenwhistle added, "we know now that you can do the rubric, which was a major part of what we needed. So we know the rubric works. Now, we need to solve the problem we didn't know we'd have."

Silas drained his glass and ignored Councilmember Roger Wrenwhistle's murmured warning that it was quite strong. "Thank you for telling me," he said curtly and then left the table.

He skirted the edge of the dance floor, sparing a brief glance at Cricket, who had turned his face away from Torquil, a blush creeping over his face as he smiled. The sight gave him a jolt of longing. He wanted to be the one putting that blush on the man's cheeks. He wouldn't have let Cricket hide his smile from him. He sighed and scrubbed a hand over his hair as he took a path away from the dance floor and into the garden. He couldn't help but notice that the councilmembers had not offered Cricket as a viable partner. He remembered Councilmember Cricket informing Mr. Emrys Wrenwhistle that she had been the one to suggest Miss Wilton-Reed as a partner for her son. And now the lady was having tea with the councilmember. It certainly didn't take much imagination to recognize that a marriage was being arranged.

He followed his feet as he ambled over the walkway and took a deep breath, relishing the crisp night air. The trees were filled with lanterns and fairy lights. Silas felt a pang in his chest, thinking of all the times his family had used fairy lights to entertain and delight him as a child. The grief he'd felt when he'd learned he would never create such things himself had been acute. He found a small footbridge and braced his hands on the railing, watching the reflection of the lights dancing on the surface of the water. He thought about how his mother had taught him his first breeze spell and his father had shown him how to use the spell to twirl the fairy lights around the room. He thought about how Quince had given him a textbook filled with information on fairy lights, so he could learn as much as possible.

He closed his eyes, the ache in his chest sharpening. It would have been so much simpler if he'd been able to bring some of his family members with him, prove that he could perform magic with a fae part-ner. But he knew the councilmembers were right: it was a good thing to have discovered such a barrier now, to better prepare for it in the future.

The sounds of other guests chattering and giggling brought him back to the present. He was newly irritated with himself for coming to another event. Now he was even farther from the townhouse, and he wasn't at all sure it would be acceptable for him to take a carriage back, not with how long it would take to return him and circle around for the rest of the group. He gripped the railing. He was stuck. Stuck in this blasted city. Stuck in this absurd garden. Stuck in this neverending project.

If he could stop being a fool about Cricket, he could at least find some enjoyment. He stepped away from the railing and stuffed his hands in his pockets. He had no idea why the man still had such a hold on him, or why he had continued to refrain from seeking pleasure else-where. All he knew was that he wished he could redo their night together, knowing then what he knew now. He wished he could hold Cricket in his arms for as long as he wished, and relish the way the other man felt in his embrace. He wished he could have spoken more eloquently about his family when Cricket had asked; he had a feeling Cricket would understand how much Silas missed them better than anyone else had. He continued into the garden, avoiding the sounds of giggles and moans as he wandered aimlessly, feeling very sorry for himself.

A lone figure in an alcove caught his eye. He would have known the trim figure anywhere, but he was surprised to see the man alone. He approached cautiously. Cricket was pacing the short length of the alcove, his brow furrowed and his arms crossed over his chest. He looked up at the sound of Silas's footsteps and hastily straightened.

"Mr. Rook-Worth," he said, his voice tight. "I did not see you there."

"Are you quite well?"

Cricket gave a humorless huff of laughter. "I am adequately well, thank you."

Silas caught the bitterness in the man's tone. The reference to his own words gave him a pang. He stepped closer, taking in the man's posture, the tension in his jaw, and the way Cricket had turned his gaze to the ground. "It seems as though Vauxhall has fallen short of the promised entertainment," Silas offered.

"We really are doing a poor job of showing off London to you, aren't we?" the man replied, meeting his gaze with a small smile.

Silas chuckled. "I'm difficult to impress."

Cricket swallowed. "I recall."

The pang in Silas' chest sharpened at the man's words. He knew he had to make things right. What better time than the present?

Cricket had offered him friendship—it would be appropriate for Silas to repay that kindness, would it not? The gentleman looked frazzled and tense— clearly a relaxing activity would help, and Silas was very good at those. It was merely a mark of good friendship to extend the offer. And if Silas got to be gentler with the man, show him a bit of tenderness, and prioritize his pleasure this time, so much the better.

The fact that Silas would enjoy Cricket's closeness, that he might get to feel the other man's magic explode against his once again, and that he might taste that sense of perfection and rightness that he'd been yearning ever since the wedding…that was simply an added bonus.

He chose his next words with care. "Although I am surprised you are not indulging in the delights of the gardens. You always seem to enjoy what the city has to offer."

Cricket seemed to consider this. "I always try my best to enjoy what is presented to me."

"And I have found you in this agitated state because you did not enjoy something as much as you feel you should?" Cricket blushed, but he did not argue against Silas' guess. "It is a pity that neither of us is having a particularly pleasant evening. It seems a shame for you to find such an enchanting night merely adequate."

"And what of you? Should you not be enjoying yourself more as well? After all, you are a guest in the city."

Silas reached up and ran his thumb across Cricket's jaw. "I can think of some ways to make this evening more enjoyable."

The other man's eyes widened. "You—I thought—" He licked his lips. "I thought you were no longer interested."

Silas moved his other hand to the wall by Cricket's head, bracketing the slighter man in. "I think I owe you an apology," he said in a low voice. "I am…unaccustomed to encountering such a gentle creature as you. I did not treat you as I ought." He tilted his face and pressed a soft kiss to the spot below Cricket's ear. Cricket let out a shuddery breath. He continued to stroke the man's jaw with his thumb and leaned close to murmur, "It seems you asked me to tell you if I want or need anything. And what I want right now is to make things up to you."

Cricket swallowed and Silas waited patiently. "Yes," he whispered. "I think I'd like that very much."

Just as it had the night of their first encounter, something snapped between them and Silas pressed into Cricket, capturing the other man's mouth with his own in a bruising kiss. Cricket moaned against him, which was all the permission Silas needed to move one hand into Cricket's hair and wrap his other arm around his waist. Silas kissed him deeply, relishing the softness of Cricket's lips, exploring him leisurely with his tongue. It was everything he'd imagined it would be, every bit as satisfying, every bit as maddening. He broke off the kiss and began kissing down Cricket's cheek and jaw, nibbling on the lobe of his ear, and nipping lightly at the tender skin of his neck. Cricket whimpered in response.

Silas sank to his knees and slid his hands up Cricket's thighs. "May I?"

Cricket nodded, a bit dazedly. "Won't your trousers get dirty?"

Silas laughed as he began swiftly undoing buttons. "I don't mind. We can return to the group separately if you'd like. No one need know who I was with." He rubbed his thumbs over Cricket's hips and grinned up at him. "It can be our little secret."

"Ever the man of mystery," Cricket quipped breathily.

Keeping his gaze locked with Cricket, he freed the other man's length and licked along the slit. Cricket shuddered. "You'll tell me if you need me to stop, all right?"

"I will." Cricket's voice was raspy. It was deliciously satisfying.

Silas took him in his mouth. Cricket's hand landed on the back of his head. But where other lovers had gripped at his short hair or dug their nails in, Cricket's grip was soft, as if to steady himself or to give Silas some sort of assurance. It made Silas curse himself all over again for not taking better care their first night together. As Silas worked his lips and tongue over him, Cricket's grip never changed.

Just before Cricket attained his climax, Silas reached out with his magic, hoping the other man would understand what he was asking. He could tell the moment Cricket felt the tickle of magic because he unleashed his own and it wrapped around them both, warm, strong, and every bit as wild as it had been in the cart. Cricket cried out and Silas swallowed every drop of the man's pleasure. When Cricket slumped against the wall, Silas buttoned him up carefully and got to his feet.

Cricket's expression was wary, and Silas's heart ached when he realized the man was bracing himself for more unkindness. Silas pulled him into his arms and kissed him as sweetly as he knew how. Cricket wrapped his arms around his neck and reciprocated. Silas wondered if the gentleman had ever tasted himself on someone else's mouth as the kiss lingered and turned soft and lazy.

Finally Cricket pulled away and glanced down at Silas's trousers. "I should—"

Silas curled a finger under his chin and lifted it, kissing the corner of his mouth. "Not tonight."

"But—"

"I'll take care of myself later. Believe me, I'll have plenty to think about so it won't be a hardship," he added with a wink.

Cricket blushed and seemed to fight a smile. "Well, if I can ever return the favor."

Silas cupped his cheek with one large hand. "As long as I'm in London, Cricket, my bed is open to you. No questions asked."

He felt rather than heard Cricket's sharp intake of breath before he closed the distance between them once again and kissed him. When they broke apart and Cricket stepped away, his lips were kiss-swollen and his cheeks were flushed. He was utterly delectable. But, thankfully, he didn't look too mussed.

"I should…" He gestured vaguely.

Silas indulged in a quick kiss to the man's temple. "Go on and join the others. I'll stay here until it's time to leave."

Cricket gave him another brief smile and then obeyed, hurrying down the path. Silas watched him go and then wandered to a bench. He sank onto the seat and spread his arms across the back of the bench, watching the fairy lights twinkle overhead.

He revisited the feeling of Cricket in his arms, the taste of the man on his mouth, the sensations of their magics colliding. Silas had spent his entire time in London feeling as if his gaze and attention was forever being pulled to Cricket, like some kind of magnetic force. The way Cricket had pressed against him felt as if they'd snapped together into place, the magnetism between them finally overcoming the distance.

Silas realized that the tension he'd been carrying ever since his magic misbehaved with his first fae partner had drifted away. He couldn't be sure if his new relaxed state was due to the pleasure he'd shared with Cricket or the feeling of his magic finally blending with another's in a positive way. The way his magic surged against Cricket's was unlike anything he'd experienced before, even with his family. It was wild and overpowering. Even though he'd just experienced it, Silas was already craving that sensation again.

It was almost an hour before Torquil found him. They gave an amused glance to the state of grass-stained trousers but didn't comment.

As Silas joined the others in the carriage, Mx. Badger-Thorp asked him if he'd enjoyed this outing better than the last one.

"Decidedly," he replied with a grin.

TORQUIL'S TRIBUNE

Greetings, ravishing readers,

Sources close to the Council have confided that the project is going well. From what we've heard of the goings on with the group of visitors, we must certainly agree. We've received multiple reports about the project volunteers paying a visit to Vauxhall Gardens last night. We can only assume the Pleasure Gardens did not disappoint, if rumors of kisses, dances, and conspicuous disappearances are to be believed.

Less scandalous were the appearances of Councilmembers Wyndham and Roger Wrenwhistle, as well as Mr. Emrys Wrenwhistle and Councilmember Torquil Pimpernel-Smith. Both couples appeared to remain very much in love. We are sure this news will be a delight to many, a disappointment to some.

The Ladies Fitzhugh entertained Mr. Cyril Thompson, Miss Harriet Thackeray, and Mx. Fern Hillcrest for dinner. Readers may recall that Lady Anthea Fitzhugh has long been a close friend of Mr. Thompson and Miss Thackeray. We like to think that Lady Imogen Fitzhugh and Mx. Hillcrest settled in comfortably with the established friend group.

Several fae families of note attended a private ball at the home of the Birches. It has been reported that Mr. Brooks danced with a variety of gentlemen over the course of the evening. Mr. Ravenwing did little dancing, but he did leave before the party was over—with another man on his arm. Sources say the two men were notably affectionate over the course of the evening.

The Applewoods had Councilmember Barnes and Mrs. Barnes over for dinner. We are pleased that the Council is socializing within its own factions, something that many deemed impossible a year ago.

Mrs. Iris Wrenwhistle and Mrs. Leonora Pimpernel were spotted promenading through Hyde Park with one of the fae-human visitors staying in the Pimpernel townhouse. By all accounts, the two ladies appeared to sit very close together on a park bench. Could the two widows be finding solace in each other's company?

Your esteemed editor,
Sal Bailey

CHAPTER 32

KEELAN

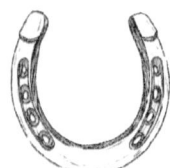

WHEN KEELAN WOKE LATE the next morning, he was certain he'd dreamed a nightmare that ended as a fantasy. He was vaguely aware that he was still dressed in the clothes he'd worn to the gardens. His arms and legs were stretched out around him as though he'd floated into his bed on a cloud. Keelan blinked up at the ceiling, fully embracing the wide grin that was threatening to cause his cheeks to ache.

Had that really happened?

He brought his fingers up to trace along his bottom lip. The tenderness he felt there only made his smile grow more. He closed his eyes again and sorted through his memories of the night before, all a bit hazy from the arrack punch, but some far more vivid than others.

Miss Wilton-Reed had kissed him. Mr. Rook-Worth had kissed him.

Mr. Rook-Worth had done *more* than kiss him.

The reality of it all settled more firmly as he sat up and moved to the edge of the bed. He looked down at his feet and wriggled his toes against his stockings. At least he'd remembered to remove his shoes.

He did the same with the rest of his clothes and washed his face at the basin, impish grin still firmly in place as he called for Marten to come and dress him. The thought of remaining in bed was tempting, but he was secretly afraid that if he did not continue on with his day, he would wake all over again and realize it really had been a dream.

Still largely in a state of bewilderment, Keelan shuffled downstairs to breakfast. Both spaniels lifted their heads when he came into the room, but neither of them were bothered enough to leave his father's side. Keelan settled into a chair. It took an embarrassingly long time for him to realize that the table was empty.

"Have Elodie and Alouetta eaten all the food?" he asked.

His father looked up from the book he was reading with an amused grin.

"The food?"

Keelan's brows pinched. "Breakfast?"

His father closed his book around his thumb and let it rest in his lap.

"Breakfast was hours ago," he chuckled. "I can have the kitchen prepare a plate for you, if you'd like?"

Keelan gasped. "Hours? What time is it?" His clambering out of his chair is what finally excited the dogs enough to bring them to their feet. They both began barking and wagging their tails, circling his legs and making it even harder for him to leave. "Why did no one wake me!"

"Settle, settle," his father soothed. He wasn't sure if it was more for him or for the dogs, but all three of them listened. "A note arrived from the Council. It seems that your late evening out left everyone struggling this morning. The meeting time was pushed back."

Keelan pressed a palm to his forehead and took the folded piece of paper his father handed him. He read over the scrawled communication twice just to be sure.

"Do you want anything?" his father offered again.

"Please," he agreed as he set the note on the table and returned to his chair.

"It must have been some night. I'm not sure I have ever seen you sleep so late before. Even the few times you came down with a fever as a child, you were awake with the sun, smiling up at me with bright red cheeks."

"Believe me, I am as surprised as you." Keelan relaxed more in his chair, grin returning to the corner of his mouth. "But it was a good night."

"Mmm," came his father's knowing response, before he continued in French. "Not with your mother's match, I take it?"

Keelan's eyes went wide as he gave the man an incredulous look, though his smirk did not fade. "Papa," he scolded softly.

"Only a guess," he shrugged with feigned innocence, returning to his book as a tray of tea and various pastries were brought in. "You look very content, that's all."

Keelan sat with that for a moment. It was probably the best word he could think of to describe how he felt. So much had happened in the past few weeks to unsettle him, and when he arrived at the Council's chambers later, he could only imagine what his interactions with Miss Wilton-Reed would be like. But this feeling had nothing to do with her.

His stranger was no longer a stranger. Mr. Rook-Worth had apologized for his behavior on the night of the wedding. Then he'd done a *remarkable* job of making it up to him. It was more than that, though. He'd been attentive and considerate; he'd extended an offer. Their magics had reacted just the same as before, and Mr. Rook-Worth had kissed him the way he'd always longed to be kissed—passionately, languidly, deliberately.

Keelan glanced at his father as he carefully adjusted his position in his chair. He knew better than to let himself think about any of this for long. For as many reasons as he wanted to hold tight to this feeling, there were just as many reasons why he couldn't. When the project was over, Mr. Rook-Worth would return home. He'd given every indication that he was not interested in being committed to anything or any*one* in London, or perhaps anywhere.

It was foolish to give life to the hope that this was more than a temporary source of pleasure. That's all Keelan had ever known, so he felt confident that he was capable of doing it again should the situation present itself—which he certainly hoped that it would. In a way, Emrys had been right after all. Mr. Rook-Worth had inevitably repaired whatever he had broken.

Bolstered by a new sense of clarity in his emotions, Keelan took a sip of tea, digging through his memory and choosing his words carefully before he said them in French.

"Has it been terrible? Life with Mother?"

The way his father brightened at his use of his native language warmed him. He set his book down and removed his spectacles, giving his son a long look.

"No," he said after the pause. "It has given me my children. For that, I will always be grateful." His grin faded a bit. "But I have never desired a connection with another person the way that you do. Romantically, you understand?"

Keelan nodded that he did, and his father continued.

"I have done the duties required of me, and I have lived my life the way I wished to live it. It has been a good life."

Keelan tried to continue in French, but found that he could not remember the right words, so he started over. "What if I cannot do what you have done?"

"You are capable of more than you know," his father said. Keelan felt his stomach drop. Maybe a future with Miss Wilton-Reed really was all he could hope for. "But just because you can do it, that does not mean it's what you deserve."

He knew this phrase in French. "What do I do?"

His father smiled and tapped a few fingers against his own chest.

"Trust your heart. Do what feels right."

Keelan sighed and let his gaze fall to his hands in his lap.

"That seems too simple."

"Ah," his father said in a tone that indicated that was precisely what he meant. "But the best things in life are simple, no?" He reached over to the tray and picked up one of the flakier pastries, tearing it in half so that he could offer one piece to Keelan. "Fresh croissants, a good book, a beautiful day, a conversation with my son. What more could I ask for?"

Keelan accepted the offering and took a bite of it to appease his empty stomach. He supposed that he would do well to take his own advice. It was what he'd told Emrys about sorting out his own future, and that's how he had ended up with Torquil. Could he really find a love like theirs?

Keelan took a fortifying breath and got to his feet again, this time with much less urgency. He studied his father for a moment, seeing him in a way that, perhaps, he never had before.

"I lost track of how many compliments I received on my waistcoat last night," he said, taking a few slow steps backward toward the door. "I may be in need of a few more, if you've got the time to make them for me." The warm sound of his father's gentle laughter stuck with him as he left to face whatever waited for him at the Council's chambers.

CHAPTER 33

SILAS

Silas knew that he ought to be dreading an afternoon of explaining his magic to someone new *again*. But he couldn't drum up the necessary frustration. As he climbed into the carriage with the other fae-human volunteers, he felt an eagerness he hadn't felt in a long time. He was excited to go to the Council chambers—it meant Cricket would be there—though he recognized that being in the same room with the man without having the freedom to pull him into his arms and kiss him again would likely be a particular form of torture.

When he strode into the room, his eyes immediately went to Cricket, whose face lit up at the sight of him. And Silas found he could bear the torture if it meant seeing Cricket smile like that.

Miss Wilton-Reed seemed to be under the impression that Cricket was grinning because of her because she greeted him with enthusiasm, patted his cheek, and promptly launched into a monologue about how Vauxhall compared to her experiences in Bath. Silas had already had to hear her opinions on the subject during breakfast and the carriage ride over, so he turned to face his new partner.

Benedict Brooks was every bit as vapid as Buckthorn, but without the other man's charm. Silas recalled Hedge-Wyck describing the fae as boring. Far be it from Silas to agree with any opinion Hedge-Wyck had put forth, but he couldn't deny it was an accurate assessment. Brooks was clearly deeply uninterested in the task at hand. When he began to punctuate his questions with sly looks and seductive smiles, Silas suspected Brooks was only involved in the project for a sampling of new entertainment. He couldn't blame the man for it, but he was irritated all the same. Brooks was an even worse note-taker than Mr. Emrys Wrenwhistle, claiming he'd remember everything Silas told him.

Thankfully, the conversation portion of the afternoon was brief and Silas got to work on another breeze spell. The moment he cast and felt Brooks's magic flash against his own, he knew it wouldn't end well. His magic fizzed inside him like a powder keg. He gave a shout and flipped the piece of parchment over to stop the spell at once. The handkerchief he had used as a focus had barely levitated into the air before it popped and shredded cotton confetti all over the table.

"Er…" Brooks said, wiping the fabric dust off of his waistcoat irritably. "Was that supposed to happen?"

Silas was saved from answering the question when all three of their councilmembers hurried over.

"What happened?" Torquil asked.

"Is everyone all right?" Councilmember Roger Wrenwhistle asked.

Councilmember Wyndham Wrenwhistle eyed the space critically before turning his gaze to Silas. "Well saved."

Silas sank into his seat. "It would appear I've successfully worked through every available fae volunteer."

Councilmember Wyndham Wrenwhistle clapped a hand on Silas' shoulder as Torquil apologized to Brooks.

"I thought you said that wouldn't happen again," Brooks said.

"Thanks to the protective spell we put together and Mr. Rook-Worth's quick thinking, it *didn't* happen again," Councilmember Wyndham Wrenwhistle said dismissively.

Brooks got to his feet. "This is absurd. You three have no idea what you're doing."

Torquil paled. "I *am* sorry, Mr. Brooks. I'm sure you must be very rattled—"

"Shall I have one of the aides fetch you a pot of tea?" Councilmember Roger Wrenwhistle asked, twisting his hands together.

Brooks rolled his eyes. "I'll take tea in the comfort and *safety* of my own home, thank you very much. Don't expect me to return."

"Convenient of him to wait until a free trip to Vauxhall before quitting," Councilmember Wyndham Wrenwhistle remarked dryly.

Torquil took Brooks's vacated seat. "Are you all right?" they asked Silas.

Silas waved a hand to waylay their concerns. "I'm fine. It was almost a preferable reaction to what my magic has been doing, if I'm honest."

Torquil's mouth quirked and they turned to look over the debris. "I must say I'm surprised. You don't strike me as the theatrical type."

Councilmember Wyndham Wrenwhistle laughed and dropped his hand from where it still rested on Silas's shoulder. "Are you joking? We've all seen the belt."

Torquil chuckled a little before giving Silas an earnest look. "I'm truly sorry this has been so difficult."

"I promised you at your wedding that I would do whatever you needed. I aim to keep that promise."

Torquil smiled. "I do so like to be right about people. Do you need some rest before starting again? You can leave early if you'd like."

Silas shrugged. "I'll only spend the rest of the day worrying what else my magic is apt to do." He turned to Councilmember Roger Wrenwhistle and grinned at him. "But if tea is still an option, I won't say no to that."

The gentleman beamed in response and scuttled off to find an aide.

When the tea was delivered to Torquil's office, all three of the councilmembers sat with Silas and chatted as he drank it. By the time the pot was empty, he was on first name basis with all of them, had learned that Wyndham had the appalling taste of liking lavender in his tea, that Torquil had taken months to learn *how* they liked their tea before settling on cream and no sugar, and Roger had a bad habit of eating while working.

Silas quickly determined that all three of them had been working themselves to the bone the past month, trying to ensure the project went smoothly. Councilmember Roger Wrenwhistle had spent hours every day reading through all of the notes and compiling them with notes of his own. His husband, who apparently found London a strain on his magic, had been working hard to keep his magic sensing in check, and had been observing the pairs mundanely. He'd also been helping his husband by rewriting some of the findings. And Torquil had been busy checking on everyone, making sure each pair got along, completing reports for the rest of the Council to read, and handling the finances for the fae-humans' stay—apparently, they'd been paying for everyone's room, board, and entertainment personally.

Sitting and chatting with the three councilmembers as he drank his tea was the most relaxed Silas had seen any of them since the project began.

He and Wyndham returned to the large room to find the workspace had been cleaned of debris by an aide. Wyndham held up a stack of papers that he had brought from the office.

"With your permission, I'll read the notes we've compiled from your other partners. Unless you're eager to describe your magic again."

"By all means," Silas said, gesturing at the pile.

Wyndham smirked and turned to his notes. Silas took advantage of the opportunity to look over at the long table at the back of the room. Cricket had his head bent over his own notes. Miss Wilton-Reed was standing beside him. She bent over the table to pick up a jar, placing her hand on his back as she did so. The touch was so casual in its intimacy. Although Silas was hardly versed in the niceties of polite society, he suspected the lady was being more openly affectionate than what was considered technically proper.

He wondered if it was a calculated choice on her part, to more pointedly stake her claim, or if, like himself, she had less experience with the behavior of the *ton* than she liked to pretend. She slid her hand away and began to prepare her next spell. Cricket watched her for a moment and then glanced surreptitiously over at Silas. When their eyes met, Cricket smiled, blushed, and then quickly bent over his notes again.

Silas turned back to his new partner to find Wyndham watching him, amusement written all over his face. Silas quirked an eyebrow, daring him to comment.

"That answers two questions I had last night," the gentleman remarked before returning to his notes.

After a quarter of an hour, Wyndham pronounced himself ready to begin. "Don't bother about the rubric," he said as Silas reached for another sheet of spellpaper. "We already know you can do it." His grin widened as he said, "I'd like to see you make use of that belt of yours. In fact, I imagine we all would enjoy that spectacle."

Silas snorted, but wasn't about to argue. While Torquil had given him the ingredients he'd requested days ago, he'd yet to use the belt for anything other than confidence. He tugged his notebook out of his pocket and flipped open to a list he'd made. Then he began preparing one of the spells he'd worked on with his family. He felt Wyndham's magic while he was still preparing everything. His fingers nimbly pulled bottles out of pockets and flipped open snaps. He found himself tucking the pencil behind his ear as he was wont to do while working, licking the tip of it before scribbling down sigils and calculations. It felt good to be working like that again, natural, *right*.

Although Wyndham's magic eddied around him, the man was silent as he watched. Silas put up his hand to cast the spell and realized he'd been sensing all along as well and his magic had yet to object to Wyndham's presence. He allowed himself a small smile and then cast the spell.

This time, his magic cooperated. Wyndham's magic did not constrict, scrape, disturb, or agitate his own. It was nothing like Cricket's magic, which felt warm and strong and steady. Nor was it like his family's, which each reacted to Silas' magic in a unique way, although all safe and sure, familiar. But Wyndham's magic was pleasantly neutral. It did not empower his magic, but it didn't weaken it either.

After experiencing so many different ways for his magic to react poorly to someone else's, Silas was immensely grateful for neutral.

The paper he was using as a focus snapped straight in response to the spell and then went rigid. He couldn't help the grin that formed on his lips. Wyndham smiled in response.

"I don't have to ask if you're relieved by that."

Silas laughed. "I thought it would never happen."

Wyndham didn't reply, but Silas could tell he thought the same thing. He leaned forward and tapped the edge of the paper with the tip of his finger. "What did you do?"

"Fortifying spell. We use it a lot in our line of work."

Wyndham's eyes narrowed with interest as he picked up the paper, which was now stiff. He drummed his fingers lightly over the surface. "Fascinating," he murmured. "Show—"

"I take it that time went better," Torquil said from behind them.

They both turned to find Torquil and Roger watching from a safe distance.

"Much better," Silas said.

"Thank goodness," Roger breathed. "Now don't get Wyn started. I can tell by the look in his eye that he's about to have you cast another spell. He'll keep you here all night if you do that."

Wyndham rolled his eyes. "Nonsense." He drummed his fingers on the paper again before tossing it onto the table. "But perhaps we had better wait until tomorrow to do more. I'll go to my office to write the notes with Roger."

Silas laughed as Wyndham stood and left the table. He watched the two men leave the room and then he caught Torquil's eye. "Will they actually write notes in their office?"

Torquil chuckled. "Probably. Roger is much more private than I am in that regard." They strode away to check on some of the other pairs.

Silas stole another glance at Cricket and found the other man watching him. Cricket was smiling, apparently having caught a gist of the situation.

CHAPTER 34

KEELAN

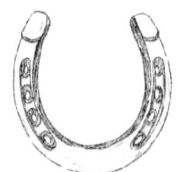

DINNER with his parents that evening was a routine affair. His mother did most of the talking, while Keelan and his father sat quietly and listened, offering practiced responses every now and again to let her know they were being attentive, even if they were not. Occasionally, she offered a bit of gossip that she'd heard, which piqued Keelan's interest, but the rest was long, drawn-out stories about what new success she'd found in some area of her own life.

Fortunately, Keelan had better things to occupy his mind. After the remarkably late start to the day and an afternoon spent exchanging glances with a certain not-so-stranger like a besotted schoolboy, he'd escaped to the Park for a ride and some fresh air. At least, as fresh as London could provide, which was perfectly fine by his standards. However, he'd discovered that even the comfort of his horse did not distract him from his fanciful thoughts. If anything, it had only spurred them on. He wondered if Mr. Rook-Worth would respond more favorably to the offer of a trot along the crushed stone paths together than his last attempt had gone.

Keelan was smiling to himself over the notion when his mother's mention of Miss Wilton-Reed pulled him back into focus. She gave him a cutting half-smirk that showed her disapproval at his lack of attention before she repeated herself.

"I asked if you enjoyed your evening with Miss Wilton-Reed at Vauxhall. It really is a wonderful place to get to know someone better. Such a lively environment to stimulate conversation."

"I would declare the opposite," Keelan muttered before he could think better of it. "Unless you are only interested in a particular way of knowing a person."

His mother powered on. "I would caution you to be mindful in the future. You never know who is watching in public spaces." Keelan's eyes widened as he stared at his half-empty plate. Had someone seen him in the alcove with Mr. Rook-Worth? "A little mouse told me today that you and Miss Wilton-Reed shared a rather passionate moment only partially hidden behind some decorative vines." She let out a satisfied chuckle. "Do think of the young lady's modesty, Keelan. She is half-human, after all."

He could not determine what forced the next words out of his mouth.

"I suppose I was simply caught up in the moment."

This earned him a more genuine smile from his mother.

"Not to worry," she soothed. "Soon you will be free to take her into your arms as often as you'd like."

Keelan asked to be excused after that. He wished his parents a good night and managed to make it to his bedroom before he let out a strangled sob against the serrated sawing of his magic in his chest. Of course he knew what was coming, but to hear his mother speak it so openly was nearly the worst thing he could imagine. Embracing Miss Wilton-Reed had felt…empty. To imagine a lifetime of that was well and truly dreadful.

He went to his window and forced it open, bracing his hands on the sill as he leaned out, drawing in lungfuls of air to try and calm his erratic breathing. He let his magic loose and closed his eyes against the breeze that picked up around him, cooling his skin where it had flushed hot with panic.

With a final, slow exhale, he opened his eyes again, coming into focus on the street below. It was mostly empty given the late hour; only a lone buggy and a handful of people taking their post-supper stroll. He watched them for a moment. Their voices carried a bit, caught between the tall rows of townhouses on each side, and though he could not make out what they were saying, he could tell by the laughter that it was a light, casual conversation had by all.

Maybe that was what he needed. A walk would give him an excuse to get out of the house for a while rather than stay in his room and continue circling over his troubles. He really was in no shape to call on Emrys or anyone else, especially at such a time of day. Keelan pulled himself back inside the window so he could shut it. A walk, he decided, was the perfect solution. It would give him time to think of something else. It would give him time to…think.

He did not want to think. Thoughts only led to worries, and he wanted no more of those for the evening. What he needed was a distraction. He needed to clear his mind completely of his imminent engagement, his meddlesome mother, of everything. And after Mr. Rook-Worth's advantageous offer, he knew exactly where to find it.

With one hand on his hip, Keelan grabbed the back of his neck with the other as he stood in the middle of his room, slowly turning as he searched desperately for something to carry. It had to be small, nondescript, easy to create a story around. He decided on the easiest option: a book. He reached for the first one his hand came to on his shelf and tucked it under his arm without giving it a glance or a second thought.

It felt like the cleverest idea he'd had in some time, all the way up until he was standing on the front steps of the Pimpernel townhouse. A footman opened the door before he could change his mind and scurry away. He was led to a sitting room and watched as the flame of a single candle found its way to several more through a human spell, lighting the room that had already been darkened for the evening. He sat neatly in a chair with his book on his lap as he waited for the person he'd asked to call on.

"Mr. Cricket."

Keelan stood at the sound. It was not a question; not quite a greeting. His pulse quickened as he gave Mr. Rook-Worth a nod and a faint grin.

"Good evening, Mr. Rook-Worth."

The man had come into the room and stopped a short distance in front of him. Neither of them made a motion to sit. Keelan kept his voice quiet as he continued. "I apologize for the late hour. I realize you were probably already in bed." Mr. Rook-Worth's clothes were much the same as they always were, plain trousers and shirtsleeves rolled to his elbows, so it was hard to tell for certain.

"I was not," Mr. Rook-Worth said calmly, taking another step forward.

"Oh, well I…" Keelan swallowed. "I wanted to congratulate you on your success today. Wyndham is not exactly known for being cooperative, but I believe he's probably the most suited of all of us for working with human magic in any capacity. You should've seen the wedding spell he and Roger performed together. But he's very much like you in that he's not easily impressed, and your spell on the paper was splendid." He forced himself to stop talking.

"Thank you, Mr. Cricket." A smirk had formed on Mr. Rook-Worth's mouth. "You really did not need to come all this way to tell me, though." His eyes dipped to the book Keelan was holding. "I would have been just as happy to hear it tomorrow at the Council's chambers."

Keelan held the book up in his left hand, only just realizing how tight his grip on it had been.

"I brought you this," he blurted, completely ruining the plan he'd come up with on his walk over. Mr. Rook-Worth accepted the book and angled it toward one of the candles so he could read the cover.

"Children's fables?" he asked.

Keelan gasped sharply and reached for the book, reading the title for himself in the low light. He went hot all the way to his toes. Of *course* he selected the most embarrassing book on his shelf. He pressed the storybook from his childhood to his chest in a pitiful attempt to hide it and covered his face with his other hand for a moment before he met Mr. Rook-Worth's amused gaze.

"I came to see if I might be able to *return* what you *offered* me," he tried again. He waited as Mr. Rook-Worth searched his face, and then as the man's expression shifted just enough that Keelan knew he'd understood.

The air between them became thick with energy, compressing as

Mr. Rook-Worth closed the distance between them. Keelan lost his breath entirely as Mr. Rook-Worth's palm found his jaw, calloused fingers splayed across the side of his face, thumb pressed under his chin to lift it.

"Here?" he whispered.

Keelan's brows pinched as he glanced at the door. It was only partially closed, and he knew that the hallway would not be completely empty.

"The staff," Keelan whispered back. "They'll talk."

"Let them." Mr. Rook-Worth leaned in, but Keelan turned his head.

"Mr. Rook-Worth, I—"

"Silas," he breathed. "At least in moments like this."

"Silas," Keelan tried on a shuddering exhale. Saying his name was somehow a sensation all of its own, one that he felt slide directly between his legs.

The man's response was a chuckle deep in his chest. He used the way Keelan had turned his face to his advantage and placed his mouth against Keelan's ear. "You'd best get creative, then."

With a thin whimper, Keelan removed himself from Silas' grip and again found himself searching his surroundings for any good excuse he could find. He looked at the book still clutched in his hand. With any luck, most of the staff had been excused for the night. He strode to the door and opened it wider. The lone footman turned to give his full attention. Keelan looked down the hall in both directions to check that they were empty before he turned back to the young man.

"Please bring this to the room Mr. Rook-Worth is staying in." He held out the book expectantly. "Additionally, this room will need more candles. Several of them have burned to nothing." The man tried to peer over Keelan's shoulder to confirm this, but Keelan shifted in the doorway to block his view. "Also, if you'd be so kind as to check the kitchen for some lemon cake. I've had a sudden craving for it."

As soon as the footman turned away to follow his instructions, Keelan shut the door as silently as he could manage. He pressed his back against it with a heavy exhale, locking eyes with Silas. The moment they met in the middle of the room with a crushing kiss, Keelan set his magic loose on the candles, their flames blinking out as quickly as they'd been lit. Darkness settled around them.

"He looks a bit too eager for my liking," Keelan panted when they broke apart. "We won't have much time."

"I do not think we'll need it," Silas replied, his confidence in such a statement bolstered by the way he already had a hand pressed against Keelan's hardening length, working him through the fabric of his trousers.

Keelan huffed out a laugh, which came out more like a moan, and he wrapped his arms around Silas' shoulders as the man hoisted him up off his feet. The shock of being picked up was strangely arousing, but Keelan had little time to enjoy it before he'd been set down on the sideboard along the far wall.

No words were needed as their kisses continued, both hurrying to unfasten the other's trousers until they each had a firm grip and worked like their lives depended on it. Their bent knuckles brushed several times; the way Silas pressed close between Keelan's spread legs left little room to spare between them. Keelan kept his hand cradled against the back of Silas' head, using the touch to keep the man from leaning away. He wanted that mouth to stay exactly where it was, steadfastly against his own, tasting, biting, teasing.

Keelan did not wait for Silas' request this time. He reached out with his magic, wishing that his natural power alone was enough to somehow bring them even closer together. The answering satin stroke of Silas' sensing prompted the first coiling of pleasure within Keelan.

His touch had gone slack on the back of Silas' neck. It allowed the man to tilt his head enough that he could focus his attention at the base of Keelan's throat, where he'd used his free hand to tug the knot of Keelan's cravat out of the way. They both knew what Silas was doing with his mouth would leave a mark on his skin. It felt dangerous and exhilarating and Keelan did not want it to end, but his breath had started trembling as much as his body and soon he could not stop the inevitable.

Silas' name escaped him on a breathy whisper that went high and thin at the end. His hand slowed on himself until there was nothing left. He managed to find enough strength to press a deep kiss to Silas' mouth as the man followed close behind. They only allowed themselves a few moments of recovery, foreheads pressed together and breaths slowing, before they each made an attempt to get themselves presentable again.

When Keelan slid off the sideboard to his feet, he almost had to catch himself because his legs were so weak. He let out a ridiculous little laugh about it that he tried to hide by pressing the back of his hand against his lips. Silas grabbed him by the arm and tugged him close for one more kiss, which sent another raw streak of desire through Keelan as though he hadn't been sated not a minute before. The kiss lingered until there was the distinct sound of footsteps in the hallway and a knock at the door.

"Enjoy your cake, Mr. Rook-Worth," Keelan whispered before he opened the door and slipped past the footman holding an armful of fresh candlesticks and a plate.

CHAPTER 35

SILAS

Silas was not overly fond of lemon cake, but he would eat a slice of it every day if it meant getting a taste of Cricket too. The man fascinated him. He was so sweet and so flustered one moment and then bold and needy the next. The combination was tantalizing.

He sat in a chair and watched as the servant lit more candles in the room that already had plenty of lighting, resulting in an absurdly bright space. Silas didn't have the heart to stop the man though. He took a bite of lemon cake and thought about the way Cricket seemed to enjoy a little rough handling and tenderness in equal measure.

While Silas had experienced repeated intimacy with people before, it had never felt like this. It had always felt convenient and mutually beneficial. This felt urgent and heated and vital. It felt as though he had finally come to learn why he had bothered to travel to London in the first place. It felt like the answer to a question he hadn't known he'd been asking. He soldiered through another couple bites of cake and contemplated the strangeness of this new experience. He *liked* Cricket. He liked his innate gentleness, the sweetness of his character. He liked the way the man wore his emotions fully on his face. He liked the man's absolute inability to lie convincingly. He liked that after a single day,

Cricket had wanted to see him again. It was all so strikingly different from his own character.

As he was sitting alone and contemplating, he heard a light knock on the door and Mrs. Pimpernel strode in. She took one look around the room and then at Silas and gave a knowing grin before taking a seat opposite him.

"I don't recall Cook mentioning I had a cake in my kitchen. What kind is it?"

"Lemon."

"A favorite of yours?"

"Absolutely not."

"A favorite of your friend's then?"

He allowed a small smile. "I'm honestly not sure."

She chuckled. "My staff is well accustomed to fae habits. They are not easily shocked. But it was a clever errand."

"Do I want to know how you figured it out so quickly?"

"There are half a dozen more candles in here than normal, I've never seen you eat dessert in here alone after dinner, it's a peculiar time of day for you to even leave your room, and your cravat is mussed."

He leaned back in his seat. "Would you like the rest of the cake?"

She took it with a grin. "Plum cake is a particular favorite of mine, in case you want ideas for the next time."

"Duly noted."

"You seemed in a better mood at dinner than usual. I take it today was an improvement in more ways than one?"

He laughed at her frankness, although it no longer surprised him. "Yes. I have successfully run through almost all of the fae volunteers, so I am now paired with Wyndham Wrenwhistle. And I'm wishing it had happened sooner because my magic likes his much better than everyone else's."

She gave a thoughtful hum. "I think the only one of you who hasn't mentioned a new partner is Miss Wilton-Reed. Is that why you say *almost all?*"

He nodded.

"And how do you like young Wyndham?"

"I like him. He doesn't attempt to soften bad news. He's clever." He shrugged. "He's amusing."

"From you that praise is practically glowing. I've always found you can tell a lot about a person from how they perceive others. I knew my grandchild was a good and decent person before I even met them, after reading their paper for years."

"I think I formed a good opinion of them when they used their position to lift up others. Many would not."

"Many, including some in this house, still don't."

"But I suspect you knew that already," he countered, "based on those people's perceptions of others."

She grinned again and finished off the cake. "You know, it isn't uncommon for fae to continue affairs after they're married. I was more discreet than most, of course, what with my husband's temperament. So I learned that there's an antechamber at the back of the ballroom. It's meant as a refuge for those who need to sit in the quiet during a crowded party. And it's always unlocked." She stood and dusted cake crumbs off her skirt. "I trust you to make of that information as you will." Then she strolled out of the room.

Silas waited for the door to close before bursting out into laughter.

CHAPTER 36

KEELAN

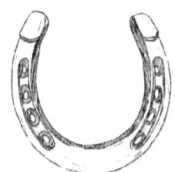

THE NEXT MORNING, Keelan kept his expression carefully neutral as Marten gave the oblong bruise at the base of his throat a long look. He politely declined the healing salve he was offered, but accepted his valet's suggestion of wearing a more elaborate cravat knot than one might expect for a workday to help cover his *injury* and avoid any unwanted questions.

Keelan finally allowed himself to smile when he was alone in his carriage. A steady rain was falling, but nothing could dampen the memory of his visit to the Pimpernel townhouse the night before. Mr. Rook-Worth—*Silas* had said something about keeping their activities a secret. Keelan had never kept a secret like that for himself before.

Of course, he supposed he'd technically been keeping the man a secret since the night of the wedding. He never expected to be adding new layers to it. He placed a gentle touch to the knot of his cravat. He never expected to have a physical representation to go with it, either.

Keelan had stared at the mark in his mirror for an absurdly long time, running his fingertips over it and remembering how it felt to have Silas' mouth on him until his breathing had become ragged all over again. In truth, he wanted to look at it more, but knowing it was there felt almost as good. Seeing the man who gave it to him would be even better.

When the fae-human volunteers arrived at the Council's chambers, Keelan was almost certain that he acted normally. Miss Wilton-Reed eyed him the moment she walked in, and he gave her a nod and a smile that, for the first time since the early days of the project, felt genuine. When Silas walked in behind the lady with his belt on, however, that warm feeling intensified more than he'd even expected.

"Good morning, Miss Wilton-Reed," he greeted his partner, though in his head he'd replaced her name with another. He held Silas' gaze for only a moment as the man walked by on his way to join Wyndham at the table in the corner, but somehow, it was enough.

"Have we traveled back in time?"

Keelan gave Miss Wilton-Reed a questioning look as they took their seats.

"Pardon?" he asked.

"You've not been this cheerful since the day this whole ordeal began."

"Oh." Keelan cleared his throat a bit and readjusted in his chair. "My apologies? I suppose I'm just feeling, er…well-rested this morning."

Miss Wilton-Reed responded with a reproving expression and then heaved a sigh that begged for someone to overhear and ask about. There were no flowers in her hair, but Keelan did notice the floral pattern on her dress looked oddly similar to the one he'd worn to Vaux-hall. When nobody else in the room paid her any mind, she continued on with Keelan as her captive audience.

"I had a horrible night. My father wrote to inform me that my grandfather on my mother's side is ill and they do not expect him to live much longer."

"I'm very sorry." Keelan felt a spark of hope. "Will you need to return home to say your farewells?"

Miss Wilton-Reed snorted. "No. He's a miserable old grump. He's been senile for years. He cannot even tell me apart from my sisters any longer." Her nose went up. "Fortunately, he and I shared a special bond before his mind failed him. I'm certain it will be reflected in the disbursement of his most valued possessions when the time comes."

Keelan blinked rapidly at the thought of caring more about material goods than the loss of a loved one. It came as no surprise that Miss Wilton-Reed was not sentimental, but he found it unsettling that she would be so brazen about such a sensitive topic with someone she hardly knew. Such things were discussed with family, or close friends.

A spouse.

Keelan realized at that moment that Miss Wilton-Reed was determined to see this through. If the impending demise of a close family member was not enough to force her to return home, there was likely nothing that would draw her away from their unspoken courtship.

Miss Wilton-Reed took in his fallen expression and smirked.

"Do not be concerned. We shall be perfectly comfortable in Bath with or without his benefaction. Now, why don't you go back to being sunny and tell me what we are working on today? I know how that thrills you."

Somewhat dazedly, Keelan picked up their copy of the rubric and let his eyes move over the words on the paper. He'd done it three times from top to bottom before he recognized that he was not actually reading the notes he had written in the blank spaces. He set the paper down and picked up one of the jars of ingredients instead, pleased that he'd started to memorize some of the spells and which materials Miss Wilton-Reed needed to perform them. He very nearly told her that she ought to use the dried blackberries to dye his cravat again since it had been so entertaining the first time, but then he remembered.

He remembered what was underneath the fabric, beneath the collar of his shirt. He remembered what had caused his good mood before Miss Wilton-Reed had swiftly ruined it. He remembered his father's advice.

Keelan could not control what Miss Wilton-Reed was planning. He likely would never understand his mother's reasoning behind what she thought a successful marriage looked like.

What had he told himself the night of the wedding, as he'd let go of his hopes for the future and followed Silas behind the stables? *Someday, but not tonight.* If he wanted to find the contentment his father had seen in him, he had to forget about what was to come. That was what Silas provided: simple, wonderful, temporary distraction. It was the only thing he could control, and it was only because he had no control over it at all.

He touched the knot of his cravat and welcomed his smile back.

FROM SILAS ROOK-WORTH TO BRIONY ROOK

19 May 1814

Dear Briony,

Perhaps my mood would improve if I did not receive countless letters from my family detailing how very sour it usually is.

As it happens, my mood *has* improved of late. I will spare you the sordid details as I am already weary from writing them out for Quince. But I can tell you that my visit to Vauxhall Gardens increased my enjoyment in the city greatly. You can ask Quince if you'd like more information about my interaction there.

Since I know you won't, I shall instead recount for you a description of the place. I am certain you would adore it. I confess that London has pleased me little, in part because I dislike all of the buildings everywhere. I vastly prefer the countryside. Give me a mile across a stretch of greenery over a half mile in London any day. Even Hyde Park, though it has its charms, is too manicured for my taste. I suppose one might say the same about Vauxhall, but you can tell that fae had charge of the gardens. The plant life is lush and vibrant. There is dimension to the flower beds. The leaves were healthy and the blossoms as merry as if it had been daytime.

Gravel paths cut through the gardens in a way as to not overly upset the plants. There are enough lanterns to provide visitors with a view of the path, but few enough to provide a sense of privacy. I'm sure Quince would have found it all very romantic. The Council reserved us a supper box and we ate some light sandwiches. They were tasty enough, but it was evident they were created for a crowd. I'm sure you would have found them wanting indeed. The punch is famously strong. I am grateful as ever for my ability to consume liquor. But many of our number were not so fortunate. Councilmember Roger Barnes was more relaxed than I've ever seen him. And even Mr. Finkle-Finch seemed to forget to apologize for everything, as is his wont. As for the punch itself, I suspect a great deal of care is put into making it very drinkable. The sweetness masked its hardness and it went down very easily. As such, multiple bowls were ordered over the course of the night, which is likely the point.

Aside from my own activities, I think my favorite part of the evening was the fairy lights—another feature that proved fae influence. They were everywhere without being gawdy, making the gardens feel serene and romantic. And since I'm saying that, you know it must have been the case. I can only imagine the number of people who have been captivated by the soft twinkling light and the fresh smell of the flowers, not to mention the overindulgence of punch, and given in to the delights of the infamous pleasure gardens.

I spent the last part of my evening in blissful silence, content to watch the fairy lights sparkle over the flowers. And before you ask, yes, of course my contentment was also rooted in other aspects of the night. Nevertheless, I daresay I would not mind another visit. That's saying something, considering there isn't a single place in London I have truly enjoyed since arriving.

I am glad to hear that you managed to keep the rabbits out of your vegetable patch. They never fail to cause you trouble this time of year.

Missing you greatly,
Silas

CHAPTER 37

SILAS

Silas had several reasons to be grateful that he was paired with Wyndham. Not only was it more comfortable for his magic and he got along with the man, but every time Wyndham caught Silas sneaking a glance at Cricket, he would chuckle and then move on. As Roger had warned, Wyndham was like a dog on a bone when it came to watching someone perform magic. Silas performed spell after spell all day, working harder than he had since he'd arrived in London. He found he didn't mind it; it was strangely gratifying to be around someone who found his magic fascinating.

As he had done the previous day, Wyndham would spool out his magic before Silas had even begun casting, magically observing the way Silas pulled out ingredients or wrote down sigils.

"Have you ever worked with raw materials before?" he asked while Silas was dusting spellpaper with ground nutmeg.

Silas cut him a glance. "No."

Wyndham gave a thoughtful hum. "We shall have to try that later."

Silas didn't bother pointing out that raw materials were notoriously dangerous. "I remember that being mentioned at the beginning of the project," he said at last. "After all of the rubric work is done."

"Do you intend to stay in London that long?" Wyndham asked,

hooking an elbow over the back of his chair. "I know you do not love the city. And I can't say I blame you."

Silas thought through his words before replying. "It has its charms."

Wyndham gave a snort. "I'm not sure I've ever heard Keelan described that way."

"Then I suppose you must not know him very well. Do you dislike London as well?"

"I do. But, as you put it, it has its charms. In my case, a husband who loves his work on the Council." He paused. "We'll be looking for a couple more members when this project is over, particularly a couple more fae-human members. Is that something you might be interested in?"

"Not in the least."

"Even if the city's charms entice you?"

Silas gave the man a steady look. "I think we both know he is not meant for me, much as he might wish to be."

Wyndham looked over Silas' shoulder at the long table. "More's the pity."

THAT EVENING, Silas found himself enjoying the company of his fellow fae-humans more than usual. He *did* actually like most of them—well, all of them with the exception of Miss Wilton-Reed. But weeks of hearing them chatter about how much fun they were having and how nice everyone was, not to mention how marvelous the city was, had been grating on his nerves. But for the second night in a row, he could actually participate in the discussion, providing his own descriptions of his work with Wyndham.

Thus he was in an unusually cheerful mood when he retired to his room for the evening. He sat down at his desk and began writing more letters to his family, particularly to his father, to describe how his work on the project had improved. He had just addressed it and moved on to start a letter to Quince, to hint that London had gotten *significantly* more enjoyable since he'd last written, when a footman knocked on the door.

"Beg your pardon, sir, but there is a gentleman wishing to see you."

Silas began putting his writing materials away and stood.

"He has been shown into the ballroom."

Silas blinked at him. "The ballroom?"

"Yes, sir. Her ladyship instructed that if your guest returned, he was to be brought there."

Silas grinned and went in search of the ballroom. He found Cricket standing awkwardly in the middle of the dimly lit room. His face transformed into pleasure when Silas walked in and closed the door behind him.

"I'm not sure why I was shown here instead of the sitting room but—"

"I do," Silas said, taking Cricket's hand and leading him to the back corner. He scooped up a candelabra on the way. The door to the antechamber was unlocked, as promised, and it featured a few comfortable looking settees and chairs. Silas set the candelabra on a nearby table and closed the door behind him.

"What is this?" Cricket said, spinning slowly to take in the space. "And how do you know about it?"

"My hostess understood the nature of your last visit and gave me some welcome advice for the future." He slid his arm around Cricket's trim waist and tugged him close. "And apparently she has instructed her staff to show you to the ballroom when you visit."

Cricket's forehead crinkled adorably. "She knows it's me?"

"No. And she doesn't seem to care who visits me. Although I wouldn't be surprised if she had guessed. She's...insightful."

Cricket's lips bunched to the side as he pondered this. Silas leaned forward and kissed the side of his mouth. This seemed to drag Cricket out of his thoughtful state. He promptly wrapped his arms around Silas' neck and kissed him back. In the privacy of the closed room, they were free to take their time and the kiss was languid and sweet, so different from the previous evening's rushed affair, but no less exciting. Silas pulled away and began unbuttoning Cricket's jacket.

"Wait." The other man put a hand on his wrist.

Silas raised his eyebrows and waited.

Cricket blushed. "Don't misunderstand me. This is why I came but…er…well I had thought that perhaps instead…"

"I'm listening," Silas said with a grin.

Cricket's blush deepened. "I thought I might reciprocate from…that is…with Vauxhall."

Silas lightly pinched Cricket's chin between his thumb and fore-finger and kissed him softly. "I'd like that. Do you always get this shy with intimacy?"

Cricket made an irritated sound at the back of his throat. "Of course not. But I don't usually discuss things this often and I…well…my partners are typically less…er…forward about things."

Silas moved his thumb to stroke along the underside of Cricket's jaw. "Is there anything I'm doing that you'd like me to do differently?"

"No," Cricket choked out.

Silas chuckled and kissed him again. "Come here." He pulled Cricket over to a settee covered in a white cloth and leaned back against the arm rest, guiding the other man on top of him. Cricket nestled comfortably over his chest and kissed him and then began to tentatively return the favor of the previous night, kissing down Silas' cheek, jaw, and neck. It did not have the same bruising effect that Silas' work had, but he didn't mind. Cricket's gentle handling suited him.

Then Cricket slid down between Silas' legs and began unbuttoning his trousers. He glanced up at Silas. "Anything particular I should keep in mind?"

Silas smiled and rubbed Cricket's cheek with the backs of his fingers. "No," he said softly. He threaded his other hand in Cricket's hair and gave a small tug. "Is this all right?"

Cricket gave a small gasp and then nodded quickly. "Yes," he said, his voice breathy.

Silas caressed his cheek again. "Go ahead."

It did not take long to realize that Cricket had not done this very much, although it was equally evident that he was doing his best. Silas remembered the man's nervousness the night in the cart and his admission that it had been a long time since he'd been on that side of things. So Silas kept lightly stroking his cheek and murmuring little words of encouragement. It was intoxicating to see the effects as Cricket grew bolder and to hear the little moans that escaped him when Silas's grip on his hair tightened due to his own pleasure.

When Silas' pleasure crested, Cricket swallowed greedily before Silas hauled him back to his chest and kissed him deeply, licking the man's lips clean.

"Was that all right?" Cricket breathed.

Silas nosed across Cricket's neck. "I think you tasted the evidence that it was." He nipped under the edge of the man's cravat, which had been tied higher than usual.

"My valet's going to think I'm doing myself an injury," he said with a chuckle. "He was quite concerned by the bruise this morning."

Silas hummed against his skin. "I don't think much of your past lovers if that's the first time you've ever had to worry about such a thing." He slipped his hand between them and began fiddling with Cricket's trouser buttons. "Should we take care of you next?"

"Well, I had thought since this was a reciprocation that I...wouldn't tonight."

Silas tilted his head to nibbled at Cricket's jaw. "Does that mean you'll be meeting me in the ballroom tomorrow night, aching and needy? I think I like the sound of that."

Cricket whimpered. "Yes?"

Silas kissed him again, relishing the way Cricket melted against him. Finally, the other man sighed. "I should probably return home."

"I'll see you tomorrow," Silas said, the hint of promise in his tone.

CHAPTER 38

KEELAN

Tomorrow could not have come soon enough, nor the next day, or the day after that. Keelan fell into a routine with Silas that felt entirely nonsensical, but in truth, it was the only thing getting him through the long hours of working with Miss Wilton-Reed. His afternoons were full of showy magic and cutting comments, but his nights brought a level of gratification that he'd never experienced before.

Similarly, Keelan had also discovered an entirely new variety of ways to pleasure—and *be* pleasured—than he ever knew possible. After Silas' positive reaction to Keelan's first time taking another man in his mouth, he'd been more than willing to try other things that Silas seemed to like. At times it had been difficult to let go of his reservations, but the man's constant reassurance and murmured words of encouragement left Keelan wanting more.

It was only when they'd discovered that someone had replaced the white sheet over the settee in the private room they'd been using that Keelan paused and gave serious thought to their behavior. He'd turned his face against Silas' shoulder to stifle his laughter.

"Stars above," he said quietly, "have we really done so much that someone felt the need to refresh our linens?"

Keelan could hear the grin in the other man's voice when he replied, "It was getting rather stiff in the middle."

Keelan used his hand on the back of Silas' head to pull him down for a kiss. It was a reflection of how he felt, and how he suspected that Silas felt too: sated and breathless and thoroughly spent. But one kiss turned into another, and soon Keelan found one strong hand pressed to the middle of his back and another squeezing his backside. He tried to take a step closer to the settee, but Silas only held him tighter.

"Perhaps we should find another place for tonight," Silas told him.

There was a roughness to his voice that Keelan found very difficult to argue with. "What did you have in mind? We do not have to worry here."

There was a silence between them that Keelan thought nothing of at first as he waited for Silas to kiss him again. When he did not, Keelan opened his eyes and found Silas staring back at him with an intensity that would've been startling if it were not for the hand still on his back-side and the other that had come up to the side of his face. Silas's thumb plucked lightly at his bottom lip.

"You never have to worry with me, Cricket."

A surge of warmth bloomed in Keelan's chest at the words, churning with his magic in a way that all but stole his breath. He'd sought the man out again and again for exactly that reason, wishing to forget his troubles for a short while. But the gentle conviction in his statement seemed to go beyond a simple promise of mutually-beneficial stress relief. It was dangerously close to a promise of security, of protection, of *more*.

Before Keelan could give any more time to this line of thought, Silas closed the distance for another kiss. Then, in one swift motion, he picked Keelan up again. Keelan let out a gasp of surprise as he landed mostly over Silas' shoulder.

"What are you doing?" he asked in a harsh whisper.

"Showing you what I had in mind," Silas answered. He reached for the door that led out into the ballroom and paused with a grip on the knob. "Be as loud or as quiet as you want, it makes no difference to me."

With one arm and hand squeezed tightly around Silas' shoulders,

Keelan pressed his other hand over his own mouth and allowed himself to be carried through the empty ballroom, into the hallway, up the stairs, and all the way to Silas' room. He loosened his grip when he thought Silas was going to return him to his feet, but instead the man turned and placed one knee on the bed, leaning into Keelan as they both collapsed onto the mattress.

"I'll have you here tonight, if that's most agreeable."

Those two words brought Keelan right back to the night of the wedding. He thought of the shame he'd felt as he said them to Silas then, and how different it felt hearing him say them now as he pressed Keelan into the pillows. There was a brush of magic; a silent request. Silas was asking for the opportunity to fix what he had done, and Keelan wanted to give it to him more than anything he'd ever wanted before.

"Most agreeable," Keelan breathed as he brought his hands to the sides of Silas' face and kissed him hard.

The moment was not unlike their first time in the back of the horse cart as their clothes were removed in a rush of desperate fingers and popped buttons. The loss of nearly every item was marked with a kiss or a scraping of teeth against skin, and it wasn't until Silas gave a final tug on Keelan's trousers that he realized it was the first time they were completely bare together.

"Let me see you." Keelan's voice trembled nearly as much as his body did in the anticipation of finally taking in every part of the man who had captured his attention the moment they'd met. There was no time for candles. Keelan snapped his fingers and fairy lights burst to life over their heads. It had always been one of the easiest parts of his magic to call on, but the intensity of the moment had created several dozen of them all at once.

Keelan shifted his head against the pillows, ready to offer an apology for being overzealous, but stopped himself when he noticed the way Silas was staring up at the lights in awe.

Before he could ask him about it, Silas turned that intense focus on Keelan again, and the details of what came after became rather difficult to remember. Hot breath, oiled fingers, long kisses pressed against damp skin. Tentative caresses of magic that quickly became too intense to ignore.

When Keelan had finally recovered enough to open his eyes, it was to watch Silas slide his tongue along his stomach and chest to clear away what they'd both spent. Despite his intense urge to shy away from such a sensual display at first, Keelan had little choice but to watch it happen; Silas had his hands on Keelan's hips and was still pressing him down into the mussed sheets. So he simply allowed his face to burn, abashed and aroused in equal parts.

Many of the fairy lights had faded or floated away, but enough of them remained that Keelan could see the moment Silas raised his dark eyes and held his gaze as he finished his last few licks. It sent a shiver through him intense enough to force out a faint whimper.

Keelan was at a loss for what to say. They'd not spent much time talking these past nights, but now that Keelan wished to, words failed him. He rolled onto his side when Silas settled next to him against the pillows and studied the man's profile in the fading light. He wanted to trace a fingertip over the curves of his nose and lips, but he lacked the energy to lift his hand to do it. A quiet voice in the back of his mind told him it would be very nice to close his eyes and rest there for a while.

"I can take my book of fables home now," he finally managed.

Silas chuckled in the darkness that had settled over them.

"I was hoping to keep it a while longer. Some of them are quite interesting."

Keelan rolled more so that he could press his grin into the pillow. Silas' arm came around his waist and pulled him closer. Keelan relaxed into the embrace with ease. His arms slipped beneath the pillow he was using and he let out a slow, contented sigh.

"Very well," he agreed, turning his face into the space between them. "You can return it when you are done. My father gave me that book."

"I noticed the inscription inside the front cover," Silas said. Keelan's brows went up, surprised that he'd actually been looking at it. "Is it in another language, or am I really so uneducated as a man from the country?"

"It's French," Keelan told him with a little laugh.

Silas made a curious sound. "Can you speak it?"

"Not as well as I used to," Keelan confessed.

There was a lull in the conversation that nearly let Keelan fall asleep.

"What does it say?"

Keelan drew in a drowsy breath. "Hm?"

"The note your father wrote in the book. What does it say?"

"I cannot recall. Something a parent would say to their child."

The arm around Keelan's waist disappeared, but he managed not to voice his protest over it. When the weight on the bed next to him shifted, he forced his eyes open. He knew he really ought to get dressed.

Suddenly there was a light from a candle, and Silas was holding the book open to the inside cover in front of Keelan's face. Keelan squinted at the book and then up at Silas before he shifted so his back was against the pillow, taking the book and reading over the words his father had written in his slanted, swirling script over thirty years before.

His cheeks went warm at the thought of reading them aloud, but Silas was watching him so intently that he felt he had no choice.

"*Keelan,*" he read, "*rien n'est petit dans l'amour. Papa.*"

Silas waited.

"It means nothing is small in love," Keelan mumbled. "My father is…he finds beauty in things very easily. And in simple things most of all."

He closed the book and handed it back to Silas so that he could get out of the bed and find his clothes where they had landed on the floor. He dressed with his back to the man because he still had not said anything, and Keelan wasn't sure what to make of his silence. It certainly wasn't the done thing to speak of love with rendezvous partners, but then, nothing about their encounters felt quite like anything he'd ever shared with another.

When he finally turned around again, he huffed out a laugh.

Silas was very clearly asleep with the book on his chest. Keelan took a moment to admire the way his serious brow had relaxed, fighting the sudden urge to place a departing kiss just above it. He sent a flick of magic into the air to snuff out the candle instead, and then left as quietly as he could, hopeful that the rest of the house was sleeping, too.

CHAPTER 39

SILAS

Silas woke up to an empty bed and Cricket's book on his chest. He lay in the quiet for a long moment, staring at the space where Cricket had lain the night before, remembering how his voice had shaken when he'd asked to see Silas, how he'd stared in wonder as Silas licked up the mess on his stomach, how he had hidden his smile into the pillows, and the way he'd looked drowsy and content after all of their activity. Silas realized, alarmingly, that he very much enjoyed seeing Cricket with a sleepy smile on his face.

He opened the book on his chest and read over the inscription, hearing Cricket's voice again. The man had said he didn't speak French very well, but Silas privately thought it was one of the single most sensual things he'd ever heard, especially with his voice raspy from pleasure and slurred from fatigue. The way Cricket's cheeks had pinked before reading it had made it even more enjoyable.

Silas sighed and placed the book beside him on the bed. The truth was, he was getting far too accustomed to having Cricket in his arms. Cricket's lips had become a taste he didn't know if he could do without. He rubbed his face and got out of bed. His body ached pleasantly from too much activity in too little time. He smiled to himself, knowing perfectly well that he'd accept the hardship easily if it meant having as much time as possible with his favorite person in London.

When he arrived in the breakfast room, he found Miss Wilton-Reed in a very fine mood.

"From what I saw of the Crickets' dining room," she was saying, "I believe my mauve dress with the white rosettes will go best."

"Oh, that would look marvelous!" Miss Gloucester-Stone gushed. "Will it be an elegant dinner, do you think?"

"I imagine so, considering the occasion."

Silas' pleasant thoughts about Cricket soured instantly.

"Do you usually try to match the dining room?" Mr. Finkle-Finch asked tentatively.

Miss Wilton-Reed gave him a condescending smile. "This is an important evening for me. I must look my best. I am sure Keelan will not notice, but his mother certainly will. And besides, it will be good for him to get a taste of what will be expected of him in Bath. I will permit no less than perfection when it comes to his appearance." She smiled and took a sip of tea.

Silas felt a lurch in his stomach at the sound of Cricket's name on her lips. He was secretly relieved he'd never called the man by his first name. It was nice to have one thing the woman couldn't steal.

Miss Wilton-Reed spent the rest of the meal monologuing about her outfit choices and whether the Crickets would serve jellied eel, which was apparently a favorite of hers. Silas bore through it as best he could. It was a relief when they were finally ready to leave for the Council chambers.

Cricket was there already, as was his wont. Silas had come to look forward to seeing Cricket's face light up at the sight of him. He felt a pang at the thought of how miserable the man would likely look the following morning. He forced a smile, allowing thoughts of the previous night to turn the expression genuine. Cricket greeted his partner with his usual formal gallantry. Silas could tell Miss Wilton-Reed did not disclose her evening plans to him because Cricket's attitude only dimmed as much as it usually did in her presence.

Wyndham was waiting at their table, watching Silas approach with an amused expression on his face. "You really are painfully obvious, you know."

Silas shrugged.

"I must admit I almost appreciate it," Wyndham went on, flipping through his notes. "In London, people tend to keep their flirtations secretive. Unless they're engaged, of course."

"Maybe you should inform Miss Wilton-Reed that," Silas remarked. They both turned to the long table, where Miss Wilton-Reed was leaning over her partner's shoulder to critique his notes. "With her, that's practically seduction," he added.

Wyndham let out a long sigh. "Keelan Cricket has never been a close friend of mine. But I must confess I pity him in this instance." He tapped his notes against his knee to straighten them. "Do you wish to keep discussing your torrid love affair or do you want to get started?"

Silas rolled his eyes.

"As I suspected. Now, what would you say to starting our work on raw materials earlier than planned?"

"I wouldn't mind it."

"Good. It will be a change from the way we've been doing things, but I'm quite satisfied with what I've seen. I think I have a good understanding of your magic. You've shown us everything we need to know about the rubric. I anticipated you being amenable, so I worked with Roger last night and we came up with a plan." He pulled a sheet of paper out of the stack and passed it over.

The paper had a list of ingredients with possible spells under each. There was also a small checklist at the bottom with the words, *Observe Roger, Observe Torquil, Observe Silas*. Silas looked up at Wyndham when he was done.

"As you can likely tell, this would involve something of a group effort," Wyndham explained. "We'd go at it two at a time with you, so one person can remain focused on the rest of the group. Although frankly, the rest of the group has been very cautious in the way they've approached the rubric, so their progress has been much slower." He leaned forward and tapped the side of the paper. "You can select whichever spell you think you'd be most comfortable with. We took care to select spells that are the least volatile. Roger will show you what it looks like when he performs those spells—he'll do them first with treated ingredients and then again with raw ingredients. That way you can see the difference. Then we'll do the same with Torquil. Their magic is, obviously, very different from Roger's. It's more similar to yours but not quite the same, so we'd like for you to get a feel for the difference in their casting with different materials."

"And then I'll perform the same spells with both sets of ingredients?"

"Exactly. You see, with Roger, the raw materials give his magic a significant boost in power. Torquil's spells are rather…quiet with treated materials. But their spells reach a level comparable to a high-ranking human or fae when they use raw materials. Your magic is an intriguing mix of both, I find—your initial power is around what Roger's is, but you use a blend of styles the way Torquil does. So I'd like to see how the raw materials impact your magic."

Silas hummed in response. It was a heady feeling to have gone from being behind the rest of the group to suddenly being ahead of them. He allowed a small smile at the thought of what Miss Wilton-Reed would say if she knew.

Wyndham, meanwhile, had turned in his chair to gesture at an aide. The aide left the room and promptly returned with a small stack of books. Wyndham placed a hand on top of the stack. "I thought today we might look over the spells in more depth so that you can decide which you prefer for the first casting. This sort of experiment can be dangerous—although, of course, we'll be safeguarding against the danger as much as possible—but I'd like you to go into it as confident as possible, with a spell you feel good about."

Silas nodded and looked over the list again.

"If it helps," Wyndham went on, "I took the liberty of marking all the ingredients that could easily be stowed in that belt of yours."

Silas laughed. "I appreciate the forethought."

"You *do* work better with it."

"Are you sure you're not just saying that because you enjoy watching me?"

Wyndham smirked. "That's certainly not a hardship. But, no, you're more at ease when you can rely on your belt. You don't even look before pulling out ingredients; you have everything mapped out mentally. You work more quickly, more steadily, with far less hesitation. I'd like to replicate that as best I can."

Silas tapped the paper. "Shade spells then. But not willow leaf. Oak leaf or holly leaf will fit into one of my pockets easily enough. And I've used the spell fairly often in my work."

"Excellent. Do you mind if Roger joins us while we prepare? He can go over the sigils he uses most to counterbalance the raw power."

"Of course I don't mind. Just keep the besotted looks to a minimum, if you please."

"You're one to talk."

CHAPTER 40

KEELAN

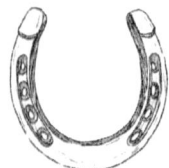

NOTHING COULD DIMINISH Keelan's mood as he spent another day working through the rubric with Miss Wilton-Reed. He'd never liked the taste of sparkling wine, but he felt as though he'd consumed an entire bottle of it as he watched her perform another motion spell. He could feel the tiny bubbles fizzling in his stomach. The thoughts in his head were a bit distant. His body was relaxed, although some movements created a jolt of sensation, reminding him of all the ways he'd been touched and used and satisfied.

Keelan grinned as Miss Wilton-Reed scolded him and pinched dog hairs off his coat sleeve. He listened as she talked about the way her magic was so much more impressive when she was not forced to work under such conditions. He offered no apology when she demanded that he bring his focus back to their table after a slight commotion had drawn his attention to the corner of the room. All three of the councilmembers had gathered around the table Silas and Wyndham were using before Torquil had resumed making their rounds.

"What do you suppose they're talking about?" Keelan asked.

Wyndham appeared to be listening as Roger was pointing to various pages in a book. The man had grown rather excited; his frown of focus had become a broad smile as he spoke. Silas' expression had not changed, but it was clear from the energy that had filled the air in that part of the room that the conversation was going well.

"How should I know?" Miss Wilton-Reed's moody response finally made Keelan turn back around in his chair. "Probably about what a failure Mr. Rook-Worth has been. Those books look awfully similar to the ones I used as a child. Perhaps they are giving him a lesson on the basics to see if they can salvage what little time they have left with him."

Keelan did not want to think about time.

"It's not a competition, you know." His voice was soft as he collected a new sheet of paper to take notes while she measured out the ingredients for what he thought was similar to one of the first spells she'd shown him. "You're all allowed to be good at this in your own ways."

Miss Wilton-Reed gave a sharp, short laugh at that.

"Mediocrity is not the way to get what you want in life."

Keelan's brows pinched as he studied the lady beside him. Small white flowers he did not know the name of had been woven into the style of her hair. They remained the only contrast to her stern personality. Her nose was small and slightly rounded; her mouth and chin were much the same. If the delicate points of her ears were more pronounced like those of a true fae, she would look very much like…his mother.

Despite this new realization, Keelan managed to not let it haunt him all the way up to the conclusion of their session. As he turned his head to try and catch a final glimpse of Silas before he left, Miss Wilton-Reed stopped him with her hand on his cheek, holding his face so that she could look directly at him.

"I recognize your preference for keeping our courtship formal, especially after what happened at Vauxhall last week. I find it rather adorable. But tonight, you *will* refer to me as Melisande in front of your parents. I wish for them to see that we are, in fact, very happy together." A small grin formed on her lips and she stroked her thumb against his cheek in an affectionate way. "Everyone agrees that we make a splendid match. Your mother thinks so most of all." There was a slight shift in her expression. "You do aim to please her, don't you?"

Somewhat bewildered, Keelan watched as she gathered her things and left the room.

"Tonight?" he asked weakly.

WITHOUT HIS KNOWLEDGE, Keelan's mother had invited Miss Wilton-Reed to a private family dinner at their home. The places at the table had been set with more care than usual, and they'd been served more food than four people could ever hope to consume in one night. Keelan's father seemed to agree. After giving the spread a small frown, he'd been sliding small bites of meat and cheese under the table to the two eager mouths waiting below. Keelan privately wished they would move over and make room for him to join them.

"It's turned out to be a marvelous partnership between us," their guest was saying, her charm thicker than Keelan had ever seen it before. "Truly splendid."

"The other members of the Council and I were quite doubtful when the project was first suggested." His mother paused to sip her wine. "It has come at an outrageous cost, keeping each of you supplied with a place to stay, all of your meals, and of course an unlimited supply of materials. I never realized human magic required so much."

Keelan and his father met eyes across the table. Such a statement was odd for anyone who had been around human magic before, but it seemed impossible coming from someone who had sat on the Council for Fae & Human Magical Relations for decades. Keelan could not claim to know anything about his mother's work. There was proof to show that the Council had done important things for both sides of society. He just wasn't sure how much of it his mother had actually helped with.

"I do hope your opinion has changed since then." Miss Wilton-Reed flashed a smile at Keelan before taking a practiced nibble of her poached mackerel. She followed it almost immediately with a press of her napkin to her lips, which she then returned to her lap as gracefully as one could manage. Keelan had never wanted to roll his eyes at something more than the act she was putting on.

At the same time, he wondered if perhaps it was not an act at all. Was this really how she behaved? Thanks to his mother's position, he'd spent his entire life existing in the world of proper etiquette and dinner parties, important social connections and extravagant balls. He had spent time with all kinds of people who held themselves to the level of personal excellence that London society demanded. Rarely, though, had he spent time with someone enough to know them well. Was it all pretense? Or had he managed to be paired with one of the few people who made it seem terrifyingly easy to hide who they really were?

"For the most part, it has not," his mother said with a sneer. "I will need to see more solid proof to know that all of the expense and inconvenience has been worth it." She paused to look between Miss Wilton-Reed and Keelan several times, a slight grin curving her lips. "However, since it appears to have been fruitful in at least one way, I cannot consider it a complete failure."

Miss Wilton-Reed gave a coy giggle at that. Her hand found Keelan's arm, and he somehow found the strength to not pull away from her touch. Instead, he used his other hand to reach for his wine. It was gone in a few swallows.

"Your mother and I have been discussing what shall come next," Miss Wilton-Reed said as she returned to her meal. "We feel it's best to wait until the project is over before we make any formal announcements. That will allow for ample planning time. I should hate to be distracted with work while also trying to enjoy the excitement of the celebrations."

Keelan felt his magic wilt in his chest. "Celebrations," he echoed faintly.

"Naturally, we can host an engagement party for you here in London," his mother added. "But it makes the most sense for the ceremony to take place in Bath with Melisande's family."

Keelan's attention snapped up at that. "So you and father will not attend."

His mother laughed blithely. "I suppose I could make the journey if you really wanted me to. We both know your father's answer."

Keelan had never seen a more pleading, hurt look on his father's face as he stared at his wife in disbelief. It had been years since the man had ventured out into society for an event or any other reason. He had only attended his sister's wedding several years prior because it had been at their estate in the country. Keelan's heart ached when his father met his gaze, knowing the war of emotions he must've been feeling over this announcement.

His father would not be there. His mother did not *want* to be there.

Was he truly about to be claimed as a prize, carted away to a place he'd never been before, to stand in front of a room full of strangers and marry a person who would never love him?

He tried to breathe through the pain of his magic in his chest.

Emrys would be there, if he asked. He was certain of it. Maybe even Torquil would come and offer some support. Newly married couples traveled to foreign places all the time and enjoyed extended stays with friends and family. Perhaps they would be able to visit for a month or two and allow him to show them around his new home.

Emotion prickled at the back of Keelan's eyes so forcefully that his eyelashes fluttered. He bit his lip hard and lifted his focus to the ceiling, blinking the feeling away.

Miss Wilton-Reed did not seem to notice.

"My family participates in the human tradition of reading the banns, so we will have several weeks to prepare for the wedding. I do not expect we will require more time than that. I have never seen the point in a long engagement."

"That's because a long engagement is for getting to know your betrothed," Keelan said, his throat working after as he continued to fight back his emotions. His jaw was tight when he looked at his mother. "Are we finished here?"

Keelan wished he hadn't asked. The four of them got up from the table under his mother's direction and followed her to the room she called her study, though Keelan wasn't quite sure what she actually used it for. Miss Wilton-Reed had her hand wrapped around the inside of his elbow despite the fact that he hadn't offered his arm. He imagined it was similar to what the weight of a shackle might feel like. After being directed to sit on the sofa near the fireplace, Keelan waited for what he knew was coming.

It happened without preamble. There were hardly any words

exchanged at all. His mother explained that she was graciously allowing Miss Wilton-Reed to make use of the ring until they left for Bath, after which she had promised to present Keelan with an heirloom piece that belonged to her family.

In fae tradition, the exchange of rings often did not happen until the ceremony, particularly between those who were not heir to the family name. He'd spent countless nights dreaming of what engagement gift he might present to his beloved when the time came, or be presented when his suitor could no longer hold back their affections. It could be anything from an impossibly romantic gesture made in public to something private and sweet, but regardless, it was supposed to be meaningful.

Keelan watched as Miss Wilton-Reed placed the thin band on his finger. It was ill-fitting, only adding to the wrongness of it. There were no words of congratulations; no expressions of joy from any of them in the room.

And then it was done.

CHAPTER 41

SILAS

SILAS WAS NOT sure whether or not to expect Cricket again that night. If Miss Wilton-Reed spoke truth—and there was no reason that he knew of why she wouldn't—then the couple was in the process of being engaged that very evening. Perhaps that very moment. Still, he wanted to be prepared. He instructed one of the footmen that if his guest returned, to bring him up to Silas' room. Then he leaned against the pillows on his bed and continued reading through Cricket's silly little book of children's fables.

He didn't entirely know why he was actually reading the book. Especially when he was well aware the man hadn't intended for him to hold onto it. But the knowledge that their time together was limited made him greedy for anything he could possibly learn about Cricket. That meant withstanding Wyndham's teasing as he stole glances across the room, memorizing the way Cricket's shoulder set when he was tense, or relaxed when he was at ease. And it meant tasting every inch of the man he was in bed with him, savoring every groan and muffled curse. And it meant reading through the stories that Cricket had likely read as a child, taking note of which pages were slightly rumpled from frequent use, where the spine cracked from multiple readings, and revisiting the inscription. It was easy to imagine Cricket as a child, just as sweet and gentle as he was now.

He heard footsteps on the hallway outside and looked up, still and alert. When the steps were accompanied by the swooshing of a skirt, he closed the book and settled back against the pillows. Miss Wilton-Reed had returned, which meant that Cricket was now engaged. Silas drummed his fingers on the book cover. Would that mean an end to their evenings together? He hoped not. Selfishly, he wanted as much of Cricket as he could get. But he also wanted to lavish the man with as much care and attention as he could, before he was married to such an arrogant and self-centered creature. Unless Cricket found lovers after marriage, Silas was fairly sure he was the last person who would prioritize his own pleasure.

Without meaning to, he began imagining how he would treat Cricket if he had forever. There would be less rushing, less urgency; he would take his time. He would learn everything about the man's body: what made him gasp, what made him moan, what made him shudder. He wondered if Cricket's voice was as soft and slurred when he woke in the morning as it was before falling asleep.

And because he was clearly a glutton for punishment, he wondered what Cricket would think of his family, and what they would think of him. He could readily imagine how his mother would spoil him with biscuits from the kitchen, even as she smacked her own son's hand away from the tray of cooling treats. He imagined the way his siblings would tease them both, how Cricket would blush in response. He sighed and closed his eyes. He had never once imagined another person entering his life in such a way; how frustrating that the first time he did, it was with a man who had already been promised away.

There was a soft knocking on his door. He slid off the bed and went to answer it, opening it to reveal Cricket. The man looked thoroughly miserable. His eyes were puffy, his shoulders slumped, and his hands curled into fists at his sides.

"I—" Cricket began. "She—" His voice cracked and he wrapped his arms around Silas' neck.

Silas locked eyes with the footman who had led Cricket upstairs. The servant swiftly shut the door. Silas slid one arm around Cricket's back and with the other, he scooped Cricket up into his arms and carried him to the bed. They were of a height, but Cricket curled himself against Silas, burying his face in his neck as he sobbed. Silas ran one hand through the man's soft hair, and the other stroked his hip as he gently rocked him where they sat. For a long time, they remained there, Silas holding Cricket as he wept.

Finally Cricket took a gasping breath. "I'm sorry," he whispered. "I didn't know what to do. I came straight here and—"

Silas hushed him softly. "You did the right thing, Cricket. I'm here. I've got you."

Cricket sniffed. "I'm afraid I won't be much good for—"

Silas clicked his tongue to stop the statement from being completed. "Did I not tell you my bed was open to you for as long as I was in London? This bed is good for a number of uses. I can't think of anything I'd rather do right now."

Silas felt a little huff against his neck. "That might be the kindest lie I've ever heard."

Silas lifted the other man's chin and pressed a kiss to his mouth. "I think you know I'm not the sort of man to offer empty pleasantries. I've never met anyone like you. I'm quite sure I never will." He kissed one damp cheek. "I'll gladly soak up every possible moment with you I can get. However that moment is spent makes little difference to me."

More tears slid down Cricket's cheeks and he leaned forward to kiss Silas with a desperation unlike anything they'd ever shared. Silas followed his lead, holding him steady, and letting Cricket take whatever he needed. Finally Cricket broke away and put his head back on Silas' shoulder.

"It's strange how I've known it was coming, yet I still felt wholly unprepared for it."

The same way I'll feel when I have to leave you, Silas thought. Instead he said, "Even bracing for a strike does not take away the pain you feel from it."

Cricket sighed. "I suppose you're right." He swallowed. "I'm in no condition to…do…anything. But can I stay here for a little while?"

Silas kissed his temple. "Stay as long as you like. Stay 'til morning. Would you be more comfortable with your clothes on or without?"

There was a small huff of laughter. "I think I'll feel more comfortable with *your* clothes off, that's certain."

Silas pivoted so that Cricket was laying on the bed and swiftly took care of both of their clothing. He was grateful that Cricket let him. Then he turned down the covers and they both slid into the sheets. Cricket laid his head on Silas' shoulder and Silas wrapped his arms around Cricket, holding him close. Cricket flicked a hand and the candles around the room extinguished. It felt so natural and so perfect that Silas felt an ache in his chest. Almost as if sensing this, Cricket laid a hand over the ache and nuzzled closer.

"The worst part," Cricket said softly, "is that I've always wanted to be married. I've wanted it since I was a child. And now—" He took another shuddery breath and Silas pulled him a little closer. "Now I will have it and it's the worst possible thing I could imagine. I'll be far from my friends, far from London, far from…everything." He sighed. "She doesn't love me. She never will. I don't think I'm capable of shutting myself up with hobbies the way my father does. I don't know what I shall do."

Silas took a long moment to think of the right response. "You bring a light with you wherever you go, Cricket. You bring out the best in people. You are gentle and kind. I haven't met a single person in this town who doesn't think well of you. She may not love anyone but herself, but I'm quite certain that everyone you meet will adore you." He kissed the top of Cricket's head. "You're going to bring that beautiful light of yours to Bath and everyone will wonder how she managed to find such a precious treasure."

A sob broke free again and Cricket turned his face against Silas' neck. Silas held him until the sobs subsided, until Cricket's breathing evened out and his weight settled with sleep. He continued to hold him until the morning sun peeked through the curtains.

TORQUIL'S TRIBUNE

Greetings, romantic readers,

Tongues continue to wag as Mrs. Pimpernel and Mrs. Wrenwhistle continue to be seen in public together. Some sources suggest the ladies are merely keeping each other company, now that they are both widowed and retired. However, canny observers have noted that friendship can sometimes be the most pure and steadfast form of love. This writer hopes the two friends have formed such a connection.

Mr. Sage Ravenwing and Mr. Benedict Brooks were seen promenading together in Hyde Park recently. Our readers may recall how the two gentlemen's names were linked as recently as last year. According to our sources, Mr. Brooks is no longer affiliated with the Council project, despite having participated previously. The pair was seen strolling arm in arm along the path and then, quite noticeably, no longer seen on the path at all. We suspect spring is in the air, in more ways than one. Could it be that the spark of love has been rekindled?

Your winsome writer,

Sal Bailey

CHAPTER 42

KEELAN

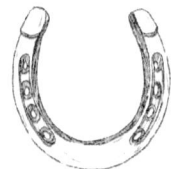

KEELAN WOKE EXACTLY as he'd fallen asleep, wrapped in Silas' arms with his face tucked in the curve of the man's neck. A kiss had been pressed to his shoulder. Silas' voice was gravelly as he told Keelan it was morning, but not yet time for the rest of the house to be awake. He understood the implication and silently appreciated the delicate way Silas had told him it was time to leave.

His eyes were swollen and the skin on his face was tight with dried tears. He tried not to think about how he must look as he hurried into his clothes. Indignity threatened at the corners of his mind as he considered his actions the night before. He'd helped himself to the bed of his half-human lover while the half-human lady he'd become engaged to only an hour before slept in a room just down the hall.

Never in his life had he imagined being in such a position. If they'd all been fae, he might not have worried so much. Fae kept lovers as naturally as plants reached for the sun, married or otherwise. But after learning the number of human traditions Miss Wilton-Reed's family observed, it felt far more serious. He was too inexperienced with the affairs of humans to know what repercussions he might now face if anyone discovered what he'd done.

As he straightened from putting on his shoes, a hand on his back made him jump. Keelan turned and lifted his chin just in time for Silas to give him another tender kiss, this time on his lips. When they broke apart, Keelan kept his eyes trained on Silas' face. He knew what he would find if he let them wander any lower. It would not be at all conducive to him leaving.

When Silas went to say something, Keelan shook his head tersely, pressing his own lips together. There was nothing Silas could say that would be better than what he'd already said. Keelan wanted to hold onto that for as long as he could.

He brought his hand to the side of Silas' face.

"Thank you," he whispered. He stole a final quick kiss and made as little noise as possible as he left for home.

NAVIGATING the Pimpernel townhouse turned out to be the easiest part. The halls were empty, save for a few members of the staff. He knew ignoring them would do no good—they were going to talk regardless. Some of the best gossip he'd ever heard had come from the mouths of servants, and he knew that Torquil had relied on them often when they were still writing the *Tribune.*

He let his final forced smile fall flat as the front door was closed behind him. He'd been lucky for the most part in that Torquil had never written anything too shocking about him in the paper. Mostly a comment here and there about someone he'd been seen with at a party. He wondered what Torquil would've written about him now. He'd certainly found himself in the middle of a situation that the people of London would love to talk about.

At first, it seemed that his house was quiet as well. He avoided looking at the door to the study as he walked by it on his way to the stairs. He'd nearly made it to his bedroom when he heard the sound of paws on the wood floor at the other end of the hall.

"Keelan," his father said in a hushed voice. He was standing in the doorway of his own room still wearing his dressing robe.

"Not now," he responded shortly.

"Please, I only want to—"

"I haven't time."

It came out sharper than he'd meant for it to, but it got his message across. He shut the door and pulled the bell cord before curling up on his chaise and burying his face into his hands. Once Marten arrived, he asked for a pitcher of hot water for his basin and allowed himself to be undressed. Keelan was not angry with his father. He understood why he had remained silent throughout dinner, and after. But that hadn't made it hurt any less. It hadn't made it easier to have someone who loved him sit by and witness the most painful moment of his life and do nothing to stop it.

Keelan looked at the metal band on his finger for the first time since it'd been put there. He noted the way that it appeared as uncomfortable as it felt, squeezing the skin just a little too much. When he tightened his fingers into a fist and released them several times, the feeling got even worse, almost painful.

"Sir," Marten said to get his attention. Keelan dropped his hand to his side. "The staff and I wish to extend a heartfelt congratulations to you and Miss Wilton-Reed on your happy news." The expression he wore was not one of good cheer. It was one of sympathy.

Keelan was saved from feigning his gratitude when two servants entered the room, one carrying the pitcher for the basin and the other a silver tray with a familiar pamphlet resting in the middle. He had never hesitated to reach for the latest copy of the *Tribune* before. By request, his was one of the first to be delivered across all of Mayfair so that he might enjoy it promptly upon returning from his morning rides, if not earlier.

But despite Miss Wilton-Reed's desire to delay making a formal announcement, there was no doubt in Keelan's mind that their news would be written in the paper sooner rather than later, if it hadn't been already.

"What does it say?" he asked with little feeling, swallowing at the burn of emotion that swelled anew at the back of his throat. "Will you read it to me?"

"You needn't devour it this very moment," Marten soothed,

accepting the gossip paper on his behalf before shooing the staff back out.

"I've never missed an issue," Keelan argued plaintively as he bent over the basin, splashing the warm water onto his face and rubbing at his tender eyelids. He wasn't sure he could manage the small print at the moment. "Please?"

Marten gave his familiar long and somewhat disapproving pause.

"Very well. But will you at least allow me to dress you first?"

DESPITE EVADING A PRINTED announcement for the time being, the felicitations continued at the Council's chambers. Miss Wilton-Reed kept a grip on his elbow as she'd done after dinner as they welcomed the stream of iterations. It seemed that everyone in the Pimpernel townhouse had been forced to listen to a retelling of the moment over breakfast. Keelan struggled to find any part of it that would have been worth repeating.

When the spectacle was finally over and everyone spread out to begin their work, Keelan glanced at the far table as he pulled Miss Wilton-Reed's chair out for her. Silas had not come to say anything to either of them. Keelan hadn't expected him to, especially if he'd already had to listen to his partner go on about it, but selfishly he'd wished for a few moments of the man being near to him again. Though it wouldn't have come close to being in his arms, at least he might've felt somewhat less forsaken in the crush of excitement from those who did not know how cheerless he truly was.

As he sat down, he met the stare of the other person in the room who had not wandered by. Emrys did not offer a nod, or his signature smirk. If anything, he looked a little pale. He had promised this wouldn't happen. He'd been so sure that they would figure out a way to prevent it. Keelan had thought that if anyone could help, it would be him. *We were wrong*, he thought bitterly as he moved his chair closer to the table.

"I've no idea how I'll focus on this ridiculous project today," Miss Wilton-Reed said with a smile. "I know I told you I've never had any interest in being married, but I must confess I am beginning to have a change of opinion."

Keelan gave her a wary look as he prepared a new piece of paper to take notes. "You are?"

"I have always enjoyed being the focus of the room. I suppose I never made the connection that an engagement would all but guarantee it." She gave a satisfied chuckle. "I wrote to Father last night to tell him. I know he'll be so pleased."

"You think he will approve of me, then?" It was another thing Keelan had not even had time to wonder about. Maybe Silas was right. Even if Miss Wilton-Reed would not love him, he could still hope that her family would.

"I doubt it," she said easily. "But he does love to see me happy. So as long as you can make that happen, I'm sure there will be no issue."

CHAPTER 43

SILAS

SILAS COULD FEEL Wyndham's eyes on him as he attempted to focus on reading through the notes from the previous day. He had gotten little sleep, having been too focused on the man in his arms. Now, he felt too aware of Cricket on the opposite side of the room and he felt as though that awareness was stretching him thin.

"Do you need to take the day off?" Wyndham asked in a careful tone.

"I don't think I'm the one who does," Silas replied.

Wyndham looked past him at Cricket. "Perhaps focusing will help to distract you."

"Perhaps."

Torquil approached their table, looking as tired as Silas felt. "Do you need anything before you begin?" they asked.

"I don't think so," Silas answered.

Torquil seemed to hesitate. "Do you need to work in our office today? It might help."

Silas gave them a measured look. "You know too?"

Their smile was thin. "I wrote the most popular gossip column in London for nearly five years. Of course I know." They paused. "And neither of you are very subtle."

Silas took that as permission to look back at the long table. Miss Wilton-Reed had scooted her chair closer and was leaning into Cricket's space even more than usual. Silas turned back to the two councilmembers. "Neither is she."

"Do you want to use the office?" Torquil pressed.

"No," Silas said, returning the notes to the table. "I want to be where he can see me."

Torquil's expression softened and, surprisingly, so did Wyndham's. Torquil clapped a hand on Silas' shoulder and then strode away. Wyndham was still watching Silas with a thoughtful expression.

Silas raised his eyebrows. "What?"

"What's your magical compatibility like?"

Silas huffed. "It's extraordinary, of course. It's warm and powerful and it feels more right than anything I've experienced. Now can we stop discussing this? I thought you had promised a distraction."

Wyndham sprang into action, gesturing for his husband to join them. Soon, Roger was demonstrating multiple shade spells while Silas and Wyndham observed with their magic. For all of his nervous personality, Roger was remarkably competent, demonstrating an academic level of knowledge of magic, supplying sigils and calculations without having to look them up. It was strange to be on the note-taking end of things for a while.

When Roger finished his demonstration, Torquil took his place and performed the same spells. They cast with a certain amount of shyness that surprised Silas. And they referred to the notes as often as Silas did. But he could appreciate why it had been useful to watch them. Their magic felt similar enough to his own, like the way distant cousins can have similar facial features.

When Torquil was done, they promptly left again and Roger reappeared, asking eagerly to watch Silas. Silas shrugged his approval and got to work. As usual, he could feel Wyndham's magic as he reached into his belt for his ingredients. The first shade spell was easy; it was the same one he always used with his work. Roger's mouth was open in awe as he watched and Silas allowed that unspoken compliment to go to his head; he needed the boost. After he cast, he waited for Wyndham to provide commentary, as he always did after a spell.

"Feels about the same as it usually does," he pronounced. "You have a flow when you prepare that spills over into your casting. It's quite remarkable."

"It's incredible," Roger gushed. "You didn't even look to see where your hands were going. You just *knew*."

Wyndham tapped at his husband's chin and then kissed his cheek. Silas felt a sharp pang at the show of affection. He wanted that with Cricket. Something in his face must have revealed what he was feeling because Wyndham immediately straightened. Although he reached over to clasp the hand of his now baffled husband.

Silas quickly turned his attention to his notes, studying the sigils and calculations Roger had provided. Carefully, he pulled out a fresh sheet of spellpaper and copied over the ones he thought best. He reached into his back pocket—the one that usually held his notebook—and pulled out the oak leaves that Wyndham had provided him. He sent out his sensing early, noting the power in the leaves and in the markings on the paper. He frowned and added another amendment to his earlier calculation. Then he cast. Their little corner of the room was plunged into darkness.

Wyndham whistled. "Impressive."

"Why do we always forget to have a candle ready?" Roger said, hurrying off to find one.

"What did you notice?" Silas asked.

"You tell me."

Silas rolled his eyes, but did as Wyndham instructed. "It sharpens my magic. The shade feels more pronounced than usual. Next time, I'll double my calculation."

"Was that what you did before you cast?"

"Yes. I could feel there was an imbalance between the two."

Roger scurried back into the shade, holding a candle. He brought it close to the spellpaper and Silas leaned over to adjust his calculation. The darkness lessened, exactly as he'd wanted it to.

Roger gasped. "You're so precise."

Silas deactivated the spell. "It's necessary in my line of work."

"Just take the compliment, Rook-Worth," Wyndham said with a

smirk as he reached for his stack of notes and began writing on the top page. Roger blew out the candle and walked away to check on the others.

Silas took the opportunity to glance back at Cricket again. As if he could feel his gaze, Cricket turned his head and their eyes locked. Cricket gave him a small smile, a shadow of his usual one, and then quickly turned away.

"You're good for him, you know," Wyndham said as Silas returned his attention to their table.

"I know. He's too good for me, though."

Wyndham tilted his head back and forth. "Perhaps just a little." He flashed a grin, then he sobered. "It truly is a shame. If he could have enticed you to stay in London, even some of the time, I might have convinced you to join the Council. It would be nice to have another voice of reason in the room."

"I'm a craftsman, not a politician or an academic. It would never have happened regardless."

Wyndham heaved a sigh. "All right, craftsman, show me your next trick."

THAT EVENING, SILAS' door was opened without the formality of knocking and Cricket slid inside the room without a sound. He was pale and his face was drawn. Neither of them spoke a word as they closed the distance and kissed. Silas knew there would be nights for urgency, for rushed pleasure, for desperate satisfaction. But tonight, without having to discuss it, they seemed to be of the same mind. They undressed each other in silence and Silas pulled Cricket to his bed and took his time, pretending the previous night had never happened, pretending it would last. It was as heartbreaking as it was necessary. Just before Cricket reached his climax, Silas captured the man's mouth with his own. Cricket slid his hands around Silas' neck and kissed him back.

It was in the silence that followed, as Cricket curled on his side, with his head on Silas' shoulder again, and Silas' arm wrapped tightly around Cricket's waist, that he realized he was falling in love for the first time in his life. And now he'd have to grieve that love before it had a chance to bloom. He pulled Cricket closer and kissed his temple, wishing for things that could never be.

CHAPTER 44

KEELAN

AT THE END of the session the following day, Emrys called Keelan's name in the hallway and jogged to catch up with him. They had not spoken since the news had spread. It was entirely unlike either of them to avoid the other, and it had only made dealing with the engagement harder for Keelan without the support of his best friend. He waited for Emrys to reach him and made an effort to return the smile he was given.

"Come to dinner tonight," Emrys said on an exhale. "My mother has decided she could not wait any longer to visit Auberon and Rose. She left for the country this morning, and Aveline has accepted an invitation to the Buckthorn residence, so we have the house to ourselves for the evening."

Keelan laughed a little at the outpouring of information.

"That sounds like a situation you and Torquil should take advantage of while you've got the opportunity."

Emrys waved a dismissive hand.

"We've also invited Wyndham and Roger to join us, so it will not be a drawn out affair. There should be just enough time between dinner ending and Aveline returning home for us to find an unexplored part of the house to *occupy* for a while."

Keelan's grin faded. "Am I expected to bring—"

"The invitation is for you," Emrys clarified. "Only you."

The words brought a wash of relief.

"Yes, I'll be there."

Keelan took his carriage home to dress for dinner and arrived well before the other two guests. He joined his hosts in the sitting room for a short while, until Torquil removed their legs from Emrys' lap and said they had better check on things in the kitchen. A short silence settled between the two men when they were left alone. Keelan could see by the look on Emrys' face that he was struggling to think of what to say.

"I am not upset with you," he offered. "About my situation. It is not your responsibility. It never was."

Emrys' brows dipped in what looked like a flash of anger.

"That does not make it any less difficult. I owe everything to you. Without your advice, I very well could have lost the love of my life. And how do I repay you? By sitting back and watching you become engaged to someone perfectly unsuitable."

Keelan winced. "Well, when you say it like *that*."

Emrys held his hand out with his palm up. "Let me see it."

Keelan moved from his chair to the open spot by Emrys on the sofa and presented the ring. Emrys grabbed his fingers and pulled them closer for inspection. He narrowed his eyes at the band and shook his head as he let Keelan's hand go.

"Disrespectful."

"It's only temporary," Keelan said as he tucked his hand between his thigh and the cushion. He wasn't sure why he was suddenly defending the piece of jewelry that had brought him such misery in so little time. A bit of embarrassment, perhaps.

Emrys turned a knowing look on him.

"Keelan, the only person I've known in my entire life who wanted to be married more than you is my sister." He tipped his chin at where Keelan had hidden his hand under his leg. "If she was given *that* ring—temporary or not—when asked for her hand in marriage, I do believe she would cry herself to death."

Keelan moved his hand from its hiding place and began to fidget with the band, a small frown curving his lips.

"Yes, that's because when someone asks Aveline to marry her, it will be because they love her." Keelan let his hands fall dejectedly to his lap. "This is not the kind of ring you give to someone you love."

Emrys let his head fall against the back of the sofa and let out a sound that began as a groan and ended more like a roar of frustration. He threw his arm over his eyes for added effect. "Torquil!"

They appeared in the doorway and propped their shoulder against it, arms crossed loosely over their chest. "You needn't shout. I'm here." There was an affectionate grin on their mouth.

"Go and fetch your engagement ring. You'll be sharing it with Keelan moving forward. I'll allow the two of you to work out who gets to wear it when."

Keelan's jaw dropped in surprise before he and Torquil both laughed. It was genuine, one that Keelan could feel lift his magic from where it had wilted with everything that had happened. One that reminded him how love came in many forms, and that it was equally as important and wonderful no matter where it came from.

"Oh, good," Wyndham's voice cut in as they settled. He and Roger had appeared in the doorway that led to the dining room. "It appears everyone has already started drinking. Perhaps this will be over even sooner than I hoped."

As they took their seats around the table, Keelan noticed the way Roger and Torquil were helped into their chairs. He watched the subtle touches and glances exchanged between each of the couples. There was no use ignoring that he was in the company of four very happily married people. The last thing he wanted was for his own unfortunate circumstances to ruin yet another dinner, so Keelan offered Roger a smile.

"Hard to believe it's already been half a year since your wedding," he said as he reached for one of the serving spoons.

Roger looked a little surprised. He and Wyndham shared a glance.

"I suppose it has been, hasn't it?"

"The way everyone still talks about your wedding spell makes it feel like it was only yesterday," Keelan added.

Emrys chuckled. "None more than you."

"Do not be jealous," Wyndham directed at his brother. "Let the man recognize greatness when he sees it."

"Your fire spell was wonderful too, of course." Keelan paused to allow Emrys time to puff his chest. "But what Wyndham and Roger did was... *revolutionary.*"

Emrys scoffed. "Whose friend are you, anyway?"

Keelan smiled when he followed the question with a wink.

The conversation continued easily as they ate. There were more questions about what it was like to be newly married. Both couples shared their plans for the summer. Roger and Wyndham told a few stories about their cat, Peony, who Keelan desperately wished to meet. By the time the dessert course was served, Keelan had nearly forgotten that he had anything to be upset about. His own situation and near future had not been brought up a single time. None of them had mentioned the project in any way.

He'd originally thought that the invitation, and perhaps the entire dinner, had been put together for his benefit alone. But he realized that they had all needed an evening of distraction. As he looked around the table, each of them had lost some of the worry lines on their faces, or a bit of tightness in their jaw. Even Torquil seemed refreshed as they sipped their wine.

A natural pause provided Wyndham the opportunity to announce that he and Roger were leaving. Keelan decided it was time for him to go, as well. Emrys and Torquil escorted them to the foyer as they said their goodbyes; soon it was Emrys and Keelan alone again.

"Thank you for the invitation," Keelan told him as one of the servants helped him into his coat. "It was exactly what I needed."

"Likewise," Emrys agreed. "We shall have to make it happen again."

Keelan could all but feel Emrys' lips press together to add '*before you leave*' at the end. He had always disliked the way saying farewells at the conclusion of a wonderful night felt.

"I'm not sure how many opportunities I'll have to say this, so I suppose now will have to do." Keelan stared at his feet for a moment before he met Emrys' gaze. "I would like it very much if you could be there. At the wedding. My wedding. It's to be held in Bath, maybe in about a month or so. I'm not certain, really. We've had little time to work out the details. I know it's a bit short notice, but I thought—"

"Are you mad?" Emrys laughed. "I wouldn't miss it for anything."

What happened next took Keelan by surprise. Emrys wrapped his arms around Keelan's shoulders and gave him the tightest embrace he'd ever experienced. It only lasted a few seconds, but it was the first time anyone had shown him such affection without the expectation of more. Something squeezed in his chest and he did not trust himself to speak. Luckily, Emrys did it for him.

"Now, get out so I can go and make love to Torquil in the library before my sister comes home."

CHAPTER 45

SILAS

SILAS DIDN'T WANT to think too hard about how he was coming to not only expect Cricket's nighttime visits, but look forward to them. While their first nights together had been thrilling and passionate, he realized he appreciated the more subdued recent evenings as well. There was something about simply holding Cricket, of communicating without words, of taking care of the man in a new way that touched his soul. He hated seeing Cricket in pain, but he wished he could always be the one to dry the man's tears and hold him while he slept. The fact that this arrangement was only temporary stung more than he liked. He had no doubt that Miss Wilton-Reed would not take proper care of her husband and he dreaded passing care of the man over to someone so selfish.

When Cricket let himself into Silas' room late that night, he was in much better spirits than he had been for days. They met in the center of the room with a kiss and Cricket promptly began removing Silas' clothes with a self-assurance that made Silas unexpectedly proud. He was relieved to note the change in mood, however brief it might be, and allowed himself to be undressed. After undressing himself, Cricket even pushed Silas onto the bed and straddled his waist before kissing him again. The self-assurance faded a little after the kiss, and Cricket's expression clouded with uncertainty. Silas grinned and took over, flipping Cricket onto his back on the bed and kissing him into the pillows.

Cricket framed his face. "I never did thank you for last night."

"There's no need. I'll take any moment I have with you, however those moments may look." He turned his face to nuzzle into Cricket's palm. "I'll take the rushed and heated nights, the nights where we don't speak as I take care of you, and anything in between. I'll take whatever you'll give me: a lifetime of you in the month we have left."

Cricket pulled him down to kiss him again, and soon the words gave way to sighs and whimpers, until they were both lying side by side on the bed. Cricket curled into Silas' side and Silas drew him close and planted a kiss on his shoulder.

"I joined the Wrenwhistles for dinner," Cricket said.

"Which ones?" Silas teased.

He chuckled. "Emrys, Torquil, Wyndham, Roger." He yawned. "It was nice. No one talked about my engagement or the project. And at the end of it, Emrys promised to come to the wedding."

Silas stroked his back. "I'm glad. You need more people taking care of you."

Cricket snuggled closer. "It's nice to be taken care of. I wish it hadn't taken *this* to bring it about though."

They were silent for a while, the words hanging heavily in the air. Silas ran his free hand through Cricket's soft hair. "Tell me about Emrys Wrenwhistle."

Cricket brightened up adorably at the request. "He's my best friend. We've known each other since we were children. Our families were in all the same circles and his grandmother and my mother both served on the Council, so we were always at the same events. We went to the same schools." He paused. "He's wonderful. We've always looked out for each other. I advised him when he was being foolish about Torquil. And he...he's doing his best to help me now. Even though neither of us can do much. I'm glad he's coming to the wedding. I don't want to be married in front of a room full of strangers..." He sighed. "But he'll be there. I hope I can invite him to visit in Bath." The last words came out soft and it was easy to discern the fear in them.

"You'll be running the house. I'm sure you'll be able to invite your friends to visit."

He felt Cricket swallow. "Yes," he whispered. "Although I have a feeling I won't have much say in the decor."

"Hm. Not unless you become enamored of florals very quickly."

Cricket burst into laughter at that and buried his face in Silas' neck. "I don't even mind florals," he said, smiling. "But, stars above, she has the most appalling taste."

"In many things, yes. She really does."

"Did you know that jellied eel is her favorite?" Cricket shuddered. "She brought it up at dinner."

"Unfortunately, I did know that."

"Abominable creature."

"Indeed."

They lapsed into silence again. Silas continued stroking Cricket's back and threading fingers through his hair. Cricket turned his face to kiss Silas' cheek. "I'm glad you're here. In London. I don't know how I would have handled all of this without having something to look forward to each night." Then he added softly, "I'll miss you when I leave."

Silas lifted Cricket's chin and kissed him as tenderly as he knew how. "I'll miss you too, Cricket. I don't think I'll ever find a light that shines as bright as you."

CHAPTER 46

KEELAN

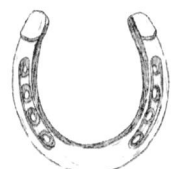

In what was beginning to feel like an endless stream of dinner engagements, Miss Wilton-Reed joined the Crickets for another meal. The mood was not very different from how it had been the night of the engagement, but Keelan was able to find some peace in the situation knowing that whatever happened next was largely out of his hands.

It was just as well, because it became evident almost immediately that his opinions on the events leading up to their marriage—and even the wedding itself—did not matter. Miss Wilton-Reed and his mother went back and forth over various details about what they should wear, what types of food would be served, and an exorbitant amount of time was spent discussing the flowers. He thought it strange that his mother would have so much interest in an event she did not even care to attend.

By the time the conversation shifted to what life would look like *after* the wedding, Keelan had stopped listening entirely. He knew he should give more attention to what they were saying. The parties and festivities would only last so long before they would be expected to settle into a married existence.

As the two women spoke, Keelan could only envision glimpses of what his parents' lives were like. They shared a name and a home, but little else. They came together for meals as a family because that was the expectation. They'd had two children because that was the expectation, too. Keelan flicked a glance at Miss Wilton-Reed beside him. He suspected that they would also be required to fulfill that obligation.

Something cold and wet pressed against his hand under the table. He leaned back in his chair far enough to find Alouetta nosing at his fingers before she gave them a few licks. Keelan felt himself grin and returned the favor, stroking the smooth fur atop her head before he scratched behind one of her silky, drooping ears.

He could not recall exactly how many years she'd belonged to his father, but the silver hairs around her eyes and muzzle hinted at her age. His father had kept two spaniels since before Keelan was born. They were an integral part of the life he'd created for himself that was separate from his marriage.

Keelan tried to imagine how he would do the same for himself. As entertaining as Wyndham and Roger made it sound, he did not think keeping the company of a cat suited him, and dogs were a lot of work, especially when they were always underfoot. Perhaps he would be able to explore his love of horses more instead. While he adored his morning rides, he'd always had an interest in learning what went into the proper care and training of such formidable creatures. He'd never been permitted to dawdle in the public stables in London, but once he had his own to oversee, he could linger and learn as much as he liked.

The more he thought about all the ways he could fill his days in Bath, he realized that it would not be so very different from the life he already had. There would still be time to enjoy riding, shopping, or attending the local playhouse. Certainly there would be a gossip paper to support, full of unfamiliar names to memorize and exciting stories he'd never heard before. The only difference was that he would just have to learn how to do these things in a new place. Alone.

Keelan sighed down at Alouetta where she had rested her chin on his knee. That was the trouble. Of all the nights he'd dreamt of what marriage would be like, spending all his time by himself had never crossed his mind. He wanted to be with someone who shared his interests—or was at least willing to endure them on occasion for the sake of companionship. He wanted all of the things he'd told Emrys about: slow mornings in bed, a leisurely ride through the Park, an evening in front of the fire together. He wanted to know that, no matter what happened, he would always have that person to turn to and never wonder if their love was true.

Unbidden, his thoughts drifted to his most recent encounters with Silas. Their nights together had meant more than he knew how to put into words. He'd even told the man as much. The handsome mason he'd never expected to see again had become a steady source of comfort and pleasure in his life. After a moment of hesitation, he allowed himself to imagine what it would be like to share those other moments he longed for with a man like Silas.

Keelan already knew how difficult it was to force himself out of his warm, sturdy embrace with the threat of sunrise. He would've gladly remained there until the entire room was flooded with morning light if given the chance. Silas cared deeply for his family, and somehow got on with them well enough to work on strenuous projects all day long and still be willing to eat around the same table for supper each night. Indeed, he was one of the most unexcitable people Keelan had ever met, but he was also secure and sensible. He was exactly the sort of person Keelan could imagine sharing a quiet evening by the fire with— so long as they were not entertaining *other* searing plans together.

Miss Wilton-Reed's hand on his arm shattered his thoughts and brought him back to reality. She asked him to escort her out, which quickly became walking her across the street and down to the Pimpernel townhouse. He decided it was because there was a greater chance for someone to see her lean up and kiss him on the cheek, which is exactly what happened. The ladies walking by all started whispering to one another, but Keelan only felt his face go hot when he met the gaze of the footman who had been letting him in to see a *different* guest of the house.

Keelan tried not to think about it as he returned home. Being called into his mother's study proved to be an excellent distraction. He was not offered a seat, so he stood and waited for whatever she had to say.

"From what I can tell, Melisande's family incorporates both fae and human traditions into their weddings rather enthusiastically. I'm sure you know this pleases me a great deal. There is nothing more spectacular than a wedding spell."

Keelan gave his mother a dubious look. "Why does it matter if you'll not be there to see it?"

"Because people talk. Even if I am not there, I will still hear about it one way or another." She leaned forward in the chair behind her desk. "I've been careful not to ask this outright, for I do not wish to offend the young lady's human sensibility, but I must know. How is your compatibility?"

Keelan gasped, only slightly mortified at his mother's question.

"I haven't—" he stammered. "We haven't—"

"Your *magical* compatibility," she clarified. "Have you not been sensing her magic for weeks now?"

Keelan pressed a hand over his heart as he tried to recover. "Yes," he told her. "It has been…a most interesting experience."

"Do you think you will be able to demonstrate a successful wedding spell together?"

He wished that he could tell her no, and that it would make everything go back to the way it had been before. There was not another fae in all of London who saw the importance of a strong wedding spell more than his mother. Keelan had not been there to witness the spell between his parents, of course, but he could only assume it must've been remarkable for them to have still gone through with the wedding despite the lack of love between them.

"I expect that we will," he said, eyes cast down. "There have not been any issues between us in that regard."

It was the truth. Despite how different they were as people, their combined magics had yet to display any sort of negative reaction. There had not been any particularly positive reactions, either, but the project had proven that to be a much better outcome than the alternative.

"Excellent." He could hear the smile in his mother's voice. "I think this is going to be a wonderful match for the both of you. The merging of two strong families is always something to celebrate."

CHAPTER 47

SILAS

Silas was in the sitting room with Mrs. Pimpernel and Mrs. Iris Wrenwhistle. He was sipping on wine while the other two chatted. There was a fire in the hearth and Mrs. Pimpernel was knitting while they talked; the whole scene felt like he was back at home, listening to his parents. It made him homesick while simultaneously easing the familiar ache of homesickness he had grown accustomed to. He listened as the conversation wound from gossip about their families to gossip about members of the *ton*, and had finally worked its way to gossip about him.

"I've heard tell that our friend here has been entertaining a friend of his own recently," Mrs. Wrenwhistle said.

Silas glanced at Mrs. Pimpernel.

"I would never betray you in such a way!" the lady said, putting her hand to her heart.

Mrs. Wrenwhistle chuckled. "Well, that is confirmation enough. Will you tell us who they are?"

"That would be indiscreet of me."

She tutted. "Nonsense, young man. You are living in a fae house, where people expect such behavior. Besides, your friend has been entering through the front door. Discretion is hardly at the top of either of your minds."

Silas took a sip of his drink and didn't reply.

"I think it's one of the volunteers on the project," Mrs. Pimpernel said.

"Well, of course, my dear. That is a most logical guess. And it certainly narrows our options down considerably, does it not? Let me think."

"I believe we can omit any of our own grandchildren and their spouses."

Mrs. Wrenwhistle hummed in agreement. "I suspect you are correct. And Mr. Buckthorn is unlikely to look away from Aveline long enough to notice anyone else, bless him."

Silas laughed. "That is certainly accurate."

"So that leaves Mr. Brooks, Mx. Hillcrest, and Mr. Cricket?" Mrs. Pimpernel asked.

"I believe Mr. Brooks abandoned the project recently," Mrs. Wrenwhistle said.

"Oh, yes. And I'm quite certain the *Tribune* would have noticed if Mx. Hillcrest's attention had diverted from Miss Thackeray and Mr. Thompson."

"Indeed, you are right."

Mrs. Pimpernel brightened. "Mr. Cricket suits you very well, Mr. Rook-Worth."

"I agree, an excellent choice."

"You do realize the gentleman is engaged?"

Mrs. Wrenwhistle clicked her tongue. "Ah, yes. How could we not? But then, anyone who knows young Keelan knows of his romantic nature. It is certainly not in my nature to cast doubt on his mother's capabilities. She's a very clever woman. Nevertheless…"

"Nevertheless," Mrs. Pimpernel jumped in to continue the thread, "it would be foolish to cast doubt on the young man's capabilities as well. One can never underestimate the power of love, can one?"

"One can when the one in love is also a person of duty," Silas argued.

"Nonsense. You'll find a way," Mrs. Wrenwhistle said.

"You are certainly very confident."

She narrowed her eyes at him. "And where is your confidence, Mr. Rook-Worth? Have you given up already?"

"Youth is wasted on the wrong people," Mrs. Pimpernel said.

Before Silas could reply, the front door opened and Miss Wilton-Reed strode in. She gave a satisfied little sigh before plopping into a chair and taking over the conversation, as she was wont to do.

"Such a perfect evening," she pronounced.

"I'm glad," Mrs. Pimpernel said.

"I quite like Councilmember Cricket. She's very practical. It makes wedding planning so much simpler when working with a practical person."

"Is Mr. Cricket not involved in the wedding planning?" Mrs. Wrenwhistle asked.

Miss Wilton-Reed waved a hand. "He was present. But that's about the best that can usually be said about him. I don't mind. That's all I really want him for anyway, so it suits me quite well. He sits there quietly while I talk to his mother." She chuckled. "A still water that doesn't run deep, if ever there was one. Not a thought in that pretty head. Perfect for a husband, really."

Silas felt his fingers clench around his wine glass so he carefully set it down and folded his hands together on his lap.

"He is a very nice young man," Mrs. Wrenwhistle said. "Very sweet."

"He is," Mrs. Pimpernel agreed. "Always was too. The most polite little child."

Miss Wilton-Reed picked at her skirt. "They have the most wretched dogs. Always under the table and getting underfoot. Disgusting creatures. I cannot abide pets. I shall have to get Keelan an entirely new wardrobe to ensure nothing is contaminated with dog hair. Of course, his dowry will help with that."

"Is it normal to discuss your betrothed's dowry?" Silas asked. "I'm afraid I'm not as well versed in etiquette as everyone here."

Mrs. Pimpernel hid a smile behind her hand.

"You are exceedingly tiresome," Miss Wilton-Reed said with a yawn. "I would hardly be marrying the man if he didn't have a decent dowry.

It wouldn't be worth my while. But as I said, his mother is practical. The contract is most agreeable. As long as he continues to behave himself as he should, I think we shall be very comfortable."

She stood and left the room without another word.

Mrs. Pimpernel heaved a sigh. "Dreadful woman," she muttered.

"I cannot imagine what Terra Cricket could be thinking, marrying her sweet boy to that creature," Mrs. Wrenwhistle said. "I think I could use some brandy after that interaction."

Mrs. Pimpernel rang for a footman and sent for a bottle of brandy and three glasses. After the footman left to fulfill the request, she turned to Silas with a cheeky grin. "Perhaps I ought to have requested four. I'm sure your friend could use some as well."

Silas chuckled. "It's early yet."

"Don't think you've evaded the topic from earlier," Mrs. Wrenwhistle said as they waited.

"I'm not sure what you want me to do," Silas admitted. "He is engaged. He has no mind to break the engagement."

"What if you offered your hand instead?" Mrs. Pimpernel asked.

"With what fortune?"

Mrs. Wrenwhistle gave an exasperated huff. "With love, of course! Good heavens. Do young people have no imagination these days?"

"Perhaps the Council ought to add it to the rubric?" Mrs. Pimpernel said.

"Mm. Just try adding anything to the rubric. I think the entire Council would combust," Mrs. Wrenwhistle muttered. "But you're not wrong." She patted the arm of her chair. "Now, be creative, Silas. You have steady work, a home, a family. You have a kind heart and a great deal of love to offer him. And considering the fact that he has visited the house many an evening as of late, it is reasonably supposed that you have other things to offer as well."

Silas barely had time to register the use of his first name and the candid reference to his evening activities before the servant entered with the brandy. He was relieved to have a chance to gather his thoughts. The spirit tasted expensive and Silas sipped it slowly, thinking about the way Cricket was being sold away for the price of his decent dowry and good behavior.

"Have you ruminated enough?" Mrs. Wrenwhistle asked.

"Nearly," he said, meeting her gaze as he took another sip. He finally brought the glass down to his lap, cupped between his hands. The brandy had warmed his chest and he allowed it to loosen his tongue. "You seem to be forgetting some very important details in your hurry to matchmake," he said at last.

"Oh?" Mrs. Pimpernel asked.

"Do elaborate," Mrs. Wrenwhistle said, resting her chin on her fist.

Silas looked down at his drink. "Our lives are not compatible. He has been raised to be a gentleman. He loves London. I know he will be quitting it when he is married, but he will still be going to a fashionable city. It suits him. It's where he belongs. And it is most certainly *not* where I belong."

"Surely he would be a better judge of where he belongs," Mrs. Pimpernel said.

Silas swirled the liquid in his glass. "I would never forgive myself if I made him unhappy by dragging him to the country and seeing him waste away there."

Mrs. Wrenwhistle scoffed. "He would hardly be dragged."

"What we have isn't permanent," he said. "It is exciting, it is passionate, it is tender. But it is only temporary. We are taking what we can of each other, knowing it will not last. It is enough. It must be."

"I wouldn't have taken you for a pessimist," Mrs. Pimpernel said.

He set his glass aside. "Simply practical."

"I guess you and Miss Wilton-Reed share a love for that virtue," Mrs. Wrenwhistle muttered.

Shame bloomed in Silas' gut. "She's bound to be right about some things," he managed. Then he got up and left the room before they could say anything else. He didn't like the way the ladies spoke as if there was actually hope for his relationship. It was far easier knowing there wasn't any. He would much prefer to steel himself for a broken heart, than hope for a change and be let down anyway. The shame and confusion mixed in his head.

He hurried to his bedroom and closed the door, leaning back against it and resting his head on the door with a soft thump. He could smell the lingering scent of Cricket's soap. And for just a moment, Silas allowed his thoughts to wander and get fanciful. He was not prone to fancies, but it was easy to imagine Cricket in his life in a more permanent way. There would be no rules for behavior, no expectations of proper dress. If Cricket wanted a dozen dogs, Silas would take him to the closest neighbor with a litter of puppies.

He wondered if Cricket's tendency to punctuality was due to being up early in the morning or due to an eagerness to please. Would he be the sort of husband to lie in bed late into the morning? Or would he be up with morning mist, trudging through the countryside, his cheeks going rosy with the exercise? While Silas was imagining the impossible, he continued to ponder whether or not Cricket would have any interest in joining the family business. He would do an excellent job at talking to the people they met. He was so good-natured and polite.

Silas rubbed his hands over his face and pushed himself away from the door. He began discarding his clothing; no sense giving Cricket more work than necessary. He settled onto his bed and waited.

He didn't have to wait long. Cricket came by within the hour. He closed the door behind him, took one look at Silas on the bed, and promptly began stripping down. Silas folded his arms behind his head and watched. Cricket noticed and went pink, ducked his head, and then continued.

"You're beautiful, you know," Silas murmured. Cricket's blush deepened. And it spread to his chest. *Interesting.* "I could just stare at you all night."

"Sounds rather boring."

"On the contrary." Knowing the other man was looking at him, Silas intentionally gave Cricket a leisurely once-over. "You're delectable."

Cricket huffed and climbed onto the bed, straddling his hips again. "You're ridiculous."

Silas cupped the back of his neck and pulled him in for a kiss, making it slow and lazy, indulgent. By the time he was done, Cricket's blush had spread even more and he was panting. Silas stroked one pink cheek with his finger. "I could look at you for years and never grow tired of the sight."

Cricket bit his lip. "You're spoiling me with these compliments."

"Just speaking the truth."

Cricket squirmed a little and looked away. "I don't know what to do when you look at me like that."

"You don't have to do anything at all."

Cricket's mouth quirked. "I confess I do always like that. When you handle things, I mean."

Silas didn't need to be told twice. He flipped them over so Cricket was on his back and proceeded to take his time, kissing, licking, stroking, until Cricket was writhing and panting beneath him. He brought him to satisfaction with his hand, sitting back so he could take in the full view. Then he eased his way back up to kiss him with the same level of decadence.

"I don't know how you manage to make every night seem different," Cricket whispered after Silas had cleaned him up and pulled him to nestle at his side.

"I'm very creative," Silas remarked. "I have a notebook full of ideas."

"For *this*?"

Silas laughed. "No, I haven't run out of plans for this yet. I might need to make a list soon, though. Make sure I get everything in that I want to do with you."

Cricket wriggled a little. "Oh."

"And I'm open to suggestions."

"Oh, I—er…I'm game for anything you have in mind."

Silas kissed him. "Good."

Cricket was silent for a long moment as he traced a pattern on Silas' chest. "Will you tell me more about your family and your work?"

Silas sent a private curse to Miss Wilton-Reed for assuming Cricket's mind was anything other than constantly churning. He stroked Cricket's back as he thought of how to condense an entire life into a single conversation.

"My father is the one who started our business. He began when he was younger than I am now, building magical items for people. It became a family business as soon as any of us were old enough to contribute."

"Do you like it?"

"I'm good at it. I like working with my hands. I like working with my magic. We work together well, and I enjoy being a part of that."

"Do you all do specific things or…"

"There is no set task for each person. But we tend to fall back on our own strengths. Although my father makes a point of giving us new tasks upon occasion, so we all gain proficiency in everything. Well, I suppose as the only one who does human magic, my tasks are a little more specific. I'm usually either the first one to lay my magic down or the last. It depends on the job, of course. But sometimes I'll start a spell as a foundation and everyone else will build on top of it. Other times, like at your friend's wedding, my family used the magic in the brick and stone, in the ground, in the trees to start. And I came after."

"How many siblings do you have?"

"Two."

"And you're the youngest?"

"I'm the youngest. Only product of my father's second marriage. Briony is the eldest. She's the one set to inherit. She's very good at the details. Notices things that no one else does that gives our spells an extra…something. I don't know how to explain it. At the wedding, the housekeeper was concerned about the trees catching fire, and Briony used the trees to our advantage, incorporating them into the protection spells. It became a benefit, rather than a hindrance. Probably why she ranked the highest."

"Is she nice?"

Silas chuckled. "They're both nice, in their way. They tease me a great deal, particularly as I'm the youngest. And they both had a part in raising me. But they're good people. I trust them."

"You miss them."

"Yes."

"That's one then. What about the other?"

"Quince. He's excellent with magic in the ground. So he usually starts off a lot of our work. And he has an uncanny ability to measure a space in his head. I get along with him best, as we're the closest in age. He's been very curious about you."

Cricket gave a soft, dismissive scoff. "Me?"

"Mm. Teases me a great deal for—" Silas broke off. He cleared his throat. "Teases me a great deal for talking about you so much. He'd like you though."

"He would?" Cricket's tone was heartbreakingly hopeful.

"Of course he would," Silas said, with more vehemence than he intended. "They all would. My mother would probably set you up permanently in her kitchen. When I was little, she would let me sit on a stool in the corner and watch her cook and bake. But once I got old enough for my feet to touch the floor, it was all *unless you're going to help me, get out of my kitchen* and *don't eat so much before dinner.*"

They both chuckled.

"She'd adore you though. I think she'd let you use the stool as often as you wished."

"Even if my feet touch the floor?"

"Mm."

"Why?" Cricket's grin was cheeky and Silas adored it.

"Because you'd thank her very prettily, and you'd compliment her cooking. And she'd probably adopt you and throw the rest of us out."

Cricket laughed. "I think I like her already."

"Oh, you two would get on famously." Silas traced a fingertip across Cricket's cheek. All of his fanciful ideas from before came flooding back. Despite what the ladies had said, Silas had plenty of imagination where Cricket was concerned. He wasn't sure if it was cruel or kind to give the man a painting of a life that could never be. But Cricket was still looking at him with such hopefulness, hungry for more. Silas had long lost the resistance to deny the man. So he continued, "And then after dinner, we'd take an evening walk and look at the stars. You can't see the stars as well in London. I miss that."

"And then?" Cricket said, voice hushed and breathless.

"And then…I'd want a cottage for the two of us. Close enough to my family to see them every day. But far enough that we could have some privacy. I'd need to fuck you in every room, you see. And we could curl up just like this every night. There are crickets out in my part of the country. In the summer, we'd fall asleep to cricket song, with my own little Cricket tucked close beside me."

Cricket's eyes were shiny with unshed tears. "And then?" he whispered.

"And then I'd never let you out of my sight again."

Cricket leaned forward to kiss him. The kiss tasted of tears and regrets and the grief of dreams just out of reach. Then Cricket laid his head back on Silas' shoulder, sniffed, and said, "I'm not sure I'd add much to your family business. But I think I'd enjoy being a part of it."

"I think we'd find a place for you in it. Everyone in the family has one."

Cricket's breath caught and his hand fisted on top of Silas' chest. Then he let out a slow breath. "Your family sounds wonderful, Silas. I could hear you talk about them all day."

"Shall I keep going?"

"Please."

So Silas continued to ramble on in a low voice, telling Cricket stories of life in the country, working with his family, and quiet days. He left out what it was like to do all of the cooking and cleaning without servants to help. He spoke of how beautiful the garden looked in the rain, but left out the exhausting practice of repairing leaky roofs.

As he detailed stories about his family, he left out how constricting it could be to live with other adults, how he sometimes felt as though he was still treated like a child, how he longed for his own space. He didn't mention the months when work was light and their purses were lighter. He left out the year that Briony broke her arm and how hard it was to fill in the gap left by her inability to contribute to the family business or work around the house.

Instead, Silas painted a vivid picture of an idyllic life. He knew it to be a false representation, as genuine as the fairy stories in Cricket's children's book. But Cricket needed a dream to hold onto, so Silas talked and talked, keeping up a steady stream of chatter until Cricket drifted off to sleep in his arms.

FROM SILAS ROOK-WORTH TO QUINCE ROOK

4 June 1814

Dear Quince,

Well, it's finally happened. I wish I could be angry with you for being right, once again. I've gone and fallen in love and it is most wretchedly hopeless. The man is perfect. You'd love him. The whole family would love him. He's sweet and charming and earnest. He's braver than he realizes. He lights up an entire room simply by walking into it. He's a breath of fresh air in this horrid, stuffy city.

And he's engaged to someone else, someone who plans to take him far away from here. She'll likely keep him in a gilded cage like an exotic bird because that is all the value she seems to see in him.

So you'd better prepare yourself now for my being in an even worse mood when I return home. I've never had a broken heart before. I've always managed to steer clear of such entanglements. But he is… different.

He brings out the best in me in ways I couldn't imagine. Perhaps it's just his way of shining light in all of the dark places.

I am not asking for your advice as I know what you will say: propose to him myself, win his heart, steal him away. But I cannot and you know it. I couldn't possibly bring such a scandal on his name. And what do I have to offer him? A life even farther from the world he knows?

All I can do is continue to store up the good memories I have with him while I can.

If you care for me at all, you'll place a nice sized bottle of ale on my bedside table so I can find some comfort when I return home.

I never would have thought I'd dread the end of this project.

Love,
Silas

CHAPTER 48

KEELAN

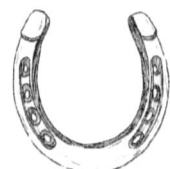

INVITATIONS to the ball had gone out days before Miss Wilton-Reed had made her declaration. Mrs. Iris Wrenwhistle and Mrs. Pimpernel were hosting it jointly at the first lady's home. All of the project volunteers and leaders had been invited, and though it was a private event, the remainder of the guest list was still expected to be impressive. There'd still been no official announcement made of the engagement, but that had not prevented the rapid spread of the news, so for Keelan, it meant sharing a room with dozens of people who had not yet given their well wishes and were eager to do so.

After nearly an hour of standing in one place with Miss Wilton-Reed holding his elbow and accepting the felicitations on their behalf, Keelan had never been happier to hear the announcement for the first dance to begin. Miss Wilton-Reed's grip on him tightened as she guided him into the ballroom; the message was clear—he was not going to dance with someone else first this time.

Following the steps of the dance with the lady felt very much like sensing her magic, or being kissed by her. It was not terrible. It was not particularly enjoyable, either. It just…was. Miss Wilton-Reed's smile was not for him as they turned and swayed, but for everyone watching. His stomach cramped and he turned his gaze away. He wanted no part in her duplicity that evening. It would have hurt less if she'd looked at him the way she usually did, with disinterest or a sense of superiority. At least it would have been real.

When the dance was over, Miss Wilton-Reed sent him to find them both a drink. He decided to take his time on the endeavor, wandering past servants with trays and pitchers as though he had not noticed them and forgetting that he had seen the table set with refreshments in the adjoining room. If she truly believed him to be so unintelligent, then he could also play a role in her charade.

Keelan found Emrys in the crowd and moved to stand quietly beside him. He was talking to a group at large about what marvelous work they'd been doing on the project, and how interesting it had been to learn about fae-human magic beyond what he experienced with his spouse. Torquil was on his opposite side and noticed Keelan first. They rolled their eyes with a small, affectionate grin. Keelan grinned back. Emrys had always had a way of speaking that made people want to listen.

After answering a couple of questions with the confidence of someone in charge of the project, rather than just a volunteer, Emrys finally paused to sip at his drink. Torquil raised their hand to his chest to get his attention; Keelan's magic swirled pleasantly at the sight of the engagement ring glinting on their finger. They only wore it to events such as this. He hesitated at his impulse to comment on it, but something stronger told him to say it anyway.

"You're a fortunate man that Torquil and I share a ring size," he said.

Emrys turned to him with raised brows, noticing him standing there for the first time, and then he followed Keelan's gaze to his chest and laughed. He lifted Torquil's hand and kissed the back of it before he inspected the ring, making the dark fire opal and even darker rubies set in a cluster around it sparkle brilliantly in the light of the room.

"Even more fortunate that you're both good at sharing."

Torquil moved their hand to Emrys' arm and hummed their agreement. "I get the first half of the night, Keelan gets the second half."

They said it with such ease that it sounded like they'd actually discussed it beforehand. Keelan grinned so hard in response that it crinkled his eyes. His own temporary band still sat snugly on his finger. He rubbed at it with the pad of his thumb and wondered what would happen if he accidentally lost it. Wilder things had gone missing at balls. He'd once returned home to discover he'd lost a stocking but not the shoe.

"You looked positively miserable during your dance with Miss Wilton-Reed," Emrys said smoothly after taking another pull of his drink. "It was quite comical paired with her dazzling smile."

"I'm supposed to be fetching her a drink right now." Keelan glanced in the direction he'd left her.

Emrys chuckled at that. "I'm certain you both could use one."

Another couple approached to speak with Emrys and Torquil, so Keelan turned his attention to the crowd. He could not deny that he was looking for one person in particular as he walked to the table set with drinks and tiny bites of food. With two waters in hand, he began the journey back to his betrothed, still searching. His magic brightened nearly on instinct as his eyes locked with a pair of dark ones across the room.

Silas had found company—somewhat surprisingly—with Wyndham and Roger. It was so rare to see the gentlemen speaking with anyone but each other at social events, but it appeared that they were enjoying themselves. Even Wyndham's characteristic expression of mild aversion had been replaced with one of cautious relaxation.

Keelan realized suddenly that he had stopped in the middle of the room to stare. He recovered with a glance around him to see if anyone had noticed before he turned back just in time to see Silas excusing himself from the small group. Keelan lifted one of his drinks and tossed it back like something much stronger before he placed both glasses on the tray of a passing servant and moved as casually as he could to follow Silas out of the room.

He searched the hallway and peered around several corners. Keelan was nearly ready to turn back when there was a sturdy grip on his upper arm and he found himself with his back pushed against the wall. He squeezed his eyes shut with a soft moan and let himself be kissed. Silas' thigh pressed between his legs brought a spark of pleasure and pain that made him gasp.

"Not here," Keelan whispered urgently.

Silas' rough palm was such a contrast to his own as he took the other man's hand, lacing their fingers together. Silently, Keelan guided them out to the garden and followed the path far beyond the view of the windows and the party inside. He did not stop until the only sounds around them were of nature. Leaves rustled gently in the trees overhead while insects sang their nighttime serenades.

Their destination became the slab of a stone bench tucked into the flowers just off the path. Silas straddled it and pulled Keelan down into his arms, leaving him with one leg draped over Silas' muscular thigh and the other stretched out haphazardly across the bench, his side to Silas' chest. They came together again as though they'd never stopped. Keelan twisted enough in Silas' grip to hold the sides of his face as their kisses continued with heat and purpose. It was everything he wanted, until Silas' hands started toward the buttons on his trousers. Keelan broke their kiss and caught Silas' wrist gingerly.

"As much as I would love for you to take me here in the flowers," he panted on a whisper, their foreheads together, "I must admit to you that I am…" He gave an awkward huff of a laugh. "I am a bit sore."

Keelan had requested a healing salve that morning, claiming a nondescript muscle ache. Marten had eyed him knowingly and instructed that he apply it and wait a day or two before exerting said *muscle* again, and that any more robust activity before an appropriate amount of rest would only amplify the issue. Keelan accepted the balm with his cheeks burning and a sheepish grin.

"You're hurt?" Silas' mood shifted instantly with his confession, and Keelan hurried to assuage his concern.

"Not at all," he promised, letting go of Silas' wrist so that he could smooth his thumb across the man's cheek again. "It's only that I've never been so…so vigorous with myself for as many nights in a row as I have with you."

It was quiet between them for a moment as Silas seemed to process this information, and Keelan let out another embarrassed little laugh as he wrapped his arms around Silas' shoulders and hid his face against his neck.

"I am sorry," he went on. He thought of trying to explain how most of his previous intimate experiences had been spread out over a much greater length of time, and that, in large part, the ladies he took to bed were not nearly as adventurous as Silas. "It's been so wonderful," he said instead. "I suppose that's part of the problem, isn't it?"

Silas did not find what he said amusing the way Keelan had hoped, but he was relieved when he was gently maneuvered so that Silas could place the most delicate kiss on his mouth.

"I am the one who should be apologizing," Silas murmured into the stillness of the night air around them. "You are too precious to be treated in such a way. It is my fault entirely for not being more gentle with you."

Keelan's lips curved in a small grin against Silas's mouth.

"I've rather enjoyed it," he whispered before he kissed him.

Wordlessly, they settled into a slow, savoring sort of rhythm that did not involve removing any of their clothes. When they were both out of breath, Keelan relaxed more against Silas' solid form and enjoyed the thrill he felt when Silas wrapped both arms around his middle and pulled him close.

"I cannot stop thinking about your mother's kitchen."

Silas snorted. "Just what every man wants to hear after being kissed."

Laughter bubbled in Keelan's chest as he traced his fingertips over the back of Silas' hand. The occasion had him wearing more clothing than usual, leaving him without access to the man's forearms, unfortunately.

"It's a marvel to me," Keelan explained. "The thought of my own mother being anywhere near a kitchen is preposterous. But the way you've described her makes me wish to see what your life is like so badly." He paused. "Your real life, I mean. At home with your family."

The silence that followed was heavier than Keelan had meant for it to be. In truth, he had not been able to stop thinking about their entire conversation. Listening to Silas speak about his family and their work, and then the life he'd dreamed up for them had been so enchanting that he'd nearly forgotten it was just that: a dream. A perfect fantasy that was everything Keelan had ever wanted.

He did not realize that his magic had crept free until it was met with a teasing brush of an answer. Keelan closed his eyes as he let it wrap around the both of them, feeling the shift in the air as they were cloaked with a gossamer sense of security and hope and something more that Keelan was too scared to give a name to.

"I see you've found yourself a refreshment after all. Good to know I'll have the sort of husband who is dull *and* disobedient."

Miss Wilton-Reed's voice cut through the thick air and Keelan gasped hard enough that a sharp pain lashed across his chest. He tried to move away from Silas' embrace, but the man held tight, and Keelan realized there was no use in trying to pretend. She'd already seen them. She was standing a short distance away with her arms crossed loosely over her chest.

"Melisande," Keelan choked out, startled into using her name for the first time. It felt as wrong as he'd always known it would. "I—"

"Save your explanations," she said, and Keelan could see now that her expression was more smug than anything. "I do not care where you find your entertainment." Her gaze traveled over them with distaste before she gave a short hum of something like pity. "Have your fun while it lasts. In little more than a fortnight, this dreadful project will be over and we will be on our way to Bath."

Something cold swept through Keelan at the finality of her words. He finally managed to work his way out of Silas' hold and got to his feet, unsteady as he felt. He was desperate to say something, but he could not make himself speak. All he could do was stare at her retreating form until she disappeared.

He did not realize his entire body was shaking until he felt Silas' arms around him again, tight and strong.

"Cricket," he murmured against Keelan's ear. The single word was comfort; it was sorrow. It was too much and not enough. Keelan's face crumpled with emotion when Silas pressed a kiss to his jaw. "I'll take you home."

CHAPTER 49

SILAS

CRICKET WAS SO VISIBLY SHAKEN from their encounter with Miss Wilton-Reed that Silas had a bit of difficulty navigating him through the party. He did not take him home, as promised, but to his own bed, though Cricket didn't seem to mind. He stood quietly as Silas undressed them both before pulling him into his arms on the bed. They laid together in silence for a long time as Silas tried to think of the right thing to say.

Before he managed to come up with anything suitable, Cricket murmured, "I suppose I should be grateful that she did not demand we stop. She would have had every right to."

His tone was wooden and it made Silas ache to hear the proof of how affected he was. He rubbed Cricket's arms soothingly. "For a woman who claims such pride in her fae blood, it would have been foolish indeed for her to protest what is common practice within fae culture. It would have associated her with human prudery, which is the last thing she wants. And besides, you are not yet married. You have a right to share a bed with whomever you please right now."

"But not after," Cricket said. "Not when I leave London. She made it…perfectly clear that I will belong to her. I don't—I don't know how —" He shuddered as a sob racked through him and Silas pulled him close.

After the tears subsided, Silas pressed a kiss to his temple and said, "Tell me what you need, Cricket."

"I need you—I need you to help me forget…at least as much as we can…until then. Please," he whispered.

Silas tilted Cricket's face up and kissed him. The moments melted into hours. The hours slid into days as Silas made good on Cricket's request.

By day, they continued to work tirelessly on their project. Wyndham continued through the list of possible spells and Silas grew more and more adept at handling raw materials. It wasn't long before he was handling them with the same ease with which he handled treated supplies. Silas was relieved by that; treated materials were expensive to purchase. And anything to increase his power and magical efficacy was a boon to the family business. He began making lists in his notebook of ways he could store more raw ingredients, besides the ones Wyndham had already marked, and how to incorporate what he was learning into his trade.

By night, Silas waited until Cricket joined him in bed, and proceeded to do everything in his power to help the man forget his impending marriage. This took the form of kisses, pleasure, hours of teasing his body, and more conversation. Silas told Cricket more about his family, his plans for his own future cottage, and his work with Wyndham. He read aloud from his little notebook, describing ideas and dreams he had for his magic. Cricket took every form of distraction with equal eagerness. He soaked up the pleasure like a man starved for it. He lapped up every word as if it were the most fascinating topic, and not Silas droning on about banalities.

Through it all, there was a sense of a clock ticking, of their time together drawing to a close. Silas cursed himself, not for the first time, for waiting until Vauxhall to make things right. They had lost so much precious time together by the delay. He did his best to make up for it, although it meant that he was sleeping less and less as he kept Cricket occupied. Cricket wasn't much better, staying awake long after the rest of the household had gone to bed, prompting Silas with questions. Though they were both fully exhausted from the lack of rest, neither complained. Sleep could wait until after Cricket's marriage. Sleep could wait until after London. Sleep would wait until they said goodbye for the last time. In the meantime, they would keep each other company into the early hours of morning, feeding each other as much love and affection as their limited time together allowed.

TORQUIL'S TRIBUNE

THURSDAY 16 JUNE, 1814

Greetings, restless readers,

We come to you today with some very exciting news. Not only is this information going to be heard by the readers of this humble paper first, but it was hand-delivered by the couple in question this very morning:

We are honored to announce that Mr. Arlen Buckthorn and Miss Aveline Wrenwhistle have been married.

Some may wonder at the speed with which this couple hastened to the altar. But those who are close to the couple will surely recognize that there is no one so impatient as a pair deeply in love. Mrs. Buckthorn, nee Wrenwhistle, is well known to be of a romantic disposition. We are relieved that she has found true love at last.

The timing may well be perfect for such an event as the newlyweds were part of the project researching fae-human magic. Sources close to the Council have confided that the project is concluding tomorrow. It has been nearly two months since the fae-human volunteers entered our fair city and this writer waits with bated breath as to what discoveries have been made in that time. We shall be sure to share all that we learn.

Your winsome writer,

Sal Bailey

CHAPTER 50

KEELAN

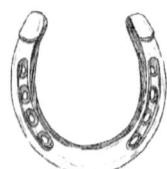

ON THE FINAL morning before what was to be the last day of the project, Keelan ambled wearily into the sitting room. He was dressed and had already taken a light breakfast in his bedroom, but he was seeking something else. Elodie, Alouetta, and his father all looked up at him and watched as he crossed the room to take a seat on the sofa. He was grateful that his father had never cared much for decorum as he allowed himself to sink into the cushion at an angle and pulled his legs up to his chest, wrapping his arms around them. He placed his chin on his knee and met his father's gaze. They had spoken little since the engagement.

His father leaned forward around Elodie on his lap and set his needlework into a basket by his feet.

"I am worried about you," he said softly in French.

"Yes," Keelan agreed.

"Everything about you says that you are miserable." His father's eyes traveled over his body. "You look exhausted. You hardly eat at dinner. I cannot recall the last time you were home to enjoy a quiet evening." There was a pause. "And yet you are smiling."

Keelan hid his grin against his knees. "Yes."

He felt as though his life had been divided, split into halves so different that he was nearly living two realities at once.

Miss Wilton-Reed had continued to make him feel useless while they worked on the project together. Her excitement for reaching the end of it had steadily increased as she focused more on what was to come after: a formal announcement in the papers, going home to her family with a soon-to-be-husband on her arm, something new to hold over her parents' and sisters' heads that made her feel more important than anyone else.

Keelan decided that it was smart to enjoy it while it lasted. In all likelihood, she would go back to being the lady she was when they first met after the wedding was over. With something to look forward to, she had stopped playing tricks with her magic. They'd been able to complete the rubric several times through, and he was actually quite proud of the notes he'd compiled. He hoped they would be useful to the Council after all was said and done. It would be the last mark he left on London before he moved away.

His magic swirled in his chest with tepid melancholy.

The project had brought him a spouse he did not want. But it had also brought him more time with Emrys. It had given him the opportunity to get to know Torquil better, and Wyndham and Roger. He'd met new people and learned a great deal about magic; human magic, fae magic, and the uniqueness of both.

He even found himself using his own magic more often. The constant exposure to it had made him feel more comfortable and confident with his abilities than he had in years. It felt natural to call on it for simple tasks again, like extinguishing candles across the room, or closing a door, or—

Keelan's smile broadened as his cheeks flushed.

Silas loved his magic. He'd told him so after Keelan had provided fairy lights for them at Silas' request the night before. They'd been tangled up in the sheets and each other, catching their breath and staring up at the last few lights that had not blinked out or floated away, and Silas had whispered it in his ear.

Keelan's magic had flared in his chest at the words. He'd been so sure that Silas was going to say something else.

In truth, several other moments just like it had transpired between them since the night of the ball. Once when Silas had a hand on his cheek and was holding his gaze for a few seconds too long, but instead of words, Silas only gave him a kiss instead. Another when Silas had slipped an orange into his pocket and saved it for them to share in bed. He'd leaned in to kiss the juice off Keelan's chin after feeding him an especially succulent slice and murmured that he loved the shape of his mouth.

Keelan's father let out a slow hum of understanding.

"*Tu es amoureux*," he said with a twinkle in his eye.

"Yes, Papa." Keelan's stomach roiled with joy. "I am in love."

The words were freedom and condemnation in a single breath.

Silas had continued to purr fantasies into Keelan's ear every night they spent together. They spoke of the life they could build, holiday traditions they thought were ridiculous and new ones they would like to form, favorite foods that Silas' mother might teach him to make someday. Silas asked him to read the silly little stories from his book of fables so they could discuss them the way scholars might and then laughed until their stomachs ached.

One more day.

A lifetime with Silas would not be long enough, but they only had one more day before the project would be over, Silas would go back to his family in the country, and Keelan would say goodbye to London.

Keelan was on the precipice of his life changing forever. It was terrifying and isolating and it made him want to scream until his lungs burst. Miss Wilton-Reed could take him away from his home, from his friends, from every comfort he had ever known. But she could not take away his friendships. His memories. Nothing could ever wipe away the time he had shared with Silas or the emotions that had grown between them. He had spent his entire life longing for the perfect love, and now he had known it, and that would stay with him forever.

He was going to ask Silas if they could write letters. Keelan had seen the stacks he sent out to his family, and he seemed to enjoy writing them, so he hoped it would be no hardship. Even a few times a year would be better than nothing at all. They could remain friends and keep in touch. Certainly Silas would agree to that?

Keelan used the heel of his thumb to quietly wipe the tears from his cheeks.

"Whoever they are," his father said after a while, "they are the luckiest person to have earned your beautiful heart, even if only for a moment."

The arrival of a footman prompted Keelan to unfold his legs and sit on the sofa as he should. He took the paper from the silver tray presented to him and sniffed back his weepy feelings. The *Tribune* had changed a bit since Torquil gave it up, but Keelan had become particularly invested ever since the project began. He felt it was only a matter of time before he found his own name printed in the fresh ink again, given his newfound proclivity for scandal.

Miss Wilton-Reed, to his knowledge, had not told anyone about what she had seen in the gardens that night. Silas had reassured him several times since that she seemed to have held true to her word. It shouldn't have been surprising. She did not care about him in any other way, so why should it matter who he found pleasure with? Her borrowed ring was still on his finger. That was all she truly held interest in.

Keelan wasted no time settling in his seat and reading over the latest gossip. Torquil had always placed the most stirring news within the first lines to catch the reader's attention, and it seemed that Sal Bailey was keeping the tradition alive. As he read, his eyes slowly got wider and wider until he gasped, slapping a hand over his mouth.

His father had never shown interest in reading gossip papers, but he lifted his head from the needlework he'd resumed and gave his son a curious look.

"Miss Aveline Wrenwhistle and Mr. Arlen Buckthorn have *eloped*," he said with barely-contained surprise. He got to his feet, holding the paper in both hands as he read over those couple of lines again. "I must call on Emrys at once." He folded the paper with little care and shoved it into his breast pocket.

His father laughed as he ran out of the sitting room.

"Their poor mother," he heard him say. "Such headstrong children."

UPON ARRIVAL at the Wrenwhistle townhouse, Keelan was led to a sitting room where there was the distinct tension of a recent family disagreement hanging in the air. Wyndham was seated on a sofa with Roger practically holding him in place. Torquil was perched on the arm of a chair, watching Emrys pace the floor with one hand fisted on his hip and the other on the back of his neck. They all turned to look at him and he offered a crooked, sympathetic grin.

"I read the news," he said.

It was met with a groan from both brothers.

"I cannot believe she's done this." Wyndham looked ready to throw his husband off him and storm out of the room, but Roger persisted in stroking a hand down his chest with a deep frown on his features.

"Can't you?" Emrys sighed and shook his head. "It was the perfect timing, with Mother gone to visit Auberon. We should have expected as much."

"Have you spoken to her?" Keelan stood awkwardly until Torquil gestured to the chair they were propped on. He accepted the invitation to sit but was surprised when Torquil did not move away. Instead, they laid their arm along the back of the chair. Keelan's chest warmed with the friendly gesture to share space so intimately.

"She just left with Mr. Buckthorn," Emrys told him. "They're off to explain themselves to his parents next, though it seems they are confident his family will be far more understanding."

Keelan's bottom lip curved with confusion. "Why would she do it? They're both of age, and I would not imagine anyone having any objections? They've been courting since winter."

Wyndham pinched the bridge of his nose. "It seems that Mr. Buckthorn proposed to her yesterday and they…could not wait."

A realization settled over Keelan. It was common enough for couples to hurry along with well-intended plans to join their families before a baby arrived.

"Are they—" he tried. "Is she—?"

Emrys snorted. "Now that *really* would have made Mother's head explode. All four of her children successfully married *and* two grandchildren on the way within a year."

Torquil chuckled at that before leaning a bit closer to Keelan. "That was Emrys and Wyndham's first question, too. Aveline very quickly indicated that it was impossible, as she and Mr. Buckthorn have never engaged in such activity before."

Keelan's brows shot up. "Not ever?"

"Apparently so," Torquil said. Everyone in the room exchanged an awkward glance in passing at the notion. They'd all had their hands in that basket long before marriage, save for Roger. "It seems that the happy couple is of the mind that a meaningful connection does not require such intimate relations."

"Aveline watched Mother take charge of all three of our weddings," Emrys explained as he finally took a heavy seat in a nearby chair. "She said that she did not want that to happen to her."

"Not an unreasonable wish," Roger added with a supportive tone that indicated his own thoughts on the matter.

"But Aveline loves weddings," Keelan argued.

"Aveline loves *romance*," Emrys corrected. "She loves love."

Keelan's gaze fell to his lap. "And an elaborate wedding means little if there is no love to show for it."

He wished he could be so brave as to defy his own mother's wishes surrounding his impending ceremony. What would happen if he broke his engagement and did what Aveline had done, running off into the night with the man he'd fallen for, nothing but wedded bliss waiting for them on the other side? The announcement was not yet official, but everyone in London—and likely in Bath—already knew. To end the relationship now without the support of his mother would be a grave decision, indeed.

Besides, as fanciful as Keelan was when it came to romance, he still wanted a proper wedding. Silas *deserved* a proper wedding so that his family could be there to celebrate his happiness. Keelan could never take that away from Silas no matter how desperate he was to spend the rest of their lives together.

Torquil set their hand on Keelan's arm and gave it a light squeeze.

He'd already cried once that morning, which meant more tears were ready to fall at the slightest provocation, but he managed to blink them back.

"Love is what you make it," Torquil said. "It is a connection between two people. How they choose to share it with the world is up to them."

Keelan lifted his chin and met Torquil's eyes. They offered him a grin.

"Wyndham and Roger fell in love with all of London watching. Emrys and I fell in love slowly, privately. Aveline and Mr. Buckthorn felt that their love was something too special to share with anyone but each other. There is no right way to love someone. But you must let it happen, if you have any hope of being truly content."

In the silence that followed, Keelan accepted that Torquil was telling him something more than what it seemed. He could not bring himself to ask what he desperately wanted to know. His heart began to race. If Torquil knew, did Emrys know? Did anyone else? Why had none of them said anything?

The moment came to an abrupt end when Torquil was bodily removed from the arm of the chair. They let out a little yelp of surprise as Emrys scooped them up into his arms and kissed them there in front of everyone.

"Why are you so bloody perfect?" Emrys demanded affectionately.

Torquil laughed and strained half-heartedly against Emrys, clearly wanting to be put down, but Emrys was not having it. They finally relented and turned their head to look down at Keelan again.

"Only trying to help a friend," they said.

CHAPTER 51

SILAS

WHEN SILAS STRODE into the breakfast room that morning, he found the table chattering with excitement. It didn't take long for him to find out why.

"I think it's so wonderfully romantic," Miss Gloucester-Stone was saying. "Don't you? Imagine such a thing happening during our project."

"And they're so beautiful together," Mr. Finkle-Finch added.

"A lovely couple indeed," Mx. Badger-Thorp said, giving him a smile. "I can't say I'm surprised. They haven't been able to take their eyes off each other since our project began."

Silas filled his plate and took a seat next to Mrs. Pimpernel. "Who are we discussing?" he asked in a low voice.

She grinned. "Miss Aveline Wrenwhistle and Mr. Arlen Buckthorn eloped this morning. It's in the *Tribune*. It's all anyone can talk about." She passed him a copy of the gossip column.

Silas had barely read the *Tribune* since arriving in London. He skimmed through the news in question. He handed it back with a chuckle. He had to agree with Badger-Thorp; it wasn't exactly surprising.

"I think it's disgraceful," Miss Wilton-Reed said. "They have brought shame on both of their families with such conduct."

"They're of age," Miss Gloucester-Stone said flippantly.

"And they're in love," Mr. Finkle-Finch added. "I'm sure their families will understand."

Miss Wilton-Reed sneered. "Love is a children's fable. It won't last. Besides, the Wrenwhistle family is famously wealthy. Buckthorn was probably just after her dowry."

"If he was, he went about it very poorly," Mrs. Pimpernel remarked.

"And besides," Miss Gloucester-Stone pressed, "anyone who watched them could see that they were in love. Dowries never entered their minds."

"Some of us lead with our hearts rather than our purse strings," Silas said. "But I don't expect you to understand that."

Miss Gloucester-Stone gasped at his comment and Mx. Badger-Thorpe patted Miss Wilton-Reed's hand. "I'm sure he didn't mean that."

The lady ignored Mx. Badger-Thorpe and smirked at Silas. "And what does that make you?"

"A fool," he replied, "because I spent too long not listening to my heart. I'm glad there are some who are wiser than I." He got up and left, his food only partially eaten.

He returned to his room and gathered up his notebook and his belt. It was strange knowing that the project was nearly over. A month ago, he would have rejoiced at the thought of returning home. Now, he just felt a familiar ache at the notion. He hated London. But now he grieved having to leave it.

When they arrived at the Council chambers, they were greeted by all six of the councilmembers.

"We've come to observe your progress," Councilmember Cricket announced. She turned a beady eye to the three youngest councilmembers. "After nearly two months of seeing only reports of this project, it's high time we took a more active hand."

Councilmember Barnes clapped his hands together eagerly. "We are very excited to see what you've all been up to. Everything I've read has been very promising."

Silas glanced at Torquil, Wyndham, and Roger. They had all, apparently, been just as surprised by the appearance of their peers. Torquil recovered first. "I'm sure you will be delighted by the results," they said.

"Although I hope you'll forgive some amount of confusion this morning," Wyndham said in a tone that suggested he was demanding understanding rather than hoping for it. "My sister and her husband will not be joining us, so we will be making some last-minute adjustments to account for that."

Councilmember Applewood beamed at him. "Of course, Councilmember Wrenwhistle. And may I offer you my congratulations on the happy news?"

Wyndham replied with a grimace that was probably meant to be a smile. "Thank you," he murmured. "Who should we start with, Roger?"

Roger snapped into action, tapping his glasses up his nose and pulling a sheet of paper out of his breast pocket. "I think it might be good for the rest of the Council to see the rubric in action. Although we don't technically need the pairs to perform together as they're no longer taking notes, I think it might make everyone feel more comfortable if we continue as we have? Perhaps if Mx. Badger-Thorp is not opposed, we could start with them and Emrys? And since you will be first, you can select which skill you'd like to perform."

Mx. Badger-Thorp strode forward and greeted Mr. Wrenwhistle. Silas was relieved to see that they had none of their initial nervousness from the start of the project. Clearly Mr. Wrenwhistle's magic did not have the same impact on them as it had on Silas.

"We'll do focus," they said. "Mr. Wrenwhistle has been very patient with me as I get more comfortable with my magic. And the glowing spell was the first skill that I felt I truly excelled in."

"They're being modest," Mr. Wrenwhistle said gallantly.

They chuckled and got to work, calmly preparing everything on the long table that had been home to Cricket and Miss Wilton-Reed for so long. Everyone watched in silence. Silas realized that after spending a month with these people, he'd really only seen Miss Wilton-Reed perform magic. Mx. Badger-Thorp was careful and methodical as they cast, which didn't surprise him. Their glowing spell was executed flaw-lessly, if a bit plainly.

Councilmember Barnes gave them a warm smile when they were done. "Excellent work. Thank you."

"Mr. Finkle-Finch, if you would?" Wyndham prompted.

Mr. Finkle-Finch looked terrified as he stepped forward. "But, my partner is—"

"Not to worry," Wyndham said easily. "I'll step in for my sister." He turned back to his colleagues. "This will be an excellent example of how things may go with a pair that have not yet worked together."

This did not seem to make Mr. Finkle-Finch any less nervous. But Wyndham was patient as he joined him at the table and asked in a low voice which spell he felt most comfortable doing.

"Perhaps a shrinking spell?" Mr. Finkle-Finch said, his voice tight with anxiety.

Wyndham patted him on the shoulder. "Very good. Mr. Finkle-Finch will be demonstrating the power skill."

Mr. Finkle-Finch was pale and his hands shook as he put everything together. Wyndham kept his hand on the man's shoulder. Silas could tell without feeling for it that the gentleman had already spooled out his own magic around the other man, probably with a mind to calm him down, considering the way Finkle-Finch's shoulders lowered as he began to work.

Finkle-Finch's nerves still came into play when he performed, over-shooting his magic and causing the pencil to shrink to a nub. But the Council seemed satisfied and Finkle-Finch hurried back to where the rest of the fae-humans were standing at the front of the room.

"Miss Gloucester-Stone, if you would be so kind?" Roger said, giving her a friendly nod.

Miss Gloucester-Stone and Mx. Hillcrest stepped forward. "I quite like the way intuition has been tested," she said. "I'd like to do that one, if you don't mind."

"Of course," Councilmember Applewood said with a warm smile.

Miss Gloucester-Stone seemed almost eager as she performed the different spells for intuition: pouring liquid from one jar to the other, and rolling pencils across the table. Mx. Hillcrest leaned forward to congratulate her on a job well done before the pencil had reached the end of the table. Miss Gloucester-Stone hopped a little in place, clearly pleased with herself.

Councilmember Barnes scooped up the pencil. "Very well done," he said. "I'm feeling quite encouraged so far. I think you're all doing excellent work."

"Why don't we see Miss Wilton-Reed and my son next?" Councilmember Cricket demanded. "I'm very curious to see what they will do together."

No one spoke as Miss Wilton-Reed strode forward with her chin held high and confidence rippling off of her. "I will demonstrate control," she said coolly.

Cricket was pale as he stepped up to her side.

Miss Wilton-Reed reached out to wrap a hand around his arm and guide him closer than necessary. Then she leaned forward over the table and got to work. Silas noticed that she seemed to still have a bit of reticence about using too much human magic. Her breeze spell was done without error, but it lacked power. He knew exactly which sigil she ought to have used to give it more of a boost, but she hadn't spent enough time writing on her spellpaper to have used the complex one he had in mind. He couldn't resist a small smile to himself that the lady's arrogance was holding her back from reaching her full potential.

"Thank you, my dear," Councilmember Cricket said. "That was… quite satisfactory."

For the first time, Miss Wilton-Reed looked a little uncertain. But she forced a smile, gave a simpering little nod, and then took Cricket's arm again.

Wyndham stepped forward. "For our last skill, I'd like to suggest we show you something a little different. But first, I'd like to explain a little about our learnings, particularly in regards to our last fae-human volunteer, Mr. Rook-Worth." He gestured to Silas, who walked to his side.

"As I'm sure you all know, magical compatibility is a complex thing. No one can ever predict how their magic will react against someone else's. We had difficulty finding suitable partners for about half of our volunteers. And they've all been remarkably patient with us as we shuffled them around with different fae, trying to find the right person to pair them with. But none more so than Mr. Rook-Worth. The gentleman has worked with practically every fae in our group, and all to different effect—most of which were not favorable." He held up a hand. "This is not to say anything slighting about Mr. Rook-Worth's magical abilities. In fact, I think I can speak for all of us when I say that he has exhibited a remarkable ability to respond appropriately to different magics, even the ones that were not favorable with his own."

"I recall reading that," Councilmember Barnes said in a musing voice. "He compensated for the constriction on his magic by adding more power to his spells."

"Exactly," Wyndham replied. "And he showed remarkable instincts throughout the whole of our project. In one case, he prevented disaster," he added with a wry smile, "and overall, he completed the entire rubric first, despite the delay due to incompatibility."

Wyndham glanced at him and then continued. "And for that reason, the three of us agreed to start Mr. Rook-Worth in the second half of our project early. Which is to say, we wanted to experiment with raw materials and see if they had a similar impact on magic as they have for Torquil. Mr. Rook-Worth was kind enough to indulge us. I've been working with him for weeks now and have only positive things to say about his abilities." He paused. "But I think for today's demonstration, it might behoove us to explore a bit of what we experienced as we shuffled everyone around. I'd like Mr. Rook-Worth to show you what he can do with raw materials. And if he will indulge me, I've been curious about the fact that only one fae volunteer was never paired with him. Mr. Cricket, would you mind?"

Cricket stepped forward, looking very hesitant.

Wyndham beckoned him closer. "If this experiment does not go as hoped, then we will ask Mr. Rook-Worth to demonstrate his impressive flexibility and I will take over in Mr. Cricket's stead. But I think it is very fitting that our last skill to show is understanding. According to our rubric, that would be shown via a fire spell. But I think we can all agree that might not be ideal for an experiment." He flashed a grin. "So perhaps Mr. Rook-Worth will indulge us with one of his other spells that we have done together."

Wyndham gave Silas a nod and stepped away to watch. Silas stared after him. There was a gleam in the gentleman's eye that showed he was, indeed, up to *something*. Silas had a pretty good idea of what Wyndham was scheming, but he was quite sure it wouldn't make any difference. Cricket was still engaged. It hardly mattered how well he performed magic with someone else.

But when he turned to look at Cricket, who offered him a hesitant smile, everything else faded away. Their magical compatibility was undeniable. It felt as though the culmination of a question he didn't know he'd been asking: what would it be like to truly perform a spell with Cricket? Would it feel as warm and vibrant as it did when they were in bed? Would it feel as steady and sure as it did when Cricket was in his arms?

"What would you like to perform, Mr. Rook-Worth?" Cricket asked, his voice shaking only slightly.

"A shade spell," Silas replied, without hesitation. Anything to shut out the people around them, to give them some space, to have a moment alone, even if it was for the last time—especially if it was the last time.

Cricket's smile was bright. "Whatever you say."

Silas wanted to kiss him, but instead he turned to the table and started a new spell sheet. He allowed himself to sink into his own comfortable rhythm, reaching for the fresh oak leaves in his side pouch, the pencil in the back pouch, his fingers working automatically, his mind buzzing ahead of his movements. He looked over his shoulder at Cricket and gave him a nod. He felt Cricket's magic envelope him, as comforting and familiar as it always was, and then he cast the spell.

After weeks of practicing with Wyndham, Silas had mastered his control with raw materials. He could tell the spell worked as planned when he and Cricket were shrouded in shadow and the rest of the group murmured in surprise. But there was no panic to the murmuring, which gave Silas all he needed to know about his spell reaching the intended scope. With Cricket's magic added to the mix, his shade spell took on more personality; it had known he wanted time alone with the man he loved and it gave him that. As always, his magic felt sharper in Cricket's presence, more precise, more intentional. He heard Cricket gasp in surprise and he pulled the man close.

Cricket wrapped his arms around Silas' neck. After nights of memorizing each other, they didn't need the light to find each other's lips in a kiss. Then Cricket stepped back and snapped his fingers. Fairy lights twirled overhead, illuminating the small space between them. Silas could still hear everyone beyond the boundary of the spell, but he paid them no heed as he took Cricket's hand and leaned their foreheads together.

"You still shine brighter than anyone I've ever met," he whispered. He pressed another kiss to Cricket's lips and then they stepped away, just before the spell ended and the room brightened once again.

CHAPTER 52

KEELAN

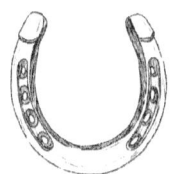

KEELAN BLINKED SEVERAL TIMES, letting his eyes adjust to the light in the room as the shade spell faded and took his fairy lights with it. His pulse and his magic were thrumming in his chest, and he could feel how wide his smile was, but he was helpless against it all. He stared at Silas even after the man had turned away to begin cleaning up the spell. He only remembered the rest of the people gathered around them when someone began to laugh—loudly.

It was Emrys.

Keelan turned to look at him, a flush racing across his face and chest. Emrys' eyes were wide with mischief. He wore the distinct expression of someone who had just made a grand discovery.

That's your stranger, Emrys mouthed at him with glee.

Keelan bit his lip and turned his head away, glancing at Silas appreciatively, before he met Emrys' gaze again with an impish nod.

The moment Wyndham had suggested that they perform the spell together, he'd known it would expose their magical compatibility to the entire group, including his best friend. There was no use denying it now. Emrys laughed again as the rest of the room came back into focus.

Everyone was still murmuring their thoughts about what they'd just witnessed, and it seemed that they were all rather impressed with what

Silas had done. He deserved every bit of it. Councilmember Barnes had formed a small circle with Roger, Wyndham, and Silas as he congratulated them all on the progress they'd made with raw materials. Torquil was standing with Councilmember Applewood and a few of the volunteers, all looking at ease as they spoke with smiles on their faces. The moment made something warm in Keelan's chest—until he locked eyes with his mother.

He did not need to wonder what she meant as she tilted her head toward the door. Keelan slipped out of the room and followed her down the hallway to her office. When her aide shut the door behind them, Keelan was instantly taken back to his childhood. He could remember standing in front of her desk, listening as she reprimanded him for his behavior at school, or politely asking if he and Emrys could go and play somewhere that did not smell of old books and furniture polish. He waited silently with his hands clasped behind his back as she sat in her chair and laced her fingers together atop the desk.

"What do you have to say for yourself?" she asked crisply.

Keelan's jaw worked as he lifted his chin a little higher.

"I do not know what you mean."

His mother gave a sharp laugh, already dropping her poise as she leaned back in her chair, gesturing with one open hand to the meeting room.

"Care to explain what I just witnessed?"

Keelan's brows pinched. "A shade spell. Silas is very good at them."

His mother went very still for a moment, before she seemed to come to some sort of a conclusion. Her eyes went to her lap as she smoothed a hand over her skirts.

"Silas," she commented flatly.

The heat drained from Keelan's face, only just realizing what he'd said.

"We've all become rather close during the project," he rushed to explain. "Many of us are familiar enough to refer to each other by name now."

She gave him a level look. "But not you and Melisande."

Keelan sighed, squeezing his eyes shut for a moment, before he opened them again and shook his head. He was only making this worse for himself.

"No, Mother."

"The spell she performed was pathetically underpowered." His mother stood from her desk and walked to the window, crossing her arms as she peered out at the view below. "Has it been like this the entire time? Her magic?"

"Yes," Keelan said cautiously. "It's somewhat of a sensitive topic for her. We have not discussed it since the earliest days of the project."

His mother huffed a laugh. "I can imagine not." She turned to him again. "Why did you not tell me that she greatly exaggerated her abilities?"

"I…thought you liked her?"

"I appreciate her shrewd mind. She and I view the world in a very similar way. But I never expected her to be the dishonest type."

"I apologize," Keelan said faintly. "I did not realize that I had a voice in the matter. I've been told by multiple people that this arrangement was your idea from the beginning."

"It was," she said, stepping around the desk. "The other councilmembers and I requested information about all of the volunteers before they ever arrived in London. I made it very clear that I wanted you to work with Miss Wilton-Reed because she comes from a good family. Every interaction I've had with the young lady has indicated that both of you were perfectly happy with the match."

"Yes, I suppose coming from her it would seem that way."

They stared at each other for a long moment before his mother sighed, rubbing at her forehead with a few fingertips.

"You have always had your father's soft heart. It's something I could never understand. We see the world in entirely different ways, you and I."

Keelan gave a small shrug. "Papa says you only want what's best for me."

His mother narrowed an eye at him. "Not that I would know. The two of you are always off having your secret conversations." Keelan was so surprised by the levity in her voice and the diminutive smirk she wore that he laughed.

"It makes him happy, I think," he reasoned.

"And you indulge him because you have always had the habit of putting others' happiness ahead of your own." She rested a hip against her desk, arms still crossed. "Your father is correct. I have only ever wanted what's in your best interest. Your marriage with Miss Wilton-Reed will provide you stability. A comfortable future. It is the most logical choice."

Keelan's chest ached.

"But after what I just witnessed, I cannot allow you to go through with it."

He knew he'd heard the words, but he could not believe them.

"Pardon?" he asked weakly.

"That was the most powerful display of magic I have ever seen from you. I daresay your sister's wedding spell was not even that impressive. I would be remiss in my duty to this Council, and in my duty as your mother, to deny you such a connection."

Keelan let out a shaky breath. "What are you saying?"

His mother pushed her hip away from the desk and walked around it to return to her chair. She began collecting the materials to write out a letter.

"I am saying that I will be speaking with Miss Wilton-Reed this evening to inform her that your contract has been revoked and that she will be returning to Bath alone." After a moment, she paused and looked up at him, setting her pen aside. She held her hand out across the desk, palm up, and waited.

Wordlessly, Keelan worked the thin band off his finger and gave it back to her. He rubbed his thumb against the indentation it had left behind. His mother inspected the ring briefly before she opened a drawer and put it inside.

"What are you waiting for?" she asked as she returned to her letter. "Go and tell Emrys your happy news."

CHAPTER 53

SILAS

SILAS WATCHED as Cricket followed his mother out of the room and into the hallway. He was too distracted to pay much attention to congratulations that were coming from all sides. So when Wyndham and Torquil pulled him aside and away from the small crowd, he was relieved.

"I knew you could pull it off," Wyndham began breezily.

Silas gave a small huff. "It was quite a gamble on your part."

"Not much. You did tell me your compatibility together was remarkable."

Silas rolled his eyes. "I knew you were scheming."

"If all goes according to plan," Torquil said, "his mother is in the process of deciding the marriage will not work out after all."

"You sound very sure of yourselves."

"We've been wanting this opportunity for some time," Wyndham said. "We didn't expect it to happen this way but—"

"Yes, the rest of the Council appearing suddenly did put us frightfully on the spot," Torquil agreed. "But we've had more brazen gambles than this one." They flashed him a grin. "How do you feel?"

Silas shrugged. "It feels strange for it to be over so suddenly." He glanced at the doorway where Cricket had disappeared through. "I've never been good at goodbyes."

Wyndham and Torquil exchanged a look.

"Are you daft?" Wyndham asked. "If we're right, Keelan will be free to marry whomever he chooses."

Silas' chest was tight. "That won't change my prospects."

"Are you aware of the way he looks at you?" Torquil asked. "I don't think it takes much of a guess to wonder what he'll decide."

Silas sighed and ran a hand over his hair. He felt wrung out from such an eventful morning. The possibility of Cricket not being betrothed to Miss Wilton-Reed made his heart feel light. But now, if Torquil was right, he was going to be faced with a decision he never expected would be his to make.

"Anyway, that's not why we wanted to talk to you," Wyndham said. He exchanged another look with Torquil. "I know we've discussed this in the past. But we really think you should consider a position on the Council. I *know* you're not a politician or an academic. Neither is Torquil, for that matter. And neither am I. That's why we need you. We need someone who cares about people and who cares about helping."

"Miss Gloucester-Stone has agreed to the second position," Torquil added. "With me as your Head of Council for the fae-human branch, I would be thrilled to have you. You are level-headed and you're thorough."

"And you don't have to stay in London all the time," Wyndham hastened to say. "Goodness knows I don't. I detest London. We're only here for a few months."

Silas glanced between them. In truth, it was a solution to the anxiety he was suddenly feeling about Cricket. If he could stay in London for part of the year, then perhaps…But then he shook his head. It wasn't fair to Cricket to tear him out of London, now that he might finally be given permission to stay. And he knew with absolute certainty that he couldn't possibly be in London and not with Cricket. "I'm sorry," he said. "I can't."

Torquil looked crestfallen. Wyndham looked annoyed. "Are you mad?"

"Perhaps. Now, if you'll excuse me, I think I'd better go and begin packing. It's a long journey home." He paused and gave them both a smile. "But I will miss you both. It's been a pleasure getting to know you."

"We'll be in touch," Torquil assured him.

"Good."

HE MADE it back to the townhouse alone and hurried to his room. He breathed out in relief at finally being alone. But being alone meant that he had no distractions from the recent events. The shade spell. Cricket. His sweet little fairy lights and his bright smile. The way being in his presence always felt so right, and the way their blended magics felt like a revelation. He thumped his head against the door. It was too painful to have everything he wanted so close within his grasp, yet knowing that it was an impossibility.

He heaved a sigh and slowly began packing his trunk. Now that the project was over, he wanted to be out of London as soon as possible. The sooner he was gone, the sooner Cricket could move on and find happiness again. He didn't even bother pretending he would ever be able to move on himself.

After about an hour, Cricket burst through the door, his smile broad and his cheeks flushed. Silas didn't have time to marvel over how easily Cricket had fit into his space before he was wrapped in a tight hug.

"It's over," Cricket breathed. "My mother is ending the contract. I'm not going to Bath. I'm not marrying that dreadful woman. I'm free, Silas!" He pulled back enough to kiss Silas.

And even though his own heart was breaking, Silas set his own feelings aside, lifted Cricket into his arms, and kissed him back.

"I can't believe it," Cricket said, when they finally pulled apart. "It's truly over. Can you believe it?"

Silas spared a moment to take in Cricket's beaming face. He wanted to save that memory forever, especially if it was going to be the last time they saw each other. "I'm glad your mother finally saw sense."

"Yes!" Cricket's eyes were bright as he began pacing the room. "She said she was disappointed by Miss Wilton-Reed's spell. 'Pathetically underpowered' were the words she used, I believe." A laugh bubbled out of him. "Can you imagine? *That* was the part that bothered her, the idea that the woman had lied about her own magical abilities." He ran a hand through his hair. "I knew she placed a lot of importance on wedding spells and magical compatibility but I never knew just how much—" Cricket stopped in front of the open trunk. He frowned and looked at Silas. "You're packing?"

"The project is over."

His frown deepened. "But—my engagement is called off. I thought you'd be pleased."

Silas took both of Cricket's hands in his and led him to the bed. "I *am* pleased. I can't properly convey how utterly relieved I am. I shall feel much more at peace now."

"At peace?" he echoed. "But—I thought—" He turned his face away as confusion clouded his features. Silas also detected a hint of fear that he'd now come to recognize. He hated that the fear was regarding him. "Did you not mean any of it then?" Cricket whispered at last.

Silas squeezed his hands. "Of course I meant it. I meant all of it." He cupped Cricket's face in one hand and tilted it to look at him. "I...I love you, Cricket. Which is why I'm leaving."

"That doesn't make any sense," Cricket said, his voice cracking.

"You were so distraught about leaving London, leaving your friends, your father, your life. I could never do that to you. It wouldn't be fair. I refuse to lock you up in a new life where you won't be happy."

"It wouldn't be the same," Cricket protested. "I love you, too. That has to count for something. What about your mother's kitchen? Your family business? You said I'd have a place in it."

Silas rubbed his thumb over Cricket's cheek. "I'd love nothing better than to have you in my life. But I would always worry that you regret it. Or that you'd come to regret it. I can offer none of the diversions London can. My family would adore you. But I have few friends. I am not so vain as to think my family would be sufficient in keeping you company, and that I would be sufficient in keeping you happy."

A tear slid down Cricket's cheek. "You won't even let us try?"

Silas tenderly wiped the tear away. "You are far too kind to admit that you're unhappy, Cricket. You would pretend. And you would be miserable. And it would be my fault."

Cricket shook his head and stood, pulling his hand free of Silas' grasp. He wrapped his arms around his chest, looking small and frightened. "And do I not have a say in any of this? My own mother realizes that we work well together. Why can't you?"

"Your mother's logic is without heart. You know that better than I do."

Cricket flinched.

"She might see that we work well together. And she might not realize that we fit together as well as we do. But all that talk, all those stories, they were dreams, Cricket. I wasn't telling you about the humble lives we keep. The lack of servants we have. You would miss your friends, but as much as I'd love for you to have them visit, where would they stay? Would you have Emrys and Torquil Wrenwhistle curled up on our sofa? It could never work."

Tears were flowing freely down Cricket's face now. When he spoke, his voice was low and raspy. "I cannot believe you would have so little faith in us. So little faith in me. You truly believe that I don't know what would make me happy? I've spent the past month or more thinking only of what I couldn't have. And now that I finally *can* have it, you would deny us both." His shoulders slumped. "Perhaps you're right then. Perhaps it was all a dream after all."

"Cricket—"

"I'll never forget you," Cricket said, turning to the door. "If you come to your senses and change your mind, you know where to find me."

He left and the door closed with a soft click. Silas leaned forward and put his head in his hands, his heart heavier than it had ever been.

CHAPTER 54

KEELAN

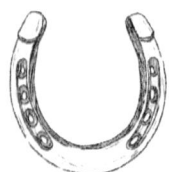

KEELAN STARED VACANTLY at the strip of sunlight stretched across the floor of his bedroom. He'd requested that the windows remain shut and the curtains drawn the following morning so that he could not hear the noise of the carriages departing the Pimpernel townhouse. He'd placed one of the smaller, more decorative pillows from his bed over his ear for good measure, holding it in place with his bent arm. He was sure he looked pathetic but he did not care, for it was a fair representation of how he felt.

He had expressly told Marten that he did not want anyone in his room, so when the door opened and there were footsteps on the hardwood, he already knew who it was. The mattress dipped with Emrys' weight as he sat on the edge.

"The visitors have gone," he said after a while.

"I wish them all a safe journey home," Keelan rasped.

His throat was raw and he could feel the stiff tracks of dried tears on his face. Even though the threat of hearing more than his heart could handle was over, he still did not want to move the pillow.

"Are you hungry? I can call for your breakfast."

"No," Keelan lied. He'd skipped tea and dinner the night before, and now he could not even guess what time it was, but he was ravenous.

Emrys sighed and tried again. "Do you want a bath drawn?"

"I want to be left alone."

"I know that is undoubtedly not true," Emrys said. "In all the years we have been friends, not once have you wished to be alone."

"Perhaps things have changed." Keelan closed his eyes and felt a new wash of grief as his magic floundered in his chest with the mess of emotions there. "All I want to do is lie here and cry, but I'm afraid I've no tears left." His voice broke on the last word. He pulled his coverlet higher to the small space that had been left open between his pillows and pressed it against his puffy eyes.

The weight on the mattress disappeared, and Keelan wondered if Emrys had actually listened to a request for once in his life. But then there was the sound of something hard being dropped on the floor. When it happened again, Keelan almost uncovered his face to try and see what was happening.

"Budge over, would you," Emrys grumbled as the mattress gave again, this time at his back. Suddenly there was an arm wrapped over his chest, pinning his arms and giving him a squeeze.

Keelan gave a weak laugh. "What are you doing?"

"Consoling you," Emrys told him casually. "Since you will not allow me to do anything else."

"You really do not have to do that," Keelan tried. Emrys was tucked against him from chest to knees to feet. The sounds he'd heard were apparently from him removing his shoes.

"Well, I have to do something. Torquil instructed that I'm not allowed to return home until I've made you laugh at least three times. I've only managed one so far."

Keelan could hear the smirk in his voice. He pushed the blanket away from his face with what little range of motion he had and welcomed the fresh air. He breathed in until his lungs ached and let it out in a rush. He stared again at the sunlight cutting a path across his rug.

"He told me that he loves me."

"Do you believe him?"

Keelan thought for a moment. "Yes."

"And do you also love him?"

His eyebrows pinched, chest tightening. "Yes."

"Then why are you so sad?"

"Because for some absurd reason, I am in your arms instead of his."

"He does have rather fantastic arms," Emrys mused.

Keelan chuckled at that. "He really does."

"I must say I'm quite upset that you never told me. How's that for a laugh, me suggesting you take him to bed when he was the one who upset you to begin with."

Keelan winced.

"I am sorry I did not tell you. I always meant to, but it never seemed to be the right time, especially when he was your partner for the project. I was worried you would say something to him about it."

"Of course I would have," Emrys said defensively. The weight of the arm around his chest lifted, and with it went the pillow over his head. Keelan shifted so that he was more on his back. Emrys was propped on his elbow on the pillow next to the one Keelan was using. "You're lucky the man left in one piece this morning. I had half a mind to make him regret ever coming here."

Keelan's eyes grew wide. "Not really?"

Emrys settled himself. "You know I've no interest in violence." He arched a brow. "However, Wyndham practically ignored him at the send-off. I think he is also hurt to see the man go. They did make a good team. Torquil said they offered Mr. Rook-Worth a position on the Council, but he turned them down."

Keelan's frown bunched to one side. "That is not surprising. He hates London. He said it was why he had to leave."

"Is that all he said?"

Keelan reflected for a moment on the memory of their painful conversation. As badly as he was hurting, he did not want to mix Silas' words.

"We talked at length about what a life together might look like. It was as if he could see into my head, Emrys. Everything I have ever dared to dream of, he made it seem like it could be real." He looked down and away. "But then he said his life in the country is not actually like that, and that he believes I would be miserable away from London."

Emrys used a finger to brush Keelan's hair away from his forehead.

"What sort of life did he describe?"

"Time spent with his family. He has a large one, and he adores his parents and siblings. His mother is always in the kitchen making the most delicious sounding food. Silas said that she would let me watch if I wanted to, and maybe someday she would even teach me to make something."

Emrys made a sound of genuine surprise. "A mother in the kitchen. What a novel idea."

"He said he would show me all of his favorite places around their home. He's known since he was a boy where he plans to build his own cottage." A small smile touched Keelan's lips. "He said we could build it together, and I could even decide how it looks on the inside. I told him I would send Papa the measurements and have him make all of the curtains for the windows."

"I am struggling to see where he thought you would not be happy."

"I suppose it's because I spent nearly as much time telling him how sad I was at the thought of leaving London, when I thought I was being sent away to be married. He told me he did not want to take me from my friends and all the things I love to do here."

"You do love London," Emrys reasoned. "But it sounds as though you have found something else you love even more."

Keelan met Emrys' gaze. "What if what he said is true? That his life is not really like what we discussed?"

Emrys' eyes narrowed as he looked away, lips pressed together in thought. "It seems to me that he is probably right. His life is nothing like you discussed. And do you know why?"

"Why?" Keelan asked warily.

"Because you are lying here in this bed instead of sitting next to him in his carriage, you rascal." He shoved at Keelan playfully. "Give me a moment. Let me think of how Torquil would say this." He closed his eyes and was silent. Lines formed on his forehead as he seemed to give real consideration to his next words. "Nearly there," he said in a slightly strained voice. Keelan laughed and rolled his eyes. "I've got it. Dreams, you said?"

Keelan nodded.

"Dreams will always remain dreams without ambition." Emrys'

brows went up, clearly impressed with himself. "It was easy for you to speak of those things because neither of you were convinced they would actually happen. I think that as soon as Mr. Rook-Worth realized that he suddenly had the power to make all of those dreams a reality, he got scared. My greatest fear is not being able to give Torquil everything they deserve and more. If he truly loves you, he likely feels the same."

"And the part about ambition?"

"How could you expect him to feel confident about making all of your dreams come true if he thinks you would not also be willing to put in the work?"

"I'm not sure I understand what you mean."

Emrys groaned and dropped forward to let his forehead land against Keelan's shoulder. "I knew I shouldn't have tried to sound intelligent without Torquil here to help me."

Keelan angled his head to rest his cheek against Emrys' hair.

"Why would he not believe me? It's all we ever talked about."

"I do not think it's about him believing you at all. It's about him believing in himself." Emrys pushed back up onto his elbow and gave Keelan a serious look. "You are the sweetest man I have ever known. When you are upset, it feels like the sun has decided to shine a little less. That is a great responsibility for one man to take on. If he truly believed that you are happier here in London, then I cannot say that I blame him for accepting a broken heart instead. I think the only way you can convince him that he is capable of making your dreams a reality is to show him."

Keelan frowned. "How do I do that?"

Emrys gave him a critical once-over. "First? Get up. Have a bath. Get dressed." His expression softened into a grin. "Then? Come to dinner. We will ask Torquil what to do next."

CHAPTER 55

SILAS

SILAS WAS MISERABLE. Even worse, he was making everyone around him miserable too. He had arrived home from London without mishap, save for the constant back-and-forth in his mind as he fretted over whether he'd done the right thing. He kept coming back to the same conclusion, but it didn't make it any easier. He greeted his family with false cheer, which none of them believed for a moment.

Days later, all he could think about was Cricket. After spending so much time imagining Cricket in his life, his home now felt haunted by memories that hadn't even happened. He would walk into the kitchen and feel a pang of sadness that Cricket wasn't in there, chatting amiably with his mother. He would gather his supplies for a task and feel saddened that Cricket wasn't there, nervous and excited to be a part of something new. He would take long walks after dinner and look up at the stars, and feel lonely in the face of the vastness.

Before a week had passed, he walked into the sitting room and found all of his family sitting together. They looked up at him expectantly as he entered the room.

"Are you going to finally tell us why you're being a miserable goosewit?" Briony asked.

Silas groaned. "I do not need this right now."

"Actually," she said, "I think you're past due for it."

"What happened, Si?" his father asked. "You've been so different since you returned from London."

"I still maintain it's that Cricket fellow," Quince observed. "He wrote me all about him, but hasn't mentioned him since he returned." He turned to the rest of the family. "He was engaged to someone else, you see."

"Oh, darling," his mother said. "That's terrible. You fell in love with a man who is marrying someone else?"

Silas felt something lodged in his throat and he tried to swallow it away. "Yes. But the engagement was broken off before I left London."

His family stared at him.

"You *left* him?" Quince shouted.

"I had to."

"You had to leave the man you'd fallen in love with?" Briony asked.

"Yes."

His father leaned back in his seat and crossed his arms loosely over his chest. "Perhaps you'd better explain from the beginning." He nodded his head toward an ottoman in the center of the room that had clearly been left open for him.

Silas sighed heavily and plopped himself down. Then he explained everything. He talked about his encounter with Cricket at the wedding, about coming to regret his behavior more and more as he came to understand who Cricket was, about them finally coming together at Vauxhall (although he was judicious about the details), and then about the evenings Cricket spent with him. He described the stories he told Cricket, the way Cricket cried in his arms, and slept with him through the night. He talked about the final day of the project, when he and Cricket performed their spell together in front of everyone, and how perfectly their magic had blended. He talked about their final confrontation and how he had reached his decision. It took a long time to explain it all, and by the time he was done, his family looked thoughtful.

"I still think you should have stayed," Quince said, breaking the silence that followed.

"I just explained why I couldn't."

"No, you just described yourself making a decision for someone else, *despite* them telling you otherwise," Briony replied.

"And what would I have done," Silas shot back, "if he had come to live here and regretted it? I could never do that to him."

"You would have figured out a solution together," his mother said softly. "The way families do."

"It would have meant taking him away from his friends and a place that he loves," Silas countered, knowing he was repeating himself.

"He has a right to choose what is more important to him," Quince responded. "And besides, I can't imagine you locking him up here. He could always go and visit London alone. He's a grown man."

Silas glanced warily at his father, who had stayed silent up until now. His father gave him a long look and said, "Explain to me again why you turned down the Council position."

Surprised by the change of subject, Silas blinked. "Because it's not for me. And I dislike London."

"It seems to me that your friends thought otherwise," his father replied. "And, besides, I noticed that in your final letters from London, you spoke less of disliking the city, and more about your work with that Wyndham person."

"I did like working with him," Silas admitted. "And Torquil and Roger."

Briony sighed and lobbed a small throw pillow at him. "You really are a prize fool. Do you know that?"

Silas caught the pillow and glared at his sister. "Care to explain that?"

"It's obvious," Briony said.

Quince groaned. "He really doesn't know. You had your answer right there."

Silas stared at him. "What?"

Quince ran a hand over his face in an exasperated way. "Marry your Cricket, work on the Council, and come home when the Council isn't in session."

"That way," Briony chimed in, "he gets London for part of the year, and you get to be here part of the year."

"And he doesn't have to leave his friends," Quince added. "And you don't have to leave us. And neither of you will have to leave each other."

"And he really seemed to like the idea of living here," his mother added with a smile. "It seems a shame to deny him that."

"And it seems a shame," his father went on, reaching over to clasp his wife's hand, "to deny you the chance to challenge yourself with new work. You thrived in that environment, Si. And you enjoyed it, despite yourself. Our work will still be waiting for you when you return."

"If that's what you're worried about," Briony said, her face serious, "it needn't be. Goodness knows I felt that way when I broke my arm and had to stay home from work. But I was still part of the business, doing what I could at home. We could even find you some ways to help from London. Think of all the contacts you could make from there."

"Or better yet," Quince said, "think of all the contacts *Cricket* could make from there. You said yourself he'd be good at that."

Silas' eyes were wide as he took in the explosion of advice. "It cannot possibly be that simple."

"It is!" they all said at once.

"You idiot," Quince added affectionately.

"But what if he doesn't take me back? What if the offer for the Council is no longer open?"

"Then you'll come home and mope until we intervene again," Briony explained calmly.

When Silas continued to sit and stew over this revelation, Quince gave an irritable groan and stood. "Come on. I'll help you pack."

SILAS SPENT the entire trip back to London in a muddled state of nerves and excitement. The more he thought about it, the more he realized his family was right, and that he really had been a fool not to see the answers all along. But the closer he got to London, the more he imagined Cricket shutting the door in his face. Cricket had forgiven his poor behavior once. Was it too much to expect him doing it again?

When he arrived outside the Cricket family townhouse, there was another carriage waiting outside on the street. It was loaded up with luggage and for a brief, horrifying moment, Silas worried that Councilmember Cricket had changed her mind and had gone through with her son's engagement after all.

But then a small crowd emerged from the house, with Cricket at the center, and he did not look like a man on his way to a dreadful future. He was flushed and smiling as he carried a small satchel in his hand. Mr. Emrys Wrenwhistle, along with Torquil, Wyndham, and Roger were all walking him to the carriage, clapping him on the back and shouting encouragement.

Before Cricket could step into the carriage, Silas shouted his name.

Cricket turned and met his gaze and it felt as if the whole world had fallen away in that moment. Cricket tossed his satchel into the carriage and then ran towards him, his smile growing the closer he got, until Silas caught him in his arms. He could feel Cricket's magic, wild and loose and pouring out of him, and their magics swirled together as they met with a kiss. Silas wrapped his arms tightly around Cricket and lifted him off the ground.

Then Cricket broke apart and rested his forehead against Silas'. "You came back." Tears were falling down his cheeks, but Silas' chest swelled when he realized they were tears of joy.

"I made a mistake," he said. "Can you ever forgive me?"

"You fool," Cricket said, smiling, "of course I can. I was on my way to you."

"You were?" Silas said, drawing back in surprise.

Cricket laughed. "I'll come visit my friends when I need to. But I love our dream more than I love London. And I love you most of all."

Silas kissed him again. He heard a whoop from the small crowd of friends behind them, but he didn't bother to check and see who it had been. Then he broke away from the kiss, gently set Cricket back down, and slowly got to his knee. With his eyes on Cricket, he reached into his belt and pulled out a small ring box.

"It was my mother's ring," he explained, opening it. "It isn't very grand or elegant, I'm afraid. But it's yours. Marry me, Cricket? I'm going to accept the Council position and you can enjoy London while the Council is in session. And then we'll return home when it's over, build our cottage, and work with my family. We can—we can have both. If you'll have me."

Cricket's face broke into a smile that was so wide and so bright, it nearly took Silas' breath away. He launched himself at Silas and kissed him again. "Yes," he whispered against his lips. "Yes to everything." Then he pulled away, laughed, and held out his hand. "And I'd very much like my ring now."

Silas took Cricket's hand, slid the traveling glove off, and carefully placed his mother's ring over his finger. His father had helped him to resize it before he left, so while it was not a perfect fit, Silas was pleased to note that it did not pinch the man's skin as the previous band had done. Cricket held up his hand to examine the ring, and beamed.

The sun came out from behind the clouds as Silas took Cricket into his arms once again.

EPILOGUE
KEELAN

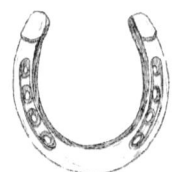

SILAS' home was even better than he had described. Keelan found that he had been doing himself a disservice by imagining anything like his family's estate in the countryside, which was more or less an extension of the residence they kept in London. Instead of high ceilings and expensive art, Silas' home was modest and full of warmth and laughter and memories. Just as Silas had warned him on the trip, he had been welcomed by the entire family, starting with a tight embrace and a kiss on each cheek from his mother. It had made him blush something awful.

The first couple of days were filled with countless new experiences. Keelan sat pressed against Silas on a bench seat around a table that was nearly too small for the number of people at it as the family shared their evening meals together. At times, they all spoke over one another, their conversations crossing the table in all different directions. The food—prepared by his mother—was not served in excess, and all of the serving bowls were empty by the time everyone cleared their plates. After, the whole family gathered in the only sitting room in the house to listen to someone play an instrument or enjoy a lively game of cards.

Each night, once everyone had said their farewells until morning, Silas took Keelan to bed and spent hours holding him, kissing him, and showing him exactly how he truly felt. The closeness of the rest of the family to Silas' small room made Keelan feel a little shy about it at first, until Silas reminded him that he was still in a house full of fae, save for his mother, but that she was more than familiar with their proclivities and would not mind.

Silas was the first to tire of his family's pokes and prods. The questions were all asked good-naturedly: when would they be married, where would they be married, would it be a large ceremony or a small one, and so on. After Quince had inspired a round of laughter at breakfast one morning by asking if their honeymoon would be as loud as their previous night had been, Silas had instructed Keelan to put on his tallest pair of boots and meet him outside.

The walk was not long, perhaps only a quarter of an hour. Silas held Keelan's hand the entire time, pointing out dips in the narrow dirt path to avoid, and then showing him the easiest way to plod through the thick grass when the path ended entirely. Keelan stole curious glances at Silas as they went, wanting to ask why he was being so quiet, but decided not to.

They finally came to a stop at the crest of a knoll. Keelan was silently grateful—he would have to spend more time walking if he hoped to keep up without breathing loudly enough for everyone to hear. Silas did not seem to mind. Instead, he lifted their joint hands and placed a lingering kiss to Keelan's knuckles.

"What do you think?" he asked.

Keelan's brows pinched. "Think?" He paused. "About what?"

Silas chuckled. "What do you think of my life? My family. Are you ready to pack your things and return to London yet?"

"Absolutely not!" Keelan said with a laugh. "Are you mad? It's even more wonderful than you described." He allowed himself to be wrapped in Silas' arms and closed his eyes briefly against the kiss Silas pressed to his lips. "I've never smiled so much in all my life."

"Even with all of the bothersome questions?"

Keelan grinned wider and placed a hand on Silas' cheek.

"It only means they care."

Something in Silas' expression softened. He searched Keelan's eyes for a moment before he turned and looked out over the land that stretched from where they stood. Keelan did the same, and for the first time realized what an incredible view it was. Even with the low clouds and generally dismal weather, he could see a great distance in all directions. He was quite certain he had never seen anything like it.

"Stars above," he whispered. "Everything is so…green."

"We are never lacking in rain," Silas told him. "Hence the mud on your nice boots." Keelan looked down and found that he was indeed sporting a fair amount of mud and grass, nearly to his knees.

"You only said they had to be tall, not inexpensive," Keelan argued.

"I suppose you're right. We shall have to buy you different ones made for life in the country."

"I would like that very much."

"I also plan to extend the path, obviously," Silas went on, turning his attention to the direction they'd come. "It will need to be widened to make it easier for the horses to pull the cart all the way up here."

Keelan nodded in agreement before he realized he had no clue what Silas was talking about.

"What will you need the cart for?"

Silas gave a genuine laugh at that, before he kissed Keelan's temple.

"Would you prefer I carry the materials by hand? I am hopeful that my family will help, but I do not think they'll appreciate doing it without some assistance from the horses. Even magic can only do so much."

"Right. Of course," Keelan said, looking at the space around them in a feeble attempt to hide that he still did not understand. Silas caught his chin and lifted it. Keelan's face went warm. He had never seen such an affectionate look directed at him before.

"This is where I am going to build you a home. Our home."

Keelan gasped. "Here?"

Silas' expression turned uncertain. "Unless you do not like it?"

"No!" he nearly shouted, before he realized that it might be taken the wrong way. Keelan took Silas' face in his hands and kissed him deeply. "I mean yes. I mean I do like it. I love it. It's…it's beyond what you described. More than perfect."

A drizzling rain had started, so Silas took him by the hand again and guided them under a nearby oak tree. Silas sat with his back to the trunk and Keelan settled between his legs. He was taken back to the night of the ball, where they'd sat in much the same way and simply enjoyed being together in the garden. There was nothing he could do to stop his grin when Silas' arms wrapped around him just as they had that night. They sat in silence for a long while, listening to nothing but the sound of raindrops against leaves over their heads.

"You know," Keelan said quietly, "we never did talk about that first night."

Silas grunted in response. "I certainly never forgot it, much as I wanted to."

"You wanted to forget about me?" he teased.

"Only the look on your face after," Silas told him. "I was already unsteady from your magic, and then you had to look at me with those eyes, and…" He did not continue.

Keelan chuckled. "What eyes?"

Silas let out a long-suffering sigh and buried his face in Keelan's hair so that his response came out muffled.

"The eyes of someone who had just had their heart broken."

"Ah," Keelan said. "I am sorry about that. I've never been very good at hiding my emotions."

"It's one of the things I find most endearing about you. I suppose I was just unprepared for it. Encounters such as that typically do not come with *feelings* attached. At least they never had for me, until you."

Keelan's grin turned smug. "Are you saying you also had *feelings*?"

Silas was quiet for a moment. "Perhaps."

The surprise of his admission made Keelan's magic swirl in his chest. He turned in Silas' arms just enough to place a hand on his cheek and kiss him.

"Who could've ever guessed that a random shag with a handsome stranger the night of my best friend's wedding would lead to a moment like this?" Keelan pulled his knees up and curled more into Silas' embrace, resting his cheek against his shoulder. "*Rien n'est petit dans l'amour*," he murmured.

"Nothing is small in love," Silas said in agreement. "That reminds me." He reached for the leather satchel he'd carried with him on their walk. Keelan sat up a bit as he opened the flap and moved his hand around inside for a moment before he pulled out what he'd been searching for.

"My book!" Keelan laughed and accepted it when Silas gave it to him. He opened the cover and traced his fingers over the inscription.

"I'd forgotten about it until I arrived home and found it packed away with the rest of my belongings," Silas explained, sounding a little guilty.

Keelan nestled into Silas again and began flipping through the pages.

"Shall I read you another while we wait for the rain to pass?"

Silas held him tighter. "Anything you'd like, Cricket."

The End

WANT to find out what happens next? Read book 4 in *Fae & Human Relations*: *Cleaning Spells Before Courtship!*

NOTE FROM THE AUTHORS

Greetings, radiant readers,

This story started to come together before we'd even finished writing *Fire Spells Between Friends*. Unlike the huge gap between writing books one and two (by "huge gap," we mean a few weeks), we started this project almost as soon as we'd typed "The end" for Torquil and Emrys.

This project has seen the most revisions out of any of our stories so far, but it has become one that we are immensely proud of. We hope you enjoyed reading it as much as we enjoyed writing it.

Your winsome writers,

Sarah & Shannon

ACKNOWLEDGMENTS

This book wouldn't be possible without our network of support. Thank you to our alpha reader, Sebastian, and our beta readers, Alexis, Katie, Anna, Becca, Bronwyn, Leslie, Kayla, and Meg, and our Sensitivity Reader, Jaida. Thank you to our amazing editor, Mackenzie! Thank you to our wonderful proofreader, Ashley. Thank you to our fantastic narrator, Maxwell. Thank you to all of our cheerleaders who encouraged us throughout the process, especially John and Ashley.

Cover art: Caras Alexandra
Editor: Mackenzie Walton
Proofreader: Ashley Scout

ALSO BY SARAH WALLACE

Letters to Half Moon Street

One Good Turn

The Education of Pip

Dear Bartleby

The Spellmaster of Tutting-on-Cress

The Viscount Says Yes

Free to Sarah's newsletter subscribers:

The Glamour Spell of Rose Talbot

ALSO BY S.O. CALLAHAN

Fella Enchanted

Fella Ever After

ABOUT SARAH WALLACE

Sarah Wallace lives in Florida with their cat, more books than she has time to read, a large collection of classic movies, and an apartment full of plants that are surviving against all odds. They only read books that end happily.

ABOUT S.O. CALLAHAN

S.O. Callahan has always been fond of sweet things, namely chocolate and love stories. When she's not writing or reading, she enjoys baking, visiting National Parks and Historic Sites, and traveling with her husband. They live in Chicago and have two very spoiled cats named Ozzy and Beau.

www.ingramcontent.com/pod-product-compliance
Lightning Source LLC
Chambersburg PA
CBHW020529020726
47494CB00006B/1693